ROYAL

K.T. HOLDER

For my Wife

AUTHOR'S NOTE

This book is a work of fantasy fiction, and while it contains magical elements and imaginary settings, it also includes themes that may be distressing to some readers.

I believe stories should be immersive, but also that you deserve to make informed choices about the content you engage with. If you'd like to see a list of content warnings for this and my other books, you can find one linked on my website:

www.ktholder.com

Please be aware that some content warnings may be minor spoilers.

Thank you for reading,
KT Holder

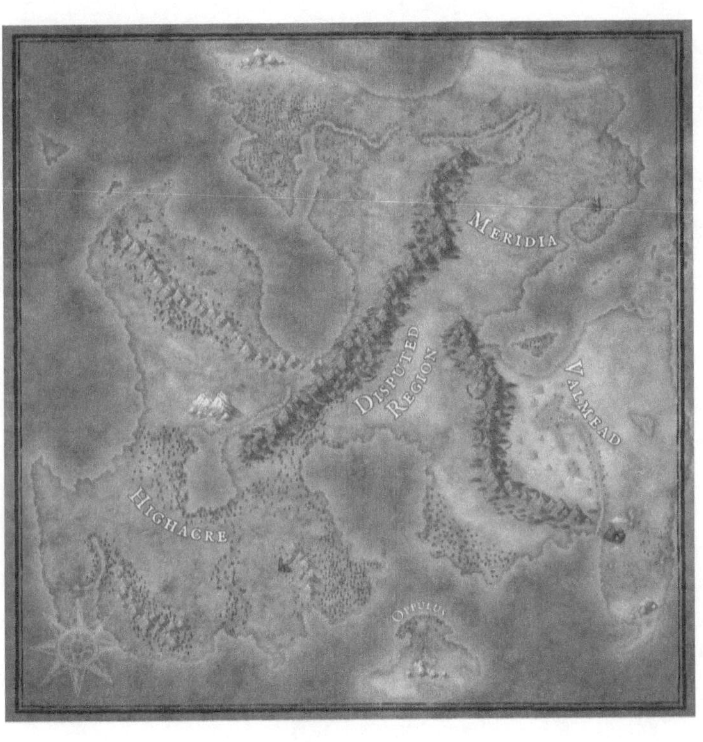

MERIDIA
VALMEAD
DISPUTED REGION
HIGHACRE
OPPULUS

PROLOGUE

THE WOMAN RUSHED through the corridors, tears streaming down her cheeks, but she had no time to focus on her fear and sadness. The men escorting her bundled her down a side hallway, seeming to take turns at random through the warren of passages, but clearly focussed on an objective.

Her cloak flapped and her hood obscured her vision, adding to her rising panic. There was no other choice. This had to happen. She thought bitterly of the men who had agreed to this plan and then simply presented it to her as a fait accompli.

They burst into a room full of those gathered to say farewell. Those she had trusted; those who had betrayed her. Her friends, and her husband.

"There is no time!"

She couldn't see who'd said it. Her escorts moved her to the machine in the centre of the room, then pushed her into its blue glow.

Everything was a brilliant blue and then... black.

1

"Your Majesty, are you okay?"

The queen looked up, pulling her hood back and letting it fall down her neck.

"Are we here?" She ignored her bodyguard's question. Of course she was not okay. How could she be?

"Yes, Your Majesty. The house is just up ahead. It's a short walk from our current position."

The three of them walked slowly up the road towards the farmhouse, which had materialised on the horizon. Despite her mood, the queen looked at the countryside around her and could not help but be taken by its beauty. In the distance, the rolling hills gave way to a thick covering of trees that failed only where sheer cliff faces prevented their growth.

Her breathing became more laboured than it should have been. She placed a hand protectively on her swollen belly, then removed it quickly. Best not to become attached.

She heard the river to her left before she saw it. It was a small thing, the kind of river that entertained children in the summer, and perhaps provided some fish for a patient angler. It gave her some comfort that this place had beauty, but that did not help ease the pain in her heart.

Finally, they were at the door, and it opened to reveal a kind face. The face of the woman who would raise her child.

1

"Thank you, Linda."

Lily smiled patiently at her director while handing her a bundle of files. She had given up correcting the woman about her name and resigned herself to forever being 'Linda the intern'.

Lily sighed and looked at the collection of folders still left in her arms. This morning's mind-numbingly boring task was to deliver folders to various people who were far too important to collect them themselves.

She continued down the corridor, smiling politely at people who had no idea who she was, and greeting those who remembered they had met before. It had been almost three months since she started as an intern in this government department, and she still didn't really understand what they did. She did know that whatever it was, she didn't want to do it.

But the problem was, Lily didn't know what she *did* want to do. The rest of her family seemed to all have their lives figured out, but Lily was yet to find her thing. Her purpose. She felt, deep down, that there was *something* she was supposed to be doing. But that feeling was frustratingly silent on what that something was.

Lily had thought she had it figured out when she left the family farm after graduating from high school. But then, when she arrived at university to begin her business and economics degree, she had very quickly discovered that she liked neither business nor economics. And so she had dropped out, much to the despair of her parents.

That had prompted Lily to panic, and instead of taking a long hard look at herself and what she might be suited to, she had applied for every government internship possible. Having secured this one, she had then tried to convince her parents, and herself, that whatever it was that she was meant to be doing here was what she really wanted to do.

"Morning, Lily." Her team leader greeted her without looking up from her computer. "Can you get started on this brief for me? It needs to be with Brooke by lunchtime."

Lily had no idea who Brooke was.

"Um, sure, but I just need to drop off these files for—"

"Perfect. Now, you should be able to figure out the gist of it from this email I'm sending you, but basically the brief should explain to the minister why we can't do a brief for him."

Lily stared at her team leader. "You want me to write a brief, explaining that we can't write a brief?"

"Exactly. Be sure to emphasise that we just don't have the time or resources to be writing pointless briefs."

Lily blinked, her brain struggling to comprehend the bureaucracy in which she found herself. In her first couple of weeks, she had asked far more questions when presented with a task like this. But now, Lily found it less frustrating to just go with it.

"Sure thing." Lily went and sat down at her desk.

"Oh, you can drop all those files off first though."

Lily closed her eyes for a beat, stood, and headed back out down the corridor.

"Oh, and bring me a latte when you're done. Please. You're a doll."

Lily wandered around the maze of corridors, delivering the files and getting most of them to the right area. She fantasised about simply dropping the pile on a desk and walking out, never to return. Only the idea of the look on her parents' faces stopped her.

"Oh love, you lost your job." (That would be her mum).

"No, I didn't *lose* it..."

"But sweetheart, maybe you just need to give it a bit more of a go?" (That would be her dad).

"I did give it a go..."

"Opportunities don't grow on trees; you have to tend your own crops." (That would be both of them).

Finally, she delivered the last of her folders and headed down to the coffee shop. Naturally, the elevator wasn't working, so she took the stairs, squeezing awkwardly past people trudging back up.

Waiting in line, Lily absentmindedly checked her phone. No messages from Brandon, her boyfriend, but his latest social media post had him at some university event with Gemma, her best friend. She felt a vague pang of jealousy. Brandon and Gemma were spending so much time together lately. Ever since Lily dropped out. Lily told herself she needn't worry, as she looked at the photo again.

A small voice in her head wondered if it would be so bad if they did hook up together. Brandon was a great guy, but Lily just wasn't sure if he was a great guy for *her*. Maybe he was the kind of great guy Gemma deserved.

There wasn't anything wrong with Brandon. He did everything right and was really kind. *But what could I say? Sorry Brandon, you're just too nice?* She couldn't shake the feeling that she was mainly with him because she felt she should have a boyfriend. *Kind of like this job.*

Grabbing the tray of coffees, Lily headed back up the stairs. She was fairly sure she had got enough for everyone, and she'd even bought an extra, in case her team leader changed her mind about the latte. Last week, by the time Lily made it through the snaking line at the café and back up to their floor, her team leader had decided that she was lactose intolerant and could only have black coffee.

"Oh, you're a life saver, thanks Lily," the team leader said, taking the latte from Lily's tray as she entered the work area. Pausing before taking a sip, she asked, "Is this skim milk?"

Lily considered lying, but her hesitation was enough. Her boss replaced the coffee in the tray. "Well, thanks anyway." She checked her watch, sighing heavily. "I'm not sure I have enough time to run and get one before my meeting..."

Unsure why she did, Lily found herself offering to return to the cafe. Her boss happily sent her on her way before sitting with the others in the break room as they enjoyed the beverages Lily had supplied. *Why am I such a pushover?*

Lily began her ascent back up the stairs, skim latte in hand, resolving to quit. This was ridiculous. She could find something else to pay the bills. Something that gave her time to consider her path in life. Something less painful. As the last thought rolled across her mind she became hyper aware of just how much her shoes were hurting her feet. She cursed her job. Why on earth, in a department that spanned several floors of rabbit-warren work cubicles, was she expected to wear shoes that were not conducive to movement? Or even standing, really.

"Cheer up darling, it can't be that bad!" called a man

Lily had never met as he and his friends passed by. They all chuckled. With an ominous feeling, Lily ducked into the bathroom and instantly saw what they'd been laughing at. The pale face that peered out of the mirror at her was frazzled. Her brown, shoulder-length hair was mussed up, as if she had been wandering in a gale rather than traipsing around an office building. She pulled it back into a ponytail and washed her face clean of the makeup that was starting to run from sweat.

Re-examining her reflection, she decided against trying to reapply her makeup. Lily often worried her features were plain, but considering no one seemed to remember her anyway, she felt no need to try and stand out.

Lily exited the bathroom, keeping an eye out for the men who had called out to her. Suddenly, she resented worrying about what they thought. And why did they get to call out to her like that? Or call her darling? Why wasn't there an equivalently patronising term to use to refer to men?

Shaking off her spurt of feminism, Lily plastered a smile on her face and presented the team leader with her coffee.

"Oh, thanks doll. But Paul got me one. Gotta run to my meeting, just send that brief straight to Brooke, okay? Oh, and can you run this file to Robert? He needs it right away."

Lily went in search of the mysterious Robert, unwanted latte still in hand.

"Oh, Linda!"

Lily almost collided with the director, who came steaming around a corner, seemingly late for something. She eyed Lily's coffee. "You've planned well—I'd kill for a coffee."

Lily offered the latte and the director graciously accepted.

"Thank you, you're a gem. Are you coming to the professional development session?"

"Oh no, I have a brief to write."

"I'm sure it can wait; professional development is very important."

"Uh, what's it about?" Lily asked.

"You know, I'm not sure," the director said thoughtfully.

Lily hesitated, then decided to go with it. She had little desire to write a brief about not writing a brief, and if nothing else it'd give her feet a rest. The delighted director linked arms and escorted Lily to the conference room, babbling happily about how good professional development was for developing oneself professionally.

I really need to get out of this place.

Once they were inside the conference room, Lily managed to slip the clutches of the director, who went to greet other people of greater import than Lily. She navigated to the back of the room and secured a seat by the window.

Eventually, the presenter managed to get his slides to work and started droning on in a monotone that made it physically impossible for Lily to concentrate on whatever it was that he was saying. Instead, she gazed out the window, watching the rain fall and tried to fight the overwhelming feeling that she just didn't seem to belong anywhere.

Suddenly, she saw the reflection of a figure standing in front of her that definitely hadn't been there a second ago. Looking up, she saw not one, but three men in front of her. One grabbed her shoulder. There was a bright blue light, and then the world was a black nothingness.

A moment later, she found herself unceremoniously deposited in a chair with the three figures still surrounding her.

At first she thought perhaps she had just blanked out for

a second, startled by the sudden appearance of the three strangers, and she looked around the conference room to see if they had shocked anyone else. But everyone else had vanished.

Weird. Since when did the conference room have this many crystals embedded in the walls? Or a holographic display?

She watched the display in amazement for a beat as figures that looked almost real paced and seemed to be talking to each other, though she couldn't hear what they might be saying.

The three men stepped back slightly and stared at her.

"Um... Hello?" Lily said awkwardly. Immediately, all three dropped to one knee, their right arms braced across their bodies and heads bowed.

"Oh. Okay..." Lily wondered whether she should also take a knee when a loud bang sounded behind her, making her jump.

"Get up, get up," chided an officious-looking man hurrying towards them from the other end of the room. Lily was temporarily distracted by the sheer volume of the hall behind her.

Enormous pillars framed the hall, which was large enough to fit a football field. The roof loomed high above them, peaking in the centre and supported by massive wooden beams. It was like the great hall of some medieval castle. With a sudden sickening lurch, Lily realized she was not in the conference room anymore, or even in the government building. This place was far, far too large and... different.

"Don't tell me they brought her back and then are just kneeling around while she probably doesn't even know what's going on," the older man muttered to himself as he ushered the three strange men out of the way.

"You are Royal Guards, for crying out loud. How are you supposed to guard if you're all staring at the floor?" None of the men responded but glared pointedly at the man, then moved to various points around the room and stood in an imposing fashion.

"Right now, there you are," he glanced at the guards, looking satisfied, then turned to Lily, his eyes and tone softening. "How *are* you, Your Majesty?"

"I'm, um..." Lily looked around. "Where am I?"

"Oh yes, of course!" He coughed and straightened up slightly. "Welcome, Your Majesty. Welcome to Highacre." He gestured theatrically around him, bowing slightly.

Lily blinked at him. The silence stretched awkwardly as Lily cast around for something that would help her understand and react appropriately. The man was staring at her, his expression shifting from a satisfied, warm one, through to surprise and concern until ultimately landing on a quizzical look, much like one wears when staring at a broken lawnmower.

"Is she broken?" asked one of the guards, who Lily realised was staring at her with the same expression.

"It can happen, I guess, but it's rare," said the older man, moving closer to her.

"Didn't seem broken when we got her here," the guard said, slightly defensively.

"No, no, it's the process." The man started palpating her glands like a doctor. "Sometimes people can have an adverse reaction to interdimensional travel."

"Perhaps she needs a shock," the guard offered.

"No, we just need—"

"It works for the hiccups," the guard interrupted, clearly put out that the older man was not listening to him.

"Yes, well, this is not—"

"Boo!" bellowed the guard from behind Lily. She

squealed and jumped, tripping on the chair and falling to the floor. Immediately, the older man and the guard were at her side, fussing and helping her to her feet.

"No, it's fine, I'm okay," she told them, trying to push them off.

"Nice one, Boris," said another guard.

"What?"

"'What?' What do you mean 'what?' You don't yell at the monarch!"

"It worked, didn't it?"

As the guards continued debating the relative merits of yelling at royalty, the older man sighed and led Lily out of the main hall and down a long corridor. Lily looked around in a stupor.

Where am I?

The walls were a light grey stone, punctuated periodically by dark wooden beams. Paintings adorned the walls at sporadic intervals, affording each a prominence that allowed it to be enjoyed without distraction. Many were landscapes, but some were important-looking people, staring in judgement at those scurrying through the halls below.

Eventually the man opened a set of double doors, and they entered a large room that looked very much like the ground floor of a hunting lodge, but without the expected dead animals mounted on the wall.

There was an enormous fireplace set in the middle of an open space. Lily could look through the flames and see the other side of the room. The room itself was filled with dark brown leather sofas and wooden tables of various heights and uses. To her left, the entire wall was a strange smooth black, and in a far corner of the room she saw a pool table.

The man murmured to a young woman dressed in a rather plain uniform, who nodded and left. He then guided

Lily to a comfortable chair and sat her down near the fireplace.

"Your Majesty," the man said gently, drawing her attention back to him. "I know you have questions, and I'll answer them, but first, are you alright?"

Lily nodded. "Yes, I'm fine. But where am I?"

"These are your rooms, Your Majesty. This room is commonly known as the Lodge. It is your personal space where you can relax and where you will take your meals unless you are attending a function. You may take visitors here, though it is more common for you to meet with them in your office, which I will show you later."

Lily looked around in dumbstruck awe.

All this is mine?

"Okay," said Lily, still gaping at her surroundings. "But *where* am I? I mean, I was in the conference room at work, and now..." She looked around in benign confusion before her eyes found the man again. "And who are you?"

"Of course, my apologies. My name is Giles and I am the personal assistant to the monarch of Highacre." Giles smiled at Lily, and she smiled back reflectively. Giles smiled more and leant in slightly towards her. "That's you."

Lily's smile froze on her face. The girl in the plain uniform re-entered the room and placed a tray on the table between Lily's chair and the one on which Giles was perched. It held some sandwiches, a glass of water, and a hot drink. The girl bowed slightly and left again.

"Why don't you eat something? It helps with the travel. And I will explain a bit about what's going on." Lily nodded and reached for a sandwich. Giles looked thoughtful, as though trying to determine where to begin.

"We are in Highacre, Your Majesty. Highacre is a large country that exists in a different dimension to the one in which you grew up."

A different dimension? Lily absentmindedly took a bite of the sandwich as she tried to make sense of what Giles was telling her.

"One of our greatest scientists developed a machine that allows for interdimensional travel; travel between worlds. Where you are now, this world—it is not the world you were in this morning."

Lily blinked and looked around the room, which was not overly helpful in trying to grasp what Giles was telling her.

"Wait, so, I'm not on Earth anymore?"

"No, Your Majesty."

"So...are we on another planet?"

"Well, Your Majesty, we are actually in a whole other dimension to the one in which Earth exists."

None of what Giles was telling her made sense to Lily and her extreme confusion was the only thing stopping her from launching into the kind of panic one might experience after being told they are in a different world in another dimension.

"But why am I here?"

"Ah yes. Years ago, your father, the king..."

"My father's a farmer," said Lily, her mouth full of sandwich.

"Um, yes." Giles looked about the room uncomfortably. "So, the king became concerned about the decline in High-acre's relations with the other large countries in our world, Meridia and Valmead. With the strong possibility of war, he took action to protect his line. Now, I should point out that Highacre is the only country to have developed the ability to travel to other dimensions, and it is a closely protected secret. Very few people here know about it, not even the Prime Minister." Giles nodded importantly at Lily, who finished her little sandwich, dusted the crumbs from her hands, and looked at Giles, hoping that he would start to make sense soon.

"The king decided to send his heir into another dimension, where they would be out of reach of his enemies and the dangers facing his country. So, he sent his wife, who was pregnant, to a dimension that, after some thorough scouting, was selected for its similarities to our own world. The queen gave birth and left the child with a family who would protect her and raise her as their own."

Lily got a sick feeling in her stomach. Perhaps those sandwiches didn't agree with her. She tried to smother a burp and reached for the water, suddenly feeling a little hot.

"That child, Your Majesty, was you."

Lily paused, the glass midway to her lips. There was a slight ringing in her ears.

My parents are not my parents?

It made no sense. They would have told her if she was adopted, or whatever it was called when your mother took you to another dimension and left you with random people.

Panic broke through the buffer of confusion. Perhaps this was a joke? Yes, clearly this was a joke. A mean joke, but someone had to be pulling a prank on her. Or maybe she was dreaming. That was it. A weird, terrible dream. Lily subtly pinched her arm. Nope, not dreaming. A prank then. That was why she'd never heard of this 'Highacre' place.

This prank is mean. Lily tried without luck to think of who she knew that would go to this level of effort to play a trick on her. That would think any of this would be funny.

Lily felt her stomach drop, unable to help but think about how different she was to her siblings. They all seemed to have everything figured out, whereas Lily had no idea what she was going to do with her life. *That doesn't mean we're not related, though. And it certainly doesn't mean that any of this is real.*

But something about her not being related to her siblings or her parents rang true and provided a cold anchor for Giles's story. On the inside, her thoughts and feelings were screaming around her head like someone with their hair on fire, but somehow Lily had so far managed to keep a relatively calm exterior.

"I know this is a lot to take in, Your Majesty," Giles said sympathetically.

"A lot?" Lily's calm exterior dissolved instantaneously. "Apparently, I've been kidnapped and taken to a different dimension and my family is not my family. Yeah, that's a lot."

Giles looked distinctly uncomfortable. "We didn't *kidnap* you..."

"You came into my workplace and took me to another world without asking!"

"We retrieved you—"

"Without asking!"

At that moment, a middle-aged, motherly looking woman entered the room, smiling warmly but worriedly at Lily.

"Is everything okay in here?"

"Yes," said Giles at the same moment Lily muttered, "No."

Giles seemed to collect himself and then stood, the woman moving to stand next to him.

"Your Majesty, this is Addison Grange."

Addison curtsied, bowing her head.

"Addison is in charge of the royal household."

"It's an honour to meet you, Your Majesty. Welcome home."

Home. This wasn't home. Lily looked grumpily around the room that had previously seemed warm and inviting, but now was dark and dingy.

"Well, I might leave you two alone for a bit," Giles rubbed his hands together, clearly eager to hand Lily over to Addison. "I'll go and prepare your office where you will soon meet your advisors. Addison will help you get freshened up a bit." Giles swiftly exited the room, leaving the two women alone.

Addison sat quietly next to Lily. When it became clear that Lily wasn't going to say anything Addison smiled gently at her. "You have your mother's eyes."

Lily immediately thought of her mother back home, then realised Addison was talking about the queen. If there was a queen. Lily needed to figure out if this was real. *How could this be real?* She leant in towards Addison and whispered conspiratorially, "Is this a prank?"

Addison's eyebrows flew up in surprise. "Gosh, no, Your Majesty. This is not a prank."

Lily nodded thoughtfully to herself as she picked up and cautiously nibbled at the corner of a sandwich. *Of course, that is exactly what someone playing a prank would say.*

Addison's eyes flitted to the strange black wall and back to Lily. "Perhaps, Your Majesty, this might help."

Addison rose and crossed to a panel on the wall adjacent to the smooth black one. Lily stood and took a few slow steps towards her, unsure of whether she was supposed to follow. Addison pressed a couple of buttons and suddenly the black wall transitioned, the glass transforming from black to clear.

Lily was momentarily blinded by the sudden light. She blinked furiously, and when she opened her eyes again, Addison had opened a door in the glass and was ushering her out onto a balcony.

The view was breathtaking. They were high up, on a hill or perhaps partway up a mountain, and she could see down into a city below. It was sprawling, but not over-crowded, and there looked to be lots of trees and parks. The buildings reminded Lily of what she imagined European cities looked like, having never visited herself. They were white with terracotta roofs, and though some looked tall, there weren't any skyscrapers.

Farther out beyond the city was a deep but vibrant green forested area that bordered a beautiful blue lake and vast mountain range, all covered in snow from about halfway up. It was like a picture. Lily had never seen anything so beautiful in her life.

There was nothing like this vista anywhere near where Lily lived, nor could she recall seeing such a sight in pictures or in movies. She had definitely moved, or travelled, what would appear to be a great distance. With a jolt, Lily realised that she wasn't in her home country anymore. She didn't even think she was on Earth.

Giles had been telling her the truth.

This was real.

2

Lily gazed out at the view, which was so beautiful that it had a calming effect. It was probably the only reason she hadn't collapsed into a full-blown panic attack.

"It's beautiful, isn't it? I often stare out at it when I need to think, or if I've had a bad day."

Am I having a bad day? Yeah, it was pretty bad. Well, her mum would say 'challenging'. Her mum was always trying to get Lily to look at things in a positive light. *But she's not my mother...*

Lily shook the thought from her head. Addison was right. The view was the kind you could lose yourself in. This was the kind of place you'd want to visit. Lily frowned.

"So, where are we?" Lily asked Addison. "Giles said we're in Hightower or something?"

"Highacre, Your Majesty. This is your country. And that," she said, pointing at the city below, "is Burlaron, the capital city."

Lily nodded, looking closer at the city. "Can we have a look around?"

Addison shook her head sadly at Lily. "No, Your Majesty. At present it's best that you stay here in the palace, where we can keep an eye on you and make sure you're safe."

Safe?

"Am I not safe?" Lily asked.

Addison pursed her lips slightly. "Yes, of course you are. However, it's best we don't take unnecessary risks." She touched Lily lightly on her arm. "Let's get you freshened up, shall we?"

Lily nodded, feeling suddenly calmer, but looked back at the city. She could hear the faint bustle of people living their lives. A bird flew past the two women, twittering a song, and landed on a tree off to Lily's left. It had feathers that were a mix of deepest black and midnight blue, and its head... Lily jumped back in alarm.

"Holy mother of— What is that thing? What is wrong with its head?"

"Oh!" Addison laughed lightly and moved closer to the tree. "It's a snufflepidgeon! Come here, little one!" She cooed at the thing in the tree, holding her hand out to it.

Lily moved cautiously closer to the barrier, peering at the creature over Addison's shoulder. It looked like a pretty little bird except that it had the head of a pig, though proportional to its tiny body. On the off chance that this was actually a dream, Lily decided that she had to give her imagination a pat on the back for creativity.

Having gotten over the initial shock, Lily had to admit it wasn't entirely ugly. Suddenly, it sprang back into the air, landing next to Addison on the barrier. Lily squealed and jumped back, immediately feeling embarrassed for doing so.

"Oh, it's alright Your Majesty," Addison said softly, holding a finger out to the snufflepidgeon. "It's just saying hello."

The snufflepidgeon regarded Lily suspiciously, as if she were the thing that shouldn't be here. Which, thinking about it, Lily decided was fair. The snufflepidgeon hopped across to Lily. Lily held her finger out as Addison had and the snufflepidgeon promptly nipped it.

"Ow!"

"They are hungry little things," chuckled Addison. "They think everything is food until proven otherwise."

The snufflepidgeon gave a loud snort and took flight, gliding down towards the city below. Lily looked at the tiny spot of blood on her finger. *Really not a dream.* Suddenly, the enormity of her situation came crashing down.

I'm in another dimension. Not the one with Earth. I am not on Earth anymore. But I need to be on Earth. I promised April she could stay with me this weekend, and I'd take her to the movies. Wait... April! Shit, what will my family think? And are they even my family? Giles said I was adopted. Why has no one ever told me I'm adopted?

"Are you okay, Your Majesty?" Addison asked, touching her shoulder. Lily felt a wave of calm wash over her.

"Yes, but I was just thinking about my family back home. It's just, they'll be wondering where I am, and I'm meant to have my little sister, April, come and stay with me this weekend. Do you think I could just pop home and let them know where I am?"

Addison looked uneasy. "I will look into it for you, Your Majesty, but I'm sure Jason's team will have let them know that you're safe."

"Or at least get a message to them," Lily continued, not really listening and oblivious to Addison's unease. On a whim, Lily asked, "Do you know much about my family? The one that raised me, I mean."

"Uh, some..." Addison looked quite uncomfortable.

"Do you know if they knew I wasn't theirs? That I was adopted, or whatever. I mean, I don't need details, but did you like, hand me over as a baby, or was it more like my mother kidnapped and inseminated. You know, like an alien abduction?"

The questions came out in a rush and Addison stared at Lily, wide-eyed. "Aliens kidnap and impregnate people where you're from?" The older woman shook her head in distaste before returning to the point. "You were given to your parents as a baby. They knew you weren't theirs, biologically speaking. But they were very happy to take you in and I have no doubt they loved you just the same as their biological children."

"But why didn't they tell me?" The question came out softly, and with much more hurt than she had intended.

Addison looked at Lily kindly. "Oh, Your Majesty. I'm sure they had their reasons. Maybe they didn't want you to feel different."

Lily nodded. She felt cold sweat bead on her forehead and heard a distant ringing in her ears. "I think I'm going to be sick."

Addison rushed Lily through the Lodge, opening another door and hurrying her to a bathroom. Lily barely made it to the toilet before losing the sandwiches Giles had provided. Addison held Lily's hair back for her and rubbed Lily's back until she finished heaving, then murmured to Lily that she would fetch her some water.

Lily got up and moved to the sink, washing her face and feeling a warmth towards Addison. The older woman hadn't hesitated in holding Lily's hair back for her despite the fact they had just met.

Patting her face dry on a towel, Lily took in the bathroom around her. It was larger than any bathroom Lily had ever been in. There was a counter that spanned the entire wall and had two sinks, and the toilet had more buttons than a toilet needed. A weird bowl thing sat next to the toilet, and a huge shower and a large tub with a bunch of jets dominated the other end of the room.

She wandered out of the bathroom and found herself in a massive walk-in wardrobe that spanned off to either side. She stared at the racks of clothing and shoes before continuing forwards and finding herself in a bedroom.

It was as big as the family room back home in her parents' house. A comfortable-looking couch and two chairs, a coffee table, and a fireplace sat off in a cosy corner. It had one entire wall of glass displaying yet another magnificent view. The bed was bigger than anything Lily had ever slept in.

"Here you are Your Majesty," Addison appeared on Lily's right with a bottle of water. She noted Lily looking around in awe. "This is your room, Your Majesty."

This was *her* room? *I could get used to this.* The luxury of the room cooled Lily's panic. It didn't seem she was in danger. At least not immediate danger. And if you had to be kidnapped and taken to another dimension, being told you were royalty and being treated as such wasn't a bad situation to find yourself in. At least she'd be comfortable for however long she was here for.

"How's your stomach?" Addison asked with concern.

"It's fine," Lily said, walking over to her dresser. "I feel much better." She ran her fingers over the back of the chair, and touched the items on the dresser's surface. Picking up an ornate hairbrush, she addressed Addison.

"Everything here seems familiar, but then slightly off, you know? Like that weird bird thing."

"Snufflepidgeon."

"Whatever." She put the brush down and walked to the bed. "It's hard to get my head around. I hadn't really given much thought to other dimensions or realities or whatnot.

That's all fantasy stuff. But I suppose that's the thing. If you'd asked me what another dimension would be like, I would have said there'd be magic and dragons and quests, you know?"

Lily turned to look at Addison, whose face had paled somewhat. Addison tried to smile and nod and wouldn't make eye contact with Lily.

"Oh crap—there aren't dragons, are there?"

Addison laughed a strange, constricted laugh. "Oh no, Your Majesty, nothing like that!"

"Then what?"

"What?"

"You've gone pale."

"No I haven't."

"Yes you have, and you're acting weird."

"You're weird." Addison clamped her hands over her mouth. "Oh gosh, no, you're not weird. You're the sovereign. The sovereign's not weird. Well, your great-grandfather was a bit weird..."

"Addison."

"Hmm?"

"Is there something you're not telling me?"

"No. I mean, yes. But it's just that I'm not supposed to... Everything's fine!" Addison was inching towards the door as she spoke.

There was a knock and Giles entered, bowing deeply to Lily. "How are you, Your Majesty?"

He frowned, his eyes running up and down Lily, taking in her unchanged appearance.

"I'm good," she replied. "Addison was just telling me about magic and dragons and stuff."

Giles looked at Addison in shock. "You told her about the magic?"

"No—"

"I knew it!" Lily cried, even though she hadn't known it. "Wait, magic? There's magic? Do I get a wand?"

Giles's face emptied of colour. Addison looked uncomfortable but seemed relieved that Giles had put his foot in it rather than her. Giles addressed Addison instead of answering Lily's questions. "The advisors are gathered. You will need to hurry up and get Her Majesty ready."

Addison paled. "They're going to be so mad. Minister Bellingham will be apoplectic."

"Indeed. I will fetch the servants and then return to the office and inform them of this...slip. Get Her Majesty ready and then meet us in her office as soon as you can."

"Does it have to be the office?" Addison asked. "Could they not all just come to the Lodge?"

"Her Majesty's office is more appropriate," Giles said stiffly. "And, well, the acoustics are better."

Lily watched Giles leave. The excitement over magic being real left as quickly as it had come, and she felt unsettled. Something about Giles and Addison talking to each other as if she wasn't there, or maybe how worried they were about how these advisors might react. Something was off, and Lily suddenly felt afraid rather than simply confused and overwhelmed. Could she trust Addison and Giles?

"Right." Addison turned to Lily, smiling warmly. She took her gently by the arms and guided her into the chair in front of her dresser. Addison had a calming presence, and Lily felt herself relax as Addison absently started brushing her hair.

"Addison, can you tell me about magic?"

The older woman smiled at Lily's enthusiasm. They were interrupted as a dozen servants suddenly entered and began fussing around her. There was an air of restraint until Addison announced to the room that the cat was out of the bag and they could all use magic. The servants perked up immediately, and to Lily's delight items began flying around the room and appearing out of nowhere.

They led her back into the bathroom, and as some started running a bath, others began undressing her. Lily felt very uncomfortable, but they were all so efficient that she was immersed and covered by bubbles before she could say anything. Addison sat on the rim, supervising the servants.

"There is magic in this world." She turned to Lily as the servants buzzed around, summoning lotions and exfoliators and towels with their minds. "I understand it does not exist in the world where we sent you, and you can't use abilities from this world there. Here in Highacre, people are born with magical power. Their power can be very strong, weak, or moderate. Each person usually has one main ability, such as extreme strength, mind control, or the ability to appear invisible. People will usually wind up in a profession that uses their specific ability, like soldiers, politicians, or spies, respectively."

Lily frowned at the idea that those with the ability to control minds should go into politics, but she remained silent, watching as a loofah began scrubbing her skin on its own.

"The abilities are only as strong as the power a person has. Giles, for example, can move objects with his mind. He uses it for cleaning or tidying up. If he could move heavier objects, then perhaps he would have gone into construction."

Lily tried and failed to imagine Giles on a construction site. Her heart sank. What if her power was weak? How disappointing to find out magic was real, only to discover that all she could do was make her bed with a click of her fingers?

Actually, that wouldn't be a complete waste. Lily thought of the state of her bedroom back home. *Wait, what if I can't do magic at all?*

Addison must have noted the concern on her face. She walked with Lily as the servants wrapped her in a soft robe and sat her back at her dresser.

"Don't worry, Your Majesty. With magic, bloodlines are important. Most people will have only one ability of varying strength. Those blessed with a second ability will usually find that it is weaker than the first. Many of your advisors have multiple abilities.

"For example, your personal bodyguard, Jason, who is standing guard outside, has enhanced strength and endurance, but is also a tracker. His stronger ability, his main ability, is strength and endurance, and his ability to track magic is relatively weak when compared to those trackers who have that as their main or only ability.

"The royal bloodline originally came to power because of the wide range of powerful abilities that it bore. In more recent times, your family members often exhibited multiple magical talents, not just one or two, though each family member displayed those talents to varying degrees. It is typical, with the royal line, to have two or more abilities that are as strong as other people's main ability."

Lily looked at her hands, as if they might suddenly reveal her power by glowing or shooting out balls of flame. A young girl seized them and ran her own fingers over Lily's fingernails. When she finished, Lily admired her newly shaped and painted nails, delighted to find they were already dry.

"But you mustn't try and do magic on your own, Your Majesty," Addison warned.

Lily looked at her guiltily, she had just decided to try and do magic if she was ever left alone.

"We don't know what, if any, effect spending so long in the other dimension may have had on your magical talents. And we are also unaware of how they will manifest since you are coming to them fully grown. Abilities are reasonably weak at birth and grow as the child grows, allowing them to learn to control them safely before the reach peak power. Yours may manifest at full strength without you knowing how to control them."

Lily's stomach dropped. What if growing up in the other dimension meant that her magical power was stunted, or that her abilities would never manifest?

"You will be fine, Your Majesty." Addison smiled at her and touched her arm. Lily immediately felt better and was suddenly suspicious of what Addison's abilities were.

"There is an extremely rare magic that usually only manifests in one person per generation. That ability allows the user to sense, and if strong enough, control, another person's power. Those found to have this power are called detectors, and they are very closely regulated.

"The current detector is Lady Octavia. You will meet her soon, and she will assess your power. This will allow us to teach you to use your abilities safely, without you inconveniently discovering that you possess destructive powers."

Lily felt a chill run down her spine. Destructive magic? What if she accidentally killed someone? She felt herself move as the chair floated her into the closet and her servants began dressing her. Someone moved behind her and she felt their fingers slide into her hair, massaging her scalp slightly. She sat back, enjoying the sensation.

She had no idea what was really going on here. Apparently, she really was in a completely different dimension to the one she had woken up in that morning. She had no idea why they had brought her here, or what danger she might be in—or who to trust, she realised, shooting a suspicious look at Addison. But, she relaxed back into the massage again, *this* she could get used to. Hurried as it was, Lily couldn't remember ever being so pampered in her life.

The fingers withdrew and Lily was prompted to stand up from her chair. She caught a glimpse of herself in a mirror and gasped.

"You look beautiful, Your Majesty," gushed Addison. The servants admired their work, nodding in agreement.

Lily took a couple of steps closer to the mirror, turning her face this way and that. She looked radiant, even to herself. Her skin glowed, and her green eyes beamed out at her, somehow highlighted though she couldn't see how they had done it. Her shoulder-length brown hair shimmered like silk, far different to the usual frizzy mess she tried to tame each morning.

She wore a red dress and heels, but the dress wasn't constricting and the heels felt comfortable, as if she were in her running shoes. She smiled at her reflection. Yes, she could certainly get used to this. Maybe being abducted and taken to another dimension wasn't so bad after all?

3

Addison and Lily exited the Lodge. Standing opposite the door was an imposing man who fell in behind the women as Addison swiftly led Lily through the palace toward her office. The halls were not what sprung to Lily's mind when she thought of a palace, which was fancy wall-paper and gold trim, with foot servants everywhere. Rather, the palace was a curious mix of modern architecture and what she would call 'rustic' or medieval. The dark hues from the extensive wooden and leather fixtures and furniture contrasted with the beautiful light grey stone walls. All the rooms she could see through open doors were well-lit, with large windows allowing plenty of natural light in.

They walked mainly in a silence broken occasionally by Addison pointing out a feature built by Lily's Great-Aunt Whosiwhatsit or doors that led to other areas of interest that Lily wouldn't remember later.

As they approached the door to Lily's office, she could hear raised voices, and Addison became increasingly agitated, casting glances behind them as if considering whether they should return to the Lodge. Lily quickened her pace slightly, and before Addison could think to stop her, she pushed open the door and slipped inside.

"...mentioned that we have magical abilities? That doesn't just come up in conversation."

An imposing woman, taller than Giles with broad shoulders was pacing in front of a large desk berating the older man. Her blue skirt was inhibiting her stride, but that just served to quicken her steps, her heels clicking angrily on the floor.

"Minister Bellingham," a petite woman who was extremely well put together spoke up politely from her position on the couch. "What's done is done. Perhaps instead of criticising Giles for this error, we should focus on how we might move forward with the plan?"

"You'll excuse me, Claire, if I don't take advice from the etiquette advisor," sneered Minister Bellingham. "Particularly one who has only been here all of five minutes."

"Yes, I must agree with Juliana," added a thin, brittle man seated in a chair and holding a glass of whiskey, which he raised in a toast to Minister Bellingham. "I really can't see what advice *the help* might provide to the foreign minister or myself. Perhaps, young lady," he learned forward with a patronising smile for Claire, "you should pipe down unless asked for your opinion."

Claire returned the brittle man's smile, though her eyes seemed to convey that she would very much like to throttle him.

"That's not what I meant at all, Jeremy," the imposing woman sighed, rubbing her eyes. "Ms Jones is a royal advisor and as entitled as any of us to voice her opinion, and it should carry equal weight." Minister Bellingham looked apologetically at Claire, clearly regretting her earlier comment.

"I dare say that I, as defence minister, might bring more

to the table than a mere *etiquette advisor*, and therefore my opinions should count for more." He sniffed, obviously offended, and took a drink.

"Minister Toot," a good-looking young man standing by the fireplace tried to interject.

"Oh no, Mr Wilcox, I will not be lectured to by Her Majesty's personal trainer," Minister Toot spat, shifting in his chair and angling his body away from the young man.

"I'm her warfare and combat advisor," the man muttered, eyes narrowing.

"Austin, ignore him," sympathised Claire. "Though perhaps we might get back to the more pressing matter at hand?"

"Yes, quite right," said Minister Bellingham, taking charge of the discussion once more. "There's nothing we can do about this error of judgement, but at least we can move forward according to the plan, and ensure that we provide Her Majesty with the appropriate information at the appropriate time."

"I *am* sorry, Minister," Giles interjected.

"Yes, but 'sorry' doesn't fix it, does it Giles? I mean really, the only thing worse would have been to blurt out that her entire family was assassinated three weeks ago and we don't know why or by whom and she is likely in very real danger of suffering the same fate herself!"

Giles looked abashed, and the other advisors all stared at the floor, feeling his embarrassment. Minister Bellingham sighed again, looking at her watch.

"And where are Addison and Jason? They really should have been here by now."

"We *are* here, Minister." A deep voice tinged with a smile came from behind Lily, startling her and making her jump. "As is Her Majesty."

The room froze for a second, Minister Bellingham's jaw

dropping and her cheeks flushing. Her advisors seemed to register the situation, and those who were sitting rose. In unison, they all dropped into bows and curtsies.

"Your Majesty," said Minister Bellingham, recovering and ushering Lily to a chair at the head of the assembled couches and chairs in the meeting area of her office.

Lily vaguely heard the woman introducing herself, but her mind was reeling.

Dead? All of them?

She had vaguely wondered why she hadn't been met immediately by these royal parents of hers, however she had just assumed that they were off doing royal things, or perhaps waiting for her to freshen up before being presented to them.

And she had said *family*. Now that Lily thought about it, it made sense for her parents to have more than one heir. And surely they wouldn't have sent her away if she was anything but a last resort. Which meant things were every bit as bad as Minister Bellingham had made it sound.

She is likely in very real danger of suffering the same fate herself. Lily felt sick.

"Ma'am?" The man with the deep voice was sitting next to her. She recognised him. He was the guard who had been standing outside her room. He was older than Lily and while he was an intimidatingly large and muscular man, his eyes were kind. Something about him made Lily feel safe. "Are you okay?"

Lily nodded and looked around. All her advisors were looking at her in concern and she realised they had been talking to her, but she hadn't heard a thing.

"Sorry," Lily said. "I must have been distracted by that whole 'high likelihood of assassination' thing."

Minister Bellingham looked annoyed at herself, and

Lily thought she saw the hint of a smile flit across Claire's face.

"I know it's a lot to take in, Your Majesty," said Jason, the guard.

"Yes, and we certainly didn't mean for you to find out like that," added Claire. She managed to sound sympathetic, rather than as if she was having a go at Minister Bellingham, but the foreign minister still squirmed.

"Your Majesty, I'm Jason." He smiled warmly at Lily. "I am the head of your Royal Guard, and responsible for your protection. I can assure you that we're doing everything possible to both investigate what happened to your family, and to find those behind it, as well as taking every precaution here within the palace to ensure your safety."

"But presumably you also took every precaution for the king and queen?"

"Ha! She's got you there," Minister Toot exclaimed happily into his whiskey.

Jason glared at the man, his muscles tensing. Lily thought Jason could probably snap Minister Toot like a twig.

"Your Majesty," Jason turned back to her, ignoring Minister Toot. "We have taken additional measures since the assassinations. We would not have retrieved you from the other dimension if we weren't confident we could protect you."

"What did happen to my family?" Lily asked quietly. The room stilled, eyes eventually finding their way to Minister Toot. It took a beat for the man to realise everyone was staring at him.

"Oh yes, this is me, isn't it?" He stood and tripped his way to a coffee table in the middle of the group. He set a small device on the table and pressed a button, muttering, "A picture tells a thousand words, yes?"

Suddenly the room around Lily faded and she found herself in a different part of the palace. Servants were bustling around but ignoring her and the advisors completely, focussed instead on a group of people who looked to be preparing to depart.

A familiarity about them struck Lily in the chest, and as a stunning woman in the centre of the chaos looked directly at her, Lily gasped.

You have your mother's eyes.

Lily moved without thinking over to the group, staring at the woman as she fussed about her four adult children, making sure they had everything they needed, regardless of their assurances that they were old enough to take care of themselves.

"Sarah and Liam, you are *not* to try and evade your security team again, do I make myself clear?"

Lily turned and found herself face to face with the king. Her father.

He looked through her at his younger children. Though his message was firm, his eyes still smiled.

"Dad, seriously." Liam rolled his eyes. "We'll be at a kid's soccer game. It's not like we need the security, but ignoring that, there's nothing there worth evading them for."

The queen crossed over and kissed each of them on the head.

"But we very much appreciate you attending," she said.

Her two children gave her a brief hug and hopped in a car that whisked them away.

"Isabella, you are too easy on them," the king chastised lightly.

"And you, Ben, are too strict," she gave him a small peck on his lips. "That's why you and my father got along so well."

"General Mortimer taught me some fine principles.

And he always said running a family was very similar to running an army."

"Yes sir," the two remaining children snapped to attention, giving him exaggerated salutes.

"Now that's more like it." King Benjamin smiled as his wife and children rolled their eyes at him. The queen addressed her eldest son.

"Daniel, please try and keep him in line."

"I'm not a miracle worker," he protested happily. "If you want him kept in line, you should send Emily with him instead."

"No way," his sister protested. "I'm going with mum. Her events are always heaps more fun."

As the siblings bantered, the queen stepped closer to her husband. He pulled her to him, and she rested her hands on his shoulders, looking him in the eye.

"Be safe," she whispered meaningfully, fear flitting across her face.

"Always." He kissed her, ignoring the groans of his children. "You know I'll always come back to you."

Lily felt intensely voyeuristic, but she couldn't draw herself away. They were all so familiar, though complete strangers. They were such a tight-knit group. As she watched, Lily longed to be a part of it, but though they were close enough to touch, she was on the outside looking in.

Lily felt a pang of loneliness, and with horror, she suddenly realised that they were all dead. Somehow this only increased her loneliness; they had even all died together.

Her longing to be a part of her biological family was replaced by guilt. She felt disloyal to her family back home. But they had never been the integrated unit that her biological family apparently was. Lily had always felt slightly left out. Different.

Why didn't they tell me?

As Lily watched two separate cars spiriting the king and his son and the queen and her daughter away, she became aware of her advisors arguing quietly behind her.

"What were you *thinking?*" Minister Bellingham hissed at Minister Toot.

"Well, it's always better to show rather than tell, don't you think?" He gestured at the scene around them with his whiskey glass.

"You will not *show* Her Majesty the assassination of her family. She doesn't need to see that. What is *wrong* with you?"

Lily looked at her advisors. Minister Bellingham looked like smoke might start emitting from her ears.

"I have to agree with Juliana," said Addison.

"We can't wrap her in cotton wool," Minister Toot argued defensively.

"Well no," Addison admitted. "But perhaps, if she does need to see her entire family murdered, we could save it for another day."

"Fine." Minister Toot poked irritably at a button, returning Lily to her office with a jolt.

"It's an immersion device," Claire explained, seeing Lily's confusion. "It allows the user to experience past events. I have one here for you that I was going to give you later. It has some happier memories of your family..."

Lily took the small device gratefully, thanking Claire as they all resumed their seats. She turned the device over in her hands. It was shiny steel and roughly the size of a battery for a torch, though lighter than she had expected. Without warning, the device collapsed in upon itself, now resembling a coin.

"Your Majesty." Minister Bellingham looked to have calmed herself, and now took control of the meeting, perhaps to bring it back in line with whatever the plan had been. "I understand this must all be quite confusing and overwhelming, and you must have many questions. If you'll permit me, I will do my best to explain the situation and why you're here, and then you can ask any questions you might have."

Lily nodded. *What have I gotten myself into?*

"As I believe Giles has told you, Highacre has developed the means of travelling between dimensions. This is a very closely guarded secret that not even the Prime Minister is aware of.

"Due to a threat to the royal line, the king sent the queen, while she was pregnant with you, to your dimension, where you were handed over to a specially selected family to raise you as their own. This would ensure, in the case of a cataclysmic event, that the royal line was preserved.

"Publicly, it was announced that the queen had miscarried. However, important figures in your father's government were told that you, in fact, survived. None were told of your true location. They were instead told that a distant cousin of the queen located in the remote island nation of Oppulus had fostered you. For convenience, the paper trail created to support this story modelled the cousin's family on your own back in your dimension. That way you can talk about them relatively freely."

Minister Bellingham paused, collecting herself. Lily felt the mood of the room dip, becoming more serious.

"Three weeks ago, immediately following the scene we just witnesses, the royal family was assassinated in an alarmingly efficient and effective manner." Minister Bellingham indicated to Jason that he should take over the brief. Jason cleared his throat.

"Your Majesty, as you saw, your family left for various events in pairs. Despite the separation, they were all assassinated at almost the exact same time. Everyone was shot except for Prince Liam and Princess Sarah, who were killed by an explosion. We are unsure how the attackers managed to get the information about where everyone would be, nor how they managed to evade security. All of that information was close hold."

"Could they have used magic?" Lily asked. "It would be easy to kill people if you could become invisible, or control the elements."

Jason smiled gently at her. "That's true, ma'am, but remember, we have magic on our side too. Some of our guards can detect invisible people, or people using any kind of magic. None was detected."

"I'm telling you, it was the Meridians," Austin piped up for the first time. "With their cybernetic implants, they can control weapons remotely and even guide bullets to their targets. I saw it in the war."

"And those Valmeadians have those enchanted weapons that never miss," added Jeremy Toot with admiration.

"At any rate," Jason continued, "we should have detected intelligence about the threat beforehand and prevented it. We should have seen this coming."

"And it is exactly that complete failure of our intelligence network that led the Prime Minister to disestablish the Highacren Intelligence Agency," said Minister Toot haughtily, clearly thinking that the complete obliteration of the country's entire intelligence capability was a good thing.

"But Minister, should we not re-establish something in the HIA's place?" asked Claire demurely. "How will we do any better in the future?"

"Well, we won't do any worse," Minister Toot shot back.

Lily wasn't entirely sure the retort made any sense, but

before anyone could respond to the minister, Giles interjected.

"The important point right now is just that. Following the death of the royal family, the Prime Minister has taken charge, enacted his emergency powers, abolished the HIA, and is in complete control of Highacre. As Jason pointed out, there clearly must have been insider help here, and it behoves us all to ensure we protect the information to which we are privy in order to keep Her Majesty safe."

"She's not safe," said Minister Toot.

"Yes she is," argued Giles.

"Well, we've screened the staff, but once everyone knows that she's back? Especially the Prime Minister—" interjected Minister Bellingham.

"The Prime Minister might hurt me?" Lily interrupted.

"The Prime Minister..." Minister Bellingham paused, considering her words. "He used to be a relatively benign man, but the vacuum left by the death of the royal family ignited a previously unknown hunger for power. He quickly invoked the emergency powers and has been abusing them. More recently, he has taken on a nationalistic bent and his rhetoric is, frankly, alarming. He appears to be trying to ensure that he has sole power over things that previously required a majority of support from the Parliament. And there are reports of disappearances..." The minister trailed off, and the rest of the advisors shifted in their seats.

Well, that settles that.

Lily made her mind up. A group of unstoppable magical, enchanted, or cybernetically enhanced assassins and a crazy prime minister out to get her? There was no way she was going to hang around here waiting to die. Even if she did like Giles and Addison. And really, fabulous as this lifestyle was, it wasn't worth dying for. She needed to get out of here.

"Thank you all so much for everything." Lily politely smiled at everyone around the table. "It's been really lovely. I've had a great time, all the food and pampering, and you've all been so kind...but I think I'd really like to go home now."

An uncomfortable silence settled over the room before her advisors all spoke at once.

"Giles, maybe you should—"

"I really don't think—"

"Jason might be best placed to—"

It was Minister Bellingham who responded.

"The thing about interdimensional travel is..." she started, but then paused and took a different track. "The discovery of interdimensional travel has provided Highacre with a significant technological edge over our adversaries. Almost a decade ago, during the war, our interdimensional travel scouts discovered advanced weapons technology that they retrieved and we were able to reproduce here. That technology was the key to our success in the war, and until that time, despite the extraordinary leadership and strategic skill of General Mortimer, the queen's father, it was highly likely that Meridia would have emerged victorious.

"Not only did we win the war, but the loss hit Meridian technological advancement and trade hard, and they have been trying to claw their way back ever since. Key to this is the Disputed Region."

Minister Bellingham placed a device on the coffee table and a holographic map emerged, clearly highlighting Highacre, Meridia, and Valmead. She pointed to an area in the far northeast of Highacre where the country bordered Meridia.

"Highacre fought hard at the end of the war to secure this area, as it contains the only known vein of felixium. This mineral is essential to power the machine that enables interdimensional travel. The area also contains several other resources that are critical to Meridia. If they were to lose access to those resources, it would devastate their economy and way of life. As a result, the fighting was fierce.

"Ultimately, both countries reached a tentative ceasefire whereby each could access the resources they required." The minister leant slightly towards Lily. "We purported to need some other resources within the region as we didn't want to draw attention to our desire for felixium, which is otherwise completely useless.

"At the same time as the assassination of the royal family, Meridian forces in the Disputed Region seized some of the land held by Highacre, aiming to secure our titanium mines. Titanium is essential to Meridian technology. Unfortunately, the land they seized also holds our felixium mines."

"Well, how much do we have in stock?"

"We used the last of the felixium to bring you home. There is no more."

THE MINISTER's words struck Lily like a hammer.

"Well, take the mines back! Is Highacre just going to roll over and let Meridia take its land?" Lily demanded.

"As we said earlier, Your Majesty, the development of interdimensional travel has been a tightly held secret. The Parliament doesn't know about it, and thus they don't know how valuable the mines are. Even the Prime Minister doesn't know. They have no intention of using force to retake our mines. They have issued diplomatic protests, but that's as far as they intend to take it."

"Tell them how important it is! Surely then they would be happy to use any means necessary."

"We cannot make the knowledge about interdimensional travel public." Minister Bellingham's tone turned forceful. "Meridia would easily develop their own machine, and any technological edge that we have been able to gain—like the edge that allowed us to clench victory from the jaws of defeat in the war—would be lost."

"Not to mention," Minister Toot piped up, "that if Meridia knew about interdimensional travel, and knew they currently possess the only known source of the mineral required to enable it, we'd never be able to recover the mines."

"Well, don't make it public then." Lily was getting frustrated. "You only need to tell the politicians needed to authorise the military."

"Your Majesty," Minister Bellingham smiled wryly. "While I would not wish to speak ill of my colleagues, telling that many politicians about something that could help them come re-election time *is* making it public. Besides, we can't tell the Prime Minister, and telling him would be the minimum required. At best, he would use interdimensional travel for himself, cement his power, and use the technology against the people of Highacre, perhaps banishing political opponents to other dimensions, for example. At worst, he would still do all of that, and then sell the technology to the Meridians anyway."

"This is part of why we need you, Your Majesty," said Addison. "When you are queen, you will be able to order the military to retake the mines without telling the Prime Minister about interdimensional travel."

Lily tried to wrap her head around everything. She hadn't signed up for this. Sure, the part of being a queen that meant being pampered was great, but she wasn't at all keen on the part that came with being the target of homicidal maniacs and having to order soldiers into battle, potentially to their deaths, just so she could go home.

"It is likely that your biological claim to the throne will be challenged. That's fine, we have the evidence to back it up, and later today Lady Octavia will assess your magical potential. But we believe the Prime Minister will challenge your suitability to be crowned because you haven't lived here. He'll argue you don't know our ways, and you could not therefore appropriately decide what is in Highacre's best interests and act for the good of the country," Addison said, then hesitated before continuing.

"In order to be crowned queen of Highacre, you need to be presented to the Council of Elders for a confirmation hearing. They will run initial tests on you to prove that you are who we say you are, that you have magical power, and then you will be questioned. The council comprises twelve senior members of Parliament, all elders and all from powerful families. They can ask you literally anything but are likely to exploit your absence from Highacre and therefore lack of familiarity with our country. It is important for us to ensure that they do not realise that you have not been raised in our world at all. We will need to do this within the next two months as, by law, if three months pass without a ruling monarch and the royal family cannot produce a legitimate heir, the Parliament is to select a new royal family."

This seemed impossible to Lily. How was she supposed to learn everything about an unknown country within two months?

"We are going to put you through an intensive training program to bring you up to speed. Claire, Austin, and I will ensure you know enough about Highacre to deal with the council's questions, and Lady Octavia will address the magical side," Addison explained.

Lily's mind drifted. She had wanted direction, purpose in her life. But this? It was too much.

Be careful what you wish for.

She rubbed her face. Did her family know she was missing yet? When they realised, they would be worried sick.

"Ma'am," Addison spoke gently and lightly touched her arm. Lily looked vaguely in her direction. "Your Majesty, I know this is a lot, and I know you probably feel trapped—"

"I *am* trapped!" Lily snapped, fear and anxiety overwhelming her.

"Not trapped as much as temporarily stalled..." Minister Toot received a sharp look from Minister Bellingham as he spoke.

"You all kidnapped me, brought me here against my will, and did so knowing that I couldn't go home even if I wanted to." Lily felt the anger rising, her voice getting louder. She knew she was about to go into a full-blown tantrum and she didn't care.

"Knowing that you were all putting me in danger, that people would likely try to assassinate me—"

"Your Majesty, we thought—"

"You thought!" Lily bellowed. "Any thoughts you had were only about yourselves, not about me. What about what I need? My safety? What I want?" Lily's anger burned itself out, and she felt dangerously close to crying. She sat back in her chair, arms crossed and blinking furiously.

"Your Majesty," Addison said quietly, reaching for her arm.

"Don't." Lily pulled her arm away from Addison, looking accusingly at the older woman's hand. "What is your ability, anyway?"

Addison looked guilty. "I have persuasive abilities, Your Majesty. I am best at making people feel better, as if all is well."

"Well, don't."

"Your Majesty?"

"Don't use your magic on me. You can't just go around making people feel better without asking."

She knew she sounded ridiculous, but they had all the power here and it frustrated her. She should be their equal. She was an adult, just like them. And, if they were to be believed, she was to be the queen. *Their* queen. It occurred to her that it wasn't helpful for them to see her upset like this.

She looked over at Jason, fighting to calm herself. "Did any of you let my family know that I'd be gone for an indefinite period of time?" Jason blushed.

"Of course we did, Your Majesty," Giles said with a smile.

Jason coughed nervously. "Actually..."

"Actually, what?" Giles's eyes narrowed.

"Boris was supposed to inform the family."

"What do you mean *supposed to*?" Giles asked, his tone dangerous.

"It was his role, but unfortunately he thought Paul had done it, so..."

Giles turned such a deep red that Lily thought steam might come out his ears. Jason turned back to Lily, avoiding looking at Giles.

"So, no one told my family anything?"

"Ma'am, ultimately it was my responsibility, and I failed. I'm sorry."

"It's okay," Lily said.

It wasn't, but there clearly wasn't anything that could be done about it now. She didn't know Jason, but something about him was reassuring, and she wanted to keep him onside. Especially if she was stuck in this strange dimension with people who wanted her dead. Plus, she remembered what Boris was like. Perhaps Jason's real mistake was trusting him with such an important task.

Lily fretted about her family not knowing where she was. Especially now that she knew there was no way to get them a message. She stood. This was all too much. She needed space and some time to process everything. As one, the room stood with her.

"I'm going to my room."

Lily headed for the door. Addison, Giles, and Jason made to go with her. Lily rounded on them.

"Alone."

She stared them down until, one by one, they backed off. Jason was the last to show that he would respect her desire, though Lily knew he would follow at a distance. For that, she was grateful, but she wasn't about to say so.

Lily turned and swept out of the room, opting not to slam the door. She decided cool displeasure was more mature. More regal. Outside of her office, Lily's emotions swamped her.

I need air.

Blinking back tears, Lily ignored the path back to the Lodge, and instead took every staircase she encountered, aiming for the ground and a way outside.

Finally, she burst through a door and found herself in warm sunlight. She closed her eyes and took some deep breaths of fresh air, trying to calm herself. She started walking without purpose, focussing on her breathing.

Her parents were going to kill her. She imagined how they might react. Lily wasn't the most reliable daughter, but she would always answer their calls. Or at least send a text message in response. Guiltily, she realised that it might be a few days before they realised that something was wrong. Probably when April reached out about their weekend together. Lily wiped at tears that began to fall unbidden. April was going to be upset. They were so close, and for Lily to just leave like this... April would think she'd forgotten.

Lily sat on a bench, staring through the beautifully landscaped gardens that surrounded a pond full of fish-like creatures, but seeing none of it. Her older brother and sister, David and Elaine, would probably assume she had just run off to have fun somewhere without telling anyone. They seemed to think she was a flake. It frustrated Lily. She couldn't figure out why they thought that. Sure, she didn't know what she wanted to do with her life, but she would never just run off without telling someone. Especially if that meant standing April up.

Oh no—Brandon.

She was meant to meet him and her best friend Gemma at the bar tonight. *Well, at least he won't be waiting alone.*

Lily leant forward, her elbows on her knees, her head in her hands. She sat that way until she felt slightly calmer, then leant back on the bench, staring at the pond.

Something in front of her shimmered slightly, and then Claire materialised without warning.

"Shit! Where did you... How did you...?"

"Forgive me, Your Majesty," Claire dropped into a deep curtsy, keeping her eyes respectfully lowered. "I thought I would check on you."

"But how...?" Lily gestured at Claire.

"It is called chameleoning, Your Majesty. I can alter my appearance to blend in with my surroundings. An ability that makes me highly suited to being a lady's maid, which is what I was before being chosen as your etiquette teacher."

Lady's maid wasn't where Lily's mind had instinctively gone. Blending in with surroundings sounded like spy stuff.

"Staff should be able to fade into the background," Claire said, seeming to read Lily's mind.

Lily looked at Claire, only to find she had all but disappeared again. It was like Lily could see through her, but that wasn't true. Claire was still there. She had just taken on all the colours and features behind her, so she only seemed to have disappeared.

"That's amazing!" Lily couldn't hide her fascination, despite the stress of the day and her anxiety. She wondered if she could do that. Or maybe disappear altogether.

"Thank you, Your Majesty. You will find, and no doubt Lady Octavia will explain, that there are usually two sides to an ability, and people within Highacre tend to manifest one side or the other. I can become a chameleon, but there are others who have the power to make the unseen seen. If they are around, they can act as a block on my power, or they can see me and alert others to my presence."

"So your ability works until one of these people is around?"

"Well, as with all magic, it depends very much on the relative strength of each person's power. If my skill as a chameleon exceeds that of the revealer, they will not be able to detect me. In your security detail are some of the most powerful revealers in all of Highacre."

Claire indicated a path, and the two women headed off to stroll in the gardens. Lily felt better moving again.

"Your Majesty," Claire began, "how are you feeling?"

"I'm feeling a bit like I'm stuck in a world where people want to kill me and everyone I'm meant to trust is lying to me. Other than that, fine."

Claire looked appraisingly at Lily.

"Your Majesty..." Claire hesitated. That hesitation, more than anything, grabbed Lily's attention. Claire did not seem like the kind of person who hesitated. She was soft-spoken, and yet she had a commanding presence and had gone toe-to-toe with some of the older advisors. "You are correct. This is an extremely dangerous time to be the sovereign of Highacre."

"Is that supposed to be reassuring?" Lily sulked.

"No, it is not," Claire snapped. Lily looked at her in shock, but Claire glared right back. "There is no time to moddycoddle you, and doing so would do you no favours. You need to be strong. Highacre needs a powerful monarch. You can hide in the corner and wait to see if we recover the felixium mines and then escape if that is your wish, but you will be in every bit as much danger as if you had taken action. So take control, Your Majesty."

Claire stopped walking and turned to face Lily, her eyes boring into Lily's, urging her to shed her fear and go on the offensive. It was powerful, and Lily felt inspired despite herself.

"I don't know how," Lily said.

To her horror, she found she was on the verge of tears again, and she would not cry in front of Claire. She already felt like a kid trying to play at an adult's game. If she cried, Claire would lose all respect for her. *Assuming she has any.* Lily turned and resumed their walk.

"We will all help you, Your Majesty." Claire's voice was soft now, and Lily risked a look at her. She was expecting to see pity, but instead found reassurance.

"You might not be able to trust us. But we will teach you what you need to know and provide you with the tools you require to succeed. It will be up to you to get to know us and determine who, if anyone, you can trust. You will remain surrounded by us, even if you hide in your rooms. But if you interact with us, you will at least start to learn who you are dealing with."

Lily thought about Claire's words. It was true. Whether she cowered in her room or jumped right in and accepted her fate, she would remain in Highacre, at least until they had some more felixium. But if she went for it, if she learned and trained and fought to become queen... Did she want to be queen?

Lily didn't know if she was the right person. Of course, she could live in the palace and smile and wave with the best of them. But being a ruler, where her decisions affected millions of people? Where her decisions could cost them their lives? Was she truly cut out for that? Could she handle that level of responsibility?

Claire was staring at her, but her eyes were softer this time.

"One step at a time, Your Majesty. Focus on how you want to respond to your current predicament. There is time enough to consider your future."

If I have one. Lily banished the thought. She couldn't spend the next however long worrying about whether she would be killed. The fear would paralyse her, and her fear of death would keep her from living.

Claire was right; she needed to decide what to do until felixium was available, and it seemed like becoming queen was the only way to regain access to the mines. She could figure out the next step after that.

"Thank you, Claire."

"Of course, Your Majesty. I look forward to our etiquette lessons together. I will spend much of our time teaching you how to conceal your thoughts and emotions to ensure that they cannot be used against you to your, and the country's, detriment."

That seemed extreme, but again, before Lily could voice her concern, Claire continued.

"It shouldn't surprise you, Your Majesty, that even aside from the assassins, you, as the monarch, will have enemies. You may not be aware of just how many people either wish you ill, or simply would prefer you not succeed. Of course, your enemies will also have other people helping them who themselves may not be against you, who may even be on your side, but who provide your enemies information, either willingly or unwillingly."

"They'd torture people?"

Claire laughed lightly. "I only meant that some people may gather intelligence simply by having a conversation with someone and asking the right questions. A member of your staff being asked about how their day is going may not realise that their response is telling the inquirer that it is a perfect day move against the soverign."

Lily noticed Claire was steering them through the garden and back towards the palace.

"How are your etiquette lessons going to help me with all of that?" Lily asked.

"Etiquette, Your Majesty, governs social behaviours and interactions, and in particular dictates behaviour in polite society. It tells us what to do and not do, say and not say. It teaches us how to hold ourselves and when and how to move. If you learn this, you will be able to interact with a variety of different people in an expected and accepted way, and keep a hold of your personal instincts and reactions.

"If someone says something that shocks or alarms you, despite whatever you feel internally, your external reaction will be the reaction required in that circumstance. Perhaps the information is only shocking if you are aware of other information. You can choose, through your behaviour, whether to allow the other person to know that you know that second piece of information."

Lily considered this. It sounded very useful, if complicated. She couldn't imagine the level of training that she would need to do that instinctively, though.

"How am I supposed to learn to do all that so quickly?"

Claire smiled and looked at Lily. "An excellent question, Your Majesty. It will be very difficult. Unfortunately, we have only been allocated two lesson per week. Perhaps you might consider mentioning this to Giles and Addison? They are in charge of your schedule."

Lily wondered whether Giles or Addison would listen to her if she did ask to have more lessons with Claire. "If you've told them how important this training is, why would they not give us more time?"

Claire shrugged. "Perhaps they are simply more focussed on ensuring you have enough information to succeed at your confirmation hearing. However, etiquette training takes time, and cannot simply be acquired after all of their other priorities are attended to. And it is possible that by then, it will be too late."

The way Claire said this gave Lily the impression that this was a favourable interpretation of Giles and Addison's reasoning. The clear implication was that one, or both, had more nefarious motivations in stunting her education. But Lily trusted Giles and Addison. *Or rather*, she corrected herself, *I like them*. She wasn't sure that she liked *or* trusted Claire. The anxiety that had been niggling at Lily suddenly swamped her, and her chest felt tight.

"For completeness, Your Majesty, as well as my cloaking ability, I have a minor talent for perception. It allows me a heightened ability to read people, and my particular skill is in identifying when someone is lying. I cannot, however, read minds."

Lily immediately felt self-conscious, even though at the moment, she knew her thoughts and emotions were clearly displayed all over her face for anyone to read, regardless of magic.

"As I'm sure you can imagine, this skill has been particularly handy in recent times when it has become difficult to identify friend or foe and everyone suddenly seems to have their own agenda."

"I can trust my advisors, though." The statement came out as more of a question, and Lily watched Claire's expression as they entered the palace. Her lips drew into a tight line.

"Your Majesty, one might observe that, despite the no

doubt extensive checks that the security team has told us they have carried out, your family also trusted the exact same group of people."

Claire opened the door to the corridor leading to the Lodge, bowing slightly and indicating that she would leave Lily here. "And that appears to have gone quite poorly for them in the end."

Lily wanted to ask more, but it was clear that the conversation was over, and Claire slipped through a door and was gone.

As she walked toward the Lodge alone, she heard voices ahead and strained to make out what was being said. Rounding a hairpin turn, Lily saw Giles and Addison having an animated discussion. Lily tried to balance wanting to hurry to avoid missing the conversation and not alerting them to her presence. Finally, she could just make out what Addison was saying.

"...and just what do you think her reaction is going to be when she finds out the truth?"

5

"WHAT TRUTH?" Lily asked with more confidence than she felt, striding towards Giles and Addison, who had the grace to look abashed. "What are you lying about?"

"Your Majesty! We didn't see you there…"

"No kidding. What are you keeping from me?"

"Your Majesty—" Giles began in what he clearly thought was a calming voice.

"Don't you 'Your Majesty' me!" Lily huffed, pushing between Giles and Addison and entering the Lodge. Giles and Addison followed her in, somewhat meekly. Lily sat on one of the leather couches and looked at them. Giles and Addison moved slowly until they were standing meekly before her like naughty schoolchildren.

Lily tried to calm herself. She was equal parts angry that no one was being straight with her and afraid. She was in a strange place, she didn't know what was going on and she wasn't sure who she could trust. Lily took a deep breath.

"So what am I going to react poorly to finding out?"

"I'm so sorry Your Majesty," Addison laughed, embarrassed. "That must have sounded so dramatic. We just received word that Lady Octavia can't come until tomorrow. I know you were excited about discovering your abilities, so I thought you might be disappointed. It would have been a fun way to end an otherwise overwhelming day."

Though there was an air of truth in Addison's explanation, Lily felt like it wasn't complete somehow. That something was being held back. She wasn't being told everything.

"Okay, well, if she's not coming then I might rest in my room for a bit," Lily said pointedly.

Both advisors sprang to their feet and gave a little nod of their heads. Assuring Lily that they were a mere button press away, they left Lily alone in her rooms.

Lily walked wearily to her bedroom, closing the door behind her. She sat on her couch and fumed quietly for a bit, the resentment she'd felt leaving her office returning. *How could they?* Lily was frustrated that the advisors had played with her life like this. That they had made the decision to bring her to Highacre—knowing that she couldn't return—without discussing it with her. It wasn't them who would be assassinated. And how did she even know that there weren't a dozen other heirs hidden in other dimensions? All waiting, just in case. If she were killed, they would simply retrieve the next on the list and continue on.

How do they even know I'm the right girl?

She felt powerless and alone, as well as slightly terrified. Lily stood. She had to pull herself together; she knew that. She could have a good cry tonight by herself, but there would be a limit to how much time they would let her have alone, and she needed to figure out what she was going to do.

She paced over to her dressing table and sat again, looking at herself in the mirror. She looked like a scared kid. That wouldn't do. She would need to look calm and self-assured if she was going to take some control back. If she was going to have her advisors treat her as an equal, and not as their doll to play with.

Something caught her eye and Lily noticed an envelope on her dressing table, propped up against the mirror. She was certain it hadn't been there before.

Lily picked up the envelope. It was stiff parchment that she associated with fancy stationery. She flipped it over and saw that it was sealed with wax. Lily ran her fingers over the seal, examining the intricate crest. Lily didn't want to ruin it, but her curiosity about what might be inside won out, and she cracked the wax with her thumb, opening the envelope.

Inside was a letter, written in ink on similarly thick, expensive paper.

> *Your Majesty,*
>
> *Forgive this mysterious approach, but it is not safe for me to come to you directly. I was a friend of your parents and feel that I owe it to them to reach out to you, no matter the personal danger that I will face.*
>
> *I must warn you that you are in great danger. The people who murdered your family know of your return. They intend to kill you as they killed your parents and siblings. You might think that you are safe in the palace. Your advisors may tell you that you are safe. I can only stress that your family also thought that they were safe, and they also trusted their advisors. The same advisors you now trust.*
>
> *You must question the level of information they are allowing you. I am sure that they have explained that they have brought you back to assume the throne to ensure that Highacre is not plunged into instability. Yes, the Prime Minister has invoked emergency powers.*

*But the entire royal family was assassinated! This does
not seem an unreasonable action in the circumstances.*

*Your advisors have enjoyed the privilege of holding
one of the most protected, most lucrative secrets in our
country: interdimensional travel. Perhaps it is this that
they are so desperate to protect, and not Highacre.*

*Unfortunately, I do not have answers for you,
though I will continue to search for them and I will
share with you what I know. In the meantime, I have
provided a map on the back of this letter to the room
that houses the interdimensional travel machine. I
know your advisors have not shown it to you. I think it
pertinent that you know where it is and how it operates.
If your life is in danger, it may well be your only means
of escape.*

Sincerely,
A Friend

Lily read the letter twice, making sure she missed nothing. It echoed some of her suspicions about not being told
the full story, and about her advisors keeping things from
her. She looked at the map and wondered for the first time
why they hadn't shown her the machine.

This mysterious friend clearly didn't know about the
absence of felixium. So he or she wasn't completely in the
know either. Nevertheless, she felt she should see the
machine and learn more about it. It would be good to know
how to operate it for when they had felixium.

On a whim, Lily grabbed a notebook that Addison had
given to her and transposed the map into it. She hid the
letter beneath the drawer in her dressing table and
decided to head off to find the machine. Lily paused, her
hand on the door. Jason would surely follow her. Should
she try to shake him? Lily doubted that she could. He

knew the palace better than she did, and had magical abilities.

Maybe keeping my bodyguard nearby is a good idea. What with the high likelihood of assassins being out to get me and all. Feeling slightly reassured about her ever-present shadow, Lily opened the door and went to find the machine.

<hr>

Claire hurried down the grassy hill towards a large and intricately decorated fountain surrounded by park benches. She was huddled slightly against the cold and windy weather, which had not yet carried through with its threat of rain. She popped the collar on her trench coat and kept one hand gently on her hat to ensure it didn't blow away.

She spotted the man easily. He was the only one there, sitting hunched over on a bench. Everyone else was apparently too smart to be outside. She inwardly rolled her eyes as she hurried towards him, the loose hair that had escaped her hat whipping around her head.

"Isn't this a bit cliche?"

The man shrugged as he threw some more small crumbs from his crumpled paper bag onto the ground for the eagerly awaiting snufflepidgeons.

"No one would think a spy would try to look like a spy," he responded, slightly sarcastically. "And besides, there aren't any spies anymore since the Prime Minister got rid of the agency." He sounded bitter and petulant. "And besides, you're not looking too 'undercover' yourself."

Claire mentally examined her outfit and decided that he was referring to her trench coat. She conveniently ignored her large, floppy brimmed hat and dark glasses. It still annoyed her that he had insisted she not cloak herself using her ability.

"My coat is perfectly reasonable in this weather." She removed her hat and smoothed her hair down before crossing her legs away from him. "And at least I haven't paired it with a detective's hat and a newspaper. Could you not find your nose glasses?"

He chuckled slightly. "Call me nostalgic. Why not dress as the failed spy that I am?" His voice grew bitter again. "Not like I can find a new career at my age."

"Oh, come on. You have plenty of skills that all sorts of companies would pay very well for. X-ray vision and low-grade mind reading? You could walk into any job you wanted. And besides, what do you think should have happened? The entire royal family was wiped out at the exact same time on the same day, and the agency didn't even have a clue that there was a credible threat against any of them?" She pulled out her phone and pretended to type a message. "Disbanding the whole thing might have been a tad dramatic, but really, what would you have done? If you kept the agency in place, you would have had to somehow recheck and validate everyone. And who would have been able to do that?"

The man scoffed and kicked at a rock on the ground with his shoe. He hated it when she played devil's advocate.

"True. But not establishing something else in its place? Is it better to have no intelligence capability whatsoever? What are we meant to do with no intelligence agency? Tell me that's not Meridia's doing."

Claire got up and strolled around the area, still playing with her phone but being careful not to trip on the cobblestones in her heels. He'd raised his voice and was talking far too openly, which made her nervous. He was sloppy now that he thought it was all over—and angry.

"And just what are a bunch of completely unregulated highly trained operatives with abilities that allow them to become invisible, control minds, and get past security going to do without a mission? Join the Peace Corps? I don't think so."

She walked past him, still on her phone, and touched his arm lightly as if, distracted, she had walked into him. *Calm.*

He sighed and emptied his remaining crumbs onto the ground. "I know, too much, too much." He got up and shuffled towards the fountain. "How's our girl?"

Claire sighed and wandered behind him, still playing with her phone, appearing, to anyone who might watch her, to be engrossed in the device. She sat primly on the fountain's edge, thinking about how to answer her old mentor's question. So far, her impression of Lily was that of a typical teenager trying to find her way in the world. Too young to have it figured out, but too old to be told what to do. She enjoyed the luxuries of her new role, but would she be up for the role itself?

She seemed willing to learn and be guided, but not blindly so. But she was too timid. There were flashes of willingness to assert herself, but Highacre would need more than flashes. And while she certainly was intelligent, she lacked confidence and largely underestimated herself, which left her vulnerable to manipulation. In fact, now that Claire thought about it, Lily underestimated herself in all areas—intelligence, capability, and looks. She was a pretty girl and Claire thought, somewhat cynically, that might come in handy. But her underestimation meant that she wasn't using all the tools she had available to her advantage. Claire made a mental note to address this during their training.

"She is naive and completely in the dark. No one went with her to that other dimension to ensure she knew who she was, let alone to prepare her for what she needs to do.

What was the point of hiding an heir to take over if the rest of the family were killed without ensuring that they prepared the heir to take over?" Claire blew her fringe out of her eyes, clearly frustrated. She was still focussed on her phone, and to any casual observer, she might be having an argument with a friend or lover.

"Maybe it's better if she is replaced, then."

Claire looked at the older man in complete disbelief, ignoring her phone and nearly blowing her own cover. She was rusty, too—had lost all her good habits and developed bad ones in their place. But she would need to be at the top of her game if she was going to both protect the sovereign and uncover the plot behind the assassinations.

Not that it was her job to investigate the assassinations. There was no agency to demand it of her. And even if she figured it out, then what? Obviously, she would turn the conspirators in, but to whom? And what would she do when it was all over? Claire deliberately turned her mind from such thoughts. Better to focus on the task at hand. She looked at the old man. He looked tired, but he had a twinkle in his eye.

"You don't really mean that," Claire said as she resumed tapping angrily at her phone, unable to completely omit the question from her statement.

"We need a powerful leader. I don't care who it is. The Prime Minister is evil. Disbanding the HIA was only the first step. He's taken unprecedented power and is increasingly spouting that nationalistic bullshit. Not to mention the disappearances. Did you hear about Dobson?"

Claire imperceptibly shook her head.

"Gone. No trace of him. He went to the bathroom and never came back. What a way to go." He shuffled around Claire to her other side, staring up at the fountain as if it were fascinating.

"Meridia is at our door. We have underestimated them for too long, and they have used that to cover their plan. We don't even know the true extent of their cybernetic abilities anymore. They are playing the long game, and they are playing it beautifully." He turned, looking at the trees. "And they will win."

"No." Claire stood angrily and walked over to another bench, brushing down her skirt. "They will not win. We will not let them."

"You'll train her then?"

"In the time we have? Impossible. We're starting from scratch and it's not even *real* to her. Grabbing a teenage girl and telling her she's royalty? It's not helping. When they're not distracting her with the opulence of her position, she's terrified about assassins. And not without reason." Claire sighed, "She doesn't need a palace, she needs a boot camp."

Claire put her phone back in her pocket and crossed her arms, looking at the fountain. "We have two months to turn her into a confident, shrewd, and wise leader. No one can achieve that. She hasn't even seen Lady Octavia. What if she doesn't have any power? Or can't use her abilities? Why wasn't having Lady Octavia assess her the first thing they did? There are too many conflicting interests at play."

The man sat heavily next to her. As he sighed, his body drooped as if he was slowing deflating.

"Then she will fail and we shall all fall into oppression."

Claire looked at her old master with disdain. He had always had a flair for the dramatic. He looked up into her eyes.

"Oh, unless you were to do something about it," he said.

"Like you are?"

The older man scoffed and looked sadly up at the fountain. "My cover's blown. With how he took down the agency, everyone knows who I am, what I did, and what my abilities are. My hands are tied and if I tried to help, I would do more harm than good. You know that. And you know I would help if I thought I could do anything useful."

He glanced in Claire's direction under the pretence of watching some squirrels. "The new assets, you and your peers, you're all still good to go. He didn't bother with identifying you to the world like he did with me and my cohort. Didn't think you newbies were a threat. I wish it were different, but it's all up to you, kid. You hold the power to determine which way this goes."

Claire considered this. He was right. The Prime Minister blew the cover of all the agency's top agents, revealing their identities and ensuring that they could never again work in the field. But he didn't reveal the identities of the junior agents. Which suddenly struck Claire as odd. Why not blow all the agents' covers? Why leave some in the shadows?

Claire thought about her peers. They had gone through the academy together and navigated the trials put before them to weed out the talent from those who would likely get themselves killed in the field. Or get others killed. That should have bonded them together, but as they had all headed out to their various assignments, they had lost touch and grown apart.

Reflecting on them now, there wasn't a single one of them that Claire felt she could trust. There had been a strong clique that was overly ambitious and self-centred, and had worked together to achieve their aim of passing the course, but had screwed over anyone else who had gotten in their way. One by one, everyone who wasn't a member of the clique had failed or dropped out. Everyone but Claire.

It made sense that the agency would be looking to recruit pragmatic people willing to be ruthless and deceitful to achieve their mission. But for Claire, the mission had always been about king and country. Perhaps she had been more alone in that mindset than she thought.

The clique bothered her now. It seemed like too many people with questionable loyalties in the one class. Had the timing been planned? They were the last class to graduate before the assassinations. Claire wondered where they were now, and what they might be up to. She made a mental note to look into their current locations, and to refresh herself on what abilities they all had.

Her old mentor stood as slowly as a man twenty years his senior would.

"Keep her, replace her. It's of no consequence. Just make sure the true power is Highacre and *not* Meridia."

The man shuffled off and Claire pulled her phone back out, reaching out with her power to see if anyone was around and, when satisfied that she was safe, blended into the surrounding environment.

"Your classmates are still out there; maybe some of them can help you," he said, pausing before turning and heading towards a nearby pub. "Though I imagine that some of them are also busy helping the other side."

6

Lily would have missed the small opening to the hallway but for the quiet muttering that drew her attention. She stepped back and looked closely at the small hallway that led off the main corridor she had been following. There was nothing overtly hiding it, but it had been designed so that the wood panelling and stone that adorned the walls of the main corridor were continued down the offshoot in such a way as to trick the eye into thinking that it was a continuation of the wall.

With only the slightest hesitation, Lily turned down the hallway and followed it until she arrived at a doorway that led into a bigger room that either seemed to have no overhead lighting, or otherwise the current occupant didn't see a need to use it. The resultant effect was that Lily felt as if she had arrived in a basement. There were an array of glowing colours in different areas of the room, each lighting the walls. All sorts of scientific equipment was set up on a bench, where beakers and tubes bubbled and dripped, giving the room a dank feeling.

The source of the muttering was a thin, elderly man with crazy white hair standing in front of a bizarre machine that was taller than Lily. It was made of a hodgepodge of different metals and comprised of two large pillars that arched up like either side of a lyre. The pillars were connected at a broad baseplate. *This must be it.*

The man failed to notice Lily enter the room. She watched him for a full minute before she started feeling intrusive and a little creepy and thought that she should alert him to her presence.

"Um, hello?"

The bizarrely magnified eyes that looked around and up at her through thick glasses would have startled Lily if they hadn't so perfectly completed the mad scientist stereotype. What did surprise Lily was that the man was not elderly at all. He was maybe in his late thirties or early forties, but his thin body and crazy hair had made him seem much older at a glance.

"Yes, yes. What?" came the hurried response.

"Er, hi. I'm Lily," Lily stammered, feeling slightly off balance.

"Yes, Lily, good," said the man, turning back to the machine. "Must get the amplifier to connect to the inductor so that... Lily..." The man pivoted to face Lily, twisting at the hips and making Lily jump.

"You have *travelled*, yes?" His intensity was off-putting, and Lily backed up slightly.

Lily nodded and the man pounced at her and started measuring parts of her body and lifting her arms and examining her hands.

"No visible signs of shrinkage..."

Lily was immediately alarmed, wondering if this tiny man had been much larger once. And what measurements was he comparing the ones he was taking to? Abruptly, he finished his examination, nodded, and returned to his machine. It took a second for Lily to realise that he had finished with her and was not coming back.

"What's your name?" she asked.

"Jenkins, Jenkins, my name is Jenkins," he muttered, seeming annoyed at the interruption. "Capacitor still needs felixium to operate, bolstering doesn't lessen."

Felixium? Lily realised he was talking about the mineral that was required to power the machine for interdimensional travel. The letter had been right.

"Jenkins, is this the interdimensional travel machine?"

"Yes, yes, IDT."

"Did you make it?"

"Of course Jenkins made it. Who else would make it?"

This was getting her nowhere. Jenkins was not interested in talking to her while focussed on his machine. She moved closer, looking at the machine itself and making sure that she had positioned herself in Jenkins's line of sight.

"How does it work?"

Jenkins snapped his head up to look directly at Lily, then vomited an explanation in the form of a bunch of scientific terms, phrases, and phenomenon, none of which Lily understood. Lily asked a bunch of questions that served only to frustrate Jenkins and illustrate that she had no idea what he was talking about.

Feeling defeated, she decided she may as well give up and continue on her way. As Lily moved toward the door, Jenkins peered somewhat suspiciously at her and seemed to be weighing something up.

"Lily really wants to know about how I made the machine?" Jenkins asked, dubiously.

"Lily really does, er, I mean..." Lily shook her head. "Yes, I do."

Jenkins considered her. "Dimensions all exist together..." Jenkins stopped abruptly. "Do you know string theory?"

Lily shook her head, and Jenkins slouched back slightly, thinking.

"One dimension is linear. You can move forwards and backwards along the line. Two becomes flat like paper, and you can move forwards and backwards and left or right. When you get to three dimensions, you get depth. A sphere as opposed to a circle."

He paused to think, having covered the straightforward part. "The fourth dimension is time, the fifth and sixth give us time travel, and the rest give us the access to the other worlds, or dimensions."

Lily considered this. It didn't make sense to her, but it didn't *not* make sense either, which in itself was confusing. Jenkins tried again.

"If time is one plane, the fourth and fifth dimensions together let us move forwards and backwards along the one plane. The rest of the dimensions together let us move side to side. Same time, but into a different dimension where the world is different."

"Okay..." Lily said.

"The machine lets us see these other dimensions, lets us go to worlds that did not start out as ours did, and see how different they are. Some are very similar." Jenkins leant in conspiratorially. "Others have dragons." Jenkins leant back, grinning like a child and nodding.

"Okay, so...wait, dragons?" asked Lily. Jenkins nodded fervently at her. "Have you seen them?"

More excited nodding. "They sent someone with me, or I'd have stayed to study them. Suspect that's why he came. Also to stop me bringing any back." Jenkins looked thoughtful.

Lily pulled her mind back to the task at hand. "There

were no dragons in my dimension," Lily said, trying to bring Jenkins back on track with her. He shook his head.

"No dragons. When we looked for a dimension for the baby, we wanted a dimension as close as possible to this one, but not this one. That way, when the baby came home it wouldn't have to learn new things or be too disoriented." He looked up at Lily. "Your dimension is basically the same as this one, but with different land masses and history. Gravity is the same, time works the same, humans are humans. I suggested we just go with time travel, but they wanted dimensions." He shrugged.

"So my world...wait, you can time travel?"

Jenkins shook his head. "Not yet. Summer project."

Lily stared at him a beat and then went back to her question. "So my world is basically the same. Same rules?"

"Same rules."

"But no magic or enchantments."

"No magic. No enchantments." Jenkins shook his head and said softly, "No dragons."

Lily thought for a while and then nodded towards the interdimensional travel machine. "So what are you doing to the machine?"

"Improving!" exclaimed Jenkins happily, throwing his arms wide and looking back at his machine as a proud parent would look at their child. "Want to reduce the amount of felixium needed to operate, and trying to establish communications so we can talk to travellers while they're travelling." He nodded happily at Lily, who returned his enthusiasm.

"That sounds great!"

Buoyed by her obvious excitement, Jenkins raised a finger and hurried over to a workbench, rifling through assorted bits and pieces before finding what he was after and hurrying back. He thrust a small disc into Lily's hand.

It looked to Lily sort of like a small circular magnet, like those her team at work had used on a whiteboard to signify who was in the office, and who was out. But it was a strange sort of metallic, reflective material that made it look liquid, though it was quite solid.

"Er, it's nice." Lily nodded at him.

"It's a communicator. When I iron out the wrinkles." Jenkins suddenly snorted a laugh, as though this was quite funny. Lily didn't get the joke, but laughed at Jenkins's sudden laughter, and he seemed happy to assume that she had appreciated whatever his joke was.

"When I iron out the wrinkles, the traveller will take this with them, and the machine will connect to it so that we can talk to them. Like the device the travellers take so they can come back."

Lily examined the disc again, impressed that this small, nondescript piece of metal would be able to do that. She started to hand the communicator back, but Jenkins raised his hands, shaking his head.

"You keep it." He smiled at her. The machine beeped and Jenkins snapped his head in its direction, the discussion clearly over. Jenkins started his muttering again and Lily turned, pocketing the disc as she moved towards the hall-way. Amid his muttering, Lily thought she heard Jenkins say, "You might need it."

Lily headed along the corridor on her way back to her room. Her head was swimming, full of everything that had happened and everything she had learned. She passed all the artwork and decorations that had earlier caught her attention, giving them barely a glance, and started down the stairs.

"How are you adjusting to life in Highacre, Your Majesty?"

Lily jumped, having been unaware of anyone nearby. On the landing, maybe ten steps in front of her, a smartly dressed, middle-aged man was holding a respectful bow. He looked like a rich businessman.

"Um, good. Thank you." Lily tried and failed to hide her surprise. The man stood and smiled disarmingly at her. Lily relaxed and returned his smile.

"I can only imagine the sheer amount of information you're having to assimilate. Rather like drinking from a fire hose! Am I correct?"

Lily laughed nervously with him and nodded, descending the stairs towards him.

"My apologies, Your Majesty, how rude of me. I am Ezra, the ambassador from Meridia." His eyes seemed to twinkle and draw her in.

"Yes. Er...how do you do?" The formality coming from her own mouth sounded strange to Lily, and Ezra smiled broadly as though understanding her discomfort.

"It will get easier," he said conspiratorially. "As will finding your way around the palace. Might I escort you to your rooms? Surely your advisors will be looking for you."

Lily bristled at the reference to her advisors and was about to respond when a voice startled her from behind.

"Thank you, Mr Ambassador. I will escort Her Majesty. You no doubt have more pressing matters to attend to."

Lily looked around to see Jason behind her. Ezra smiled at Jason and dipped his head.

"Indeed I do, and forgive me; I should know better than to think the sole heir to the throne would be wandering around unescorted." He turned to Lily and dipped his head. "Your Majesty." The ambassador slipped through a doorway and was gone.

As they started back towards the Lodge, Lily looked at Jason, and despite Claire's warning and the fact that Jason was in charge of the security that had so overwhelmingly failed her parents and siblings, Lily decided she did trust him. Which she knew she shouldn't. She didn't even know him. But he just had an air about him that made Lily feel safe.

"So, Jason," Lily began awkwardly. "Tell me a little about yourself."

Jason laughed, clearly uncomfortable being asked to talk about himself.

"Well, ma'am, what would you like to know?"

"I don't know. What brought you to this job?"

"Okay Your Majesty, let's see. I was in the army. Joined up as a young lad. It seemed like an adventure, you know? Apparently I was good at it, and my sarge told me I should try out for special forces, so I did. Got in. We mainly trained and dealt with some little skirmishes in faraway countries. I never thought we'd actually have to defend our own. When the war first started, we went and did missions like usual. Covert ops, you know?"

Lily nodded even though she was pretty sure she didn't really understand.

"We were pretty successful at weakening the military power on the other side." He chuckled ruefully and shook his head, then looked at Lily. "That's a more acceptable way of saying that we killed high-ranking Meridian officers and officials, and a lot of people in general."

Lily found Jason's blunt description jarring. She couldn't picture this sweet, quiet man stalking and killing others. But she also had a newfound respect for Jason. Here was someone who was willing to go and do the tough jobs to keep others safe. Others like Lily, who could never imagine heading off and killing people. Except now she might have to send people like Jason to go and do just that. How could she possibly do that if she wasn't willing to do it herself? Jason broke into her thoughts.

"Anyway, I did well and after the war I was offered a job here in the palace."

"And then you worked your way up to be the head of the Royal Guard?"

Jason grimaced. "Uh, no, Your Majesty. I was offered this job straight out of the army."

Lily looked at him. It seemed like a pretty good job to fall into after the army. But then, why was he embarrassed?

"Sounds like there's a story there." Lily prompted. Jason nodded but seemed reluctant to go into it. "I'd really like to hear it. After all, I need to get to know you all pretty quickly. How you wound up as head of the Royal Guard and my personal bodyguard seems a good place to start."

Though Jason's reluctance didn't lessen, Lily could see understanding on his face. He took a deep breath and told her.

"The war was tough. Like Minister Bellingham said, it wasn't going well until we got the new technology in. The fighting was hectic, and they needed to give soldiers—particularly special forces soldiers—a break from the rough jobs. But we weren't doing well enough in the war to have a proper break. So, they'd rotate us out and spread us around in conventional units. The ones doing more mundane jobs, like logistics or guarding towns.

"I was working with the 5th, and we were looking after a small inconsequential town down south. They'd had some shelling early in the war, and really, we were just there to fix a few things that were broken and drum up some support for the troops. Real hearts and minds stuff." Jason steered them through a door Lily had never been through that led to a dark passageway.

"I was trying to fit into the unit, showed them a few of the tricks and tactics we use, and let them teach me some things. There was a girl, woman," he corrected himself, "just promoted to corporal, and she was clearly going places. She had complete control of her troops, and it was clear that she managed that through respect. And I could tell they respected her, not just the rank.

"I was young, thought I was hot stuff. Thought I could help develop her." He scoffed. "Like she needed my help. She was a much better soldier than I was ever going to be. And officer material, if she'd wanted. Anyway, we got word that our little holiday task was over. A Meridian unit was on its way to capture the town. I wasn't sure at the time why they were coming. Not a particularly special town." Jason shrugged.

"Anyway, we started preparing, looking to evacuate the town and prepare for the assault. Williams, that was her name, came up to me and said she had a plan. I mean, it was a good plan. There was nothing wrong with it. It was unusual, and I thought why not give it a go. I told her to go for it, that she was in charge, and shelved my own plan.

"It was too late by the time I realised the unit was Meridian SF." He looked at Lily's blank expression. "Special Forces. It wasn't there to capture the town. It was there to destroy it. That particular unit was very brutal. That was why, in our mission before our respite, we had been sent to kill its commander." Jason paused and looked at Lily.

"The town, as it turns out, was the secondary objective. They were hunting me and my guys." He guided Lily past some statues that looked to be likenesses of ancient kings and queens of Highacre and out another door.

"I ran to find Williams, but I was too late. They had killed her and wiped out her entire team. I cobbled together the rest of the unit and we fought like dogs and somehow pushed the Meridians back, taking out enough of them to force the rest to withdraw. We saved most of the town; the civilian casualties were much lower than they should have been in such an assault. But over half the 5th was dead or wounded. And they gave me a medal."

He said it with such disgust that Lily had at first thought that 'medal' must be some military jargon for a reprimand or something.

"What really gets me, though, is that I can't figure out whether if we'd gone with my plan, we'd have done better, and maybe Williams would still be alive, or if we'd all have been wiped out."

Before Lily could respond, Jason opened a door and Lily realised they were near the Lodge. They'd taken a shortcut.

"Anyway, Your Majesty, my 'valour in combat'," he said with air quotes, "saw me offered a job by the palace as CPP —close personal protection—for the royal family. And here we are."

Lily was impressed, though she knew that wasn't the point of Jason's story. Again, she noted how safe he made her feel. It seemed wrong that the royal family could have been wiped out with him in charge. The thought caused a pang of nausea in her gut.

"Jason," Lily began cautiously. "Where were you when the royal family was assassinated?"

7

Jason stopped walking and turned to Lily, though he didn't meet her eyes, and turned a soft shade of pink.

"Ma'am, my apologies. I was absent. I wasn't there when I should have been, and that was my fault. I will take the shame of my failure to the—"

"No Jason, sorry," Lily interrupted. "I was wondering where you were. Physically, I mean. Did you...did you see it?"

Jason shook his head and cleared his throat. "I was on leave, ma'am. My wife was having our third child, and having missed the births of the first two..."

"Oh, how old are they? What are their names?"

Jason, taken aback by Lily's genuine enthusiasm, relaxed slightly and smiled.

"John is thirteen, Lance is nine and Sara is one month, no—two months now." Jason looked embarrassed. "It's been a little while since I've been home."

Lily's smile faded. "When were you last home, Jason?"

Jason's face darkened slightly. "I've not been home since the assassinations."

Lily sighed and looked at him. "Jason, your family..."

"Are just fine, ma'am," Jason insisted as he drew himself back up to his full height.

"Are they? What about your wife? Three kids, one of them a new baby. That sounds pretty rough. I think I'd want my husband at home," Lily added gently.

Jason nodded, looking around, scanning for threats as was his habit.

"I told her I'd be away for a bit. That with you coming back, I was needed here. She understands. She had the first one while I was deployed and the second while I was with your father during his first post-war visit to Meridia."

Lily pursed her lips. "I'm sure she understands. I'm just wondering whether it's necessary. Surely you could go home for a night?"

Jason shook his head, looking at his feet. "Your Majesty, if anything happened, I'd never forgive myself."

Lily patted his arm, surprised at how muscly it was. Jason looked like a bodyguard, but not a meathead. He was clearly strong. His arm felt like steel.

"Isn't there another bodyguard we can trust that could look after me for the night?" Lily smiled, trying to make him feel better. "I mean, if there isn't, that seems like a big problem."

Jason paled slightly, his silence answering Lily's question. He opened the door to the Lodge, entering first to ensure it was clear. They walked to a leather couch by the window and sat down.

"Claire said something to me earlier," Lily began cautiously. "She said that my family trusted the same group of people that I'm trusting now, and that didn't turn out too well for them."

Jason nodded and sat back. "Ms Jones is a relatively new member of staff," he mused. "She makes a good point.

Actually, she was the first one I looked into when I started investigating the close staff."

Lily looked at Jason in surprise.

"I didn't really think she was involved," he explained. "But she had turned up the week before the attacks and I had wondered if there was a connection." He looked over at Lily.

"Clean, as it turns out. She was still being set up in our systems and hadn't been given access to anything that could be manipulated to give her the information that the insider must have been able to obtain."

Lily looked at her hands, slightly uncomfortable about suspecting the people who had taken her in and treated her so well.

"Are you investigating everyone?"

"Yes ma'am." Jason nodded vigorously. "There had to have been leaks, if not actual help, from within. I have been systematically vetting everyone who had access to your family, and particularly those who now have access to you. But I haven't found anything. At first I was relieved, thinking that we had not been betrayed by anyone who had been trusted to protect the family. But the further I go without uncovering anything, the more I think someone has contaminated the vetting process." Jason looked pained.

"Ma'am, you can't trust anyone, not completely. Not until we can sort this out." He looked around the room. "It would be easier if we still had the HIA, and now I'm even wondering if disbanding them was part of this whole sordid mess."

Lily looked at him. With a closer examination, she could see the exhaustion that he hid so well from passing glances.

"So, what are you doing about vetting my CPP? Obviously, if we have an issue with them, then any measures we put in place for my safety are pointless. And you need to be able to go home at some point." She smiled at him, and he returned a wan, stretched smile.

"Ma'am, I am currently looking for a female bodyguard for you. I have a strong candidate, and once I have her fully vetted, then she and I can share the load, both in ensuring your safety and looking into the others. It's just taking a while because not having an intelligence agency is making it more difficult, and this is kind of the key decision. If I get this wrong, then not only am I entrusting your safety to the enemy, but she will be able to vet anyone she wants and the enemy will further infiltrate our ranks."

It still all just sounded so over the top and paranoid to Lily. Everyone kept telling her she was in danger, but it didn't feel real. Not yet. *Hopefully not ever.*

"Is there anyone from that agency thingy who we could get in to help you?"

Jason shook his head sadly.

"That's just it, ma'am. The minute they disbanded them and sent them home, we lost most of the checks that are in place as a matter of course on all our agents. They have now been operating outside the secure system, and there's no way for us to check what they've been doing. I'd have to vet them before I vetted the bodyguard, so I may as well just start with her."

"Right. Okay, well, how much more vetting do you have to do on your preferred candidate?"

"A bit," admitted Jason. "I'm trying to vet a backup as well while continuing to look into the potential insiders."

"In all that spare time you have when you're not tailing me all over the palace?"

Jason smiled at Lily. "The plan is to keep you here, in the palace, and that will help. I won't have to organise and run security out in public."

Lily frowned. "Seriously Jason, is there anything that I can do to help?"

The bodyguard considered her request. "Keeping unnecessary risks to a minimum is good. And if you notice anything weird with those closest to you, let me know. Doesn't matter how small, and don't just think it's because you're new and you don't understand. Your lack of familiarity with things will actually be really helpful in identifying anything ...off."

"You got it, boss." Lily gave Jason a brief salute, and he smiled.

Should be simple enough. I just have to help Jason find them before they get me.

Lily excused herself and went to her room, suddenly completely exhausted. It had been a long day and the encounter with Ezra had unsettled her. He seemed harmless enough, but his popping up like that seemed weird. And convenient. And perhaps a little creepy.

Should he be able to wander around the palace like that? Lily had thought she would be more protected, what with her entire family being murdered and all. And didn't her advisors keep saying that even the Prime Minister didn't know about her yet? Then why on earth would they let the Meridian ambassador know?

Something was going on that Lily didn't understand. A tiny alarm began buzzing in the back of her brain, and though it wasn't calling for panic just yet, she would need to start figuring it out, or she might end up like the rest of her family.

Later that night, Jason was working alone on the operations room floor of the security office. He had set himself up in front of the wall of screens that showed the views from different cameras throughout the palace. Jason had keyed the two big screens that sat directly above his borrowed desk to show the cameras outside the Lodge and Lily's bedroom.

He heard the beep of someone swiping their card outside to gain access to the operations room floor and immediately began minimising windows on his computer monitor, before pulling up a spreadsheet just as Richard Berryman, his second-in-command, walked up to his desk. Jason was almost certain that Richard would have seen enough of his reaction to know that he had hidden what he was doing.

"Alright boss?" Richard pulled a chair over from a neighbouring desk and sat down, resting his boots on the desk that Jason was using and crossing his legs. Richard was in his late twenties and kept his blond hair exactly as long as it was allowed to be before Jason could tell him to get it cut. He was in uniform, but somehow wore it so it looked fashionable. Jason wanted to tell him to roll his sleeves down, but as Richard had reminded him last time, there was nothing in their regulations that said he couldn't roll them up. Jason swept Richard's feet off the desk with his arm.

"Not bad, you?" Jason didn't want Richard to make himself at home. The sooner he left, the sooner Jason could get back to work. Richard chuckled at his feet being battered away and rested them instead on a nearby box.

"Not bad. About to head off for the night, heading out with some of the boys. Figured I'd come back in tomorrow though, and perhaps you could duck home for a bit."

"Thanks, but I'm on another overnighter. You should make it a couple of extra days. Get some proper rest."

Richard looked at his boss with a raised eyebrow. "Another overnighter? That's like three in a row, boss. You can't keep that up, and what about Gwen and the kids?

You've barely seen what little Sara looks like, and I'll bet Gwen would appreciate you being home."

"Thanks Rich, but I'll be home soon enough."

"How about I stick around tonight and you pop home?"

"Thanks mate, but I got it."

Jason felt Richard studying him as he stared resolutely at the spreadsheet on his screen, only glancing up occasionally to check the camera feeds. He refused to make eye contact with Richard, who was clearly waiting for him to do so.

"Requisition form," Richard said, nodding at Jason's screen. "Important."

Jason nodded, and started tapping away, adding in supplies that were needed.

"You don't trust me." Richard failed to keep the hurt from his voice. Jason knew Richard took pride in the fact that, while Jason as the boss kept a professional distance from the rest of the team, he let Richard in. He also knew Richard thought they were much closer than they actually were. Richard sniffed and sat up straight, removing his feet from the box. He looked around the room, now trying to avoid eye contact with Jason.

"Mate, I don't trust anyone right now." Jason gave up the pretext of working on the spreadsheet and turned to look at Richard. "It's not personal, I just can't afford to assume anything based on what I think I know about people."

Jason's explanation didn't seem to help; in fact, Richard looked even more dejected as he stood. "Well, you can't do it all by yourself, so let me know when you trust me again and then you can get some sleep." He turned to go. "You look like shit."

Jason waited until he heard the door shut before looking around to confirm that Richard had gone. He didn't like making Richard feel like they weren't partners, but truthfully, even if he was going to clear someone based only on his gut, it wouldn't have been Richard.

Jason vaguely wondered why he had accepted him as his second-in-command. Just easier than fighting the brass, he supposed. And really, it wasn't as if he'd had a choice in the matter.

Richard's family was old money and some sort of minor royalty, but Jason never really understood how all those titles and relationships worked. Everyone had expected that this was just a bit of a lark for Richard before he went off and found a real job. And the powers-that-be had decided that having 'second-in-command' on his resume would be good for Richard. And no doubt giving him such a sought-after position had put the higher-ups in better standing with Richard's powerful family.

Jason had begrudgingly accepted the situation, and to Richard's credit, he was a good worker and hadn't once complained about the long and sometimes short-notice hours. He was also willing to learn and always seemed interested in why they would do the things they did. Richard had told Jason that this wasn't some in-between gig for him, like everyone thought; that he really wanted to make something of it. He'd even joked that he might have Jason's job some day. Or at least, Jason had assumed that he'd been joking.

Still, there was that air of ambition that the upper crust had that made Jason slightly wary. Maybe it was just that Richard was aiming for Jason's job and Jason, perhaps unfairly, found it insulting that Richard, with all his privilege and pampered lifestyle, thought that he could do it.

But anyone who was looking to get themselves ahead was dangerous in Jason's book. If they were focussed on an end state, then everything they did would relate back to that end state, and in Jason's mind, protecting the royal family was the be all and end all. Not a promotion to a cushy job.

He supposed that was probably unfair. Maybe Richard's ambition really did only extend to one day having Jason's job. Maybe he was just trying to do his best. Jason blew his breath out and ran his hands through his short hair, bothered that it was longer than he liked. Being suspicious of everyone was exhausting.

Jason sat back in his chair and stared at the camera feeds. Maybe he should let Richard have his job. Certainly, that would give Jason more time to focus on his investigation.

Richard also had a point. And Her Majesty had said the same thing earlier. How was he going to do it all by himself? It was impossible, but Jason's tired mind couldn't process the situation well enough to find a solution. Instead, he just focussed on the word 'impossible' until it repeated over and over again in his head, a sick feeling of anxiety growing.

He shook his head to clear it and took a sip of the now-cold coffee from the mug on his borrowed desk. After minimising the spreadsheet, Jason pulled back up the security footage he had been watching, along with an email inbox. The inbox was labelled *"Addison Grange"* and a little blue bar told Jason that the computer was halfway through restoring her deleted messages from the server.

This would be so much easier with some proper tech support. Jason felt a twinge of nostalgia for his army days. Working in a team with people you could trust with your life. Though now that he thought about his old crew who he'd lost touch with after the war, he didn't know that he would call them. They were probably all off doing private contractor work or being muscle for some billionaire somewhere in the world. Jason was old school and believed in serving his country, but while a lot of the guys he'd served with felt good about serving the nation, they were often more interested in the pay packet that came with it. He shook his head.

There was one of his old buddies that he'd trust with his life, but he couldn't call him. He hadn't spoken to him since the disaster that was the attack on the town down south during the war. Jason didn't know why he hadn't called him. Or gone to see him. Shame, he supposed, but what kind of jerk prioritised his own comfort over what his buddy needed?

Jason pulled out his phone and stared at it. He unlocked it and pulled up his buddy's number.

Probably not even his number anymore.

No harm in trying it then.

His rational brain had a point, but even so, Jason put the phone away and went back to sifting through the footage and waiting for the computer to tell him that the emails were ready. All the while, he tried to ignore the little voice that told him he wouldn't be able to do it all on his own.

8

Lily ate her lunch quietly in the Lodge, thinking over everything they had taught her in her lessons during the last couple of days, and trying not to get too excited about finally meeting Lady Octavia that afternoon. The meeting had been twice delayed and Lily was half expecting Addison to enter and tell her that it was again postponed.

She was nervous. What abilities would she have? What if she didn't have any magic at all? What if her abilities were stunted by her time in the other dimension and all she could do was trivial tasks? Would they still let her be queen? Or would she be cast aside, no longer useful to her advisors? The initial shock having worn off, Lily was enjoying having a purpose, if not feeling important. But if she had no magic...

Casting around for a distraction, Lily mused on the fact that the whole royal family had been murdered, but everyone, except maybe Claire and Jason, seemed convinced that she was in little to no danger. Shouldn't she be the next target? What would be the point of killing everyone else and then just leaving her to become queen? Lily decided to press Giles for an answer, or perhaps ask Jason the next time she saw him.

The door opened and Lily bounced to her feet, all concerns fleeing her head. It was time! Addison smiled at her excitement and gestured to her to follow, and after one last nervous bathroom break, the older woman led Lily through the hallways, down the stairwells, and out onto the grounds.

Lily took in a deep breath, enjoying the fresh air and the sun on her face. Addison took her alongside the palace wall and into a courtyard that was about the size of half a basketball court. It was plain with stone walls that reached just above Lily's head, and was paved with broken grey stone tiles. Unlike the rest of the palace that she had seen so far, the courtyard showed signs of disuse, with leaves and other small debris hugging the borders. It looked like someone had hurriedly tried to tidy the place up.

The courtyard was also empty. Lily felt herself deflate slightly, having worked herself up on the way down from the Lodge. Lily was standing in the middle of the empty courtyard when she sensed rather than saw Lady Octavia enter. Addison startled, bowed, then moved off to the side and sat on a bench, trying to look small and inconsequential. Giles, who had escorted Lady Octavia to the courtyard, gestured towards Lily grandly, bowed, and joined Addison.

Lady Octavia scrutinised Lily over the top of half-moon glasses perched precariously on the tip of her nose. Lily tried to pull her shoulders back and stand confidently, looking at Lady Octavia, but she had the strangest feeling that Lady Octavia could see right through her to her very soul.

"So, this is Isabella's daughter?" Lady Octavia asked the courtyard at large.

Lily returned Lady Octavia's gaze, unsure of how to

respond. Lady Octavia shuffled closer to Lily, still peering at her.

"Yes," she said finally. "I see it."

Lily stared back, assuming Giles or Addison would jump in, but when no one did, she asked, "See what?"

"You are of the royal line," Lady Octavia nodded slowly.

"So I've been told," Lily said, slightly awkwardly.

"You look like them." Lady Octavia looked Lily directly in the eye, and Lily shrank back slightly. "And you have the blood."

Lily heard Addison make a high-pitched excited sound and gave a little clap, and Giles sighed with relief.

"But what about the magic?" Lily asked. Lady Octavia raised an eyebrow, and her gaze slid over Giles and Addison, who immediately became interested in the courtyard tiles.

Lady Octavia stared at them for a beat.

"Leave us."

Both stood immediately, but hesitated.

"The guard may stay," said Lady Octavia, nodding her head towards the wall. Lily couldn't see Jason but knew he was there outside the courtyard.

"Yes, of course," Giles bowed. "Thank you, Lady Octavia."

After they left, Lady Octavia looked at Lily. "Take a seat, child."

The two women walked slowly to the bench that had been vacated by Lily's advisors.

"Highacre has always had magic," Lady Octavia began. "Our histories first record it in the times where the nomadic tribes roamed our land. Each tribe had mastery of a specific type of magic, but that's what inbreeding and a lack of innovative thinking or experimentation will do."

Lily stared at Lady Octavia, but the old woman simply waved her hand and continued.

"As time went on and Highacre turned into a country with more fixed settlements, finally our people generated some genetic diversity, and with that our magic also grew.

"Your line is the first to have developed secondary powers. Thanks to some very carefully arranged marriages a few hundred years ago, your line progressed in magical development at a much faster rate than the rest of Highacre. In fact, most Highacrens are only now displaying a level of magical ability akin to that found in your ancestors three hundred years ago."

Lady Octavia scrutinised Lily for an uncomfortable minute.

"You have the power," Lady Octavia said, standing abruptly and locking Lily in a steely gaze, "now let's see what you can do."

They moved back to the middle of the courtyard.

"Concentrate," Lady Octavia urged Lily. Lily had no idea what she was supposed to concentrate on. She closed her eyes and tried to focus on producing some kind of magic. Maybe she could fly or turn invisible, or shoot balls of energy out of her hands!

"No, no, your focus is scattered," criticised Lady Octavia. "Try not to imagine what you think your abilities might be, but just focus on finding your power."

Lily blew her breath out in frustration. "But how can I focus on my power if I don't know what it is?"

"Think of your power as your life force. Your life force isn't your heart or your lungs, though they are necessary for you to stay alive. Your life force is more about you, *who* you are. Your essence, not your body."

Lily thought she understood what Lady Octavia was

saying, but she wasn't entirely sure how it helped her figure out how to focus on her power.

They spent another thirty minutes in the courtyard, with Lady Octavia running Lily through various exercises designed to help her connect with and use her power, but nothing seemed to work.

Eventually, Lily collapsed back onto the bench. Lady Octavia sat quietly beside her.

"What if I can't do magic?" Lily asked quietly.

She was getting frustrated and slightly panicked. Lily didn't even know why she was so worried about it, other than it would be cool to have magic. She had managed pretty well without it all her life. Perhaps it was the self-imposed pressure of not wanting to let Giles, Addison, and the rest down. She looked over at Lady Octavia, who was watching her quietly.

"You have power, I can sense it. Once you connect with it, the magic will come."

Lily felt relieved, but it was immediately swallowed by concern that growing up in a non-magical dimension had blocked her ability to access her power. That might even be worse than not having magic at all.

"Breathe in deeply and connect with your centre."

Lady Octavia led Lily through a meditation, urging her to connect with herself. Lily tried to banish all the thoughts about how stupid it was and how ridiculous she felt, and instead focus on Lady Octavia's voice. Following Lady Octavia's direction, she concentrated on her breath, breathing in deeply, holding it, and then slowly releasing it. Slowly, Lily relaxed.

"Ow!"

Lily's eyes flew open, and she jumped up, rubbing her arm. Glaring at Lady Octavia, she eyed the cane that had somehow appeared in her hand.

"Focus on your centre!" Lady Octavia urged.

"I'm focussed on my arm! That hurt!" Despite herself, Lily was suddenly aware of a warm feeling towards the bottom of her chest. Like a ball of light had grown there. She closed her eyes and tried to focus on it. She felt it grow, engulfing her whole body, and then radiating out.

Lily opened her eyes excitedly, looking for whatever magic must have emerged. Lady Octavia was looking at her with a curious expression. Before Lily could ask any questions, voices from outside the courtyard broke her concentration, and she lost hold of her power.

"No, no, I'm fine. Must have just tripped. Getting old!"

Beyond the wall, Lily watched Jason attempting to help and usher away a familiar-looking middle-aged man. She returned her attention to Lady Octavia, who was hurriedly packing her large handbag.

"That's enough for one day. We will continue our lessons in due course." Lady Octavia bustled towards the exit, then turned and seemed to catch the look on Lily's face. She hesitated, then walked over and placed a reassuring hand on Lily's arm.

"Don't worry, child. You have power. This is a good thing. Together we will help you master it." Lady Octavia clutched her handbag and rushed out of the courtyard.

Lily felt slightly better. She had felt it, and Lady Octavia confirmed she had power. But why hadn't anything happened? She had thought there would have been something, anything, that would hint at what she could do. And wasn't Lady Octavia meant to be able to sense and tell her what her magical gifts were?

Lily started to go after Lady Octavia to ask, but the woman had vanished. Lily suddenly realised that she was alone. She had no idea where she should be, or how she was supposed to get there. Lily looked around for Jason. Not immediately seeing him, she tentatively stepped farther through the archway and out onto the grass.

Lily looked out across the lawn and manicured gardens, both fenced by the tall trees that were the beginning of a vast forest. She took a step forward, thinking if no one was waiting for her, she might have a chance to explore the grounds. Suddenly, she noticed two figures off to her left, huddled together in whispered conversation, moving slowly towards her. The shrubbery around the courtyard hid her, and they hadn't yet noticed she was there, so Lily moved slowly backward, using the shrubbery to further block her from sight while peering through the branches to make out the people approaching. With a start, she realised it was Addison and Minister Bellingham.

"No Minister, she didn't say."

"But the whole point was for Lady Octavia to evaluate her and tell us what her abilities are!" The minister sounded as exasperated as Lily felt.

"She said she had power, but that she had to consult the oracle."

"Oracle?" Minister Bellingham's voice rose. "What oracle? Are we in ye olden times?"

"I don't know—"

"If there was an oracle, I would know about it," Minister Bellingham said confidently.

"Of course, Minister."

"Should we be worried then? Does the girl have no magic?"

Lily bristled. *Girl.*

"She said Her Majesty had power—"

"Yes, yes, but what of her magic? What can she *do*?"

"I don't know, Minister." Addison was getting exasperated too now. "She just said she needed to consult the oracle."

Minister Bellingham scoffed. "Well, what do we do now?"

"We wait for Lady Octavia's report, and we train her so she can pass the confirmation hearing."

"But—"

"Business as usual, Minister," Addison had a warning tone now. "No one must know. Not until we're ready."

The minister nodded. They had arrived outside the courtyard. Lily had quietly moved back inside as they approached.

"Where is she then?" the minister asked Addison quietly.

"She's here," Lily said as she walked out of the courtyard with more confidence than she felt.

"Your Majesty."

Both women dropped into curtsies and Lily nodded in their direction, as Claire had taught her.

"How was your lesson with Lady Octavia, Your Majesty?" Addison asked kindly.

"It was good. Lady Octavia was...interesting."

"And what did she tell you?" Minister Bellingham asked, a little too eagerly.

"Oh, nothing I'm sure the two of you don't already know." Lily tried to keep her tone light, but she saw a look of frustration brush the minister's face. Lily felt a slightly vengeful pang of satisfaction.

"Very good, Your Majesty," Minister Bellingham said brusquely, shooting a glance at Addison before addressing Lily. "Please excuse me. Duty calls."

And with that, the imposing woman strode away. Addison looked at Lily, slightly embarrassed, and gestured for Lily to follow her.

"She's a very busy woman."

"I'm sure she is."

They walked together in silence for a while before Addison tried again.

"So now that it's just us, how was your lesson really? Did she tell you what your abilities are?"

Lily hesitated. Clearly Addison and the minister had failed to get the information out of Lady Octavia as well. But Lady Octavia had already told Addison that she had power. No harm in reiterating that. And if she tried to imply that Lady Octavia *had* told her what her abilities were, Lady Octavia might contradict her. How long did it take to consult an oracle? Maybe she'd be back tonight.

"No." Lily decided on the truth. "She told me I have power, but then hurried off. I don't know what abilities I have. Or if I even have any..." Lily finished moodily.

"You do, Your Majesty," said Addison sympathetically. "Everyone with power has abilities. Perhaps they're very powerful or new."

"Has anyone ever spent nineteen years in another dimension without magic before?" Lily asked.

"Well, no..." Addison admitted.

Lily's face fell. Addison reached for her arm, then thought the better of it.

"Never mind all that, Your Majesty. The main thing is that you have power. Minister Bellingham looked into it, and technically that is all that's required for you to be confirmed. It says nothing about abilities!"

Lily didn't really care what *it* said. Power with no abilities seemed pointless to her. And if there was this big conspiracy, she imagined that anyone who wished to oppose her confirmation would use that lack against her. But she smiled weakly at Addison.

"So, what's next?"

Addison led Lily back to her rooms, keeping up a constant stream of chatter about the lessons to come and the work they needed to do. Lily would need to continue to learn all about the world around her, as well as the countries and key people involved.

She would need to keep up her etiquette lessons with Claire so she would talk and act like a queen, which would not only help her as queen, but allow her to look the part during the confirmation hearing, which would hopefully sway some politicians to her side.

She would need to be briefed into all the matters that she, as queen, would need to know about or have an opinion on or get involved in. And Austin would teach her martial arts and how to use weapons and how to run a war.

Lily still wasn't sure exactly why she needed to learn martial arts and how to use weapons, but of all the things she was supposed to do, it sounded the most fun and at least involved *doing* something rather than being talked at. Lily had never thought that she would look forward to exercise so much.

Upon arrival at the Lodge they were met by Giles, who was equally animated about Lily's upcoming schedule. Lily sat at her dining table and ate her dinner quietly, half-listening to Giles and Addison detail her life for the next couple of months, and half-wondering where the day had gone. Eventually, Giles and Addison seemed to realise that Lily was not quite as enthused about her schedule as they were, and excused themselves so she could rest.

Lily plodded into her bedroom, suddenly exhausted and feeling quite lonely. She felt a wave of homesickness for her family and the farm. She wondered what they were all doing, and pictured her father and brother working out in the fields while her mother and older sister tinkered around in the store they had set up. She missed her little sister April the most. She hoped April wouldn't be too mad at her for missing their weekend together. She would have been worried; Lily would never ghost her like this. She could imagine April going to the city anyway to look for her.

That thought worried her. April was resourceful, but she was still a farm girl at heart and hadn't spent much time in the city. Maybe Gemma would have taken care of her. She felt a pang in her heart for her best friend. They had been growing apart lately. Each finding new interests. If April hadn't let Gemma know Lily was missing, Gemma might think that Lily had just forgotten about her.

No, she told herself, *she's at university with Brandon. And he would have noticed I was gone.*

Thinking about Brandon made her feel guilty, but still, Lily would have given anything for anyone from back home, even him, to be here with her. To help her. Someone she could trust and bounce ideas off.

Lily flopped onto her bed and felt something beneath her pillow. Reaching under, she found a crisp envelope. *Another note!* Lily propped herself up on her pillows and examined the envelope eagerly. It was the same as the last one, heavy parchment with the same wax seal. She broke it gingerly and carefully pulled out the letter within.

> *Your Majesty,*
>
> *By now, you will have seen for yourself that your advisors are hiding things from you. What that is I don't yet know, but I implore you, for the good of the nation, do not trust them!*
>
> *You will hopefully have met with Lady Octavia and have some answers about your heritage and your abilities. Lady Octavia should be able to help you develop and control your abilities, and the sooner you can do that, the less reliant you will be on your advisors for everything.*
>
> *My sources inform me that Minister Bellingham is*

gathering her allies in Parliament. For what purpose, I cannot say, though if she were wishing to challenge the Prime Minister for power, having the sole heir to the throne in her pocket would surely be a boon. Perhaps she will accept you as her queen, or at least her equal, and seek to work with you.

While I cannot say that Minister Bellingham is up to no good, I must implore you—do not trust Ms Jones! I seek answers on your behalf and of all your advisors, her past is the most mysterious. Though there is information to be found as to where she lived and worked, when the surface is scratched, her alibis crumble. I will continue to investigate, but please be careful.

Sincerely,

A Friend

Lily reread the letter. She was buzzing, but slightly disappointed. The last letter had contained a map to the interdimensional travel machine, and she had been hoping that this letter would also contain something exciting, but all it held was more questions and worries.

Lily stood to go to the bathroom and get ready for sleep. A thunk on the floor drew her attention. She bent down and felt around under the bed. A cold metal object caught her fingers, and she stood up and looked at the key in her hand. *A key to what?*

She looked again at the letter on her bed and picked up the envelope. Had the key been inside? It was thick parchment for sure, but the key wasn't flat. She would have felt it. Or would she? Lily began to doubt herself. Where else would it have come from? It must have been in the envelope with the letter. Or perhaps under her pillow and she had bumped it when retrieving the letter, and then it had fallen.

Lily took the key with her to the bathroom and examined it, wondering where its lock was. It was a small key, cylindrical in its stem and ornate at its head. It looked to Lily like a key for an old wardrobe or drawer.

She finished getting ready for bed and snuggled down under her covers, staring at the key that she had placed carefully on her bedside table. Suddenly she jumped out of bed, snatched up the key and letter, and hid them with the last letter beneath her drawer before hopping back into bed. It was better that no one saw it when her servants or Addison came to wake her tomorrow.

For now, it would be her secret.

A small voice nagged at her again that she should tell her advisors. At least Jason. But Lily stubbornly silenced that voice. If her advisors could have their secrets, why shouldn't she have hers?

9

The days that followed passed in a blur of information and activity. Lily had lessons with her advisors, and between Austin's workouts and Addison trying to cram the history of Highacre into her head, Lily ended each day exhausted and ready for sleep. She read and reread the mysterious letters, though no more arrived, and look though she did, Lily was no closer to finding a lock for her key.

She observed her advisors and moved around the castle as quietly as she could, hoping to overhear more conversations, but nothing she saw or heard gave her any more information. Of course, nothing she saw or heard reassured her either. More often than not, at her approach, her advisors would separate from huddled, whispered conversations and greet her with broad smiles. She would hear the ends of discussions showing that they were worried, or unsure, but about what, Lily was none the wiser.

One thought plagued her more than all her concerns about her advisors, their aims, and their loyalty: When would she see Lady Octavia again? Lady Octavia had not appeared again since their first lesson and Lily was getting frustrated, eager to develop her magic.

She was still too afraid to *do* anything, lest she break something or hurt someone, though she was starting to wonder if that was a line they had fed her to keep her compliant. Most evenings, she would sit on her bed and try to connect with her power like she had with Lady Octavia. Once or twice she felt it, but in her excitement she lost the connection and hadn't been able to get it back. Lily felt like she was regressing, and she really didn't have anywhere to regress to.

She had asked Giles and Addison when she would see Lady Octavia next, but both waved away her concerns about learning magic with platitudes that it wouldn't take her long to get the hang of it and that she would see Lady Octavia again soon.

Frustratingly, Giles and Addison were solely focussed on preparing Lily for the confirmation hearing, which was understandable, given how little time there was to prepare. But Lily remained far more interested in finding out how to use her magic.

She also asked Claire about Lady Octavia, but the woman had responded mysteriously that she would have thought that Lily would be seeing Lady Octavia every day, which did nothing to ease Lily's anxiety.

Ultimately, Lily had stopped asking, but it had added to the mounting evidence that her trusted advisors could not actually be fully trusted, and that made her feel increasingly isolated and alone. She questioned what they really wanted from her.

Despite the frenetic pace and the pressure from her advisors to learn so much so quickly, Lily was enjoying the break from her real life. While she missed her family, she no longer had to worry about what she was going to do or be. She would be a queen! Everything was done for her. She had no bills to pay or housework to do, and she lived in a palace with everything she could ever hope to need.

Looming over her was the spectre of unstoppable assassins, but having now been in Highacre for over a month without incident, Lily was no longer jumping at shadows and was finding it difficult to maintain a vigilant attitude. Perhaps the people behind the assassinations thought that they had eradicated the royal family and gone home, leaving Lily safe in the palace.

Today she was trudging up the stairs towards the classroom where she had her lessons with Addison. She liked the room; it wasn't that big and much of the wall space was covered with floor-to-ceiling bookshelves. One entire wall was a floor-to-ceiling window, offering a beautiful view of the harbour when the days were clear.

There were a couple of large desks, the leather-topped kind that Lily associated with a fancy study rather than what you'd find in school. There were maps and a globe and a board to write on. Something about the room was cosy and intimate, and Lily felt like Addison was telling her stories rather than instructing her in the sense of formal education. Which was good. Lily had never really liked school.

As she headed towards the classroom, Lily tried to remember everything Addison had taught her so far. Highacre, Meridia, and Valmead were the dominant countries. Highacre and Meridia shared a border, which currently sat somewhere in the aptly named Disputed Region. Valmead was separated from Highacre by an impenetrable mountain range. The only known entry-point a tunnel, accessible by a single-lane highway and rail.

Highacre was a monarchy, but the current Prime Minister was pushing for the abolition of the monarchy, wishing to replace it with a republic of which he, no doubt, would be the first president. Meridia was a republic and used their technological edge and money for power. This was being threatened by Highacre's technological boom as a result of interdimensional travel, which Meridia didn't know about.

Valmead, on the other hand, was a dictatorship who favoured military might and power. Their current dictator had been in power for over thirty years, and if the nepotistic streak was to be a guide, his son, Alexei, would take over whenever he died or stood down. Apparently there was an election, but rivals to the dictator seemed to have an unusually high likelihood of suffering some sort of fatal misfortune.

Suddenly Lily found herself at the door to the classroom. She had been so focussed on trying to remember her lessons that she hadn't been paying attention and was slightly startled to find herself at her destination so quickly. That brief hesitation was the only thing that stopped her from bursting through the door as she usually did. Instead, she heard the whispered voices and paused to listen.

"...not ready, it just won't work."

"That's not fair, we have time."

"There's not enough time! We have one chance to get this right, otherwise he'll take over and nothing will stop him but revolution."

"You don't think that's being a little dramatic?"

"Dramatic? You've heard the speeches, and he's clearly a puppet. No, we need to be steering the ship."

A pause.

"What makes us the right people to do that?"

"It's better than the alternative. And besides, when things settle, we'll hand everything back over to the right person."

A scoff.

"Said no one ever. And who decides who is the *right* person? Us?"

Jason approached Lily, a questioning look on his face, clearly wondering why she had paused outside the classroom.

"Is everything alright, Your Majesty?"

The voices in the room ceased, and Lily forced a smile at Jason.

"Yes, sorry, I was just trying to remember the name of the Valmead dictator in case Addison quizzes me on my previous lessons."

"Nicholai Rosovski," Jason whispered, smiling and opening the door for Lily.

Thanking Jason, Lily entered the classroom to see a harried-looking Giles and frustrated Addison. Both sunk into respective bows and curtsies, avoiding her eyes.

"Are you joining us today?" Lily asked Giles.

"Regrettably no, Your Majesty. I have other matters to attend to. I was just discussing a household matter with Addison, but I will leave you both to it." He bowed again before leaving.

Addison busied herself with a large screen positioned in front of Lily's chair. Lily walked over to the chair and stared at Addison's back, waiting for her to turn around.

"Hello, Addison," she said pointedly when the older woman failed to look at her.

"Hello, Your Majesty," Addison said. She turned, a smile plastered across her face. "Are you ready for your lesson? Today we're going over the key players that you'll need to know."

"Is everything alright?" Lily decided to push it. "I heard you and Giles arguing."

"Oh!" Addison laughed nervously. "We weren't arguing, Your Majesty. No, he just has his ideas of how the household should be run and I have mine."

Lily smiled back at Addison. "Who usually wins?"

Addison's smile froze slightly as she met Lily's eyes. "It's always best, ma'am, when we can compromise. I find the best solution usually lies in the middle." Addison went to turn back to the screen.

"And if you can't find a compromise?"

Addison turned again and studied Lily's face for a beat. Her eyes, initially suspicious, softened a little. "You remind me of your mother."

Lily was determined not to be distracted, but she couldn't help it. "The queen?"

Addison broke eye contact and turned back to the screen. "Yes. Her Majesty was always straight to the heart of any issue, and not easily dissuaded from her mission. *Your* mission," Addison said, turning back to Lily after finishing with the screen, "is to learn all about Highacre so you pass your confirmation hearing."

Lily really wanted to get to the bottom of the argument. Who was the puppet? And what wasn't working? But one look at Addison's face made it clear that Lily wasn't going to get anywhere, so she nodded at Addison and looked at the screen.

"Okay," said Addison, "let's start with... Oh! The Meridian ambassador."

The picture that had appeared on the screen was a familiar man, maybe in his forties, who looked to Lily like a snappy businessman. He had neat white hair, receding slightly, but seemed very energetic. The picture didn't quite capture the twinkle in his eye that Lily remembered from their meeting on the stairs.

"Ezra Brown is fifty-three and his background is in intelligence. As such, we know little about his early career.

However, he was, at thirty-five, the youngest ever director of the Meridian Intelligence Agency. His cybernetic implant includes a cloaking ability which is similar to the magical ability to become invisible."

"Do they only get one ability?" Lily asked, curious about these implants.

"Meridia does tightly control and regulate the implants," Addison said. "While people can have more than one ability, from what I understand, if they try to give someone too many abilities, or abilities that are too strong, that person gets overloaded."

"Overloaded?"

"An overload can cause damage like a stroke. Sometimes it is fatal."

"Whoa."

Lily had been thinking cybernetics were the way to go. Guaranteed ability, you can pick what you want, and have as many as you want. Apparently not.

"It also depends a lot on the person's own capacity. There's an implant that lets you learn and retain information really easily..."

"That sounds like it would be useful right about now."

"Uh, yes. But Your Majesty, we in Highacre don't allow cybernetics."

"Why is that? Wouldn't that be the best of both worlds?"

"Some have tried it," Addison admitted. "However, our abilities cause increased malfunctions with the implants. For the lucky ones, the implants just shorted out and didn't work. The less fortunate suffered overloads."

"Oh. Okay, maybe I'll stick to learning the hard way."

"Yes, that's probably best. What was I saying? Oh yes, if you did get an implant that lets you learn quickly, you're still limited by your own ability to retain and recall knowledge. If you can only keep, say, the information of three books in your mind, then even if you skim seven with your implant, your mind will only retain three."

"Why don't they make an implant that stores the knowledge for easy retrieval?"

"I think they're working on it, but so far it's not been successful. Something about how fiddly it is trying to connect it to the neural pathways so it acts like your memory. Anyway, back to Mr Brown. We think his implant also has some charm boosts, but the only registered ability is the cloaking.

"He was stood down from the Meridian Intelligence Agency over a scandal and emerged in the business world, where he has done extremely well. Mr Brown is a known golfing buddy of the Meridian president and is understood to have accepted the post of ambassador to Highacre as a personal favour to him. He's been here for two years now."

Addison barely took a breath before continuing, "I understand the president asked Ezra to be a consultant for the Meridian Intelligence Agency, and he lectures on their training courses, as well as recruits for them if he sees talent."

"Sounds like he's landed on his feet," Lily commented. She wondered what could have defeated such a formidable man. "What was the scandal?"

"Well," began Addison, leaning in, seeming ready to gossip, "what I heard was that he was running the agency during the war, and there was an attack on Meridia that everyone thought should have been prevented. The president at the time declared that it was Ezra's fault, as his department failed to identify the threat and report it, and so he asked Ezra to stand down. The rumour is that Ezra *had* briefed the president, but the president ignored it. When there was a public outcry, the president sold Ezra out."

"Wow, he must have been really mad," Lily said.

Addison nodded enthusiastically. "He was. But then he made a fortune in business and became a big supporter of that president's competitor, who wound up winning the next election."

Addison smiled at Lily, clearly impressed with Ezra's comeback, before turning back to the screen and changing the picture.

Lily stifled a yawn. It was interesting, but Lily had never been a fan of classroom learning. And the sun streaming in the window, which offered an amazing view of the beautiful day they were missing, didn't help.

"There aren't too many to get through, Your Majesty," Addison reassured her sympathetically. "Now, each ambassador is accompanied by one ambassador to court. While the ambassador travels around and attends functions and has a broad range of duties, the ambassador to court remains here with the primary function of forging good and productive relations with the royal family. The ambassador is the 'official' representative." Addison used her fingers to make air quotes around the word 'official'.

"However, for the sovereign, often matters can be resolved more expediently, and sometimes more subtly, through the ambassador to court. They are usually younger, and this role is often to prepare them for future positions."

Addison clicked her button. "Like the ambassador to court from Valmead, Alexei."

A good-looking man, only slightly older than Lily, appeared on the screen as Addison wiggled her eyebrows at Lily, making her laugh.

"Alexei is twenty-one, and the eldest son of the dictator,

Nicholai Rosovski. It is unusual for Valmead to send a likely heir to another country for an extended period like this, however, they insist it is to best prepare him should he wind up taking over from his father." Addison replaced Alexei's picture with that of a beautiful young woman.

"Ava Harrington is the Meridian ambassador to court. She is a graduate of the Meridian Army's Officer Training Academy and their Intelligence Officer Training School. Following a deployment with the military, the agency recruited her."

Addison turned to Lily. "The Meridians typically send an intelligence agent as the ambassador to court. However, Ava, who is only twenty years old, is much more junior an operative than what they normally send. Anyway, she seems lovely." Addison's smile turned thoughtful. "Which I suppose she would be if she needs to get people to give her information..."

Lily yawned again, trying but failing to stifle it. Addison looked at her thoughtfully. "Okay, come on, Your Majesty." Addison started for the door.

"Where are we going?" Lily asked excitedly, jumping up and following Addison.

Without answering Lily, Addison swept out of the room and down the stairs, Lily hurrying to keep up with her. Addison held an impressive air of mystery and purpose, which she promptly ruined by turning suddenly, almost bumping into Lily.

"Oh shoot, I forgot my wire. Your Majesty, you keep going. We're heading for the grounds. I'll meet you by the fountain."

And with that, Addison took off back up the stairs, leaving Lily staring after her and wondering what on earth a 'wire' was. Turning, Lily headed on down the stairs and through the maze of the palace, eventually finding the ground floor corridor that led to the side door to the gardens that they had used when going to her lesson with Lady Octavia.

Lost in her own thoughts, Lily didn't notice anyone approach, so when the man to her left greeted her, she gave a high-pitched squeal and jumped.

"My sincere apologies, Your Majesty. I thought you saw me coming."

"Oh! No, sorry Mr Ambassador, I didn't see you there. I must have been lost in my own thoughts."

"Of course! Your poor brain must be swimming. I do so often wonder how you Highacrens do without cybernetics. I can't imagine being without my implant now. Though I suppose that means I'm far too reliant on it!" Ezra Brown said.

He laughed genially and Lily joined in, vaguely recalling Addison mentioning something about augmented charm.

"Mr Ambassador, about your implant," Lily began, eager to hear more about them from someone who knew. But she was interrupted by Jason's arrival. The large man loomed imposingly over Ezra, a displeased look on his face.

"You should not be here, Mr Ambassador."

"My apologies, Jason. You're right, I know better. I should stick with the door to the gardens that is closer to my rooms, but I was trying to sneak in a shortcut to the mountain path." He smiled at Lily. "No real excuse when I'm being lazy on my way to exercise."

"Nonetheless, Mr Ambassador, you are not to be in the Royal Wing. Harry will escort you back."

Another guard that Lily had been unaware of materialised, and without protest, Ezra bowed at Lily and made to follow.

"Oh goodness, what's going on here?" Addison bustled up, flushed from hurrying through the palace. Before Jason could speak, she continued, "Ezra! What are you doing here?" She seemed surprised by his presence, but not alarmed or annoyed as Jason was.

"I'm being bad, Addison," Ezra said, playing the part of a naughty schoolboy. "I was taking a shortcut which, as Jason rightly points out, was completely out of bounds. Harry will take me back." He smiled at the group, completely nonplussed.

"Well, but you're here now." Addison said, shooting a look at Jason that was half-smile, half-pleading. "You'd be headed for the mountain path for your walk, yes? Surely there's no need to go all the way back to the diplomatic quarters before heading out again."

"Addison," Jason started, uncomfortable with where this was going.

"It's okay with me," Lily added, trying to help, then immediately realised she had undermined Jason. "But I mean, yeah, he shouldn't have been here."

Jason bowed at Lily, avoiding her eyes. "By your command."

He gave a sharp jerk of his head and Harry went to guide Ezra outside, but Addison held out her hand to stop them.

"We're heading outside, so we can escort him."

She quickly looped her arm through Ezra's and headed for the door. Lily looked apologetically at Jason and mouthed, "Sorry."

The large man shook his head at her, his face kind. Lily hurried after Addison, watching her walking in close discussion with the Meridian ambassador and wondering what they were talking about. As Lily came into earshot, the two said their goodbyes and parted ways.

"What were you two talking about?"

"I reminded him to stay out of your house." Addison smiled. Lily did not believe for a second that had been the subject of their whispered discussion. "Now, with me, Your Majesty. We have much to get through."

10

"So you're saying that a country so technologically advanced as to invent interdimensional travel, can't build a plane?"

"No, Your Majesty, not that we can't—"

"Well then, why don't you have planes?"

"We don't really need—"

"Everyone needs planes! How do you travel long distances?"

"Well, we have the—"

"And you've all just had a war for crying out loud! What does your military use?"

"Well, I know the Air Force has hot air balloons. I think they use them for surveillance. Or perhaps they just like the view... In any event, they're really quite pretty."

"But how do you bomb each other?"

Addison sighed, smiling at Lily's enthusiasm. The conversation had been going on for a while now, and she didn't really know to answer Lily in a way that would satisfy her. Yes, they understood about flight. Clearly, they had seen birds and insects that fly. And yes, they had seen planes in Lily's dimension, and a couple of others, so of course they could build them if they wanted. It's just that no one had thought it necessary to encase a bunch of people in a bundle of metal and hurtle them into the sky.

"I don't know what to tell you, Your Majesty." Addison said. "But if it's this important to you, maybe when you're crowned you can have some planes built." Addison inwardly cringed. Giles was going to kill her.

Thankfully, Lily dropped the subject. Addison had been happy when Lily latched onto it instead of asking more awkward questions about what she and Ezra had been discussing. But then it had become something of an obsession, though she suspected that Lily was just enjoying a robust discussion. Which was probably a good thing; she would need to be assertive.

Addison was pleasantly surprised when Lily looped her arm through Addison's and smiled, closing her eyes and breathing in the fresh air. She looked around, smiling too. It was a beautiful day.

"Safety's one thing, but it's not good for you to be cooped up inside all the time," Addison said, leading her along the path in the 'extended grounds', as the woods near the palace were known.

She watched Lily look around happily. The trees were tall and sturdy, their bark a deep rich brown and their leaves a light and vibrant green. They rustled gently in the breeze, and Addison could smell a comforting earthy scent, but she couldn't exactly figure out what smells came from the trees and what came from the soft underbrush they were walking on.

Occasionally, they heard the soft rustling of small animals on either side of them, but none appeared. Lily confided in Addison that she missed the animals on her family farm and was hoping, much as she knew it wouldn't happen, that perhaps some of the woodland creatures would run up to her and let her pat them as if she were a cartoon princess.

"What else would you like to know about Highacre, or this world, Your Majesty?"

"How come we're all speaking the same language?" Lily looked thoughtful for a second. "Or *are* we speaking the same language? Maybe my ability lets me understand all languages?"

Addison laughed at Lily's hopeful tone. "No, sorry Your Majesty, while that may be an ability you might develop, I can assure you that we are speaking what you know as English. We selected your world for its similarities with ours, language being a big one. Imagine if you had to learn our language as well as everything else."

She considered it for a beat. "Jenkins says that it's possible our worlds are connected by a multi-thingy." Addison clicked her fingers. "Multi...oh, multiverse! Something about your world is one of the infinite possible worlds that our world could have been? I don't understand half of what that man says though!" She laughed, and they followed the path in silence for a bit.

"So does everyone here speak English, or whatever you call it?"

"We call it Fengstein, but yes. Well," Addison caught herself, "it's the main language, but it wasn't every country's native language. I think we had a few other languages in ancient times. Valmead spoke something else, and I gather some people can still speak it. And I've heard that some tiny countries speak other languages, but I've not been to any, so I don't really know."

"Well, you probably would have gone to some of those countries if you had planes."

Lily nodded in a slightly patronising manner. Addison rolled her eyes, then grabbed Lily's arm, declaring a race to the stream. They ran through the woods, off the path now, jumping over logs and finally arriving at a small stream that was hurrying its way through the woods off to some lake somewhere as if it were late.

Addison led Lily along the edge of the stream to a deeper part and then took off her shoes and socks, sat on the edge, and dangled her feet in the water. Lily hurried to join her, sighing as her feet hit the refreshingly cool water.

They relaxed there for a while, enjoying the sun and the water. Addison heard a rustle and looked up. She touched Lily's arm and quickly raised her finger to her lips, then pointed into the bushes. Lily strained to see what Addison was pointing at. A small branch snapped and Addison held Lily's arm, keeping her seated. Seconds passed, and just when Addison was sure that the animal had left, a tiny, tan-coloured dog emerged from the bushes. It was about the size of a hamster and very fluffy.

"It's a tiny puppy!" Lily whispered excitedly to Addison.

"It's a pelotromo," Addison whispered back. "They're very cute, but you don't want to make them mad."

Addison was watching the pelotromo warily, and before she could stop her, Lily had risen and was creeping towards the little dog. It kept a suspicious eye on Lily but continued snuffling around the undergrowth like a pig looking for truffles. Addison got up too as Lily crept closer and closer. She considered calling out to her but didn't want to startle the pelotromo. *Where are those guards when you need them?*

As Lily reached down to pat it, the tiny fluff-ball bared its teeth and growled at her. It was a funny, whiny sound, like a tiny, angry weed eater. Addison jumped and moved towards them as Lily pulled back, but once the pup was satisfied it had put Lily in her place, it trotted over, licked her leg, and looked up at her expectantly. Lily cautiously patted it, and when her hand wasn't bitten off, she rubbed its chest, and it promptly flopped over onto its back, allowing Lily to rub its tummy.

It was tan all over except for its snub of a nose, which was black, and it had a white streak on its chest and white-tipped paws. Abruptly, the pup rolled back over and bounded off into the woods and was gone.

Lily stared after it for a beat, then she whirled around to look at Addison. "I want one of those."

Addison laughed, sighing in relief as she sat back down and splashed at Lily with her feet. "Yes, Your Majesty. Of course you do."

"Was it wise to take her into the extended grounds?"

"She was half asleep in the lesson, and we had Jason and his team nearby. Besides, there hasn't been a sniff of a threat." Addison looked out of the window of her small ground floor office.

"Yes, but there wasn't last time either." Giles was focussed on disposing of his tea bag without dripping and missed the look Addison shot him. "We need to make sure she's safe. At least until the coronation."

"And what then?" asked Addison, appalled. "She's disposable?"

"Now, that's not what I meant," Giles said. "Obviously her safety remains of utmost importance, but our current focus *must* be on the removal of the Prime Minister."

Addison remained silent, still uncomfortable with the idea that they should decide who ran the country. Of course, she was pretty sure that most people wanted the Prime Minister gone. And if they didn't already, they soon would. An affable, friendly man before he came to power, the Prime Minister had become power hungry following the assassinations, pushing the limits of his emergency powers and posturing to remain in charge indefinitely.

His speeches of late were less speeches and more nationalistic ranting. And if the rumours were to be believed, the arrests and mysterious disappearances were increasing in number, as was the distinct lack of justification for those disappearances.

"And in the meantime, we all need to be more careful about what we discuss and where. She's clearly suspicious, and has now several times almost overheard things she shouldn't."

"But why shouldn't she? She knows about the Prime Minister. About why we need her to get rid of him. Why can't we tell her the rest?"

"Because we don't know her, Addison," said Giles. "We know next to nothing about who she is and what her values are. And even if she is as nice as she seems, we don't know that she won't say the wrong thing to the wrong person."

"But if we told her who the wrong people are—"

"Addison." Giles took off his glasses and looked at her, his eyes tired. "We've been over this. Jason is doing his very best, but he doesn't know who all of them are, and he can't guarantee that they can't get to her. All it would take is for one person on the other side to win her trust and we're finished. She can be told what is necessary to achieve what is required of her, and no more."

Addison sighed and turned back to look at the gardens. "I wish I knew where Lady Octavia has gotten to," she said, almost to herself. "And what or who is this oracle? Have you ever heard of an oracle?"

"No," said Giles, frowning. "I can't say I've ever heard reference to an oracle. It is troubling that we can't reach her, though."

"You don't think something has happened to her?"

"I suppose it is possible." Giles saw the look of horror on Addison's face. "Oh, I'm sure she's fine. Honestly, I think Lady Octavia will always do what Lady Octavia wants. You know she turned down a position as a royal advisor? Oh yes, the king asked her himself, but she politely declined. No one's turned down a position in...well, ever! It's completely unheard of."

"Why'd she turn it down?"

"Who knows? Who knows what goes through that woman's mind. In all likelihood there is no oracle and she's just told us that to keep us from bothering her."

"She is very wise, though," said Addison, somewhat defensively.

"She certainly is that." Giles smiled at her. "No one doubts her intellect and wisdom. That's why she was offered a spot as an advisor to begin with. But she's just so unpredictable."

Addison sat in a chair across from Giles, both seats angled towards the cosy fire. She admired Lady Octavia. Had since she was a little girl. Everyone held her in such awe and respect; Addison had dreamed of having people look at her like that too. But when she told her mother that she wanted to have Lady Octavia's ability, her mother had just laughed and told her that only very special people had that ability. Addison had thought she *was* very special, but apparently that wasn't the case.

Her own abilities had their uses. Her powers of persuasion came in handy on an almost daily basis, mainly in calming situations and avoiding conflict. Addison hated conflict. And everyone loved a healer, even one whose ability was as weak as hers was. But she had to admit, she often looked around at everyone else and wished her powers were as impressive or revered as theirs were.

Her discussion with Lily had left her pensive. She remembered as a child wishing she had been born Meridian so she could choose her own talent. In a rare rebellious phase in her twenties, she had even investigated getting an implant, convinced that the risk was worth it, and she would be the one who could handle it. Maybe that would have been her third ability—surviving an implant unscathed. But she had chickened out at the last minute, overwhelmed with guilt about how her mother would feel if it all went wrong.

Still, if she couldn't be as important as Lady Octavia, she could at least be grateful for her privileged position and her regular exposure to such amazing people. *Giles should be too.* The older man did not seem to appreciate his position or revere her idol.

"Oh, by the way, Her Majesty would like a pelotromo..."

Giles sprayed his mouthful of tea over the table in front of him. Addison sipped hers, a satisfied smile on her lips.

"I assume you told her no."

"Of course not! She is the sovereign."

"Not yet, she's not," Giles muttered.

"Anyhow, will you procure one, or shall I?"

"Don't you dare! No, I mean it Addison. We cannot have one of those...*things* in the palace. What if someone made it mad? No, you are under no circumstances to buy Her Majesty a pelotromo."

"But if she asks...?"

"If she asks, you will tell me, and I will address it."

Addison sipped her tea and wondered who would prevail in that battle of wills. With a tiny smile, she thought perhaps the butler was underestimating the princess.

11

LILY WOULD NORMALLY BE happy with an interruption to her routine, which was by now both reassuring and monotonous. However, the level of alarm in her advisors was contagious, and Lily found herself on the brink of blind panic.

Giles burst into the room while Lily was having her etiquette lesson with Claire, said something about the Prime Minister, and insisted that Lily must immediately return to her rooms to 'prepare'. Prepare how and for what was not immediately forthcoming, but Giles and Claire had preceded her in the flight to her rooms in huddled, urgent discussion, none of which Lily could hear. By the time they reached the Lodge, Lily was about ready to shout, demanding to be told what was going on. Instead, she was met by Addison, who swept her into her room where a bevy of servants pounced upon her to prepare her for, as she was finally informed, her meeting with the Prime Minister.

"What!" Lily exclaimed over the hubbub of activity surrounding her. "But he's not meant to know that I'm even here! I'm not ready! You said that I'm not ready!"

"It would be our preference, Your Majesty, to have

some more time preparing you before you meet the Prime Minister," Addison said, clearly choosing her words carefully. "But you have been working hard in your lessons and you will be fine."

Addison's eyes didn't completely back up this sentiment, but Lily didn't question her further. This was happening. She would just need to mentally prepare and do her best.

"How did he find out I'm here?" Lily asked Claire, who had joined them to give her some last-minute advice on the protocol for meeting the Prime Minister, and some tips on how to deal with questions she didn't feel comfortable answering.

Claire thought before answering. "We're not yet sure, Your Majesty, though we are looking into it. It's possible someone with knowledge of your return told him, or conversations were overheard and passed on. He was informed upon the death of your family that efforts were being made to retrieve you from the country in which you were hidden. To be fair, I'm surprised that story held up as long as it did."

Lily pondered Claire's answer. Now that she thought about it, there *were* a significant number of people who knew she was here in the palace. It did seem surprising that the secret had held so long.

The servants finished getting Lily ready. Once her hair and makeup were done and she was in a fancy dress and heels, she was ready to meet the Prime Minister.

"Now, Your Majesty," Giles offered Lily his arm and escorted her from the Lodge. "The Prime Minister is a little...upset. Following the death of the royal family, the Prime Minister directed that every effort be made to find you and bring you home. When you weren't immediately located and retrieved, it was thought that perhaps you had perished also, and ever since, the Prime Minister has been posturing for the abolition of the monarchy and the installation of himself as president.

"Even if he were happy to see the continuation of the royal line and the monarchy, which, from all accounts he is not, he would still be in an awkward political position because of his posturing and is no doubt expecting a lot of uncomfortable questions about his position on the monarchy now, and his loyalty to you."

Minister Bellingham bustled up to them in the corridor, and Giles greeted her with surprise.

"Minister, I'm glad you could make it, but we were hoping you would be in Her Majesty's office with the Prime Minister, calming him down."

"Jeremy is with him," Minister Bellingham said, slightly dismissively.

It took Lily a beat to remember that 'Jeremy' was Minister Toot, the defence minister. Minister Bellingham caught the look on Giles's face.

"Jeremy and Reginald are old classmates; Jeremy can handle him."

Giles didn't look entirely convinced but let the matter drop.

"Your Majesty," Minister Bellingham turned to Lily. "This may seem overwhelming, but Reginald, the Prime Minister, is just a man, and his major frustration here is going to be about political capital. Answer the questions you are comfortable answering based on your lessons, and anything else can be deferred to one of your advisors, or until the confirmation hearing."

With that and a curt nod to Giles, Minister Bellingham strode away towards Lily's office. Lily looked anxiously at Addison, who immediately took her other arm, and the procession continued slowly in the foreign minister's wake.

"Don't worry, Your Majesty, you'll be just fine,"

Addison soothed her. "And as Juliana said, the Prime Minister will be squarely focussed on himself and his career. At this stage, he won't be looking to trip you up and poke holes in your story. That'll be at the confirmation hearing."

Oh, great.

Claire moved in front of the group as they reached the doors to Lily's office. Lily was distracted by muffled raised voices inside.

"Your Majesty," Claire brought Lily's attention back to her. "Remember our lessons. Poise and posture. Hold yourself as if you are the most important person in the room, which you are, and people will respond accordingly. It is not his place to question you. You are to be queen."

Lily nodded, holding herself up straighter and lifting her chin.

I am the queen. Well, technically not yet...

She banished the unhelpful thought with a shake of her head and focussed on getting in the right mindset. Finally, she nodded at Giles, who was poised with his hand on the door handle. He returned her nod and opened the door.

Immediately, the voices hit them. Clearly, her office was well insulated.

"I shouldn't be kept in the dark. It doesn't do well for the prime minister to be ignorant of matters going on in his own backyard."

"You want me to ensure you aren't ignorant? For goodness' sake Reggie, I'm good, but I'm not a miracle worker."

Minister Bellingham and the Prime Minister were standing toe-to-toe in the middle of the room. The Foreign Minister was leaning slightly away from the Prime Minister, her arms crossed. The Prime Minister's face was beet red, and he was glaring at Minister Bellingham, his hands balled into fists by his side. Jeremy Toot was sitting casually in an armchair, looking completely nonplussed.

Minister Bellingham noticed their arrival and cut the Prime Minister off from his rant about her responsibilities to him and their political party.

"Pull yourself together Reginald, the queen is here."

The Prime Minister looked over at Lily and her entourage, clearly wrong-footed by their sudden arrival. He recovered quickly and muttered, "She's not the queen yet."

Minister Bellingham looked like she was about to respond, but Giles then announced Lily's arrival formally.

"Ladies and gentlemen, Her Royal Majesty, Crown Princess Lily, fifth of her name, heir to the throne of the lands of Highacre, all her isles and protectorates, the First Sword of the Land, and protector of all who inhabit her realm."

Lily barely had time to register her full title when Giles proceeded.

"Your Majesty, may I present the Prime Minister, the honourable Mr Reginald Toth."

"Your Majesty." The Prime Minister took a step towards Lily and bowed deeply, but curtly.

"Prime Minister." Lily inclined her head. "Shall we sit?" She gestured towards the lounge setting where Minister Toot was standing, having risen when Giles announced Lily.

"As you wish, Your Majesty."

The group had barely sat down when he began, "I must say, Your Majesty, delighted as I am at your return, I must object to being kept in the dark like this. I cannot run the country in your stead without being kept in the loop."

"Well, you won't need to burden yourself with running the country for Her Majesty much longer," Minister Bellingham shot back.

"Juliana, I must insist..."

"Oh, calm down Reginald," Minister Bellingham said, then seemed to remember the formality of the setting. "My apologies, Your Majesty. Mr Prime Minister, all Her Majesty's advisors agreed that those who would be made aware of Her Majesty's return would be kept to a bare minimum because of the security situation. Obviously you were to be told soon, as we need to arrange for the confirmation hearing."

The Prime Minister scoffed. "How do I even know she is who you say she is?" He glanced at Lily. "Apologies, Your Majesty."

Lily shook her head to indicate that she was not offended but could not get a word in before Minister Bellingham responded.

"Yes, yes, she's been assessed by Lady Octavia."

Minister Bellingham produced a document that looked like a certificate and handed it to the Prime Minister. It annoyed Lily that she had not seen whatever was being shown to the Prime Minister and briefly empathised with the man.

"There was obviously no need to bother you before we could ensure that she is the heir."

The Prime Minister scanned the document briefly before putting it aside.

"And what abilities does she have then?"

Lily felt the room tense, but Minister Bellingham continued, undeterred, "Oh, I don't know Reginald, she's working with Lady Octavia. I assume the woman can do her job and don't ask for updates every five minutes. What matters," she continued, quickly cutting off a protest from the Prime Minister, "is that she is the heir and she is of the royal line inclusive of the power. We can cover everything else at the confirmation hearing."

The Prime Minister scrutinised Lily, who tried her hardest to channel her inner Claire and appear aloof and unworried.

"Fine," he said eventually. The room let out a collective breath. His lack of protest confused Lily, and she sensed she was not the only one.

"Good. I'm glad that's settled." Minister Bellingham went to stand.

"We'll hold a press conference. I'd prefer the steps at the Tower, but I'm happy to come here if that's what you want."

"Stop, stop, stop. Reginald, no." Minister Bellingham leant closer to the Prime Minister. "Are you mad? A press conference? We cannot alert the public to her return. The investigation into the assassinations is ongoing. We must keep her existence secret for as long as possible so that we can ensure security."

Lily expected the Prime Minister to argue, but again he simply nodded and sat back.

"No, you're right, my apologies. I forgot myself in all the excitement over Her Majesty's return."

He did not look excited. Instead, after a beat, he stood and bowed at Lily.

"Well, I'd better be off. Can't be hanging around here all day. It'll raise suspicions."

He smiled, but it didn't reach his eyes. Lily's advisors all politely farewelled the Prime Minister, and a guard escorted him out.

"Well, that went better than expected!" Minister Bellingham announced.

Lily's advisors all began excitedly debriefing about the meeting and the next steps. Lily sat back, noting they did not seek to involve her in their discussion. It was not lost on her that for all the excitement before the meeting, she had been largely ignored by the Prime Minister, and Minister Bellingham had taken charge.

Not that she'd tried to take the lead herself. Lily reflected that she had been content to sit back and let her advisors take charge. If she continued to allow them to take control, they'd never see her as a true queen. And *would* they ever see her as a queen? Their queen? Or was she just a prop? She certainly felt like a prop right now. A real live doll that they had pulled out, dressed up, and wheeled out to show the Prime Minister she existed. *Smile and wave.*

Lily resolved to be more active in her lessons. To ask questions and figure out what she wanted to know, as well as what they thought she needed to know. And she needed Lady Octavia to return. If she could develop some of her abilities, then she could take more control. All she needed was a little mind reading, and all of this would be so much easier.

Eventually, the advisors calmed down and Lily was escorted back to her room to change for her afternoon lesson with Addison. Despite her new resolution, Lily mainly listened to Addison and took in the information rather than asking questions.

Tomorrow. I'll start tomorrow.

Tomorrow started in another flurry of activity. Her servants woke Lily and allowed her some privacy to visit the royal bathroom. When she came out of the bathroom, her servants had not yet returned, so she wandered back towards her bed.

Something huffed at her, and she looked up to see the tiny dog she'd met in the extended grounds sitting on her bed and looking at her expectantly. Lily looked around her room. The pelotromo hadn't been there before, and she couldn't see who might have delivered it.

The pelotromo huffed again. Lily wrapped her robe around her and cautiously approached the little dog, holding her hand out for it to sniff. The dog grabbed her finger with its paw and pulled it towards its chest.

"Oh, you want pats, do you?" Lily smiled. She obliged, and the little dog looked very pleased with itself. Lily heard the door behind her open and, without thinking, picked the pelotromo up and hid him in the deep sleeves of her robe. He didn't seem to mind.

Though her servants tried valiantly to distract her and take her through her routine to get ready for her lessons, the raised voices out in the Lodge took Lily's attention, and she brushed them off and went out to see what the fuss was.

"...should have known! That stupid little man!" Minister Bellingham ranted.

"What's going on?"

Lily approached, realising too late that she was still in her robe and pyjamas. Her advisors didn't blink at her attire, all paying the appropriate compliments.

"Your Majesty," Giles began, but immediately floundered, looking for the words.

"Oh here, let her see for herself." Addison took a newspaper from Minister Bellingham's hands and thrust it at Lily.

The page was slightly crumpled from where Minister Bellingham had gripped it angrily. Lily smoothed it out and was greeted with an enormous picture of the Prime Minister on some steps in front of an impressive building.

WELCOME HOME

A delighted Prime Minister announced today that the

"'So her security could be assured', give me a break." Minister Bellingham was clearly animated about the Prime Minister getting the upper hand and taking all the credit.

"What happens now?" Lily asked, less concerned about the political jostling and more about her own safety.

"We stick with the plan, Your Majesty," said Giles. "We will continue with your preparation. Only, we will now have less time, as we will also need to arrange time in your schedule for you to meet with dignitaries and move more publicly into matters of state."

"Now that the public know you are here, we need to ensure they see you in the role," Claire added. "People need to see that you are capable of being their queen."

"And what about my security?" Lily asked, feeling slightly cowardly.

"Have no worries, Your Majesty," Jason startled Lily, who hadn't realised he was behind her. "My team and I will increase our efforts, and your second personal bodyguard has been selected. She is a powerful revealer and highly competent in protection. She'll be available to start shortly."

Lily nodded. It was not lost on her that her advisors

seemed singularly focussed on their aim, and were less concerned about Lily's safety, or even her comfort, now that everyone knew she was here. She absentmindedly stroked the pelotromo, who purred.

The room froze.

"Your Majesty." Giles shot a dirty look at Addison, who looked bewildered but amused. "Where did you get that?"

"What? This little guy? He was in my room." Lily lifted the pelotromo to her face and cooed at him. The advisors gasped, but the pelotromo didn't seem to mind.

"I think I'll call him Pumpkin!"

The little bundle of fluff let out a menacing, weed eater growl.

All her advisors stepped back.

"No, okay, not Pumpkin. Um, how about Lord Fluffybutt?"

If anything, the growl was more intense, though of a higher pitch.

"Your Majesty, maybe you shouldn't..." Giles's voice wavered.

"You're right," Lily said. Giles looked slightly relieved. "I'll call him Kevin."

Her advisors flinched back but were surprised to find that the little dog simply started licking its paws. Lily nodded at them and headed back into her room to get dressed.

12

Lily looked in wonder around the great hall. It had been beautifully decorated and was full of men and women, all in marvellous, colourful suits and gowns. She looked down at her own pyjamas. The immersion device had taken a little getting used to, but Lily no longer had the pang of anxiety akin to dreaming of turning up at school naked.

Most nights Lily found herself plunging into scenes from her family's past, and today, having been told that tonight she was hosting a royal ball, she had grabbed the device, wanting to see what was in store. It was addictive and strangely comforting, being able to be with her family like this and experience the key events and moments in their lives. Though she couldn't completely shake the feeling of separation. Of literally being on the outside looking in.

Nonetheless, she felt like she knew her family. She recognised the smirk her brother Liam had when he'd played a prank and the difference between the expression on her mother's face when she appreciated Liam's mischief but felt he needed to be told off, and when she was actually mad.

She sighed and moved towards Sarah and Emily, who were standing by a table of hors d'oeuvres, giggling and whispering to each other. She felt a familiar pang of guilt but pushed it away. She wasn't cheating on her family back home. She had every right to try and get to know her biological family. It wasn't her fault that she couldn't talk to her parents about it. And besides, they should have told her about her being adopted.

Before she could reach her sisters, her mother's voice caught her attention.

"...annoying man. He's up to something, I'm sure of it."

"Oh, Your Majesty," Addison smiled. "He's up to nothing. He's a lovely man. You just don't like him because your father wouldn't have liked him."

"My father would have had the measure of him. Smarmy little bast—"

"Your Majesty!"

Lily laughed at Addison's shock at her mother swearing. She took in the queen, elegant in a beautiful red and gold flowing gown. Lily was sure she would never look that graceful.

The smile fell from the queen's face. "Do be careful Addison."

"Ma'am?" Addison's face fell, a concerned expression replacing her smile.

"There is something off about him, and after the briefing we just got from—"

A disembodied hand on Lily's arm startled her, causing her to jump and squeal. Suddenly the image disappeared, replaced with her bedroom once more.

"Apologies, Your Majesty," said a maid, dropping into a curtsey. "Miss Grange said I was to start getting you ready for the ball."

"Stop fidgeting, Your Majesty," hissed Giles for the fifth time in the last three minutes.

"You have no idea how uncomfortable this stupid dress is," Lily shot back, her patience waning.

She had plenty of clothes in her closet that, in her opinion, were more than appropriate for an occasion such as this, so when Addison had appeared in her room with the monstrosity that she was now fighting against, she had questioned why her advisors hated her so much. *I can't even breathe.*

"Your Majesty," Addison had laughed, "it's tradition!"

"It's a stupid tradition."

"Your Majesty!"

"Probably made up by some man who would never have to wear something so hideous and uncomfortable."

Lily's very least concern, now that she was imprisoned in the outfit, was her appearance. The ornate beading and the sheer number of jewels plastered all over it made the dress heavy. Lily felt like someone had gone crazy with a bedazzler.

It was also just long enough to catch her feet as she walked, and was long-sleeved and high-necked. The neck was tight and frilly, so Lily felt like she both couldn't breathe and was constantly being tickled. Of course, due to the bedazzled sleeves, she couldn't really bend her arms to scratch the itches or adjust the frills.

Though she didn't often wear them, Lily did enjoy wearing dresses, but there was nothing redeeming about *this* dress. She thought fondly once more of her closet, full of beautiful gowns that were both stunning and comfortable.

Lily had asked Addison whether she would have to wear a similar outfit to her confirmation hearing, and

Addison had laughed no. But when Lily asked about the coronation, Addison had blushed and said that Lily would not have to wear that particular dress again, then had quickly left the room before Lily could ask any more questions.

"My first act when I am officially queen will be to abolish these traditional dresses and have them destroyed."

Giles looked at her, shocked at first, but his expression softened as he took her in. "But Your Majesty, you look so beautiful. Regal!"

If Lily could bend her arms, she might have punched him. Perhaps that was why they made the sleeves like that...

Claire moved behind her and Lily felt some pulling, some pressure, and suddenly the dress was a little more tolerable.

"Is that better, Your Majesty?" Claire asked.

"Much, thank you," said Lily in surprise. Claire nodded and moved away as Giles ushered Lily out of her room and off to the great hall, where she found herself standing in front of about a hundred people.

As Lily squirmed, Claire made a small sound of disapproval and shook her head at Lily. Lily rolled her eyes. Being a queen seemed much more like being a schoolgirl than being in charge of everything.

Lily's eyes wandered around the great hall. All the fireplaces along the walls had been lit, giving the enormous hall as much of a homey feeling as it could manage. The hall itself was full of people who Lily was informed were a veritable who's who of Highacren society. Dresses and tuxedos and coiffed hair abounded. Lily had always hated formal events. That she was the centre of attention made it significantly worse.

Lily waited what felt like an age as she was announced and they went through all of her titles. When the guard finally stepped aside and bowed, the room followed suit, and Giles escorted Lily into the great hall.

"Now remember, Your Majesty, we start with the nobles. Some will be loyal to you, others...less so."

As they moved through the room, men and women nodded respectfully as they passed.

"The important thing," Giles said, smile plastered to his face as he nodded in greeting to various people around the room, "is that you remember who you are, and what you are. It doesn't matter that you did not grow up here. What matters is that you are the rightful heir. Act like it, and they will respect you."

They arrived at what seemed to be an ill-placed receiving line, but Lily quickly realised that it had been positioned to the rear of the room so that those not important enough to be granted an audience with the heir could see exactly who was that important. Several of the nobles seemed to spend more time glancing around the room haughtily than looking at Lily as they spoke.

"The Duke and Duchess Silvercolt," announced Giles, guiding Lily in front of a short, rotund man and his tall skinny wife.

"Your Majesty," gushed the duke, taking Lily's hand and kissing it. "May I say how delighted we were to hear that you were alive and well. And home!"

"Delighted," agreed the duchess, nodding emphatically. "And relieved."

"Oh gosh yes," the duke nodded back at his wife. The reminded Lily of the bobblehead figures that people put on their car dashboards. It was almost mesmerising. "But the important thing is you're here. And gosh, if you don't look like your father." The duke beamed at Lily, his eyes tearing up.

"Oh yes," agreed the duchess. "But those are definitely the queen's eyes."

"Such lovely people." The duke sniffed and produced a large red handkerchief. "Such a tragic loss."

Lily didn't quite know what to do as the duke and duchess devolved into sobs, so she murmured what she hoped were comforting phrases, patting them gently on their shoulders. Unfortunately, her display of kindness only set them off more, and Lily looked to Giles in alarm.

He guided Lily away from the sobbing couple and along the line as Addison and Claire appeared to usher the duke and duchess away. Lily looked up to see she was in front of a severe man dressed in a tuxedo that was completely black except for a dazzling emerald green silk pocket square.

"Count Blontoy," said Giles curtly.

"Charmed," the count took Lily's hand limply and bowed slightly, a lazy parody of kissing it.

"It is good to meet you Count Blontoy," said Lily, smiling widely. Claire had advised her to kill with kindness when met with those who either supported the Prime Minister or simply did not recognise her claim.

"Well yes," the count raised an eyebrow. "So kind of you to return to Highacre. And to now deign to meet us."

"Of course. In light of the recent tragedy, it has been my priority to be brought up to speed so as to best serve the people of Highacre."

"Perhaps they are best served by the Prime Minister? He has been running things in your absence. And doing a fine job too, I might add."

"And I am, of course, grateful to Mr Toth for stepping up during such a tumultuous time. I look forward to working with him in the future."

"You'd be better off staying out of his way and letting him go about the business of running the country," the count sneered, his mask slipping. "Keep to your balls and fancy dresses and let the man lead."

Lily was shocked by the venom in his voice, but held her smile on her face, forcing herself to maintain eye contact. "It's been a pleasure, Count Blontoy. I look forward to seeing you again soon."

"Well done Your Majesty," Giles whispered as he guided her to her next dignitary.

"Ah," Giles perked up. "Your Majesty, it is my pleasure to introduce Brigadier Sergei Romanovich, the ambassador from Valmead, and Alexei Rosovski, the ambassador to court."

Both men snapped into respectful bows.

"Your Majesty," Sergei began. "Great Leader Rosovski sends his best regards. He is pleased to hear of your return and welcomes open relations between Valmead and Highacre."

"Thank you, Brigadier Romanovich. Please be sure to convey my gratitude to the Great Leader, and that I hope to meet him personally soon."

"Your Majesty." Alexei took Lily's hand and kissed it. *Oh, this one's a charmer.* "It is my pleasure to make your acquaintance. I look forward to working closely with you."

"Oh, yes... I'm sure we will work closely." Lily blushed, unsure why she felt so flustered.

"And here," Giles said, moving Lily quickly down the line, "are the ambassador and ambassador to court from Meridia: Ezra Brown and Ava Harrington."

Both dropped into deep bows, and Lily caught a brief look of disdain flit across Claire's face at Ava bowing rather than curtsying. She had a feeling she and Ava would get along very well.

"Your Majesty," smiled Ezra, his eyes twinkling. "May I

offer the warmest welcome home to you from President Taylor, and all Meridia. We share the joy of all Highacrens at your safe return and eagerly anticipate your assumption of the throne."

"Thank you so much, Mr Brown. Please convey my appreciation to President Taylor and tell him I very much look forward to meeting him soon."

Lily turned to Ava, trying not to be intimidated by her confidence. Ava couldn't be more than a year older than Lily and yet looked to have no issues meeting a foreign dignitary so publicly, nor hobnobbing with nobles and politicians and whoever else was here tonight. Ava smiled warmly at Lily, a gleam of mischief in her eyes.

"Your Majesty, it's an honour to meet you at last. I look forward to working with you." Ava eyed Lily's dress. "And lucky for me—I almost wore the same thing. I wouldn't have been able to pull it off as well as you are."

Lily almost snorted at the unexpected joke and looked jealously at Ava's beautiful dress that looked like it flowed, rather than constricting the wearer. Giles nodded at the ambassadors and moved Lily along the line.

She quickly lost count of how many people she met, and felt she had no hope of remembering all their names.

As Lily completed the receiving line, a feeling of relaxation pervaded the room. Everyone started milling around freely, chatting in groups and snatching glasses of different liquids off the trays being hovered around the room, directed telekinetically by attendants concentrating hard from a balcony overhead.

Minister Bellingham startled Lily, appearing from nowhere and grabbing her elbow to steer her over to meet some politicians. They chatted politely for a bit, but before long the politicians became more engrossed in themselves and the conversation turned to work and other matters familiar to everyone in the little group but Lily. She smiled politely, vaguely following the conversation while she tried to subtly scan the room to see what else was going on.

A booming laugh caught her attention and she saw the Meridian and Valmeadian ambassadors over in a corner, clearly having a great time. She turned back to her circle and politely laughed at whatever political quip the minister for fisheries and agriculture had made.

As the group's attention moved to the minister for transport and communications, Lily took her chance and slowly backed out of their circle before making for the ambassador's corner.

"Your Majesty." Sergei saw Lily first and greeted her, alerting the others to her presence and seeing them all straighten up immediately.

"Please," she raised her hands, indicating that they should remain as they were. "I'm trying to escape the politicians, and you all seemed to be having the most fun."

"Damn straight," said Ava. "And that's despite Alexei being here."

The group laughed as Alexei mimed being stabbed in the heart.

"Ah, this is the best thing about Highacren parties," declared Sergei, grabbing a drink off a floating tray.

"My good man! I can offer you a great deal on some hovering trays," said Ezra.

"But don't you need an implant to make them work?" asked Sergei.

"Ah yes," agreed Ezra, thinking. "Well, I'm sure we can send one of our people over to run them for you."

Sergei laughed loudly. "I'm sure you can. I'm sure you have just the person to run your electronic gadgets in all our state buildings."

"I won't even charge you for it!" Ezra joked.

"You can control electronic devices with your implants?" Lily had been dying to find out more about the Meridian cybernetics as well as the Valmedian enchantments, and this seemed like the perfect opportunity.

"Of course. That's a basic function of all implants," said Ava. "When you're young, you get the base-level model. It comes with a heads-up display that provides you with basic information about the world. So you can see the weather report, search for information, get directions, and communicate with other people."

"Like a smart phone," said Lily.

"Exactly. It also lets parents keep an eye on their children; see what they're up to and tell them to come home."

"Our more modern implants now also have health monitoring," interjected Ezra. "Which means we're able to detect and treat childhood illnesses more easily."

"So do you just keep that same implant forever?" asked Lily.

"Some do," said Ava. "Depending on the capability of the model you get as a child, you might be able to simply update the firmware and attach the capabilities you want or need. But sometimes you will need to replace it. For instance, if you get into a top-level school or university, you may need to get a more advanced model that will let you run programs that help you with learning and retaining information.

"Otherwise, it will depend on your job. Your employer might provide you with a better implant that can support the skills required, and of course, if you get into government work, you must use one of their secure implants."

"Years ago, back in my day," Ezra winked at Lily, playing up his age, though not looking old at all. "People would just keep adding implants. As the person and implants aged, this could cause all sorts of issues. Nowadays, it's more common to replace the implant, or upgrade the existing implant. This is why Meridia is working to provide children with the best possible implant from the beginning. Hopefully, in a few years, Meridians won't ever have to remove an implant or add another. It will all be done through adding functionality wirelessly to their existing implant."

Lily was impressed with the passion in Ezra's voice. Clearly this was something he cared about.

"So, if your employer gives you an implant, what happens if you quit?" Lily was imagining how many implants she would have gone through already if she had been born in Meridia.

"A good question, Your Majesty," Ezra said. "Usually this is covered in the contract of employment. Some employers will take a portion of the employee's wages each pay cycle to cover the implant, and when it is paid off, the employee owns it and may take it when they leave. Others will have a certain time period after which they may keep the implant if they leave. Many government implants must be recovered because of the sensitive information in them, or the nature of the implant. It is usual for government employees to be offered a range of different implants when they leave based on the time they served and the position they held."

"Fascinating," Lily said. No doubt somewhat influenced by her lack of success in developing her abilities, Lily was quite envious of the Meridians and their ability to choose, to some extent, what they could do and what talents they could access. She wondered what it would be like having a heads-up display.

"Boscht," said Sergei with a good-natured smile. "Your cybernetics are simple machines. Our enchantments are much more good." His accent sounded similar to an Eastern European's from Earth.

"Much better," Ava corrected him instinctively.

"Finally, you agree," said Sergei, a twinkle in his eye.

"Why, you underhanded—" Ava stopped herself. "If Her Majesty wasn't here, I would finish that sentence, Ambassador, but out of respect for her, I will simply register my diplomatic protest at your behaviour."

Lily enjoyed the banter between the ambassadors. It was a relief from all the formality.

"Your Majesty," Sergei addressed her with a sharp bow. "Please forgive my poor language skills. I am just a simple soldier and so lucky that Ambassador Ava is here to help me."

"You have superior language skills, Sergei, and since when was a brigadier a 'simple soldier'?" Ava said.

"You see! She helps me again!"

They all laughed. Lily felt relaxed for the first time that evening. Really, for the first time in a while.

"Cybernetics sound amazing," said Lily wistfully.

Alexei scoffed. "Silly machines. Enchantments are far superior."

"In what way?" Lily asked.

"For one, they don't malfunction."

"Our cybernetics do not malfunction!" Ava exclaimed.

"Oh, that's not your implant? That's all you?"

Ava was about to bite back but saw Alexei's smile and settled for rolling her eyes at him and sipping her drink.

"Our enchanters train from a young age to ensure that they are masters of their craft. They can imbue any object with various powers and abilities. Our master enchanters can even put two enchantments in one object." Alexei was clearly proud of his country.

"Can they now?" asked Ezra. "I had heard that was still very limited."

"Your information is old, Mr Ambassador," Alexei told him. "We have advanced quickly in recent times." He turned back to Lily. "With our enchantments, the skill comes from the object. If a soldier dies in combat, his fellows can pick up his enchanted rifle and benefit from the enchantment. The unit's abilities are not degraded. With cybernetics" —he gestured towards Ava and Ezra— "the person dies and the ability is lost."

"So, if I picked up an enchanted object—" Lily began.

"They usually won't work for someone with magical power," Alexei interrupted. "Or an implant." He added, looking again at Ava. "The enchantments seem to interfere with the implant, or vice versa. I don't really know why it doesn't work."

"Okay, well then, let's say you pick up an object enchanted with super strength, and then you pick up one with super speed. Do you get both powers?"

"Yes," said Alexei proudly.

"Do you really?" asked Ezra, fascinated. "I thought the enchantments don't work together, and you only got the power from the stronger enchantment?"

"Well, sometimes that is the case," Alexei admitted. "But our enchanters are learning new ways and we are developing means of enchanting that will allow multiple enchanted objects to work together."

"Drink?" Sergei thrust a drink into Alexei's hand. Lily got the feeling Sergei was shutting Alexei up.

"How about a demonstration?" suggested Alexei, putting the drink Sergei had handed him back on a nearby tray. "Sergei, may I borrow your belt?"

Sergei reluctantly began to remove his thick leather belt. Lily saw it had some dull, rough-cut gemstones on it.

"Now, Sergei's belt boosts the wearer's strength and endurance. If I take this..." Alexei cast around for something metal, eventually eyeing a spear mounted on the wall. He crossed to it and pulled it down, returning to the group and ignoring the surprised looks of some of the Highacren nobility.

"Without the belt, I can't move it." Alexei made a show of trying to bend the spear, even grasping it either side of his knee and pressing. "But with the enchantment," he put the belt on, "it's like butter."

Lily gasped as Alexei bent the spear easily with his hands, twisting it as if it were a paperclip. Alexei smiled impressively around the group.

"Not a bad trick," admitted Ezra. "But really, the utility is lacking. How many spears does one need to twist?"

He reached into his pocket and pulled out a small ball, about the size of a marble.

"With this little fellow, I can increase my field of view exponentially." He tossed the ball into the air, where it hovered for a moment before flying up towards the roof of the hall and out of sight. "Your Majesty, I can share my heads-up display with you if you'd like. Do you have your phone?"

Lily rummaged around in her handbag for the phone her advisors had given her. It was thinner than her phone back home, and could be folded up into more convenient shapes, which just meant that Lily was more likely to lose it. Not that she was worried about that. It only held her advisor's contact details, and had they had limited the functionality so she could look up information, but couldn't really interact with the outside world. This was apparently for her own protection.

"Here it is." Lily brought it out and presented it to Ezra.

"Ah, excellent. Just click 'accept' on that little link. There we go. And now you can see what I see."

Lily and the others watched her screen as it suddenly showed them a top-down view of the great hall. Lily was amazed as little squares appeared over different people, scanning them and then displaying who they were, and bits of information about them.

"Incredible! I could really use something like that for these kinds of events."

"Indeed, Your Majesty," Ezra nodded. Suddenly his face fell slightly. "Uh oh. I think I've been bad again."

The group snorted, trying to suppress laughter as Lily saw two guards approaching. One pointed towards the roof, gaining control of the ball, guiding it back down, and snatching it out of the air.

"Sir, surveillance devices are strictly prohibited in the palace."

"Of course, of course. My apologies. I was just demonstrating our technology for Her Majesty, but I should know better."

The guard glared at Ezra, unimpressed with his apology. They both turned and left, heading for Jason to no doubt update him on the security breach.

"There you are, Your Majesty!" exclaimed Minister Bellingham. "I wondered where you'd slipped off to. Please excuse us." She smiled politely at the group and guided Lily away.

"Your Majesty, you really shouldn't wander off like that," chided Minister Bellingham. "Now, your suitor will be presented to you, and then you will dance with him, and that will conclude the official ball. You will remain and mingle for a further thirty minutes before retiring to your rooms."

"Wait a minute, hold on." Lily stopped walking, forcing Minister Bellingham to stop too.

"Don't make a scene, Your Majesty," said Minister Bellingham. The older woman had a smile plastered to her face and she nodded politely at people walking past.

"I wouldn't dare," hissed Lily, hitching her own smile to her face. "What suitor?"

"We need to secure your, currently somewhat tenuous, hold on the throne. Not to mention ensure succession. Look around, right now you are simply some girl who hasn't lived here and who, the people are told, was the child of their beloved late king and queen.

"We need them to want the royal line to continue, to feel like you are one of theirs. Securing an appropriate betrothal will inspire them to follow you. New life after such a terrible tragedy. A good news story, if you will. And, with the appropriate Highacren house by your side, people will be less likely to doubt your claim."

"Sure, but you've picked someone? This is definitely something I should have been involved in. Or at least consulted on."

Minister Bellingham, fake smile still in position, grabbed Lily's elbow and started guiding her to the platform at the far end of the hall. "You simply do not know these people or their families. This is not a decision to be made based on looks or other superficial factors, and so it would simply have been a waste of your valuable time to involve you in the discussions."

"Perhaps," Lily hissed, pulling her elbow away from Minister Bellingham and smiling politely at a group of elderly women. "It would have been valuable for me to learn about the more powerful families in Highacre. And at any rate, the ultimate choice should have been mine."

"Of course, Your Majesty," Minister Bellingham said

tightly. "My apologies. Unfortunately, the decision has been made, and you will meet your suitor now. Should we require a new suitor, you may be involved in that selection."

She glanced at Giles, who had been anxiously waiting for them.

"She's all yours."

13

"I CANNOT BELIEVE you would do this!" Lily hissed at Giles.

Giles was more worried about the nobles who were starting to turn their attention to the stage Lily and Giles were standing on. He tutted at her to be quiet and stop fiddling as he smiled beside her.

"There's no harm in meeting people."

She glared at him, and he simply nodded at the door, indicating that Lily should turn and face the front. Lily did so, annoyed.

A smartly dressed soldier marched to the centre of the hall, halting abruptly.

"Your Majesty," the man bellowed, causing many nobles to flinch, "may I present the fourth son of the Count of Marquiss de Plompy Fleur and the Baroness of Stable-market, the Viscount Edmund Armeganon Maximillian Remington Breckenridge Blatherington."

The man finished with a sharp nod and performed a flawless about-face before indicating to his fellows standing on either side of a scared looking young man.

Lily had to stifle a giggle. *Those can't be real names.*

Both men snapped to attention and escorted the young man who was dressed in the kind of suit that someone who has half a dozen names, the last of which was Blatherington, would be expected to wear. As the man drew closer, Lily could see that he wasn't unattractive. However, he had a weak chin, and his nose was a touch too big. Seeing Lily appraising him, Viscount Blatherington drew himself up straighter, looked Lily in the eye, winked, and promptly tripped over his own feet, stumbling into one of his escorts.

Lily held back another chuckle as Edmund untangled himself from the escort, who had barely moved despite the younger man having used him to break his fall, apologising profusely. They all took a few more steps, and both escorts stomped their feet, coming to a halt. Edmund jumped at the crack that their feet made on the highly polished floor and looked about, seeming lost. Giles cleared his throat and tried to subtly wave Edmund forward.

"What? Oh yes, er, yes okay," Edmund spluttered and then half-walked, half-jogged to the bottom of the stairs before Lily.

"Your Majesty," he said grandly, performing a strange bow-curtsy mix and managing to hit his nose on the stairs. He stood quickly, rubbing his nose, a blotchy red making its way up his neck.

Lily could see a well-dressed older couple standing in front of the crowd off to the left of the platform, rolling their eyes and rubbing their foreheads, clearly embarrassed.

They must be the count and baroness.

There were three young men standing with them, all very good-looking and slightly older than Edmund, trying to stifle laughter.

His brothers, perhaps.

Lily suddenly felt very sorry for Edmund and quickly descended the stairs to meet him.

"Viscount Blatherington," Lily said loudly, holding her hand out for him to take. "A pleasure to meet you."

Edmund took her hand gratefully, kissed it, and responded, "I'm pleasure to you charmed." He went completely red. "Very happy meeting, so nice, so much yes."

The courtiers around the room broke out into tittering laughter and Edmund looked as if he wished the floor would open up and inhale him. Before Lily could do anything to try and help Edmund feel more comfortable, Giles stepped forwards and clapped twice. The small orchestra started playing, and Giles ushered Lily and Edmund to the middle of the floor. Edmund, still beet red, looked to be desperately trying to recall what they were there to do. Lily had the feeling that she would not enjoy this dance.

Edmund bowed to Lily, and she curtsied in response. He then thrust his hand out for her to take and misjudged the distance between them, awkwardly jabbing her breast. Mortified, Edmund then tried to excuse the jab by patting the offended breast, causing the complete breakdown of decorum around the room. Most of the crowd roared with laughter, though a few were incensed by the manhandling of the monarch.

Lily grabbed Edmund's hands and placed one firmly on her shoulder, the other on her waist, and pulled him into a lazy slow dance, giving up on the traditional waltz that Giles had spent the last several nights trying to teach her.

"I'm so sorry, Your Majesty." Edmund still looked like he wanted the ground to open up and swallow him.

"It's fine, really. Could have happened to anyone."

Edmund did not look like he believed that but relaxed slightly as Lily tried to keep his attention on her and not the jeering crowd.

"So, what do you do, Edmund? When you're not

dancing with royalty." She smiled at him, and he returned it.

"Ah, well, um, my father runs several companies that produce all sorts of things, from cans to electronics. And my brother Julius is his vice president and helps him with that. And my other brothers run some of the other operations. Marketing the products or dealing with other companies to get the raw materials or components."

"Impressive," said Lily. "But what do you do?"

"Oh! Um, well, I am kind of an all-rounder. I help all of them from time to time with discreet tasks and projects." Edmund puffed out his chest importantly.

You're their minion. Not trusted with your own part of the family pie. She felt a stab of pity for Edmund. His family didn't seem to have much respect for him, and while he seemed nice enough, he really wasn't her type, and she couldn't see them getting married, no matter how much sense it made to her advisors.

"That sounds impressive," Lily lied. "Will you take over one of the companies one day?"

"Maybe." Edmund looked doubtful.

"If you weren't going to take over one of the companies, what would you want to do?"

Edmund thought for a while as they twirled around the hall. Gradually, some couples had joined them, and Lily realised that most of the audience had now taken to the dance floor, the intense scrutiny over.

"Well, if it were up to me," Edmund began tentatively, "I think I'd quite like to be in the military." He smiled nervously at Lily, waiting for a rebuke.

"You! In the military? We're not that desperate for soldiers, are we?"

A strapping young man twirled his beautiful young partner up beside Lily and Edmund, who blushed bright red again and physically deflated. Lily glared at the young man. It was one of the three who had been laughing at Edmund's entrance.

Lily, throwing caution and the protection of her feet to the wind, pulled Edmund into a series of twirls that saw them finish well clear of the couple.

"Your brother?"

"Yes, sorry."

"Don't apologise. I have an older brother, David. He's not *that* bad, but he does think I'm a flake."

"Julius and Trish think I'm pathetic. But they've been much nicer since mum told them I was selected as your suitor." Edmund beamed at Lily, whose stomach dropped.

There was no way she was going to marry Edmund. And while she knew she should nip this in the bud, Lily couldn't bring herself to do it now and have Edmund face the fallout of being dumped after just one dance.

"Come on, Eddie, let's find Giles. Perhaps we can have your brothers kicked out. Or at least uncomfortably searched."

"It's Edmund..." he muttered as she led him away.

14

"Ma'am, I really must—"

"Jason, you said the problem was that someone on the inside leaked information about movements. So if you're the only one who knows, and I've only just decided to go out, I should actually be safer out with you than if I stayed in the palace, where everyone expects me to be."

Jason considered her point, struggling to find a flaw in her logic. Lily hurried on. "Please Jason? I'll go crazy if I have to stay cooped up in the palace any longer. It's been weeks of the same thing. Training with Austin, followed by lessons, then I'm wheeled out for some meeting or other. I need something *real*."

He looked at her sympathetically. "Well...okay. But I will have to at least tell Giles and my second-in-command that I'm taking you off the grounds. If they can't find you, they'll panic."

Lily smiled. She was so excited to be getting out of the palace, even if just for a little while. The idea had come to her in the previous session with Claire, which had been a particularly boring lesson about different types of forks. As soon as she got out of class, she had called to Jason, who she knew was lurking nearby, and asked if he could take her for a drive.

Jason reluctantly led Lily towards the garage, which, as it turned out, was underground. Lily looked at the fleet of vehicles in wonder, unsure why anyone would need so many. There were at least two dozen sedans, as well as three limousines, eight SUVs, and two buses.

Jason selected one of the sedans. Of all the vehicles, it was the one that screamed "I'm royalty" the least. Jason opened the rear passenger door and Lily was about to protest, preferring to sit in the front, when she saw the look on Jason's face and decided not to push her luck.

As the garage door opened and the car slowly emerged into the dying afternoon, Jason said into his sleeve, "I have sparrow. We are leaving the nest."

"Sparrow? Sparrow! That's a terrible codename! Why can't I be something cool? Like 'Eagle' or 'Hawk'... 'Nighthawk'! I want to be Nighthawk."

Jason glared at her in the rear-view mirror and hit a button on the dash. Lily heard a dial tone.

"Hello?" Giles's voice boomed in the car and Jason hurriedly adjusted the volume.

"Giles, it's Jason. I'm taking our friend for a drive."

"You're taking who...wait, what? Taking them for a drive? Whose stupid idea—"

"Mine!" interrupted Lily loudly.

"I'll check in on our return," said Jason and abruptly hung up. He looked again at Lily in the mirror.

"Where would you like to go, ma'am?"

"To your house."

"Ma'am?"

"I'd really like to meet your family. And I'm sure they'd like to see you too."

Jason looked conflicted and stared at the road for a bit, jaw clenched.

"Look," said Lily gently. "I really just want to be somewhere normal for a little while. I figure that this is a win for both of us."

Jason considered this for a beat and then raised his eyes to the rear-view mirror again. "Thank you, Your Majesty."

Jason lived relatively close to the palace in a quiet and understated residential area. It reminded Lily of nice, quiet suburbs back home. Trees lined the streets and the houses all seemed to have neat front yards with pretty flowers and fences.

Jason pulled into the driveway of a modest one-storey home, the smallest in the street. It had a well-cared for front garden with blue flowers in beds behind a white picket fence. As they pulled to a stop and Jason turned the car off, Lily noticed the curtains move.

Jason and Lily exited the car and were moving towards the small path leading to the front door when the front door flew open and two young boys barrelled out, jumping on Jason, hugging him and crying out in excitement. A pretty thirty-something woman holding a baby stood in the doorway beaming at her husband, and an old dog that Lily thought looked like a German shepherd stood in front of her wagging its tail.

The woman noticed Lily and smiled reflexively before a shadow of recognition crossed her face, and she started to look slightly horrified.

"Gwen, hi, I'm Lily, I'm so sorry for the unannounced intrusion, but I thought Jason should be able to come home for a bit and he wouldn't come without me, and well...here we are," Lily finished, slightly feebly.

She had moved towards Gwen as she spoke and now

offered her hand. Gwen panicked, curtsied, then took Lily's hand and kissed it.

"Love, it's fine. Relax," Jason said. He tried not to laugh as he walked towards them with his sons hanging off him. "But let's go inside now, eh?"

They all moved inside, Gwen handing the baby to Jason, who immediately started making faces at her to her extreme excitement, and then she darted through the lounge room, picking things up and uselessly trying to tidy.

"You have a beautiful home, Gwen," said Lily, trying to reassure her.

"I'm sorry it's so messy, Your Majesty..."

"It's perfect," Lily interrupted. "I was telling Jason how much I miss normal things, and this is just what I needed. It reminds me of home."

Gwen seemed to relax, looking at her husband before surveying the room once more. "Can I get you something to drink?"

"John can do it," Jason said, looking at his eldest.

"I'll help!" said Lance excitedly, not wanting to be left out.

Both boys rushed off to the kitchen without taking orders, and before Gwen could try to rescue the situation, Lily said, "I love surprises!"

They all took a seat, Jason and Gwen on the couch and Lily in a very comfortable padded recliner. A slightly uncomfortable silence fell over the trio, though Jason, still making faces at his daughter, seemed oblivious to it.

"Did you have a big family, Your Majesty? I mean, the people you grew up with. I mean, back...er...home?" She looked at Jason in alarm.

"Your Majesty," Jason was blushing furiously. "I might have...that is to say, I, um... Gwen knows. I told her about you being hidden in another dimension. I know I shouldn't have, but..."

"It's fine, really." Lily was surprised to realise it didn't bother her. She trusted Jason and he trusted his wife. She knew she should be worried about it, but it seemed right that he would share everything with this woman, who was truly his partner. Seeing them together gave her hope that there might be someone out there who fit her as perfectly. It took the edge off the pang of loneliness she felt.

"I call them my family." Lily smiled at Gwen. "That's who they are to me. And yes, there were four of us for Mum and Dad to deal with."

"Oh gosh! I only had my brother to put up with. I can't imagine having two more siblings. And these three are more than enough for me!"

"Oh, it wasn't too bad." Lily smiled, thinking about her family. "My brother David, the eldest, is the only boy, so he was always the protective older brother, rather than picking on us. And he's always been so keen on taking over the farm that he mainly followed our dad around and didn't have time for pranks.

"My older sister used to get up to all kinds of mischief, and, of course, I would always toddle off with her if she let me. Drove my mum mad." Lily smiled ruefully, not realising until now exactly how much she missed them all.

Reading her mind, Gwen said, "You must miss them."

Lily nodded. "It's funny, I didn't really appreciate them enough when I was there. How we all loved and cared for each other, no matter what. I was so focussed on not letting them down that I distanced myself from them, and all that did was take away the last few months we could have spent together."

Gwen nodded sympathetically. The re-emergence of the boys, who were trying to carry an array of drinks and seemed dangerously close to losing them, broke the sombre mood.

"John! Lance! Jason, help them!"

Jason laughed. "I have the baby. What do you want me to do?"

Somehow, the boys managed to land the drinks on the coffee table with minimal spillage. They looked at each other, clearly pleased with themselves. Lily looked at the concoctions and thought she saw some tea, judging by the little tea bag tabs draped over the side of the mugs, some hot chocolate hidden beneath mounds of marshmallows, and a mystery drink topped with about two inches of whipped cream.

The adults all selected various beverages, and Gwen shooed the boys out to play while putting Sara in her bassinet. Jason sat back, looking more relaxed than Lily had ever seen him. Gwen sat back on the couch and, as Jason put his arm around her shoulder, she too seemed to finally relax.

"Jason talks about you all the time," Lily said. "And he's very proud of his kids. How's John's soccer going?"

"Oh, he bores you with all that, does he?" Gwen smiled up at Jason.

"The kid's a natural. I'm simply bringing everyone up to speed on the next national star." Jason smiled and took a sip of his tea.

"Well, he did score the winning goal in the final last weekend."

"He did?" Jason beamed at her. "That's my boy! He's just like his dad."

"You never even played soccer!"

"So what? Still my boy!"

Lily smiled, following the exchange. The old dog

walked in front of her and presented himself for patting, his tail wagging and thumping against the chair.

"Mr Jingle Paw, leave her alone." Jason saw the look Lily gave him and shrugged. "The kids named him."

"Uh huh. Sure, blame it on the kids," Lily teased as she patted Mr Jingle Paw.

"So your parents have a farm?" Gwen asked.

Lily nodded. "It's only a small one, but Dad looks after the crops and animals, and Mum has a little shop in the front where she sells whatever is left over from whatever contracts they have. My older sister Elaine helps her and uses some of the leftover produce to make candles and other knickknacks to sell."

"And you said you have another sister?"

"Yeah, April, she's the youngest. Still in school, but she'll kick butt with whatever she does."

"Sounds like you have a wonderful family, Your Majesty."

Lily nodded, still patting the dog. "So do you, Gwen, though it must keep you busy!"

Gwen laughed and told them both about all the antics the boys had been getting up to, at times having to wait while Jason and Lily roared with laughter. Eventually, Lily excused herself for the bathroom, and afterward, instead of heading back to the lounge room, crept towards the back of the house where she could hear the boys playing.

They were in the backyard kicking the soccer ball around, having made up some game with rules that were beyond Lily's understanding. She sat on the steps and watched them for a while, homesick for her siblings and trying to give Gwen and Jason a little time together before Jason decided they needed to get back.

She eventually heard the door open behind her, but

before Jason could tell her it was time to go, the boys spotted him and cajoled him into their game.

This is what it was all about. Family. Lily thought of how much time Jason had already missed with his family because of the war. She wondered what would have happened to them if Highacre had lost. Would Meridia have similarly left Highacre to their normal way of life? Or would a Meridian puppet leader have been installed and Highacre's people become oppressed?

Lily's thoughts turned to the current predicament. Apparently, the Prime Minister was already oppressing the people. Lily's daily briefing increasingly mentioned strange and mysterious disappearances and reports about a new police force. Her advisors were convinced that the only cure for this disease was for Lily to take the throne and get rid of the Prime Minister. She looked again at Jason and his kids, laughing and playing. What would happen to Jason's family if Lily did not take the throne?

For the first time, Lily realised that the risk of inaction was too high. Her advisors, for the most part, seemed to have the best of intentions. But they all had different ideas about what was important and how best to go about their plan. They needed a clear leader. Someone to listen to all of their advice and opinions, and decide the way forward.

And it looks like that person is me.

Lily thought of Claire's warnings and concerns. Perhaps she was right. It was too late to say 'oops' when they were all shackled. She couldn't gamble with the future of these children.

Lily had previously been persuaded by Claire to not curl up in her bedroom and wait to be sent home. Since then she had been going through the motions. Attending her lessons, and doing what her advisors asked of her.

Sitting on Jason's back step, watching his sons insist it

wasn't too dark to see the ball, Lily resolved to fight to assume the throne and to keep her people safe. At least until an appropriate, more permanent solution was found. She thought about her own family. If they were in danger, she would want someone to help them. Her chest constricted. She missed them all so much. They were her people too. The people who had accepted her, no matter what. Who could tease her, yell at her, argue with her, but would still love her and have her back. They would understand. They would want her to stay and help.

Once they had some felixium, she would see about going home to visit. *But what then?* Would she return and assume the throne for good? It was her birthright. Literally what she had been born to do. She had never really fit in back home, but here... Highacre was strange and different, and while she still had so much to learn, something just felt right. But could she leave her family and friends forever?

Lily shook her head. That was a later problem. For now, she had to address the immediate concerns, including her advisors. Not only were they divided, but there was at least one among them who was not on the same team. They needed to find out who was against them, then unite to defeat the common enemy. If she could not trust anyone but herself, then it would have to be her to lead them through this.

15

LILY WAS DISTRACTED during her workout with Austin that morning. She had been joined by the ambassadors to court and Edmund, which normally made the session fun and engaging, but today Austin had taken her off to the side for some one-on-one training. As she practised sword drills on the dummy, her mind drifted to the letter she had found on her dressing table that morning and the warning within. *"You might wish to learn more about your advisors' pasts"*, it had urged. *"Not all is as it seems."*

It was frustrating, these mysterious letters telling her that her advisors weren't being straight with her but doing so cryptically rather than being direct. Still, she had told no one about the letters. Partially because she didn't fully trust anybody, a distrust that the letters were encouraging. But also because her advisors would surely put a stop to them. And the little information that the letters provided was still more than what she was getting from those supposedly on her side.

Lily felt guilty, though. Her entire biological family had been murdered and now someone could apparently access her room, even with her in it. She knew she should tell Jason. It would be the right thing to do. She wasn't safe if some stranger could come and go as they pleased. But she hadn't been hurt. And the letters didn't threaten her.

"Ow!"

Lost in her thoughts, Lily had not seen Austin come up beside her and bat her on the head with the flat side of his training sword. She glared at him, rubbing where he had hit her. She was still having difficulty understanding exactly how being able to sword fight was a skill she needed in a world with guns and other modern weapons. And magic. Not to mention she had an ever-present shadow waiting to protect her at all hours of the day.

"I still don't get why I need to learn to sword fight. It seems a little extreme," Lily said grumpily. Austin chuckled a little and shrugged.

"I suppose it does. Most of it is tradition, I guess. Ages ago, the king..." He looked at Lily appraisingly. "Well, usually the king, but sometimes the queen, would ride to war with the army onto the field of battle. These days you wouldn't do that, but we still train the sovereign as if they would fight."

"Why wouldn't they fight?"

"The sovereign would be too much of a target, and with modern weaponry, Meridian cybernetics, and Valmeadian enchanted weapons, too easy to kill." He stopped pacing and looked at Lily. "The obvious reason is that we don't want the sovereign to be killed. The more, I guess, logistical or practical reason is that we would have to put so much effort and so many resources into protecting the sovereign that we would degrade our fighting capability and split our focus between attacking the enemy and defending the sovereign. If we were to do that, we would risk losing the fight. But if you're going to send troops into battle, it's good for you to understand what you're going to be asking them to do."

"Sure, but do you have to hit so hard?"

Austin smiled broadly and winked at Lily. "Situational awareness ma'am. It's important."

He was boyishly handsome, and his smile highlighted his eyes, which twinkled cheekily, and his firm jaw. His hair was short enough to hint at military experience, but long enough to show that his military life was behind him.

Lily sighed and turned reluctantly back to the training dummy. Austin burst out laughing at her complete lack of enthusiasm. "Alright, Your Majesty, come on." He adopted a fighting stance and gestured with his free hand for her to advance. "We'll spar together. It's more interesting than the dummy. Well..." Austin stood back upright and cocked his head to one side. "At least, I hope I'm more interesting than the dummy."

Lily chuckled and squared up to face him. The sparring began. It was slow and awkward, Lily still not used to the weight of the sword or the movements.

"No, Your Majesty! Block, duck, and then move!"

Lily swore under her breath.

"Come on, Your Majesty! You're doing well," called Alexei encouragingly.

"Yeah!" added Edmund quickly, "Your...wrist technique is superb."

Ava snorted, and Edmund glared at her.

The ambassadors to court and her suitor, for she had not yet been able to bring herself to cut Edmund loose, had begun joining Lily for her lessons almost immediately after the ball. Apparently, her advisors had decided that more time with Edmund would help them grow closer. And including the ambassadors to court, under a guise of teaching them about Highacre and their traditions, ensured that it was less awkward and reduced the need for chaperones.

Lily enjoyed having people her age with her, and they were becoming friendly, if not friends. However, Edmund had decided that Alexei was his competition, and whenever Alexei, who seemed to simply want a friendship with Lily, interacted with her, Edmund made it his mission to deride Alexei and impress Lily. The constant bickering and one-upmanship was grating on Lily's nerves.

Austin engaged Lily again, and again bested her quickly, smacking her on her arm.

"Ow!" she cried again, glaring at Austin. "Kevin!"

The tiny pelotromo let out his weed eater growl and began trotting over towards them from the bushes he had been snuffling in.

"Okay, okay." Austin put his hands up in surrender and looked at Kevin, slightly panicked. "I'm sorry, Your Majesty. I won't tap you again."

Lily stood Kevin down, and the tiny pup bounded happily back to his bushes, nipping at the leaves and rolling in things he probably shouldn't roll in before suddenly jumping up with an excited yip and darting off towards the forest. Lily knew she shouldn't use her advisors' fear of Kevin against them, but it really was amusing to see them cower at such a cute little fluffball.

Feeling pleased with herself, Lily raised her sword but completely missed Austin's feint and then tripped over her own foot. She remained on the ground swearing softly, reluctant to get back up and try again.

"Ma'am," Austin said gently, sensing her frustration, "for someone who hadn't even touched a sword before we started, you are doing extremely well. You can't expect to be a master swordswoman overnight, but I can say you are advancing at a rate on par, and often exceeding my top students." He smiled at her reassuringly.

Lily looked at him doubtfully, but sighed, stood up, and raised her sword again in preparation for his attack. He was so fast, she almost didn't see it coming, even though she was looking right at him. One second he was standing there, relaxed and looking at her, the next his sword was swinging at her left shoulder.

Somehow, she got her sword into the block position in time, and she pivoted to her right, bringing her body around so she was facing Austin's side. Instinct and training took over, and she swept her sword through the block and then around, aiming to hit Austin squarely in the back. Her aim was off and she was tired from the hour that they'd already spent drilling the basic moves, so her sword simply brushed him across the back of his left knee.

"Very good, ma'am!" Austin lowered his sword and looked at Lily, clearly impressed. "We haven't covered the weak points of the body yet, but if you get your opponent behind the knee like that, you could absolutely hobble them and win."

"Brilliant, Your Majesty!" cried Edmund sycophantically. "Ow!"

Alexei had prodded Edmund in his fleshy midsection with his training sword, taking advantage of his inattention. Ava laughed and Alexei smiled at Edmund's annoyance and shrugged, provoking a string of expletives from Edmund, attacking everything from Alexei's character through to his rugged good looks.

Lily sighed and turned back to Austin, who was watching her.

"So, where is your mind this morning, Your Majesty?" Austin asked.

"I was just thinking, I've been here so long, but I still

don't really know anything," Lily said as she parried Austin's slow, sweeping attack. "Even all of you—my advisors. I'm with you every day, but I know nothing about you."

"I am yours to command, Your Majesty." Austin blocked Lily's clumsy attack, bowed politely at her, then spun around and tapped his sword gently on her thigh. "What would you like to know?"

"How old are you?" Lily asked more suspiciously than she had intended. "And what did you used to do before humiliating royalty at swordplay?"

Austin laughed, stepping easily out of Lily's range, and then lunged and lightly sliced her across her stomach.

"I'm thirty-eight, Your Majesty. And before this, I was in the army. I joined at eighteen, completed officer training and eventually became the OC of Charlie Company, 5th Battalion of the Royal Mountaineers." The way he said it and looked at Lily made her think she was supposed to be impressed, so she tried to arrange her face into an appropriate expression. She vaguely wondered what an 'OC' was.

"During the war, our CO was killed. I was field promoted and led the regiment for almost a year before they reassigned me to be the MA to General Mortimer."

That name was familiar. "The queen's father? My... grandfather?" Lily asked. Austin nodded proudly. "And, er, what's an OC, CO, and MA?" Lily asked, slightly embarrassed.

"Oh!" laughed Austin. "Sorry! Officer commanding, commanding officer and military assistant." Lily was glad she'd asked, but she wasn't sure the explanation had given her any greater understanding.

"So anyway, while I was no longer leading my own people, I was fortunate to be exposed to, and occasionally involved in, the strategies that the general developed, as well as his discussions with your father that informed the higher-level political decisions." Lily was genuinely impressed this time and didn't have to fake her reaction.

"After that, I went to Command College and studied strategy, but at that time I was already thinking about getting out of the military." He looked over at Lily. "It had been a long war, you know?"

Lily didn't know, but she nodded anyway, and Austin continued.

"Your father called me and asked if I'd come and be his advisor and train his kids. He'd barely finished making the offer before I said yes." He grinned at Lily and she grinned back, grateful for his down-to-earth, relaxed manner. All the formality of being royalty was difficult to get used to. Something suddenly occurred to Lily.

"So, in the army, do you still fight with guns and stuff?"

"Yes ma'am. We are very good with guns and stuff."

Lily rolled her eyes at him. "Yes, but what about magic? You don't fight with, I don't know, fireballs or something?"

Austin laughed and lazily jumped over her low sweep. He didn't have to jump, but he did anyway.

"We use both. They teach everyone to fight with weapons and basic infantry tactics for three reasons. First, our foes don't have our abilities and so use physical weapons. We learn to fight as they do so that we know how they fight and can defeat them. Second, the strength of powers and talents varies. If there is someone in your section who can only fire one elemental blast per hour, you want them to be doing something else while they're waiting for their power to recharge. More powerful soldiers will usually spend most of their time using their powers, but the baseline soldier skills are just as important. And third, some cybernetics or enchantments can block certain powers. You don't want to rely on your powers only to have them taken away."

Austin slapped Lily's attack away and led her over to their water bottles. Lily wiped the sweat from her face and gratefully guzzled her water.

"They group us according to our talents. Some talents are spread among different units, such as area talents." Seeing Lily's confusion, he added, "Some magic has to be specifically targeted at a person or thing, but area talents can work on anyone or thing in a certain area. Like sensing abilities. If we have enough people available, we put one person who can sense enchantments or cybernetics in each unit. That way, it's easier to find the enemy. My apologies, Your Majesty, I would have thought Lady Octavia would have covered this with you."

Lily felt irrationally embarrassed not to know the basics of magic. She wondered again why Lady Octavia had abandoned her. Or was she being kept away from her?

"I haven't seen her since that first lesson."

"Oh." Austin dropped his guard briefly, eyebrows raised. "Well, I'm sure Giles has a good reason for that." Lily could see on his face that he couldn't think of a good reason for Lady Octavia's absence.

"It's not his choice—" Lily heard the crack at about the same moment Austin dove on her, slamming her to the ground and covering her with his body.

"What's wrong?" she gasped, out of breath from being knocked down.

But Austin wasn't listening to her. He kept his body covering hers and was looking around, his eyes darting here and there, looking for something and calculating distances. Lily felt two thuds, one on either side of her body, and saw Alexei and Ava both similarly scanning the area and feeding information to Austin.

"On my go, we're going to crawl to that tree." Austin's eyes directed them to the gigantic tree about twenty metres from the training ground.

Lily nodded, her heart pounding. She didn't know what was going on, but was reacting to Austin's demeanour. After another crack, Austin bellowed, "Go!"

Lily had never moved so fast in her life, flying along the ground with ease and racing towards the tree as if her life depended on it.

Which it did.

Those cracks, she realised, were gunshots. Lily knew what a rifle sounded like from her childhood on the farm. She slammed herself against the tree and Austin slammed into her, pinning her with his body and looking over her shoulder, trying to see where the shot had come from. Alexei and Ava piled in, Austin getting them to crawl to another tree and the palace wall respectively so they would have better cover and be able to see more of the grounds to look for the threat.

Lily suddenly realised Austin was talking to someone and looked to her right. Jason was there behind a wall, and several other guards were beside him.

"...don't know, probably up in the west tower."

Jason nodded at Austin and turned to his guards, giving orders, and then they all moved, fanning out like liquid, moving swiftly through the grounds.

Jason and another guard sprinted to their tree, diving on the ground at Lily's feet and crouching on either side of her. Luckily, the ancient tree's trunk was big enough to shelter all of them. They remained there as Jason spoke with his guards through his radio, the microphone in his sleeve, and the receiver in his ear.

"All clear," he muttered, and Austin and the other guard relaxed. "Okay, Your Majesty, we're going to get you back inside. I will lead, and Austin and Richard will follow you. We're going to move swiftly, but calmly." He motioned to some other guards who had appeared and were protecting the ambassadors to court.

"Wait for me!" came a high-pitched cry. The group looked over and saw Edmund emerge from a pile of dirty straw that the gardeners had left. With a small cry he sprinted over to where the group was gathered, crouching behind a burly guard, much to the guard and Alexei's amusement.

The group prepared and then moved at a slow shuffle towards the wall of the palace, and a door that Lily hadn't seen before. She felt like they should be sprinting and was anxious about how slowly they were going. Before she realised, they were in the door and moving along a corridor. Jason kept talking into his sleeve in a low voice that Lily couldn't make out. They turned this way and that, and climbed stairs until Lily was completely turned around and unaware of where in the palace they were.

Suddenly they emerged into the Lodge, the guards all immediately fanning out and searching the room and balcony. Lily, Edmund, and the ambassadors to court stood awkwardly in the centre of the room, watching the flurry of activity around them.

"What stinks?" Alexei asked, wrinkling his nose. Ava gave him a little poke and indicated to Edmund, shaking her head to tell Alexei to leave it. Edmund had dirt and straw sticking to his clothes and through his hair. He was pale and staring out the window with wide eyes. Alexei looked like he was about to say something more, but caught the look from Ava and seemed to think better of it. A moment later, Edmund turned to look at the group.

"I thought we were all hiding," he said to no one in particular.

"We were, Eddie," said Ava.

"Edmund," he corrected her out of habit. He shook his head. "You all sprang into action. I hid. I always thought I would react well in a crisis. Take the lead. I suppose my brothers were right . . ." he drifted away from the group and flopped into a chair. Ava started warning Alexei to leave Edmund alone, but Alexei protested he had no intention of making the poor guy feel worse. Lily went over and sat beside him.

"I didn't spring into action either."

"No, but you don't have to."

"What? Because I'm a girl?" Lily barked, nerves still frayed.

"No, because you're the sovereign. You're not supposed to spring into action, you're supposed to be protected."

Lily squashed her retort, deciding that while it didn't sit well with her, Edmund might have a point, and at any rate, arguing with him to make herself feel better certainly wouldn't help make him feel better.

"You're not a coward, Edmund."

He looked at her as if she had slapped him across his face. "I know I'm not a coward. Is that what you think of me now?"

"No, I just meant—"

"It was a mistake, and one I'll not make again."

"Of course—"

"If the others had been standing in my position..." he hesitated. "The distance to you was too great. The smarter move was to take cover, assess the situation and then move to protect you. I knew Austin was with you," Edmund said, clearly trying to convince himself that he had done the right thing.

"Edmund, I don't—"

He stood suddenly. "If you'll excuse me, Your Majesty.

You seem well-protected here, and I should clean up." And with that, Edmund swept out of the room, leaving Lily slightly open-mouthed in his wake.

16

JASON

Jason took a swig from his coffee mug, only to discover that it was empty. He looked at the dirty bottom in disappointment and considered the fifteen-step trek to the coffee machine for a refill. Somehow that seemed like too much, and he checked his screen to see how the search was going.

Tonight, he was doing a deeper search into Richard, who had become increasingly distant and insubordinate lately. Jason conceded that this could be due to him cutting Richard out of things, but still. He hadn't ever completely trusted Richard. Although, now that Jason thought about it, Richard had taken everything that Jason threw at him and run with it, and with good humour. And Jason had given Richard a bunch of tasks that he never would have given a second-in-command who he felt had earned the position. Jason now wondered whether he had discriminated against Richard, never giving him the respect he deserved because of where he had come from. Perhaps that had something to do with the insubordination too.

Jason's computer pinged, signalling that it had finally completed the search it had been running for the last three hours. Then it crashed.

Jason swore loudly, slamming his fists on the desk, before sinking his head down onto them.

Rebooting the computer, he begrudgingly made the trek for coffee. As he poured a lukewarm cup of the terrible, cheap liquid, he thought again about his old friend Hudson. An ex-signaller, Hudson had gone into IT after the army, and once he finished his rehab.

Whatever computer system he is using wouldn't crash. Hudson had unimpugnable integrity and even after so long, Jason would have no hesitation trusting him with such a sensitive matter as this investigation. He knew he should call Hudson, but still he hesitated. *What's the worst that could happen? He tells you to piss off? Then you're no worse off than you are now.*

Returning to his desk, Jason logged on, restarted his search task, and sighed in despair as the progress bar appeared and told him that the search would take two hours. He pulled out his phone, looked at it for a few minutes, then nervously entered the number.

"Hello?"

"Hey mate, it's Jase."

There was a prickly silence. "Jase. Long time, no hear." Hudson's jab landed home. Jason should have kept in touch and he didn't. He hadn't even called him once to see how he was.

"Mate, I'm so sorry. I'm a complete arsehole and there's nothing I can say to change that or make it in any way okay that I haven't called you."

The silence extended as Hudson considered this. Jason wiped his brow.

"Ahhh..." Hudson exhaled loudly. "It's okay. I mean, it's not. You *are* a complete arsehole and you absolutely should have called. And I'm still pissed. But I can't say that I wouldn't have been too much of a coward to have called you either if the situation was reversed."

Jason breathed a sigh of relief. If the worst he got was Hudson calling him a coward, which was fair, then he'd gotten off lightly. "You're a legend. How are you, anyway?"

"Come off it mate, you didn't finally call me after all this time without really needing something. And while that would normally piss me off even more, I know you and I know it must be something pretty important. So come on, out with it."

Jason smiled. Typical Hudson, always mission first. He felt even worse that he hadn't been in contact with him, and half-wondered if that wasn't what Hudson intended.

"Mate, I'm trying to do background checks on everyone here in the palace. But our IT system..."

Hudson laughed. "You're trying to run searches on *that* system? No wonder you called."

Jason laughed with him, and suddenly the tension and the years fell away, and it felt like old times. As if they were both still in the army and Hudson still had both legs. Jason described what he had already done, and the latest computer issues.

"It still says the search has one hour and fifty minutes to go," he said, finishing his explanation.

"Okay, what you're going to do is cut and paste these commands that I'm going to email you into the command box, and that should fix your current search. Then you're going to give me the name of your next target, and I'm going to concurrently run a search on them."

Jason gratefully gave Austin's name to Hudson, pointedly not asking how and on what system Hudson would be searching, and followed his instructions with the commands for his search on Richard. Jason cut and pasted the gibberish that Hudson sent him into the command box and hit enter.

To his great surprise and enormous relief, the search bar sped up, showing that it would be complete in a few minutes rather than hours.

"Thanks mate, you're a legend."

"I know. So this is about the assassinations, huh?"

"Yeah. We did a scrub of everyone immediately afterward, but I feel like it was compromised, so I'm doing it again."

"Well, if you've got an insider issue, then they absolutely would have compromised any vetting you did."

Jason's computer pinged that it had finished its search. He stared at it suspiciously for a beat, and then, satisfied the computer would not shut itself down again, shared the file with Hudson. They started going through it together while Hudson's computer ran its search on Austin.

Jason opened document after document, discussing anything he found with Hudson, grateful for someone to bounce ideas off. Nothing in the file seemed out of order, and Jason felt equal parts relief and guilt that he had distrusted Richard. He clicked on a document about Richard's finances, more out of completeness than anything.

"Hey Hudson, can you open the finance doc for a tick?"

"Yep, wait one...okay, got it."

"This company, ModTech. Know anything about it? Rich seems to hold a lot of shares, and is getting regular payments. I guess that could be dividends from the shares, though..."

"Nah, that's not just the shares. More like he's got a side gig working for them. Hang on, searching...ah! ModTech, blah, blah blah...ah, okay, their director is someone called Ezra Brown."

The Meridian ambassador? Jason was shocked, but this wasn't exactly the smoking gun he was looking for. In fact, it was unlikely that Richard even knew Ezra had anything to do with the company, but Richard hadn't disclosed that he owned a large interest in the foreign company, let alone that he was working for them, and he was definitely supposed to declare that—even if he was working for them in his own time.

The dishonesty worried him. At least the new female bodyguard would start soon. Then he would reassign Richard and remove his access to the queen, at least until this was all sorted out. A thought occurred to him and he asked Hudson to look into the new bodyguard for him. Hudson promised he'd have something to Jason by morning.

"Ah, Jase?" Hudson's voice broke into Jason's thoughts.

"Yeah mate?"

"Open the folder on Austin and then open the document I've put at the start."

Jason clicked through until he had the document Hudson wanted him to look at in front of him. It was Austin's service record from his time in the war. Jason scanned the document, looking for whatever had caught Hudson's attention.

"I mean, it all looks okay..." Jason wondered what he was missing.

"Yeah, so I looked at the file size, 'cause a service record is relatively simple and so it should be relatively small. This guy's is like twice, three times the size of what it should be. So I looked at it. It's been overwritten a couple of times," Hudson finished his statement as if he'd just landed a winning argument.

"Sorry mate, I don't get it..."

"Someone's tinkered with it, dummy. They've changed the content."

Jason sat back in his seat. That was definitely unusual. Why would anyone need to change their record unless there was something they needed to hide?

"Hudson, can you..."

"Already done mate, open the second file. That should be the original. I'm going to look for anything else that's been altered."

Jason opened the file and started scanning. Most of it, he already knew. Austin's unit had performed well under his command, he was transferred to work for the queen's father, General Mortimer, did well there too, and then went to Command College. He brought the new record up to see what was different. The only thing he could find was that the new one was much more glowing. Maybe he doctored it to boost his reputation?

"Uh, Jase, you have a problem, man." Hudson sounded worried.

"What is it?"

"Okay, I'm going to need some more time, but it looks like this guy was not so much 'specially selected' to go work for the general, as much as sent there so the general could keep an eye on him. Leave it with me, and I'll dive a little more into this and see what really happened."

"Yeah, but just from the documents you have, Hudson." Jason knew his friend well enough to know that he would be quite comfortable going to less-than-legal means of getting the information. "Nothing questionable that we can't use later."

"Yeah, yeah."

Jason wasn't exactly reassured as he said goodbye to Hudson and opened another document in the file. Should he stand Austin down now? He didn't think he had enough to do that, and he should wait for all the information at any rate. Austin had also recently protected Lily when the unknown person, who obviously couldn't be Austin, shot at her during their training session. However, he decided not to leave Lily unattended at training anymore. The ambassadors to court attending would help, but either he or the new female bodyguard would have to be there too.

He looked at the clock, depressed and trying to remember the last time he'd gone to bed before midnight. Jason closed the file on Austin and opened an email, addressing it to the selected female bodyguard's current boss. Hudson was helping him now, but he still needed another set of eyes to watch the queen. He felt like they were only just scratching the surface of whatever malicious forces were operating against the royal family, and he had the sense he was running out of time.

A couple of days later, Jason sat in his office, stiff and straight-backed in his chair. He tidied the papers in front of him on his desk and then did the same with the pens, the phone, and the keyboard. He had barely been in his office lately, instead choosing to work late on the ops room floor so he could watch the camera feeds while he investigated the queen's advisors. A slightly disturbing layer of dust had settled on his things, and Jason wondered where it came from. He continued his nervous straightening of his desk until there was a knock at the door.

It opened a crack and Richard poked his head through. "You wanted to see me, boss?"

Jason cleared his throat and told Richard to come in, pointing at the seat across from him. Jason could tell that Richard was picking up on his nerves; he kept flicking his eyes from Jason to the female standing behind him, over his left shoulder.

"Richard, this is Naomi. She's the new second personal bodyguard to the queen." Jason was primary personal body-guard to the queen, and a member of the close personal protection team was always designated as second. It was a coveted position. Until now, it had been Richard.

Richard stood, smiling warmly at Naomi, and moved to shake her hand. "Pleased to meet you, Naomi. Welcome on board." Naomi nodded back at him, returning his firm handshake.

"Richard, since Naomi will be working with me regarding all things to do with Her Majesty's security, it makes sense that she will also be the Royal Guard's second-in-command."

This was Richard's primary job, and he looked at Jason as if Jason had just punched him in the face.

"I'm reassigning you to lead the Overseas Visits Team."

"Overseas Visits!"

"It's another leadership role with your own team—"

"Overseas Visits is where you park passed-over old jerks."

"No, it's a valued position—"

"Bull!"

"Richard," Jason said warningly.

"No, this is garbage. You've had it in for me from the start. You've been looking for an excuse to get rid of me, and now you've found one." Richard gestured towards Naomi. To her credit, Naomi didn't look at all uncomfortable, but she did ask Jason if he'd prefer for her to wait outside. Richard answered before Jason could.

"No, stay. You need to know what you're getting your-self into. Who you're working for." Richard looked at Jason in disgust.

"Richard, this is not a demotion."

Richard scoffed. "Which is exactly what they say when they're demoting you. Look, I know you've never liked me. Had some chip about my background or whatever. But I thought we had a relatively good professional relationship.

You could have discussed this with me. You could have told me."

Jason looked Richard in the eye. "I'm telling you now."

Richard's eyes narrowed and flicked up at Naomi pointedly, his meaning clear. Jason should have spoken with him alone.

"Right," said Richard, suddenly standing. "I guess I'll get my things and move to my new barracks." He walked to the door, put his hand on the doorknob, and opened the door before turning back and looking at Jason with venom in his eyes.

"This is a mistake. Everything's changing. Can't you tell? The power is shifting, and things are in motion. You're backing the wrong horse."

"What do you mean by that?" asked Jason, quickly standing.

Richard smirked. "Don't worry, *Jase*. You'll find out." He looked Jason up and down with derision. "Probably too late." An evil smile crept across his face as he added, "As usual." And he left, slamming the door behind him.

Jason exhaled loudly and dropped his head, leaning on the desk. What had Richard meant? Was it just a generic threat because he was angry that Jason had replaced him, or something more sinister?

"That went well," said Naomi sarcastically. Jason looked at her, and she shrugged.

"What do you think about his threat?"

Naomi thought about the question. This was one of the reasons Jason had picked her. Naomi considered things first rather than giving a snap response from the hip. She was young, but she was mature. All her reports contained phrases like 'despite her young age...' Now that he thought about it, that was probably a slightly patronising thing to say about a thirty-three-year-old woman.

Naomi looked younger than thirty-three, but she had a serious air about her that people often found imposing. She had mocha skin, and her straight black hair was pulled back in a sharp ponytail. Her clothes were practical, and while she was well put together, everything about her appearance screamed 'I don't care what you think about me'. Jason had liked her immediately.

"Normally I'd say he's just angry. But with everything going on, 'backing the wrong horse' was an odd turn of phrase. Does he mean the monarch? The royal advisors?" Naomi moved around to the front of Jason's desk, taking the chair vacated by Richard. Jason sat with her, waiting for her to continue.

"And he didn't quit. I'm glad he didn't," she added as Jason looked sharply at her. "But he doesn't need the money. Both with his family being rich and what he's getting from ModTech, he doesn't need this job. So if you were treated the way he was just treated—no offense—why would you stay?"

Jason thought about this. It was true; he'd been harsh. He hadn't needed to have that conversation with Richard with Naomi there too, and he should have given Richard the respect of speaking with him one-on-one. He had decided to have Naomi there to provoke Richard. That maybe if he pushed him, Richard would somehow reveal himself to be dirty. But if he was really honest with himself, the tactic had also been a little about Jason hoping that Richard would quit and then Jason wouldn't have to deal with him anymore. He felt like a coward. He felt like every boss he'd had who he'd sworn that he would never be like. He felt ashamed.

"Good point, well picked up."

Naomi nodded at him. "Well boss, if that's it, I was going to take these and start going through them." Naomi held up the thick files Jason had given her. They contained the printed information from the searches he and Hudson had done so far into all the royal advisors, including all the information that Hudson dug up on Austin.

Hudson had sent Jason a bunch of files about Austin in an email telling Jason to read them in detail. Hudson had only just skimmed them and said they looked 'dodgy', but he was going to focus on completing more searching, since that was what Jason was really struggling with.

Jason had printed the material, intending to read it, and then had gotten caught up with accompanying Lily wherever she went, a task that had become significantly more time-intensive since the Prime Minister revealed her existence to the world.

The documents had remained untouched on his desk, and he was yet to read them. So he had decided to give them straight to Naomi while he read the latest tranches that Hudson had sent through earlier that evening. He asked Naomi to meet back with him the following evening and be prepared to discuss what they'd each read. By that stage, they should be able to go over each of the advisors and get a better idea of whom to focus on in more detail.

As Naomi closed the door behind her, Jason sat down and opened the file Hudson had sent. It was enormous. He was going to need more coffee.

Lily sat on her bed, patting Kevin and absently turning the mysterious key with her fingers, wondering again how someone got into the palace grounds, shot at her, and got away without anyone seeing or stopping them. *Unless they didn't enter the grounds, but were already here...*

Morbidly, Lily thought it odd that she was still alive. All she kept hearing about magical abilities, cybernetic implants, and enchantments seemed to indicate that if someone had wanted her dead, she would be dead. They would either have magical accuracy, an implant that turned the person into a sharpshooter, or a failsafe enchanted weapon that shot what the person saw. Anyone who didn't have any of those things probably wouldn't try to shoot her. Unless they were stupid. Or didn't want her dead.

But why shoot at her if not to kill her, like they had her family? And from all she'd heard about the plot against her family, if those people wanted her dead, there seemed to be nothing that would stop them. Surely, with the high levels of organisation that they had shown in the attack against her family, they wouldn't have botched the job as badly as this would-be assassin?

There was a knock at her door. She startled, dropped the key, picked it back up, hurriedly hid it in the drawer, checked her hair, and in the calmest voice she could muster, called, "Come in."

"Ma'am," Jason opened the door and poked his head through. "I have news about our investigation into the recent attack. Is now a good time?"

"Of course," said Lily. "What did you find out? Did you find who did it?"

They moved into the Lodge, walking to the leather couches by the window. Jason sat across from Lily, his back straight and his forearms resting on his knees as he leant forwards to brief her.

"Your Majesty, I am pleased to report that we found the culprit and have them in custody."

"Who was it?"

"Bruce Dilson."

Lily strained her memory, trying to see if the name rang any bells. It didn't. "Who's that? Is he linked to the attack on the royal family?"

"No, Your Majesty. Mr Dilson seems to be a lone wolf actor. He has ties to the Highacren Nationalist Movement. We have evidence of him attending several rallies."

"Nationalist? You think the Prime Minister hired him to kill me?"

"No, Your Majesty." Jason paused. "Our evidence suggests that Mr Dilson acted completely alone. He appears to have attended a rally the night before the attack and had several drinks there. After the rally, he and some acquaintances went back to one of their houses where they all continued to drink. One of the people present described Mr Dilson as becoming more and more agitated and oscillating between praising the Prime Minister and cursing the 'royal family's globalist platform'."

"My what?" Lily was very confused. She was sure, with all the concern about super-efficient assassins, that the attempt on her life would have to be connected to the larger conspiracy somehow. And what was a 'globalist platform', and how was she supposed to have one? She didn't think she had any platforms. Did she need a platform?

"The Prime Minister has been quite critical of your father's efforts after the war to rebuild diplomatic relations with Meridia and Valmead. Recently, he's been implying that you would naturally continue that focus, and has hinted that in not expelling the ambassadors and ambassadors to court, you are signalling that intent."

"But," Lily cast around for the words, "that's stupid."

Jason smiled. "Yes, Your Majesty. But politics usually are."

"So, because the Prime Minister thinks I want good diplomatic relations, this random guy decided to try to kill me?"

"It appears that way, Your Majesty. The men he was drinking with, who claim to know him from their attendance at rallies but would not describe him as a friend, say that as Mr Dilson became more and more agitated, they, in their drunken states, encouraged him to 'go do something about it'."

"They told him to kill me?"

"No, Your Majesty," said Jason patiently. "They claim they kept urging him to leave because of his increasing agitation and propensity to yell. By 'do something about it' they thought they were encouraging him to write an angry letter. Or at most, they thought he would pass out back in his own apartment and forget all about it."

"But he didn't."

"No. Instead, Mr Dilson returned to his house, retrieved his rifle, which he owns legally—"

"Is it a special rifle?"

"No, Your Majesty. Mr Dilson owns a normal, non-modified forty-five calibre bolt-action rifle."

"But..." Lily cast about again, "how did he get in and out undetected?"

"Mr Dilson can move and operate objects by telekinesis. Essentially, Mr Dilson arrived outside the palace walls, levitated the rifle, and pulled the trigger with his mind."

"How did he know where I was?"

"We're still questioning him, but we think that his powers of 'operating an object' extend to using the scope. So he would have levitated the rifle, looked around through the scope, and then fired at you. Thankfully Mr Dilson was still quite inebriated, however from what we can gather, he is also a fairly terrible shot at the best of times."

Lily sat back in her chair. It had just been some drunk idiot, not the slick assassins that killed her family. There was a level of relief to this revelation, but still—now she didn't just have to worry about the assassins. She also had to worry about drunken idiots. And probably also other random angry individuals. Who wasn't trying to kill her at this point?

"Your Majesty, I know this was scary—"

"Jason," interrupted Lily in a low, calm voice. She didn't want to upset Jason, but she had to ask. "If some random drunken guy could fire shots in my direction without being detected or stopped, how would we ever prevent the kind of people who killed my family?"

She used 'we' on purpose. She didn't want Jason thinking that this was an attack on his capabilities. To his credit, he nodded and considered her question before responding.

"I have reviewed our security protocols and the number of guards we have protecting the palace. We had not returned to the staffing levels that were in place when the royal family was alive. The numbers required to provide security for six people seemed unnecessary for one, and I was trying to minimise the amount of people with access to you. But there's no reason we can't increase the staffing now. I believe we have enough vetted guards that we can pair them with those yet to be fully vetted, and that will give us the numbers we need without compromising your safety. I have asked my new second-in-command to develop a new security plan. She is not tainted with knowledge of how we've always done it, and she's not... as likely to make a mistake as I am." Jason blushed slightly

Lily reassured Jason that she did not blame him, that she thought he was doing a great job under the circumstances, and that anyone as exhausted as he was could not be expected to be operating at their peak. He shook her reassurance away.

"Your Majesty, you are kind, but a mistake like this is unacceptable."

"I'm not accepting your resignation," Lily got in before he could offer.

"As your advisor, ma'am, I'm not sure that is the best decision."

"You have my best interests at heart, Jason, and you said you have a new second-in-command. That means she's finally here? Now you have support. Everything will be fine," she concluded with a confidence she didn't necessarily feel. "When do I get to meet her?"

Jason got up and moved to the door, letting in a woman who seemed to ooze efficiency.

"Your Majesty." She gave a sharp bow rather than a curtsy. "I am Naomi Faulkner. It is my honour to serve you."

"Pleased to meet you, Naomi. I'm glad Jason has some help."

"Yes ma'am. The ambassador to court for Meridia arrived just before I did. Are you available to meet with her?"

"Ava? Of course!" Lily had grown to like Ava and enjoyed her company in their shared classes. Ava was friendly, down-to-earth, and not afraid to speak her mind. Lily missed her friend Gemma, and though Ava and Gemma couldn't be more different, Ava was someone she felt a strong bond with, despite not knowing her for long. Lily found she looked forward to the classes with Ava and even noticed that she was disappointed whenever she arrived and found that the ambassadors to court were not joining her, as had been the case in the last week or so since the attempted shooting.

Jason went to the door and let Ava in, escorting her back to where Lily and Naomi stood.

"Ma'am, I'm going to take Naomi through some of our protocol and procedures, but we'll be right outside the Lodge if you need anything."

"Thank you Jason."

Ava gave a small bow as the bodyguards left.

"Your Majesty, I wanted to come and check on you and see how you're doing after the eventful training session the other day."

"Oh, I'm fine," said Lily, her expression growing dark at the reminder of the danger they had all been in because of a drunken idiot. Seeing Ava's look of worried surprise, she hurriedly added that she very much appreciated Ava coming to check on her.

"But of course, Your Majesty..."

"I think you can call me Lily when we're alone together." Lily wasn't sure of the protocol about that, but she decided she would prefer to ask forgiveness than permission in this case.

"Okay... Lily." Ava smiled.

Ava followed Lily out to the balcony. Lily leant on the balustrade and gazed out at the lights of Burlaron. She was feeling frustrated and restless. Here she was, cooped up in the palace to protect her from a threat that so far seemed to consist of one drunken idiot. Who had been able to shoot at her here anyway.

"What's the city like?" she asked Ava.

"Oh, it's great. Tons of shops with all sorts of marvellous stuff from clothes to gadgets to weird Highacren things to send to people back home. During the day there are heaps of lovely cafes, and at night there are pubs for relaxing and clubs for dancing." Ava's face lit up as she spoke, and she realised too late that this might not have been a helpful answer with Lily's current mood.

"I could do with a trip to the pub," Lily smiled wickedly, suddenly excited.

"Yes, but—"

Lily darted back into the Lodge, casting a glance at the door as she made for her bedroom.

"Lily, what are you doing?" Ava looked on in confusion as Lily stripped her bed. Kevin, curled up in his miniature copy of Lily's bed, huffed judgementally, clearly of the opinion that whatever Lily was up to was a bad idea.

"Come on," said Lily, hurrying back past Ava with her bundle of sheets and snatching a pair of scissors from a drawer in the Lodge. "Are you in?"

"Am I in, what?" Ava followed Lily anyway and looked on with a bemused expression as Lily began to destroy her sheets and tie long strips of them together.

"Girls night out. I want to see the city. Not to mention get out of here for a bit. Come on Ava, it'll be fun."

"I'm sure it will be, but I really don't think you're meant to wander around town unescorted."

"I won't be unescorted," Lily said, tying one end of her hastily assembled rope to the balustrade. "I'll be with you."

Before Ava could stop her, Lily tossed the rest of the sheets over the railing and climbed over herself. "Now, wait until I'm at the bottom and then follow me down. If Jason or Naomi come back, try not to let them see the sheets and tell them I'm in the bathroom."

With that, Lily took a deep breath and started climbing down the sheets. Her stomach dropped a few times as the sheets tightened under her weight and she thought they might come apart. Lily had never been more grateful for Austin's strength training as she found that she could grip the makeshift rope and lower herself relatively easily.

She breathed a brief sigh of relief as her feet touched the ground. "Okay Ava, your turn," she hissed up at the balcony.

"I really did not think that would work," Ava said from beside Lily, making her jump.

"Ava." Lily goggled at her. "What are you... how did you..."

"I took the stairs." Ava examined the rope, intrigued.

"You took... but Jason and Naomi—"

"Are not charged with keeping *me* in the palace. I left and told them you were taking a long soak in the tub and going to bed."

Lily stared at Ava, feeling slightly embarrassed, and then rallied, thinking of the excitement that awaited. She started to head off, but Ava grabbed her arm.

"Lily, you do need to think about this. It's not the safest thing to do. Especially under the circumstances."

"I've been playing it safe since I got here, and some drunken guy was still able to take pot shots at me. I can't live my life bundled in cotton wool and locked in the palace. I'll go crazy." She looked pleadingly at Ava. "I'm meant to be queen, but I've not seen any of my own country. Not really. How am I meant to be queen without knowing my people?"

Ava looked at Lily sympathetically, but clearly was still not convinced that this was a good idea.

"Okay, but you stay with me at all times. Promise?"

"Are you my new bodyguard?" Lily asked playfully. "Okay, yes, I promise." Lily saw Ava acquiesce and squealed, clapping her hands. "This is going to be amazing."

Lily started off down the hill, but Ava again grabbed her arm. "Where are you going?"

"To the city," Lily said, pointing at the lights.

"I don't know what things are like where you were raised Your Majesty, but here, we have things called cars." Ava produced a set of keys, dangling them from her fingers.

Lily snatched the keys before Ava could pull them away. "Great, I'll drive."

***

Lily gawked out the window as Ava cruised through the city centre. Having sat in the driver's seat for a full two minutes and remaining completely ignorant of how to start the car, she had reluctantly shuffled across to the passenger's seat, leaving Ava to drive. Which had worked out for Lily in the end, because she had no idea where they were going, and now she got to take in all the sights.

It was early evening, and there were a myriad of different people out wandering Burlaron's streets. Some were in business attire, having just come from work, while others wore more risqué clubbing outfits and some seemed to have a punk rock motif. Ava pointed out the different styles and factions as they drove, as well as the best places to eat, drink, or hang out.

Lily watched enviously as a girl her own age with intricately styled hair and fluorescent clothing took a huge bite out of something that looked to be the love child of pizza and a kebab. Ava promised they could get one on the way home.

Though initially nervous, Ava was relaxing, and now it felt like they were a couple of old friends heading out for a fun evening.

"It's a little too early for the clubs," Ava said, perfectly executing a difficult reverse park. "So we'll head to this pub I know and have a couple of drinks."

Lily got out and admired Ava's car, impossibly squeezed between two others.

"I'm an excellent driver," Ava boasted. She tapped the side of her head. "And I have a little help."

"You can drive your car with your implant?"

"I mean, I could. I prefer to drive manually. It's more fun. But I do use my implant for tricky parking jobs. Particularly for a better field of vision."

They headed down the street, Lily stopping to look in every window. Eventually, Ava grabbed her arm and kept her moving, though at a relatively slow pace so that she could still take everything in.

The wooden sign over the pub's door was jarring given all the surrounding shops used electronic signs and holographic displays to announce their wares. With a name like The Leaky Dungeon, Lily had been expecting the bar to be grubby and full of nefarious characters, and so she was pleasantly surprised to find it had a rustic, homey feel.

Ava led her past wooden tables lit with candles where people were tucking into hearty meals and drinking from what looked like wooden tankards. A sign at the bar told customers to order there, and their food and drink would be delivered to their tables. Lily stopped abruptly, almost walking into someone's dinner as it flew through the air to a table in the back.

"Sorry!" someone called from the kitchen, and the middle-aged barmaid smiled apologetically at Lily, rolling her eyes.

Lily felt more relaxed than she had in a long time. She sat on the bench seat across from Ava, beaming. "This is amazing."

"I thought you'd like it." Ava smiled at Lily's obvious joy. "Why don't you tell me what you want to drink, and I'll go and order."

Lily's face fell. "I don't have any money."

Ava just laughed. "I figured. I mean, someone as important as you would have someone to perform such menial tasks as paying for things, right? Relax," she stopped Lily's protest. "You can buy the drinks next time we go out."

Lily relaxed again and looked at the menu, marvelling at how easy it was to be with Ava. None of the names meant anything to Lily, and she was gripped in a bout of decision paralysis wanting to try everything. Eventually she told Ava to surprise her, and Ava left for the bar.

Lily looked around at the patrons. There were a few people in suits, but most people wore relaxed clothing, and there were a number of families scattered around the room. Everyone was talking and joking loudly with each other, creating a not-unpleasant din.

A group of men occupied the table next to Lily. They'd clearly just finished work and were having a couple of rounds before heading off home, and Lily heard plenty of references to various wives not being happy if their respective husbands were late or drunk or both.

"Yeah, alright. One more. But no more than that

because Lizzie will kill me if I spend too much. She's already on a rampage about the price of groceries."

"Oh, don't get mine started. She never liked Toth, but now it's like he's her personal nemesis."

"Well, he is an arsehole."

"He's a politician."

"Isn't that what I said?"

The table dissolved into laughter and a round of general politician bashing.

"I mean, money's one thing. A big thing—you don't have to tell me that with my youngest, Rita, heading off to school next year—but I'm more concerned about the disappearances."

"Oh Keith, you know that's all conspiracy rubbish."

"It's not, Greg," Keith said. "My neighbour's cousin works at the police department and he says they haven't seen the chief in weeks."

Greg scoffed. "Well, I mean, if your neighbour's cousin says so."

"I'm serious, Greg. I don't want Rita heading away with all the rumours. And I heard there were protests out west that got violent. I tell you, without the royal family, this country's going to the dogs."

"I'll agree with you on that, Keith. Things were definitely much better with the royals around. The king kept them honest."

Keith downed the rest of his drink in one big gulp. "On the bright side, I suppose if the Prime Minister has his way, I might not need to worry about Rita going away."

"What do you mean?"

"He's wanting to bring in stricter regulation for university admissions. Cut the numbers. Regulate what's being taught. Something about ensuring we focus on the right professions, not frivolous degrees feeding the 'education corporation'. Charlie reckons he's cutting the number of places available at uni to support a return to compulsory military service after high school."

"How does he figure that?"

"Apparently if there are a bunch of school leavers without jobs or education, then people will be crying out for them to have something to do. He'll swoop in with his compulsory military service idea and everyone will be on board."

"Sounds far-fetched to me." Greg finished his drink.

"Yeah, I don't know. But if Rita doesn't get to go do her course, I sure as hell don't want her conscripted instead."

Greg offered to get Keith another drink, and despite the earlier concerns about better halves, Keith gratefully accepted. Lily wondered how much of what they'd been talking about was true. She couldn't imagine her younger sister April being told that she couldn't go to university, or that she couldn't study whatever she wanted to. Or being conscripted. The thought made her feel slightly ill.

She looked around the room at all the people and the families. Looking closer, she saw some worried expressions mixed in with the laughter and frivolity. A family off to her left were counting coins onto the table, making sure they had enough to pay for their meal. Lily's eyes followed the woman as she went to the bar to order, and saw the barmaid wave off her payment. The woman was embarrassed, but didn't protest.

"Sorry," Ava broke into her thoughts, sitting back down and dropping a mug in front of her. "They're short-staffed tonight. Apparently they've had to let some people go."

Things were clearly worse for the people of Highacre since the death of the royal family. Lily felt a stab of anger at the Prime Minister. Did he know what he was doing to them? Did he care? And these people—*her* people—deserved better.

Lily felt guilty for sneaking out. All these families were suffering, and she had slipped her security so she could go to the pub for a night out when she should be preparing for the confirmation hearing.

"What's up?" asked Ava. "Did I get the wrong drink?"

"No, sorry. Thank you for the drink. I just... this was a bad idea. I shouldn't be so childish. Sneaking out like this."

Ava looked at Lily sympathetically. "Being cooped up like that isn't great, though. It's normal for you to want to get out and about. This is *your* country. You deserve to see it. You need to see it. And don't worry about your safety. Bodyguard." Ava pointed at her chest. "Remember?"

Lily laughed and settled in, chatting with Ava and relaxing again. A few hours later, they walked back up the street to Ava's car, having decided to give the club a miss.

"A successful outing, Your Majesty," said Ava.

"Indeed. And despite your concerns, nothing bad happened."

And at that moment, a hood was pulled over Lily's head and everything went black.

18

Lily woke, her head fuzzy, and she instantly regretted drinking too much. Though in her defence, she hadn't thought that she had that much. *Alcohol must be stronger here.* She felt something cold and hard under her cheek. Different from how her plush pillows usually felt. She blinked her eyes open and stared at the dirty concrete floor she was currently lying on.

Suddenly remembering a hood being pulled over her head, Lily tried to sit up, only to find her hands were tied behind her back, and she flopped back down, jarring her shoulder.

"Try using the wall," Ava suggested, startling Lily. She rolled over onto her stomach to see Ava sitting propped against the wall, her arms behind her back and legs bound at her ankles.

"Where are we?" Lily asked.

"A dark, dingy basement, it would appear," said Ava, scrunching her nose in distaste. "Such an overused stereotype. Speaks to a lack of imagination."

"I'm sorry our kidnappers' lack of ingenuity upsets you," huffed Lily as she inched her way to the wall, much like a worm. "Personally, I think I prefer my kidnappers to be lacking in imagination. And stupid. And maybe incompetent."

"Tied these ropes well enough," complained Ava, pulling at her arms.

With a great effort, Lily swung herself up until she was mirroring Ava's position. She blew her hair out of her eyes and looked around. It was a small room, like a dungeon cell big enough for two prisoners if they each had a bed. The room did not, however, have any beds. It didn't have anything except dirt, dust, debris, and a suspicious-smelling puddle in a corner.

"Any ideas about—"

"Shhh." Ava hushed Lily urgently, straining her head towards the door, listening. A few seconds later, Lily heard the men walking outside talking in low voices. She turned her head, trying to make out what they were saying, but she couldn't pick up a single word. She looked at Ava questioningly, but Ava shook her head, telling Lily not to talk.

The voices were getting louder, and Lily strained again to hear.

"... a week or so. She'll either miss the confirmation or it'll mess up her preparation, so..."

Lily kept straining, but the men moved out of hearing range again. Ava kept concentrating for a beat and then relaxed slightly.

"What did you hear?" Lily asked.

"Nothing useful. They snatched you to mess with the confirmation hearing."

Lily felt that Ava might have heard a little more than that, but she didn't push her on it. She watched Ava pull at her bonds again, and tentatively tried her own. Lily struggled and pulled and twisted, but to no avail. She cast around the room, looking for a nail or a jagged rock, but nothing vaguely sharp caught her eye.

Both women eventually gave up, and a depressed silence engulfed them before Ava broke it. "So I've been meaning to ask, how's it going finding yourself suddenly being the heir to the throne of Highacre?"

Lily laughed at the irony of the question, and Ava joined in. For a couple of minutes neither could stop the increasingly hysterical laughter, and it broke the tension and eased the panicky fear that had been growing in Lily's stomach. As they recovered, Ava looked at Lily expectantly, awaiting her response.

Lily considered the question. Current circumstances excepted, this new world hadn't been too hard to adjust to. She figured it must be like moving to a new, but similar country, not that she'd ever done that. Everything was slightly familiar, but she didn't really have all the background, and missed a lot of the cultural references.

Being queen though? Lily still felt a bit like a work experience kid, or perhaps a 'queen in training'. She was learning a lot, but she wasn't necessarily ruling the country in any proper sense. Lily felt so isolated in the palace, and so drawn to Ava that without thinking, she began to unload on her.

"It's rough, you know? I feel like I'm just a figurehead. My advisors are running everything, and I'm just sort of here. They don't seem to respect me, they just respect the institution. They don't even ask for my opinion before making decisions. Decisions that should be made by me. I mean, I don't think that they believe I'm incompetent or stupid. Well, I hope they don't, but it's more... they don't even think to ask me." Lily coughed to cover her voice cracking and dropped her head, staring at her lap.

"But otherwise I'm adjusting fine."

Ava smiled sympathetically. "I moved around a lot when I was young, and each time I felt like I had to start all over again. Learn the people, learn the 'in jokes'. Break into the different groups. I always felt a bit like I didn't fit."

"Why did you move around so much?" Lily wondered if Ava's parents were in the military.

"Oh." Ava blew out her breath. "Where to start? I went to live with my aunt when I was young, but after a few years it was too much for them, so they gave me to the state and I went into foster care." Ava caught sight of Lily's expression. "They already had three kids of their own. All boys. Massive handfuls; they were always getting into trouble. So anyway, I went through a few foster homes, and bounced around the countryside a bit with that.

"Eventually, when I was about sixteen, I was allowed to live in supervised accommodation, so I got my own apartment. I stayed there until I was old enough to join the army. I decided to try for infantry."

"Infantry!" Lily's look of surprise and horror made Ava laugh.

"What? Don't think I could hack it?" Ava teased.

"No, I'm sure you could. But why would you want to run around in the mud and pee in a hole?" Lily felt her face flush, but Ava just laughed easily again.

"Fair point! No, I think it was more the challenge. I wanted to see if I could. But I wound up hurting my leg, and so I joined intelligence instead. After a few years of that, they offered me a job in international relations, and here I am!" She looked pointedly around their current accommodations. "Enjoying all the luxury of being an ambassador and hanging out with royalty."

Lily looked at Ava with a new level of respect. Ava had glossed over the details, but clearly she had lived a hard life.

Yet she wore it well, and didn't seem to have a chip on her shoulder about any of it.

"Ava, that's... wow. You've been through so much."

Ava shrugged. "Everyone's been through difficult times. It's all about how you approach the difficulties, and what you learn from them. What was your childhood like?"

Lily reminded herself that she was supposed to have grown up with the family of a fake distant cousin of the queen in Oppulus, one of the smaller countries to the south. Luckily her advisors had modelled this family on her own back home.

"Oh, nothing like yours. I was so lucky growing up with... Belinda and Bruce, my surrogate mum and dad. They never treated me any different to their own kids. Sometimes I even forgot that I wasn't theirs! But I guess I always felt slightly... separate. I don't know if that's just something I projected on the situation, but... Perhaps everyone feels that way sometimes."

They lapsed into silence, each lost in their own thoughts. Suddenly, the door slammed open and a man in a creepy ghoulish mask entered, tossing a plate with a couple of husks of bread on the floor and placing a mug of water next to it. He went to leave without a word.

"I need to pee," Ava said quickly.

"Me too," Lily added.

The man paused and then left the room briefly before returning and throwing a bucket into the corner. He slammed the door shut as he left and they heard the key turn, locking them in.

Ava glared at the bucket, then shrugged. "Worth a shot."

"I do need to pee now though," Lily said ruefully.

Ava considered her thoughtfully.

"What?" Lily asked after Ava's consideration became uncomfortable.

"I'm just wondering why you haven't used your magical powers to bust us out of here yet."

Lily felt her face flush. "I'm not... it's just..." She closed her eyes, telling herself there was no need for her to be embarrassed. "I can't use my abilities yet," she confided. "Lady Octavia says I have power and the abilities should come. It's just... they haven't yet."

"Oh," said Ava simply.

"Well, why can't you get us out of here?" Lily asked defensively. "Aren't you supposed to be a soldier and a spy and have some fancy cybernetic implant thingy? Surely you can escape some simple rope bonds."

"Of course I can," Ava said, bringing her arms to the front and untying her legs. "I just wanted to see if you could too."

Lily's jaw dropped. "You were able to do that this whole time?"

"Yep," said Ava, rubbing her legs before moving over and dropping down next to Lily to get started on freeing her arms.

"They why—"

"Tactical patience, little one. Never hurts to wait and gather intelligence. Well..." Ava paused, thinking. "It almost never hurts. Anyway, by waiting we know that they're not meant to hurt you, and now that they've checked on us, they probably won't again for a while."

They stood, Lily rubbing her wrists. Ava went to the door, listening and staring intently at it.

"No one on guard. These guys are terrible."

"I'm fond of terrible kidnappers."

"Well, you can leave them a good review."

"How do you know no one's outside?"

"X-ray vision." Ava tapped her head next to her eyes. "And now, I'm doing a quick search for floor plans... Hmmm. Nothing official, but according to this, the exit should be to the left."

"Left, huh. Well, let's go then," Lily said sarcastically. Ava turned to look at her.

"Your Majesty," she said, a playful smile on her lips, "you have nothing to fear. I, your illustrious bodyguard, will keep you safe. I am, after all, a soldier and a spy and I have a fancy cybernetic implant thingy."

"Shut up." Lily pushed her gently.

"By your command." Ava bowed.

Lily laughed and nodded at her. "Alright, let's get out of here."

Ava fiddled with the door and had it open in a flash. She popped her head out, checking what her implant had already told her, then motioned Lily to follow her into the hall. They moved swiftly but silently, Ava checking each turn before they took it.

As they moved along a musty hallway, a door farther along opened and they ducked into a small alcove and hid behind some wooden boxes. Two men exited and began walking away from Lily and Ava. Lily examined their hiding place. The wood was rotting and Lily picked at it, wondering what was inside. Ava tapped her hand to get her to stop and focus on remaining undetected. Lily rolled her eyes at Ava, then scooted back in alarm as what looked like a large cockroach crawled out of the box. Ava grabbed her, clapping her hand over Lily's mouth to keep her quiet. The men moved out of sight and the women relaxed.

"Are you ready?" Ava asked Lily, and Lily nodded. She was embarrassed by her reaction and determined to get it together.

Ava scanned ahead and, comfortable that the way was

clear, emerged from their hiding place at the exact time a huge masked figure emerged from a side corridor behind them.

"How did you get out?" he demanded.

"Look, I'm sorry, I just really needed the bathroom," Ava apologised.

The man glared at her, and Ava attacked him without warning, trying to catch him unawares. Unfortunately, this kidnapper wasn't as incompetent as his friends, and he blocked Ava's punches. As she swung at him again, he caught her fist and twisted her arm, pinning it behind her back and wrapping his other arm around her neck.

"Pretty *and* feisty, eh? Reckon you and me can have some fun."

They had moved down the hallway away from Lily during the fight and Lily poked her head out, seeing Ava struggle as she insulted her attacker's manhood.

"That so?" He was angry now. "Well, when I've finished with you, you won't have to worry about—"

Lily ran at the man and, with all her strength and momentum, punched him as hard as she could in the kidneys. He took a step forward as if merely jostled, and turned his head trying to see what had bumped him. Ava took advantage of his distraction and stomped as hard as she could on his foot. The man doubled over and Ava drove the heel of her palm into his nose before slamming his head against the wall. The man slid to the ground and didn't move.

"Are you okay, Lily?"

"Yeah, you?"

Ava nodded. "Thanks for the assist. Alright, let's get out of here."

They resumed their escape, moving faster now to find the exit before someone found the unconscious man. Eventually, they found themselves at some concrete stairs that seemed to lead to street level.

"One guard outside the door," Ava frowned. "I mean, better than the no guards outside our door, but still."

"Mail them a critique," Lily hissed. "Besides, that one guy before was more than enough trouble. Can we take this one?"

Ava looked offended. "Of course we can take him."

"Then let's go."

As they exited the door, Ava started chatting to Lily as if they were simply two women heading out to go to the club. The kidnapper started towards them but stopped, unsure and wrong-footed by Ava's demeanour.

"Oh my god, and then Rachel..." Ava chopped her hand into the man's throat and slammed her fist into his stomach as he doubled over.

"Well, that's that. Shall we get you home?"

"Your Majesty!"

Lily turned to see Jason, Naomi and a team of guards sprinting down the street towards them.

"Jason! What are you doing here?"

Jason stopped in front of Lily, breathing hard and looking at her in confusion. "Me? But... what are you... I mean. Your Majesty, you are not meant to be out of the palace. What if something happened?"

"It did." Ava nudged the kidnapper with her foot.

Jason took in the scene, eyes pausing on Lily's raw wrists, and turned to his guards, ordering them into the basement. The guards moved like an elite unit, disappearing down the stairs as Jason led Lily and Ava away.

"Your Majesty, what happened?"

Lily guiltily told Jason how she had snuck out, trying to minimise Ava's involvement, though she noted he glared at her, no doubt remembering the line she had fed them about

Lily going to bed. When she mentioned she had been unconscious, Jason snapped his fingers at one of the guards, who jogged over and raised his hands near Lily's head.

"Minor bump... no concussion... minor abrasions. No major injuries, sir."

Jason nodded and the guard went to leave. Lily stopped him and had him check Ava too, before he left having similarly given her the all-clear.

"Look Jason, I'm sorry. I know it was stupid. But I just—"

"Why did it take you so long to find us?" Ava asked Jason.

He glared at Ava. "Excuse me, ma'am?"

"I mean, I know I told a teensy little lie, but I figured you would have realised she was gone within the hour. Two tops."

Jason, still angry, dropped his gaze, an angry red blush making its way up his neck. When he responded, he addressed Lily.

"We should have realised you were gone earlier, Your Majesty, that's my fault. Naomi and I assumed you were in bed" —he glared again at Ava— "and because we were outside the Lodge, the guard who normally monitors your room assumed you were elsewhere."

"Well, she was," said Ava unhelpfully.

"Legitimately elsewhere," Jason snarled before trying to control himself. "Again, that kind of lapse is unacceptable. It will not happen again."

"I know, Jason," Lily said, trying to diffuse the situation. "And I promise not to sneak out of the palace again."

Jason sighed heavily and tilted his head side to side, cracking his neck. "Let's get you safely back to the palace."

An hour later, Lily was back in the Lodge, wrapped up in a fluffy robe over her flannel pyjamas and curled up on the couch with a mug of hot chocolate. She had enjoyed a hot bath and felt better having washed the dingy basement off her.

Ava was sitting across from her wearing a soft tracksuit and nursing her own mug. Jason had been reluctant to let her into the Lodge, but Naomi had diverted him to the operations room before sitting herself in a far corner by the door, seemingly engrossed in some files. Lily knew Naomi was keeping a close eye on them and saw her occasionally looking around, scanning the area.

There was a sharp rap at the door, and Naomi was answering it before Lily could even think to get up.

"I wondered if I might visit with Her Majesty..."

Lily could hear Alexei at the door and signalled to Naomi to let him in. Alexei marched towards them, formality dripping off him until he saw Ava and visibly relaxed.

"Ah, Your Majesty," he said with a sharp bow, "I wanted to come and check on you. Word of your evening exploits is the buzz of the palace. But I was concerned it would be improper to visit with you alone. Now I see our friend Ava is here, and all is well." He smiled and took a seat at Lily's insistence.

"Were you worried about Edmund's fury if you were inappropriately visiting his girlfriend unsupervised?" Ava asked, straight-faced.

Alexei scowled at her while Lily said reflexively, "I'm not his girlfriend."

The three fell into easy laughter, Lily feeling slightly bad that the joke was at Edmund's expense. Though Alexei was curious about their escapades, Lily kept the discussion to a brief overview of events. She didn't want to think about what had happened. What could have happened. She felt so stupid and foolish.

"Let's not talk about it anymore. I'm sure I'll hear all about it from my advisors for the next week at least. I'd rather pretend it didn't happen for a bit. Then maybe I'll be able to sleep tonight."

Seeking to distract them, and inspired by the mention of Edmund, Lily asked them both about their relationship statuses. Both informed Lily that they were single and a discussion of past romantic interests ensued. Ava told them about an almost comical string of failed relationships, and Alexei shared with them a tale of a girl who he didn't realise he was dating until she had told virtually everyone he knew.

"I looked like a complete jerk saying that we weren't together after she'd been telling everyone what a sweet boyfriend I was for two months!"

Lily told them about Brandon, who she admitted she had barely thought about since arriving in Highacre.

"Well," said Ava. "I mean, now you have Eddie, so your love life's sorted." Lily threw a handful of salted nuts at her. They joked for a bit about his escapades in his quest to win Lily's heart.

"Poor Eddie," said Lily, recovering from another bout of laughter. "He's such a nice guy, and he means well, he's just..." Lily shrugged.

"Not the guy for you?" asked Ava

"He's definitely not my type," Lily admitted. "But he's so lovely, and funny—when he's not trying to impress everyone."

"He's not trying to impress *everyone*," said Alexei.

"I know." Lily picked at a stray thread on her cushion. "I'd love to have him as a friend. I just don't know how to call off this courtship thingy without hurting him."

"I'm not sure that there is a way," Ava said sympathetically. "But you know it won't get better the longer you leave it, right?"

Lily nodded. She knew she needed to grow up and sort the situation out before Eddie got any more hurt than he was already going to be. Tomorrow. She would totally do it tomorrow. With a slightly guilty sense of déjà vu, Lily turned the discussion back to easier things, like what Ava did for fun back in Meridia. Before she could answer, there was another knock at the door.

As Naomi permitted Edmund entry, the room fell to the guilty silence that loudly informed the entrant that everyone had been talking about them prior to their entry. Edmund's eyes fell first on Alexei and he scowled, straightening up and marching towards them.

"Hi, Eddie," called Ava pleasantly. Seeing Ava took the indignant wind out of Edmund's sails. Lily watched as his face turned to relief that Lily hadn't been hanging out alone with Alexei to hurt that the three of them had been hanging out together without him.

"My apologies, Your Majesty," he stammered with effort. "I didn't know you already had company. I just wanted to see for myself that you were alright and check if you needed me. I'll come back..." He turned back towards the door. Lily jumped up and grabbed his hand, pulling him over to join the group. Ava looked pointedly at Lily holding Edmund's hand with an expression that warned she wasn't making things any easier.

"Actually," Lily turned to Ava and Alexei. "Would you two mind giving us a minute?"

Edmund puffed out his chest, shooting Alexei a smarmy look.

"Of course," said Ava, getting up and grabbing Alexei's hand and dragging him towards the door. "We'll leave you to it. It's getting late anyway. See you at training tomorrow."

"Edmund," Lily began after the door shut. Edmund closed his eyes and leant in to kiss her. Surprised, Lily pushed him away. "Wait, no."

Edmund looked confused and hurt. "I thought... I mean, you sent them away so we could have some alone time. I could comfort you..." He went to embrace Lily, but she put a hand on his chest.

"I sent them away so we could talk." Lily felt uncomfortable, but she fixed her resolve. She kept her voice gentle but firm. "Edmund, it's not going to work out with us. There's nothing wrong with you. I think you're a great guy, and I'd love for us to stay friends. I just don't feel anything for you. Not in that way."

"You're traumatised. It's natural to try and push away those closest to you after such a horrific experience."

"Edmund, this is not new. I'm just not interested."

He looked at her hopefully, and then seeing her resolve, Edmund physically deflated and floated towards the couch before dropping onto it. "Everyone always just wants to be friends." A look of horror swept over his face. "My brothers. Oh no. They're going to be insufferable. 'Couldn't keep her more than a month'." He groaned into his hands.

"Don't tell them," Lily suggested.

"They'll find out. Your advisors will find you someone else immediately." Edmund stood and began pacing the length of the room.

Lily hadn't considered that. She didn't want another suitor. Not yet, anyway. She had more than enough to be getting on with. *Perhaps we can help each other.*

"How about this then, Eddie—"

"Edmund."

"Neither of us tells anyone. We can put on a charade going forward, at least until my coronation, and then we end it. I'm even happy if you want to tell people that you dumped me."

Edmund considered her offer. "You'd do that? For me?"

"Of course, Edmund. Like I said, I *do* like you. Just not in that way."

He considered her proposal.

"Just not in that way... yet." Edmund had an unnerving gleam in his eye.

"Huh?"

"Until coronation... that gives me a couple of months. I can change, you'll see. I can become the man you want me to be. A man you'd be proud to be with."

"Oh, Edmund, I don't think—"

"No, no." Edmund raised his hands as if warding her off and headed for the door. "I get it. You're not into this version of me. I understand that it's all smoke and mirrors until the coronation, but I'm going to become the man of your dreams. If you still don't want to be with me then, I'll bow out gracefully. But just you watch, Your Majesty. I'm not the kind of guy who loses."

Edmund tried to sweep grandly out of the Lodge, but pushed the door when he should have pulled and bumped his head before rectifying the situation and leaving slightly more sheepishly than intended. Lily thought she heard a quiet snort from the corner where Naomi remained engrossed in her files.

Lily retired to her room and snuggled into her bed. Kevin hopped up and snuggled in beside her. Lily patted him, grateful for his company, and thought about the evening's events. She wasn't sure what had been more trau-matic, being kidnapped or trying to dump Edmund.

19

"Ow! Watch it!" Lily scowled at the girl whose task it was to turn her hair into something presentable and regal for the state dinner she was to host that evening. The girl muttered an insincere apology, singularly focussed on her task and clearly more interested in satisfying whoever had given it to her than worried about upsetting the future monarch.

Lily was frustrated with all the fussing around her and the masses of palace staff seemingly required to make her presentable. It was particularly irritating to her because, as they all got started, she had noticed another crisp envelope on her table and had snatched it away before anyone else saw it. She had not had a moment to herself since, and the curiosity over what was in it was killing her. She had tried pleading to Addison, Claire, and Ava, who were all somehow involved in preparing her for the dinner (Ava, she suspected, for her own entertainment, as the more the servants' fussing annoyed Lily, the wider her smile grew), but none of them had proved an ally.

"I need to go to the bathroom," Lily announced loudly, standing to the frustration of her hairdresser. "Alone," she added after at least five servants made to accompany her. Lily closed the door behind her and waited a beat to listen in case anyone thought to follow. She decided that taking the opportunity to relieve herself shouldn't be passed up and after washing her hands, sat on the side of the bathtub and retrieved the envelope she had hidden in her clothes.

She examined it with reverence, seeing the now-expected calligraphic lettering proclaiming the letter hers, and the wax seal with the mysterious crest. She cracked the seal carefully and pulled out the letter, which began in the now familiar way the others had.

"Your Majesty, I just need..." As Ava burst into the bathroom, Lily scrambled to hide her letter, eventually settling for shoving it under her leg, and turned to look at Ava, fixing her best innocent expression on her face. The result was that Lily looked far guiltier and drew more attention to the letter than if she'd done nothing.

"What's that?" asked Ava suspiciously.

"What's what?"

"That."

"What?"

"That letter." Ava was clearly getting annoyed.

"It's none of your business." Lily tried and failed to come across as regal and aloof, instead succeeding in appearing like an obstinate child. It did, however, break the tension, and Ava smiled and sat next to Lily.

"Okay, have your secrets."

It was this backing down and allowing Lily to be in charge more than anything that caused Lily to show Ava the letter and explain how they'd been turning up mysteriously since she arrived in Highacre. Ava studied the envelope, frowning.

"And you've told no one?"

"No."

"But they've been turning up in your room, which indicates that someone we don't know, whose motivations we don't know, has access to your room. Despite your security." She looked meaningfully at Lily.

"I know," said Lily guiltily. "But it's just..." she paused. Saying 'it's just that they aren't telling me everything either' suddenly sounded childish and stupid. "I don't know which of my advisors I can trust."

Ava considered this as she examined the envelope.

"This is expensive stationary. It's from Remington's."

"How can you tell?" asked Lily as she looked over Ava's shoulder, trying to see what she was looking at.

"I'm scanning it with my implant."

"Oh." Lily stopped trying to look.

"What does the letter say?"

"I don't know," said Lily, taking the envelope back from Ava and pulling the letter out. "I didn't get to read it before you came in." Lily opened the letter.

Your Majesty,

You are in significant danger. I have uncovered information that shows they will make an attempt on your life at the state dinner this evening. I do not know who the assassin is, however, my sources tell me they will carry a dagger and their ability allows them to guide it through the air into their target—you.

I believe that at least one of your advisors is aware of this threat. I do not know which one yet, however, my sources tell me a very well-informed and high-ranking member of the palace staff is involved, and that can only be one of your advisors.

I can't stress to you enough, Your Majesty, that you

Lily thrust the page at Ava, her mind reeling. Despite the warning, Lily thought she should tell Jason. Ava finished the letter and handed it back to Lily, asking what she was going to do.

"I'm not sure. I might tell Jason—"

"But it says that might be risky."

"I don't think Jason is the bad egg," Lily said, thinking.

"I can scan people with my implant to see who's carrying a dagger."

"You can see that level of detail?" Lily suddenly felt slightly exposed.

"Yeah, it's pretty cool!" Ava smiled at Lily. "I can scan specifically for metal, but I can also kind of see the shapes of what people are carrying in their bags or pockets. If there's a heap of stuff it's trickier, obviously."

A knock on the door interrupted them, and Lily shot a panicked look at Ava, having not sworn her to secrecy. Ava gave her a reassuring look that Lily took to mean her secret was safe, and Lily allowed herself to be swept back out into her bedroom for the staff to work on her.

Finally, Lily took her seat at the dinner after a traditional Highacren dance display and a very long speech from the governor, who Lily was told had no real power or responsibilities, but was a figurehead often rolled out at functions to give very long speeches.

Lily was relieved to find Ava sitting across from her. She didn't know whether this was a lucky coincidence of the seating plan or whether Ava had managed to adjust the plan in her favour. Either way, Lily felt safer with Ava in her line of sight, and she could see the other woman gazing intently at people, which Lily assumed was her using her X-ray abilities.

Lily was less thrilled to find the Prime Minister had been seated to her right. She knew he had to be afforded a place of prominence, but with all she'd been told by her advisors and what she'd heard in the pub, she really didn't like the man, and wished she didn't have to interact with him. The Prime Minister for his part was clearly aiming to get his taxpayer money's worth and had been inhaling red wine like it was going out of fashion.

Lily made polite conversation with a diplomat from Oppulus who had been seated to her left. She was trying to avoid drawing the Prime Minister's attention. Unfortunately, having drained the carafe directly in front of him, as well as the one to his right, the Prime Minister's gaze drifted to the carafe to Lily's left and slid a little farther, landing on her face.

"Your Majesty," he slurred, "lovely dinner. Very good work." He couldn't have been more patronising without patting her on her head.

"Thank you, Mr Prime Minister. I do so appreciate your approval."

He looked at her, his eyes struggling to focus and clearly trying to determine if she was being sarcastic. "You should enjoy it while it lasts," he sneered, his small beady eyes narrowing. "Be such a shame if you didn't make it through the confirmation process. All this effort for nothing."

The Prime Minister then secured a full carafe from a staff member, who looked slightly conflicted about his actions in providing it, and sloshed a good helping into his glass. He smiled evilly in Lily's general direction.

"But then you could just toddle off back to wherever it was that you came from. You'll be happier, we'll be happier, and everything will just go back to how it was before you got here." He was slurring his words significantly now, and his voice had the rolling pitch of a drunk. Ava was watching with interest, finding his current state amusing even if his words were not. Seeing Ava distracted, Lily looked furtively around the room, as if a knife-wielding maniac might jump at her from the shadows. Ava gave her a light kick under the table and indicated that she had not forgotten her duty.

"We were doing just fine," the Prime Minister rambled on, oblivious to anything other than the point he was struggling to make, or possibly remember. "This country is mine."

Lily looked at the Prime Minister. This last comment was not as slurred as the rest, and he had said it in a quiet, dangerous voice. He met her eyes, his own less cloudy now. "I have worked all my life to make this country great. Sacrificed, struggled, and all for the good of Highacre. I am what it needs. We are finally coming into our own and focussing on ourselves, our needs, and not trying to kowtow or please foreigners." He spat the last word, gesturing at Ava, who continued to scan the room but stiffened at the Prime Minister's comment.

"And finally, I was positioned to see my plan through to fruition, and then you turn up. Well, let me tell you *Your Majesty*, your father couldn't stop me, and neither will you."

"Mr Prime Minister, are you threatening me?"

He laughed as if Lily had made an extraordinarily funny joke, drawing some amused looks from around the table. "Of course not," he leered. "I have no need to harm you. When presented with confirming a little girl with no leadership experience and no actual knowledge of Highacre and what this country needs, and me with decades of proven ability in protecting Highacre, I am completely confident that the council will find a reason to block your confirmation."

Ava stood suddenly and moved to the servant's corridor, gesturing to Jason to follow her. Jason indicated to Naomi to assume his position behind Lily, but Naomi was already moving. Lily went to stand, but Naomi gently touched her shoulder and Lily resumed her seat. It was not her job to chase after the assassin. Her role was to remain at the table and keep everyone's attention diverted from the action.

The sounds of a scuffle emerged from the corridor, drawing some curious looks, and Lily decided that now was as good a time as any to give the speech she had been dreading. She stood and spent a good five minutes greeting all the dignitaries and thanking them for coming before getting into the main body of what her advisors had prepared for her to say. She paused, running her eyes over the page in front of her. It was a lot of surface-level waffle that sounded like it should be important, but really didn't say much of anything. Was that the type of queen she wanted to be? Lily took a deep breath and put the speech away.

"I never thought that I would be a queen."

There was a small intake of breath around the table, and Lily caught the shadow of a scowl pass over Minister Bellingham's face.

"The last of five children, I think I can safely say that no one expected that I would ever sit on the throne of Highacre. No one would even have imagined the tragedy that had to occur for me to be here today, preparing to be crowned your queen. Though, clearly there were concerns, else I would have been raised here in the palace rather than being sent away for my own safety and that of my family's line.

"While I loved growing up in Oppulus," Lily said, nodding at the diplomat on her left, who smiled broadly, "I do wonder what my life might have been like growing up within these walls. Living and playing and exploring Highacre's forests and cities; lakes and mountains; plains and beaches. Though I've not been home long, I can honestly say that I have fallen in love with my country, and I am proud to be Highacren.

"I am proud to be a part of a country that has a strong tradition of leaders who put service before self." Lily stared pointedly at the Prime Minister. "Who care about our people and put their needs before personal gain."

The Prime Minister snorted and drank deeply from his glass of wine.

"I am proud to join a leadership team that ignores self-interest and is not governed by fear."

The Prime Minister glared at Lily now.

"For fear can cause people to make weak decisions. Decisions that adversely affect the people they govern *just in case*. Just in case of war. Just in case they lose power.

"I am grateful for the experience Highacre's current leadership team brings." She smiled back at the Prime Minister, saccharine sweet. "And look forward to bringing a new perspective. Together, we will drive Highacre forward in a new and exciting direction. A direction that considers the best interests of all Highacre's people."

Enthusiastic applause met Lily's speech, and she nodded at her guests as she resumed her seat. Even

Minister Bellingham tipped her head appreciatively in Lily's direction. Lily focussed on keeping her face a mask of impassive confidence, as if she gave speeches like that every day, as she wiped the sweat from her hands surreptitiously on the tablecloth and tried to slow her pounding heart.

After they had finally farewelled the official guests, Lily and her advisors gathered in the Lodge, joined by Ava due to her participation in the evening's events.

"Are we sure?" asked Minister Bellingham, fiddling with her pearl necklace.

"Yes ma'am," reported Jason. "We've run a thorough background check. The individual is one Peter Gladwell, forty-two, from East Shore. He is a regular attendee at nationalist rallies. Lives alone. Until recently was employed by Hasham Tech, but was let go three weeks ago after the company invested in some Meridian technology that made his role redundant."

Minister Toot let out a disgusted scoff and looked accusingly at Ava, who ignored the man completely.

"So, another lone wolf, also with connections to the rallies?" Giles asked with a note of sceptical disbelief in his voice.

"And another one missed by our security," added Minister Bellingham in an under-her-breath tone that was clearly audible. Lily saw an angry red flush creep up Jason's neck.

"Yes Minister, although this person was detected prior to launching an attack—"

"Thanks to the Meridian ambassador to court," Minister Bellingham nodded at Ava, who kept her expression neutral.

"Yes, thank goodness you saw him, Ava!" gushed Addison. "Is your scanner on all the time?"

"No, the X-ray functionality has several features and so has to be actively engaged."

"Curious. And why did you decide to engage it and scan our guests?" asked Minister Toot pointedly.

"I was bored," Ava replied boldly, meeting his eyes. Lily smiled to herself when the minister looked away first.

"The real issue here," Minister Bellingham said, bringing the attention back to her, "is the seeming inability of our security service to protect the monarch." She glared at Jason, who opened his mouth to respond.

"Yes, forgive me Jason, but this does seem problematic. How did this man not only gain access to palace grounds, but make it all the way to the royal wing?" Giles looked at Jason slightly accusingly.

"We are running checks. It's possible he has some tele-portation abilities."

Minister Bellingham scoffed, and the advisors looked slightly embarrassed for Jason, who did sound like he was reaching.

"Or," he said loudly, "it's also possible that someone let him in."

A slightly stunned silence settled on the room, and the advisors looked shocked at the implication.

"Unlikely." Minister Toot recovered first. "And even if that was what happened, it doesn't account for him moving, at least partway, through the palace unaccompanied, and that you and your men," he said, ignoring Naomi, who shot him a dirty look, "failed. If it wasn't for the girl" —he gestured at Ava, who also gave him a dirty look— "Her Majesty may have been killed."

There was an uncomfortable silence. Jason looked as though he wanted to reply but set his jaw and remained silent.

"It seems to me," said Lily, "that it is very unlikely that

random attendees at these rallies are periodically taken with a sudden desire to attack me. More likely that something nefarious is going on. Some wider plot. But so far, it seems like a pretty terrible plot if the aim is to kill me. So, perhaps there's another aim entirely. Perhaps, contrary to current opinion, my security in the wake of the assassination of the rest of the royal family is pretty good." She looked at Jason. "You beefed it up, I assume?"

"Yes, Your Majesty."

"So then maybe these attempts are testing the systems—"

"And finding them wanting," muttered Minister Toot.

"Or are really aimed at discrediting Jason and his team, hoping that he will resign or be replaced, which would leave my security vulnerable, at least during the handover period while the new lead was getting up to speed, thus providing a window in which to successfully assassinate me."

Lily's advisors looked at her with a mix of surprise and respect that Lily found slightly offensive, as she didn't think it so unlikely that she might have something intelligent to say.

"I mean," Minister Toot began what was no doubt a dismissal of Lily's theory.

"That does make sense, Your Majesty," Claire said loudly. The rest of the advisors nodded in agreement and Minister Toot, sensing that the weight of the room was against him, wandered over and sat in a leather armchair, sipping from a glass of whiskey that Lily hadn't realised he had.

Resolving that it was, in fact, foolish to even consider standing Jason down in such uncertain times, Lily's advisors filed out. Ava said goodnight and told her she would see her at her training session with Austin in the morning. They finally left Lily with Jason and Naomi. She pre-emptively cut off any words of apology or appreciation.

"For better or worse, Jason, I trust you," Lily said sincerely. "And you, Naomi. You're the ones I am confident are on my side. The rest... I do like them. Most of them," she corrected herself, thinking of Minister Toot, "but one of them must be dodgy. Everything from the assassinations through to these latest incidents needs support from a well-placed person. Find them," she implored the guards.

"Yes, Your Majesty, you have my word. We will not rest until the traitor is uncovered."

"Resting is allowed, Jason," Lily called on her way to her room. "It might actually help."

"Okay, so what have we got?" Jason sat heavily in his chair while Naomi made herself comfortable on the other side of the desk. He watched as she dumped her files on the desk and took a swig of coffee. Her files were neat, ordered, and he could even see little flags highlighting areas of interest. He glanced guiltily at his mess of scrunched and slightly stained papers and tried to tidy them up as inconspicuously as possible.

"I reckon we start with the suspects," said Naomi, ignoring Jason's fiddling. "Your mate Hudson was right; there's something dodgy about Austin."

"Agreed. People first, and then," he said, checking his watch, "Hudson will call in to tell us what he's found. He's been reviewing our security systems around the times of both lone wolf attacks."

"Great, and then perhaps we can all chat about those notes and the key," Naomi nodded at the letters and key that Lily had begrudgingly passed to Jason, admitting that they had been turning up in her bedroom and that she did not know how they got there.

Lily had become agitated when Jason reminded her that

in Highacre, people could be invisible, but after he promised to have a revealer positioned at her bedroom door at all times, she had relaxed and even been gracious enough not to ask why that hadn't been routine since her return.

Jason *had* put a revealer on the door to the Lodge, and there were other revealers around the palace at strategic locations. It concerned him that someone had still managed to access Lily's rooms, and he intended to source someone who could sense the mere use of magic to layer their approach.

"So," began Naomi, "the stuff Hudson found on Austin includes a bunch of recovered files, emails, and what I think are notes from his supervisors. Some of it had been deleted, some of it amended. But essentially what we have is a random bunch of files, rather than an ordered service record. I've gone through it all and tried to make sense of it, but bottom line up front, what we have shows that something is off and we need to look closer at him, though none of it as it stands would form a reliable basis for us to take any action."

Jason acknowledged her caveat, and she began her brief.

"Austin's unit was very successful during the war, however, he was sent to work for the general because of some uncomfortable rumours about how they went about their success."

"What kind of rumours?" Jason interrupted. He wasn't aware of any rumours and hadn't heard any himself during the war.

"It's not clear in the documents, but the implication is that they committed war crimes. Unnecessary collateral damage, mistreatment of civilians. Some cowboy stuff. Some people implied they were a group of nationalistic young soldiers out to kill all the Meridians they could. Anyway, they sent him to work for the general with the idea that if the rumours were true, the general would deal with him and if they weren't, his career wouldn't suffer.

"Here's the kicker. Some documents indicate the general came to the decision that Austin *was* dodgy. There are some emails that Hudson found—not going to ask how—where the general basically says as much."

"Basically?" Jason did not want to assume Austin was a war criminal based on innuendo.

"He's cagey in his language. But if you read all the documents together... Anyway, that's not all. Hudson also pulled all the firsthand witness statements about the attack on the command post where the general died protecting his troops. From what I can see, no one but Austin witnessed the general's final act of bravery."

"What?"

"Yeah, no one saw it, and if you read Austin's description along with what the contemporaneous witnesses say they heard happened, it couldn't have happened the way Austin said without a bunch of people seeing it."

Jason knew the story of General Mortimer's bravery well. All soldiers did. General Mortimer was said to have run out into the firefight raging around his command post, which was under attack from the Meridian Special Forces, and pushed several soldiers out of the firing line, saving their lives, before jumping in front of a bullet meant for someone else. That sounded like it should have several witnesses. Like the people he pushed out of the way, and the person whose life he saved.

"So," Naomi continued, "I asked Hudson if he happened to have a copy of the general's autopsy—"

"Naomi!" Jason didn't doubt that Hudson had acquired a copy for her, but he was concerned about the means employed to do so.

"It was on file," claimed Naomi with a straight face. "At

least, it is now. Anyway, the general was shot in the head and had no other injuries."

"It's possible that they got him in the head with a lucky shot," Jason said.

"With a nine-millimetre round?" asked Naomi.

"Meridian officers have pistols. And if their rifle jammed, or ran out of ammo, or they were close—"

"With one of *our* rounds?"

"They may have picked up a Highacren pistol off a fallen soldier."

Naomi looked at Jason and sighed. "I thought of all those possibilities too. That's why I also asked Hudson to pull the records from the quartermaster. They took stock of everything after the fight ended and they evacuated the survivors." Naomi pulled out a poorly photocopied reproduction of a handwritten ledger.

"Austin's pistol only fired one round during the fight." She looked at Jason, anticipating his next question. "His rifle ammo was almost empty. Look, I know that it's all circumstantial. But, in the context of our current investigation, we have someone who *may* have committed war crimes, and then *may* have killed a general, who also happened to be the late queen's father, and there *may* be a nationalist undertone."

Jason looked at Naomi. "A war criminal teaching the new queen about war. Yeah, probably not a good look. At the least, I will stand him down as her trainer. We're a week away from the confirmation, so I can talk to Giles and Addison about prioritising her studies to minimise attention."

Naomi nodded. "Speaking of which, I reviewed both of their files and did a quick audit of their inboxes. Giles seems fine. He's been here forever and is nothing but loyal to the royal family. Addison is similar." Naomi opened her file to a tabbed page. "She's been working here for twenty years or so, always directly for the royal family and with no issues. Routine security checks never flagged a thing. Everyone reports that she is lovely and friendly."

"So they're both fine."

"I think so," said Naomi slowly. "The only thing with Addison is that there was very little information about what she did before joining the royal household. There's something in there about a temp agency, but I couldn't find it online, and there's very little reference to where she lived or what she did."

Jason reached for the file, and she handed it to him. Skimming it, he muttered, "No issues with her clearances to work here... was vetted by the HIA... hmmm, you're right, that is pretty thin." He handed it back to her. "If there was anything dodgy in her past, I'd think the HIA would have picked it up in the checks over her first few years of working here. That would have been proximate to whatever she was doing before. And if not, what are we saying? This is a plot twenty-odd years in the making?"

"Yeah, it doesn't fit, but it is a bit odd," Naomi said without a trace of defensiveness.

"Agreed. We'll keep an eye on her. Perhaps get Hudson to give us something to monitor her emails and phone."

"Or we could ask Claire about her," segued Naomi, "since she used to be an HIA agent."

Jason stared at her. Naomi smiled back, clearly enjoying herself. "Oh, you didn't know? So, our palace file on her is a bunch of blacked out pages saying 'classified', which isn't suspicious at all." Sarcasm dripped from her words. "But your mate Hudson managed to get us the unredacted version. She had just started at the agency when it was disbanded. But the interesting thing is that she got her job here while she was still in the HIA. Which means that it was the agency that sent her."

"They disbanded the HIA for failing to identify warnings about the assassinations," Jason thought out loud. "But what if it was deeper than that? Could they have been behind the whole thing?"

"What would be their angle?" Naomi asked. "What would they get out of removing the royal family? Surely if the agency had wanted to interfere in politics it would be better to target the prime minister?"

"Unless it was the prime minister controlling them," Jason mused. "But Claire was a new agent. Surely if the agency was going to murder the sovereign, they would have put someone more experienced in the palace?"

"I suppose it would have depended on her role. But the main thing for us is—whether or not she was involved in the assassinations—following the disbandment of the agency, we don't know where her loyalties lie."

Jason looked at Naomi, trying to think it through. If Claire had trained as hard as he understood recruits had to train to graduate from the academy, let alone how difficult it was to even get into the academy in the first place, what would her reaction have been to the agency's abolition? Agents joined the agency to serve Highacre, so surely her loyalties remained to Highacre, perhaps strengthened by the destruction of the agency she had worked so hard to join? Maybe she could be an ally? Unless the agency *had* been replaced by something? Something set up by those behind everything that was going wrong? In which case, she could be their worst enemy.

"I'd say let's get Hudson to help us monitor her too," Naomi broke into his thoughts, "but with her background, that probably won't help."

"No," said Jason, "but let's watch her anyway. Try to figure out who's side she's on."

"Surveil the highly trained spy. Got it." Naomi busied herself looking in her files and missed the look Jason shot her. He pulled out his files on Ministers Bellingham and Toot.

"Last thing before you get started boss. I looked into Richard too. For completeness. He's clean. He accessed nothing he shouldn't have, and nothing in his official or private communications raises a concern. Except of course his working for a Meridian company after hours." She shot a sympathetic look at Jason. "I understand our investigation might have brought his activities to the attention of the brass. I heard he's been stood down."

Jason nodded and focussed on pulling out his summary of the files that he had looked into. He felt his face burning, and his stomach churned. It wasn't his fault that Richard had done the wrong thing and been caught. And he should have been caught. The rules were there for a reason. So why did he feel so guilty?

"You did the right thing," Naomi said quietly.

Jason nodded and cleared his throat, signalling that he didn't want to talk about it.

"Okay. I had the politicians. I know more than I had ever hoped to know about both of our ministers. Minister Bellingham is ambitious and has her eyes on being prime minister one day. From what I can tell," he said, flipping through some of the pages of the file, stopping at a printout of parliamentary voting practices, "she is loyal to her party, but will side wherever she thinks the power is or with whomever she thinks will come out on top. She does seem to hate the Prime Minister, though. So if he's on the bad side—"

"Which he seems to be—"

"Which may be possible. Keep an open mind." He ignored Naomi's scoff. "Then she will be on our side."

"I mean, it sounds more like she's on her own side. Which is good, since she doesn't seem to want to be the dictatorial leader of a highly oppressed state, but may not be so useful if the queen is in her way once the Prime Minister has been dealt with."

Jason nodded. She was right, but he couldn't worry about that now. That was definitely a future-Jason problem.

"Toot does not seem to be a concern at the moment. He's not ambitious. Been a politician forever and seems to just be marking time until retirement."

"Could he be vulnerable to a bribe, then? Something to make retirement more comfortable?" Naomi asked.

"Possible," Jason said. "He does seem to be buddies with the Prime Minister. Not close, but of late he seems to be attending more of his functions, and has even voted with the Prime Minister a couple of times. Not for anything too controversial, but still. I'll put him in the 'watch' pile."

"Do we need to worry about the ambassadors?"

"I mean, yes, but I think we focus on them later. They may well be involved, but if they are, they are using one of the advisors. No one else has the necessary access. So it's most important that we find the tainted advisor first."

The phone on Jason's desk rang, and he answered it, putting Hudson on speakerphone. As was typical, Hudson jumped right to business without worrying about pleas-antries.

"Okay, so I've pulled all your system info as it relates to the timings of the attacks, like footage, sensor data, and guard rosters. There's definitely interference, and from the looks of things, it's got to be pretty high level."

"What kind of interference?" asked Naomi.

"You mentioned that there was no footage, but it's more complicated than that."

"Of course it is," muttered Jason.

"Your cameras and sensors go dark from ten minutes before the attacks until ten minutes after. I'm running some programs, but at the moment I can't figure out whether the interference occurred at the time of the attacks or was done to the footage and data after. Or both," he added.

"What do you mean by 'dark'?" Jason asked, trying not to be frustrated with Hudson's typical assumption that everyone knew what he knew.

"Just that, mate. The footage is black. It's there, as in it's not been cut out. The counter is running in the corner throughout, but the screen is blank and there is no sound. Same for the sensors throughout the castle; they just flatline during the relevant periods in the relevant areas. I can't tell if they actually failed at the relevant time or if they were working, but now the information is gone. For the attempt at the dinner, the entire palace goes out. I can't even use the blank spots to track the guy's path through the palace. I'm running a program to see if the information is still there, since if it's been wiped it can still be restored, but I'm not hopeful. I've never seen anything like this."

Jason and Naomi looked at each other with mirrored expressions of concern and dismay. Hudson was usually a magician with technology. Literally, since his ability was to interact with and control machines with his mind. He had a weird affinity with them. If he was having trouble retrieving the information, it likely could not be retrieved.

"Does it look like the work of someone with a similar ability to yours?" asked Naomi.

"Good question." Hudson paused, considering it. "It's possible. Again, I've not seen anything like this so am not aware of an ability that would let someone do it, but it's so seamless that it could well be someone who can connect to the system in a similar way as me."

After concluding their call with Hudson, Jason and Naomi sat in a contemplative silence, Naomi turning the mysterious key with her fingers.

"So we have a person who can move about the palace without being seen, who can interfere with our surveillance to enable others to move about relatively unseen, and while he or she doesn't yet seem to be making a genuine attempt to kill Her Majesty, he or she does at least seem to be probing our security and trying to separate her from those of us trying to protect her," Jason summarised with a fatalistic tone.

"Yep, that's about it," agreed Naomi. "So until we sort this out, we'll have to go back to basics with security. Line of sight presence, revealer with her at all times, and obviously one of us should probably be close by whenever possible."

Jason was grateful for Naomi's practical focus. He got them some more coffee as they settled in to work out a roster that enabled them to protect Lily, work together to find who was behind the plot, and possibly even get some sleep now and then.

21

Lily felt exactly as she had before every exam she had ever taken in her life. It was simply not possible that the requisite time had passed; she felt she should be more prepared than she currently was. Had it really been almost three months? How could it be time for her confirmation hearing already? In fact, she disbelieved it so much that she had even asked Addison that morning whether time moved differently here, wondering if Jenkins had been wrong or joking, though neither seemed likely.

Lily missed most of the last-minute advice that Giles and Addison rapid-fired at her. As they sped through the city, Lily was glued to her window marvelling at how different it looked during the day. The buildings and people felt so familiar, but had just enough differences to be unsettling. Like a weird dream that you couldn't quite remember.

She focussed on the different fashions and shops, trying to drown out Minister Bellingham's tirade about a newspaper article that had appeared on the front page that morning. A 'source close to the Prime Minister', that Minister Bellingham had assured them all was code for the Prime Minister himself, had said that there was little point in the council confirming Lily as queen of Highacre, since she had only been back for a few months and there had already been two attempts on her life. The suggestion was that she clearly wouldn't be around for long, and so this was all a waste of time and resources. Lily had been quite offended, pointing out that she had in fact survived both attempts, whereas Jason and Claire had been far more interested in how the Prime Minister knew about the first attempt.

The drive passed far too quickly, and before she was ready, Lily saw they had arrived at the Tower. Suddenly her mind was blank, save for the sheer terror at what was about to happen.

Jason helped her out of the car. Lily knew his eyes were darting everywhere behind his black sunglasses. He murmured into his sleeve and touched his ear, clearly nervous about the plan, which he had disagreed with.

Jason had wanted Lily to arrive in the undercover car park beneath the building, but Prime Minister Toth had insisted that 'Lily's people' should be allowed to see her, and Lily's advisors had decided it wasn't worth pushing back against the Prime Minister on the matter. Now that she thought about it, Lily couldn't remember who exactly had been the one to decide not to push back. It seemed like an awfully big risk just to keep the Prime Minister happy.

Lily glanced up at the Tower, the building where Parliament sat, which, true to its name, towered above her. One tall spire extended almost to the clouds and could be seen from miles around. Marble stairs led from the footpath up to the enormous white building set far back from the road. It had pillars framing its entrance that reminded Lily of Roman or American buildings, but they looked like they had been made with sandstone.

Above the entrance to the building were two elephant-like creatures depicted rearing up, along with words in a language that Lily didn't understand but was told said "tremble ye who enter and be awed", which seemed to Lily like an inappropriate quote for a government building.

Lily hadn't really noticed the shutter flashes that had been going off since the car pulled up, and as she noticed them, they suddenly seemed scary and oppressive. The public cheering, jeering, and general yelling seemed loud and sinister, and Lily immediately felt claustrophobic. Jason started steering Lily slowly up the stairs as Claire followed close behind, whispering to Lily to smile and wave.

Lily tripped on the stairs, only briefly stumbling before Jason caught her, but she couldn't help noticing that the shutter flashes increased in volume and wondered if something as simple as the queen stumbling was front-page news. *Maybe not newsworthy, but definitely front page for tabloids and magazines.*

Lily swore in her mind and forced herself to lift her head and walk with purpose. She even listened to Claire and acknowledged the crowd. After smiling and waving, she darted in to shake some hands and accept some gifts that the people had brought her, but before she could really engage, Jason was steering her back up the stairs and into the building.

Lily, flanked by her advisors, advanced at pace down the hallway, heels clicking on the tiles and the material of their suits swishing. Her advisors kept up a constant urgent murmur of last-minute advice, a mixture of what she should do and what she shouldn't do. Lily was already in such a heightened state of panic that all she heard was frantic white noise.

Don't get upset, don't be provoked, don't make up responses, don't panic. *Sure.* Lily felt drops of sweat making their way down her back in small individual trails and she thought she might throw up or faint. Or both.

Lily stopped in the middle of the hallway, causing her advisors to stop quickly, some of them tripping and running into the backs of other advisors. The persistent murmuring stopped, and they all stared at Lily.

"If I don't have it now," Lily said slowly in a calm, low voice, "I don't have it."

Silence followed her pronouncement. She knew they meant well, and they were nervous too, but she was the one in the firing line. As one, they all resumed walking, but more purposeful now. Heads high, they continued down the hallway towards the determination of Lily's fate.

The door shut behind Lily, severing her link to her advisors and the strength that she had been drawing from them. The room felt cold and sterile. Lily looked around and saw that it was a large, cavernous room, dark despite the lighting from the perfectly spaced chandeliers. There was a large, long bench in the front of the room that seated her would-be interrogators, and all the other politicians were sitting behind it in a semicircle of tiered seating.

Everyone in the room was facing one seat that was on a raised platform and reminded Lily of a witness chair in a courtroom. Rather than its stature being promoted by its height, as a throne would be, the effect that had been created was accusatory, as if the person who would sit there was to be judged. *Which is true.*

"Your Majesty, please, take a seat." The Prime Minister spoke into his microphone, and his voice boomed around the room. Lily looked for him and found him in the middle of the twelve people seated along the front bench.

Lily felt all the eyes in the room on her as she moved to her seat on the raised platform. The walk took forever, Lily feeling as if she was moving through quicksand, her one aim to ensure she did not trip as she had outside. She took the seat gingerly, noting that it was uncomfortable. She looked at the Prime Minister, who was staring intently back at her, the smile on his face not reaching his eyes.

Lily took several deep, slow breaths. *I can do this.* She had learned so much about herself over the past few months. She was stronger than she had thought she was, and smarter. A much better sword fighter, though of course, she had never considered herself to be a sword fighter at all.

Lily refocussed her thoughts and found even that was easier for her than ever before. She was in control. She might not remember all the facts and figures, or be able to recite the entire history of Highacre off the cuff like Giles, but what had surprised Lily the most was that she was calm under pressure. And it occurred to her that this had always been the case; she just hadn't realised it. She had always been better at exams than essays, and this was just like an exam. She was going to kill it. She looked up at the Prime Minister and smiled sweetly.

"Thank you, Your Majesty. Now. Normally a confirmation hearing is held in one of the more private committee rooms, where you would be questioned by the Council of Elders, who you see before you." He gestured grandly to his left and right. Most of the politicians nodded importantly, but a few smiled at Lily. "Following that meeting, a report is usually then delivered to the Parliament, who then vote on the recommendation. However, I thought, and the Parliament agreed, that the whole Parliament should be able to hear your responses directly, and so we have moved the confirmation hearing into this room.

"We will all vote immediately after the panel has finished questioning you. Each member of the Parliament has two buttons in front of them, and the results will be calculated immediately and will appear on the screen at your rear. Do you have any questions, Your Majesty?"

The Foreign Minister had warned Lily and the other

advisors that the Prime Minister was likely to try and change things up, both to shake and distract Lily, but also to try to ensure that the vote fell his way. Minister Bellingham had told Lily that the senior members of Parliament who made up the Council of Elders would likely either be supportive of Lily or fearful of a change in government, especially when the only current viable option was the Prime Minister, and most were wary of him because of his recent actions. Therefore, Minister Bellingham had predicted that the Prime Minister would try to involve the rest of the Parliament more directly, as that was where he felt he had the majority of his support. *Well, he certainly achieved that.*

In a way, Lily was glad he'd sprung it on her like this. There was no time to be nervous about it. Actually, had he told her a few days ago, he probably would have achieved the impact he was after, as she would have been stewing on it and probably would have worked herself into a nervous wreck. *Exams rather than essays.* That thought made Lily happy and gave her a small boost. She looked back at the Prime Minister with a demure smile that would have made Claire proud.

"No, Mr Prime Minister, thank you. Shall we begin?" Lily asserted her dominance. She was the queen. This was *her* Parliament. The smile left the Prime Minister's face completely, and he nodded curtly at a severe-looking man at the end of the bench to Lily's left.

The questions started and came in thick and fast. They were a mixture of inquiries about her opinion on past issues —ones that required Lily to have a solid knowledge of High-acre's political history—and questions about current policy that required Lily to both understand the current circumstances and give an appropriately circumspect response so as not to alienate half the Parliament, and everything in between.

Lily fell into the zone, recalling her lessons about the relevant subjects, as well as the hours spent with Claire learning how to hold herself and how best to present her answers. Minister Bellingham and Minister Toot were both on the panel and gave Lily relatively straightforward questions, but they could only ask one question each, and the other members did not hold back. Predictably, the Prime Minister went last.

"Your Majesty, I would be interested to hear your views on my proposal regarding the royal family and possible new methods for succession." He sat back in his chair, smiling at Lily and lacing his fingers over his plump stomach.

Lily returned his smile and considered his question. Addison had briefed Lily well on the Prime Minister's plan to abolish the monarchy and install himself as Highacre's first president.

"Well, Mr Prime Minister, I believe that any system of government should be that which best serves the people and the national objectives. I also believe that it's never good enough to keep any system or practice because of sentimentality and tradition, or because it is simply the way it has always been done." Lily paused and looked around the room.

"You have all been selected by the people of Highacre to represent their interests and govern for the good of the country. I, of course, have not been chosen by the people of Highacre. However, my duty by virtue of my birth is to act in the peoples' best interests, and to protect them.

"Is it in the people of Highacre's best interest to significantly alter the system of government? The truth is, I don't know. How could I? But I also don't think it could properly be said that this was something that they contemplated when electing any of you. And I think that it also follows that none of you could be completely sure that it is in the people's best interests. Well," Lily reconsidered, "you may, of course, *think* it is in their best interests, but I believe that you have a responsibility to ask them. That *we* have a responsibility to ask them.

"Therefore, Mr Prime Minister, in answer to your question, I am interested in your ideas about a new system of government. I believe it is healthy to consider and discuss new ways of doing things. And if the people of Highacre themselves wish to pursue a new system of government, I would support them and do whatever was in my power to make it so."

A somewhat stunned silence followed Lily's answer. Clearly, no one had expected that response. The Prime Minister recovered himself quickly.

"Yes, well, thank you, Your Majesty. An admirable response, particularly from someone so new to Highacre. Ladies and gentlemen." He quickly turned and addressed the floor of the Parliament. "You have heard Her Majesty's answers to our questions, and now the power is yours. You have two buttons in front of you. One will allow you to vote to confirm Her Majesty as the queen of Highacre, and the other will let you register your support for change for the good of Highacre. Vote now!"

Lily's face flushed with anger at the Prime Minister's attempt to influence the vote, but otherwise steeled herself not to react. Minutes seemed to take hours as the room busied themselves with deciding her fate. Lily felt bizarrely like a reality show contestant. Would she lose, or win the grand prize? Perhaps the best she could hope for was to progress to the next round.

It struck Lily definitively that she truly did want to be queen. The idea that in a couple of minutes she might be told it was no longer a possibility made her feel physically ill. Like she had let the people of Highacre down. They were counting on her to protect them from the Prime Minister, and she felt a strong sense of responsibility to them. She thought of the families in the pub. Of Rita potentially being conscripted. Had she done enough?

Suddenly, both all too soon and after what felt like an age, the Prime Minister rose again and announced that the voting was complete, then theatrically gestured to the screen behind Lily.

Lily heard the gasps as she turned to look. The numbers were close—only five votes separated the results. She heard the applause before she was able to comprehend which way the vote had gone, and wasn't sure if it was celebrating her win, or her demise.

As the screen behind Lily lit up announcing her successful confirmation, the Prime Minister, red-faced with anger, stood and settled the room.

"Colleagues, please. I feel it important to note that yes, Her Majesty is biologically the deceased king's daughter. And yes, Lady Octavia's report confirms that she has magical power. But it is certainly concerning to me that, in these troubled times, Her Majesty is yet to manifest any actual magical abilities."

How does he know that?

The room descended into animated discussion at this revelation. The Prime Minister letting them talk amongst themselves, nodding and looking about the room self-righteously.

As the talk died down, the Prime Minister made a show of calling for silence before adding, "I remind you all that the confirmation process does not require Her Majesty to have abilities, just magical power."

The room burst again into concerned whisperings, and this time the Prime Minister quickly called for quiet.

"In these dark days, Highacre needs to be at its most powerful. Indeed, this is why Her Majesty's family has ruled for so many years. They were the most magically powerful family Highacre has ever known." The Prime Minister was laying his admiration for Lily's dead family on a little too thickly, and by inference his sadness at their loss.

"It is for this reason," the Prime Minister said, raising his voice a notch to silence the few whispers that continued, "that I now, in the presence of you, my esteemed colleagues, invoke the Trials."

There was a collective intake of air, and the room began babbling excitedly again. Lily had no idea what this meant, but the entire Parliament seemed to like it. She watched as the council began talking to each other in urgent whispers, some even getting up and walking around to the front of their bench so they could all discuss the Prime Minister's invocation.

After what felt like an age, one of the council members, a thin, wiry lady, stood up, and a hush fell over the chamber. She nodded at the Prime Minister, and Lily had a distinct feeling that she would not like what the woman had to say.

"The council acknowledges the Prime Minister's invocation of the Trials. We have concluded that the confirmation of Her Majesty will be subject to her successful completion of the Trials." The woman sat back down without once looking at Lily.

Lily was ushered out of the chamber and into an anteroom, where her advisors were waiting. They gushed about her performance until Lily silenced them, demanding to know what the Trials were.

"Er, the Trials," stammered Giles, "are an ancient method of determining whether someone has abilities and, if so, what they are. They were in vogue for a while hundreds of years ago when an unpleasant sect tried to challenge the detector for the privileged position they hold in society because of their gift."

"And why were they abolished?"

"Well, some found them quite... er... barbaric."

Lily tried to process this information, her fists clenching. "So first we all bust our arses to make sure I can pass this confirmation hearing, and I do, and now there's another hoop to jump through? Why hasn't anyone mentioned these 'Trials' before? Surely you might have expected him to pull something like this? And what's next, then? I pass the Trials and suddenly there's some 'Ordeals' that I need to complete?"

"Oh no, they abolished the Ordeals *centuries* ago," said Minster Toot casually, sipping whiskey and sitting comfortably in an armchair. Lily was distracted from her rant, wondering yet again where his whiskey had come from. She couldn't see a drinks trolly in the room. Did the minister have a magical ability to conjure whiskey at will? Lily found herself slightly envious.

"Your Majesty," said Addison in a friendly tone. She reached for Lily's arm, then seemed to think the better of it. "The Trials haven't been around for almost a hundred years, and the invocation of them in the way the Prime Minister has just done exists in statute merely because no one has actively repealed the law. But you're right, we should have thought of everything."

Addison apologised in such a genuine way that Lily's annoyance at her advisors melted immediately, and she even felt bad for having expected them to have foreseen the Prime Minister's actions. She sighed. "Alright, well, we'd better start preparing."

22

LADY OCTAVIA

LADY OCTAVIA HAD BEEN STILL in her chair for a long time. Unmoving, she hunched over an ancient text, surrounded by scrolls, books, and various writings. The single candle she had lit had melted to an inch-high nub without her noticing. She finally reached the end of the tome she was reading. Some of her predecessors were overly wordy. Really, all one needed to do when recording a prophecy was to ensure the salient points were easily discernible to those who would read about them later. Flowery language was completely unnecessary, and if she read one more prophecy written in rhyming couplets, she might set fire to it.

She pushed the book away and picked up a significantly shorter scroll and read it quickly, giving it a satisfied nod. Short, sharp, to the point. World in peril, chosen one to protect it, chosen one is Lily.

Lady Octavia frowned. If she was reading these correctly, and she had no doubt she was because Lady Octavia knew, without false modesty, herself to be one of the greatest minds Highacre had ever seen, then Lily was the subject of no less than one hundred and eighty-three prophecies recorded over the last several hundred years. No one person had ever even come close to being the subject of as many prophecies. It was rare to find two about the same person, but Lady Octavia was certain that the 'chosen one' in each of the recordings that she had found and studied over the past couple of months was the same person. And that person was Lily.

Lady Octavia sat back in her chair, letting out a breath with a small sigh. She had hoped to find more answers than questions, but that hadn't been the case. It seemed odd that Lily could be the single subject of so many prophecies over the years, but that no other detector had recognised that the prophecies all referred to one person. Confident as she was in her intellect and abilities, she also knew that her predecessors had all been wise people. They should not have missed something this simple. Something this big.

She looked around the library where she had now spent the best part of a month, having first located all the prophecies that she recalled and thought might be relevant. How many had she missed? It was just so much work for one person, but that had always been the case.

She closed her eyes and remembered the fateful day that they had brought her before her generation's detector. He had been an old man. Unthinkably old to the then four-year-old Octavia. She had been focussed on his skin, so wrinkled and thin it had felt like paper. He had held her on his knee and looked into her eyes. His eyes had surprised her. A brilliant blue. They were at complete odds with his body. So young, full of life and mischief.

"You are special, little one," he had said, and her parents had gasped. "You are like me."

Four little words, and her parents had collapsed into tears. Little Octavia hadn't known what was wrong, but she had cried too. It was odd; she had been so focussed on her parents in that moment, and now she couldn't even remember their faces. She knew now the anguish had come from the fact that the old detector had identified Octavia as his replacement and this, for her parents, had started a countdown on when she would be taken from them.

Her mother had, from that day, distanced herself from her daughter, who had not understood why and had cried each night from the sting of rejection. When Lady Octavia looked back now, she was happy with her life, had no regrets, and was proud to be a detector, but she still occasionally felt resentful that her mother had not fought to keep her.

She would not have succeeded, of course. Detectors were taught many secrets from a young age, and as such could not simply return home, where they might tell their parents. And so, on her fifth birthday, clutching the cloth doll that her father had thrust into her hands, trying and failing to hide his tears, little Octavia had gone with the old man, and had not seen her parents again.

It had been strange, at first, living in the large, dusty house with the old man. The wind got in through all the cracks and howled and moaned and made everything cold. But the old man had been kind and had told her his name was Theodore and they were going to be friends.

He taught Octavia how to identify other people's abilities in general, and how to identify specifics, such as whether a mental power was mind control as opposed to mind reading.

He also shared great secrets with her. The first was that she had more than one special ability. "This is very special and very secret," Theodore had told Octavia. "Everyone knows you can see their abilities, but no one knows you can see their dreams."

"Cool!" said Octavia, and Theodore had smiled.

"Very cool."

He taught her how to visit people's dreams. She enjoyed it mostly. She would appear in their minds, invisible and unknown to them, and could walk around and watch and listen as if she were really there. Sometimes the dreams were weird, or downright scary. She didn't like those, but Theodore was with her, and he told her that sometimes the most unpleasant ones were the most important.

The second secret was that they were not the only special people. There were three people per generation that had unique abilities. Detectors, soothsayers, and reassigners. The detector and the soothsayer worked together, sort of.

"We get to be told what our role is, Octavia, and with that comes great responsibility and expectation, as well as loneliness."

Octavia had nodded wisely, gripping her doll tighter.

"But the oracle, while they are every bit as important as we are, they never get to know."

Theodore explained that the soothsayer, who was referred to as the oracle by the detectors, could see the future, but only in their dreams. It was almost unheard of for an oracle to remember their prophetic dreams, but those who did usually wrote them off since they always required interpretation.

"That must be our job!" little Octavia had said excitedly.

"Right again! You are very smart, little one." Theodore smiled back at her. "Our job is to identify the oracle and then visit their dreams regularly. We write their dreams down. You will soon get the hang of identifying the prophecies from the rest, and then you will interpret them to discover what is to come."

Theodore told her that over time, detectors had discovered that prophetic dreams have their own language.

Dreams about alligators almost always meant that the crops would be bountiful; dreams about needing the bathroom meant that conflict was imminent. And so on. Octavia had considered this and then asked who they told about the prophecies. Theodore had smiled at her and simply told her they were sworn to use the knowledge of the future 'for the good of all the world' which he explained meant that they could use the information to try to avoid a war, but not to favour one side in a conflict.

It had taken Lady Octavia a number of years to query this premise.

"But to whom are we sworn?" she had asked Theodore one day, as they walked along through the field at the top of the cliffs, the ocean crashing against the rocks below.

He had smiled his toothy grin at her and simply said, "The reassigner."

Theodore had refused to be drawn in on the matter further, insisting that Octavia focus on her lessons, but that evening after dinner, as they sat by the fire with mugs of hot chocolate, Theodore said it was time for a story.

Octavia loved story time with Theodore. Instead of telling her a tale, he showed her. As the room around them faded to black, Theodore set the scene.

"Years and years ago, a boy was born in a small village in the north. It was common in the village for people to discover their powers in the old way. On their own. The detector rarely went to tiny villages like this one, and the villagers saw little reason to visit the city. So when little Cyril failed to manifest any abilities by the time he was eight, the villagers just decided he was slow, and saw no reason to ask the detector to examine him."

Octavia looked around in wonder as the village materialised around them. It was as if they were there, but invisible. Just like the dreams they visited. Life continued around them ignorant of their presence. She saw the young Cyril in front of her, playing on his own. Some children were playing together in a field just outside the half wall that surrounded the village, and the adults that passed Cyril shot him sympathetic smiles.

"Had Cyril been born in the city," Theodore said, "his family would have rushed him to the detector with excitement. They would have been hoping that he had some new, not-before-seen ability, and that this was why nothing had manifested."

Octavia watched as four boys approached Cyril, sniggering at him, a mean glint in their eyes. The largest of the bullies picked up a small rock with his mind and threw it at Cyril, catching him on the shoulder and startling him.

"Oh dear, did I scare you, simple Cyril?" he taunted the smaller boy.

"No, I—"

The large boy sent another rock flying, hitting Cyril square in the forehead. The four boys fell about laughing as Cyril pulled out a handkerchief and dabbed at the small cut the rock had left.

The large bully concentrated again, but nothing happened. Frustrated, he stared pointedly at a stone a few feet from Cyril. Cyril watched him, intrigued, and then suddenly the stone flew up and hit the bully on the head. The bullies fled, the largest panicking, and Cyril resumed playing, a large smile on his face.

"He's a reassigner!" said Octavia excitedly.

"Exactly," Theodore said with a smile. "After that, Cyril was treated with more respect in the village, and he began to experiment with the bounds of what he could do. Cyril found he could take other people's abilities for himself, or give them to another person. There didn't seem to be any limit to his gift. If Cyril had been a power-hungry maniac, he could have travelled around Highacre, stolen everyone else's abilities and crowned himself king.

"But Cyril was a gentle boy, and though he liked to think a lot about the possibilities connected to his ability, he was content with the simple life of his village. This was not to be his future, however. Though word of his gift never reached the capital, Cyril's village being so isolated, the detector saw him in the oracle's dreams. The king sent his advisors and the detector to travel to the tiny village and assess this little boy."

Octavia looked around in fascination. They were now in a small hut with an older Cyril who was being poked and prodded by a man wearing fancy robes. Five similarly dressed men and women were standing, slightly cramped, at the other end of the hut, looking about their surroundings with disdain.

The man pulled down one of Cyril's eyelids and peered into his eye. "He can definitely reassign abilities," he announced, adding under his breath, "but we already knew that."

The man tilted Cyril's head to the side and examined his ear, before telling Cyril to stick out his tongue and staring down his throat.

"What's he doing?" asked Octavia.

"Examining him for abilities," replied Theodore.

"But we don't have to do all that to see someone's abilities."

"No, but back in those days, people needed more of a show to convince them that detectors knew what they were doing."

"He's also immortal," announced the detector. The group of advisors immediately put their heads together, discussing this revelation in hushed tones.

"Am I really?" Cyril asked.

"To a point," the detector said quietly, casting a quick look at the advisors to check that they weren't listening. "You won't die of old age as the rest of us will. But you may still succumb to unnatural death. You can be murdered, for example, but failing that, you will live forever."

Octavia watched as Cyril exited the hut and joined the detector and king's advisors as they got into carriages and rode back to the palace. They introduced Cyril to the king and the detector told the king what he had told the advisors, once again omitting Cyril's vulnerability.

"The king offered Cyril a place in his court," Theodore resumed his narration. "Cyril, used to living in a small hut, was intoxicated by the extravagance of the royal lifestyle and agreed. However, Cyril was unaware, from his relatively isolated village life, that Highacre at the time was on the brink of civil war. A challenger for the throne was making the king's life difficult, and the king saw in Cyril a powerful weapon.

"Conflict broke out and Cyril was sent forth, both to the front lines and to the homes of the king's enemies, and ordered to take their abilities and reassign them to the king's men. Cyril did so but had not been prepared to see the now-defenceless people whose abilities he had taken slaughtered before his eyes."

Octavia found herself back in the king's throne room. The king was sitting lazily on his throne. Advisors flanked him and eager nobles watched greedily from the main floor.

". . . and give the duke of Irvine the ability to fly."

"Your Majesty," interjected an advisor. "The duke already has the ability to levitate."

"Does he?" the king chuckled. "Oh well, then give it to Count Schriver."

"No."

The stunned silence that met Cyril's refusal was laced

with danger. Several of the king's courtiers took a step backwards, while others inched towards the doors.

"No?" the king glared at Cyril.

"No."

The king's face became an ugly, splotchy crimson. "You
ungrateful backward little— We. Are. At. War. You will do
what I tell you to do."

"I will no longer enable massacres. It's not right."

"Not right?" The king's rage boiled over. Some courtiers
left the room, others subtly ensured their fellows stood
between themselves and the king.

"Boy, we are fighting for our very survival. Those
people are marked for death. Whether they die quickly in a
group or individually over time, die they shall. Without you,
their abilities die with them, wasted. If you transfer them to
our side, we shall win the war much faster and this will
mean less people will die."

Cyril considered the king's argument. "I hear the logic
in your words, my liege. However, the faces of those who
have died as a direct consequence of my actions remain
with me. I see them in my dreams, and they haunt my
waking hours. My assistance may make your war more efficient, but I don't think that makes my actions right."

"Lock him up!" the king roared. "We'll see how long it
takes for you to change your mind."

The scene surrounding Octavia became one of a
dungeon cell. It took her a little while to pick out Cyril, who
was sitting against a wall, and was now so dirty he blended
in. He had grown a scraggly beard and was thinner than
before. He had clearly been there a while, and Octavia
wondered how long.

The door opened and the detector entered, carrying a
small candle. He ordered the guard to leave them and the
guard did so, albeit reluctantly. Once the detector was sure

the guard had left, he pulled a small husk of bread from one sleeve and a flask of water from the other. Cyril gratefully accepted the gifts and polished them off before the detector could warn him not to rush.

"I'm sorry to have put you here my boy," the detector said eventually.

"You didn't. It was the king."

The detector smiled sadly at Cyril. "Yes, but it was I who told the king of your ability. I knew what he would demand of you. It's my fault you languish in this cell."

"It's not so bad," Cyril said simply, looking around. "Though I did want to ask; is starvation an unnatural death, or will I just survive in here forever?"

"What if I said you didn't have to worry about either? What if I can get you out?"

"But where would I go? I can't go back to the village."

"No, my dear boy. I will help you vanish."

Octavia watched as the detector visited Cyril again, but this time with another person.

"You remember Lord Fontain, don't you Cyril? He has a wonderful ability. He can alter memories."

Without further explanation required, Cyril took Lord Fontain's ability and used it on the lord and the guards, and any others who interrupted his escape. They borrowed some horses and rode across the countryside until they arrived at a large house atop some cliffs.

"That's our house!" said Octavia excitedly.

"It is indeed," said Theodore, smiling.

The men entered. Octavia looked around in wonder, taking in the run-down house and gaining a new appreciation for the current state of it.

"We'll hide here until the war's over," the detector told Cyril as he lit some candles and started a fire in the fireplace. "Without you, the king will lose, and his brother will take the throne. I'll let the new king settle in before I approach him with our terms."

"How do you know he'll accept?"

"Because I've seen it." The detector looked at Cyril's blank expression. "In the oracle's dreams."

"What were their terms?" Octavia had asked Theodore.

"They agreed that the reassigner, the detector, and the oracle should be neutral and only use their abilities for good. The detector would now keep the existence of the oracle a secret. In time, memory of the oracle would fade, and the detector would simply hold themselves out to be extraordinarily wise.

"The reassigner would act as a check on the detector. If the detector were to stray, or someone sought to influence them, then the reassigner would take the detector's ability. The detector would tell everyone that Cyril had died—noting that everyone else who knew of his immortality would perish in the final battle—and keep his existence secret. With Cyril safe, a new reassigner should not emerge. Cyril could then fade into the reclusive lifestyle he still enjoys today, where he also remains protected from attempts on his life."

Octavia watched their plan play out. The detector rode to the palace for an audience with the new king. He eagerly accepted the proposed terms, perhaps inspired by the hints dropped by the detector about important prophecies that he had knowledge of. True to his word, the detector also reported that Cyril had perished.

The throne room faded, and Octavia found herself back in front of the fireplace.

"Now we two are the only people who know that he is still alive today."

The overhead light came on, bringing Lady Octavia out of her reminiscing as if she'd had a glass of ice water splashed on her face. She blew out the candle and tidied the prophecies into some semblance of order. How was any one person supposed to achieve so much? And, though she liked Lily well enough, how was that young girl supposed to do all of this? She was a nice girl, but 'nice' wasn't enough.

"She's just so young," Lady Octavia muttered to herself.

"Age is but a number," a small voice said gently from behind Lady Octavia, careful not to startle her.

"You needn't worry, I had a hint you were coming when the light came on." Lady Octavia smiled down at the little girl. She was small for her age, and thin. Her arms and legs looked like twigs that would break at the slightest pressure. Lady Octavia liked her successor.

"And I wasn't referring to physical age. You and I both know that means very little. I just worry that she hasn't had the life experience. She lacks the self-confidence and, well, cunning that she will need. She could do with a dose of your ability."

"I did grow up fast," the little girl said. "She will have to as well."

"Yes, but she can't just quickly live a few lifetimes like *some* people."

The little girl returned Lady Octavia's smile, and they walked through the library and out into the sitting room, where a cosy fire was crackling away in front of two chairs.

"The Prime Minister invoked the Trials," Lady Octavia said, lowering herself into her chair. "As we knew he would. But the good thing is that I will have unrestricted access to train Her Majesty, and her advisors won't be splitting her attention as they would have while preparing her for the confirmation."

"Which we know she would have failed if she had been

taken with the excitement of learning her abilities," added the girl.

"Precisely. And a bit of positive stress can't hurt. It might cause Her Majesty to get her shit together."

Lady Octavia saw the girl cringe at the curse.

"Oh, I'm sorry, I forget you don't like vulgar language."

"Well, I am only five years old." She sipped her hot chocolate, summonsed from the kitchen. "The time pressure will be useful." The young girl frowned, putting the mug on her side table and worrying a thread on her sleeve.

"Go on, out with it."

"I visited the oracle last night."

"Upsetting, was it? Oh, you didn't see her fantasising about the Meridian ambassador again, did you?"

"No!" the girl flushed with embarrassment.

"That'd be enough to put anyone off their chocolate."

"It's not funny." The girl crossed her arms and sulked.

"Oh, come on now. I'm sorry, just trying to cheer you up." She smiled at the little girl, a twinkle in her eyes. The girl couldn't keep it up and smiled briefly before taking her mug and drinking a big gulp.

"I saw you die."

23

Addison left Lily the minute they returned to the palace from her confirmation hearing to track down Lady Octavia. She had eventually returned to the Lodge and informed Lily and the advisors that she was unable to get a hold of her. Her advisors then decided amongst themselves that they would take on Lily's training in Lady Octavia's absence.

"Tell me about these Trials," Lily said loudly, cutting off their discussion. She did want to know about the Trials, but she was also tired of her advisors assuming control.

"They originate from the tactics of Meridian witch hunters," Claire explained. "Centuries ago, some early Highacren travellers and explorers found themselves on the wrong end of some fairly conservative Meridians, who, having witnessed feats previously thought impossible, had then travelled throughout Meridia enthusiastically searching for other witches to torture and kill.

"What piqued Highacre's interest was that one of the Highacren travellers seemed to have developed a previously unknown ability to freeze things when the witch hunters tried to burn them."

"Not that Meridians were torturing Highacre's citizens?" Lily asked.

Minister Bellingham waved Lily's question away. "Conflict between Meridia and Highacre is not uncommon."

"Highacren scientists wondered if Highacrens had several latent magical abilities that could be awoken by extreme circumstances, or if the torture in this case had caused the spontaneous development of a completely new magical ability. They sought to discover if the employment of these and similar tactics, though perhaps crude, barbaric, and largely ineffectual when wielded by the Meridians against their own people, could see most Highacrens develop multiple abilities." Claire concluded.

"So, they just started setting people on fire?" Lily asked, slightly alarmed.

"They tried several witch hunter's tactics. Burning, freezing, suffocating, drowning, intense pain—"

"Okay, yes, I get it," interrupted Lily.

"—and some of their own design. They ultimately found that significant stress tended to result in the development or appearance of abilities that related directly to the stress. Ultimately, the scientists concluded that the range of traumas that an individual would have to be subjected to in order to cover the field of possible abilities outweighed the benefit, and noted that there were some abilities that couldn't really be tested for. Mind reading, for example, rarely manifests because of one's finger being amputated—"

"Yes, thanks Claire," said Lily quickly, feeling that the young woman's enthusiastic interest in the subject was slightly unnerving.

"Unsurprisingly these tests were not favoured by the sovereign," Claire continued.

"Because they didn't like their citizens being horrifically tortured?" Lily asked.

"Because their claim to the throne rested in no small part on the bloodline having multiple powers. If everyone suddenly had several abilities, why should your family rule?" Claire said simply. Lily shifted uncomfortably. "And so the Trials were created. Under certain specific circumstances, someone could be put to the test to determine their abilities and worth."

"Worth?" Lily queried, objecting to the term. "So what were the circumstances?"

"The most common were challenges to the fitness of a monarch, or potential monarch, to rule, and convicted criminals seeking to have the punishments of life imprisonment or death overturned. The argument being that if they were particularly magically powerful, there was a greater benefit to Highacre to rehabilitate them back into society."

"Wouldn't being more magically powerful make them more dangerous?"

"There were a number of other boxes they would have to tick to be released, but none of that mattered as there's not one recorded case of a criminal succeeding at the Trials."

"Oh."

Addison then explained that there were three Trials; the Trial of Courage, the Trial of Endurance, and the Trial of Illusions. They were all conducted one after the other, and there was no limit on how long they could go for. The longest the Trials had lasted, Addison told Lily, was three weeks.

"So if I fail the Trials, I can't be queen, right?" Lily asked, fearing some previously unmentioned sixteenth-century punishment that would also be attached to failure.

"If you fail the Trials, you will die," proclaimed Minister Toot as he sat dramatically in an armchair, having just somehow topped up his whiskey.

"What? Isn't that a bit extreme?"

"It is tradition." Minister Toot nodded solemnly, drinking from his glass, the ice clinking softly.

"No, no, really Jeremy." Addison hurried to Lily's side to reassure her. "They haven't killed anyone for failing the Trials since the late thirteenth century."

"Oh? Shame, really," said Jeremy Toot, thoughtfully. "It'd make the whole affair much more exciting."

<hr>

A couple of days later, Lily found herself outside in the grounds with some of her advisors, the ambassadors to court, and of course Edmund, who insisted on doing 'everything in his power' to help Lily prepare for the Trials. They were all relaxing on the lawn, with each participant taking a turn to use their abilities, or in the case of Ava and Alexei, their implant and enchantments respectively, to provoke a magical reaction in Lily. So far it wasn't really working, however, it was enjoyable lazing around in the sun, and no one seemed too worried about the lack of progress.

Edmund had initially taken the opportunity to impress Lily. However, his ability turned out to be the control of small birds and between Alexei's laughter and the women proclaiming his tiny-winged army cute, he had become quiet and now sat with Addison discussing Highacren history.

He was clearly still paying attention though, as Lily saw him react when Claire suggested Ava and Lily move away from the group to practice with minimal distractions. She thought he might protest, however he simply relaxed and continued his discussion. *Maybe this arrangement will work after all.*

Claire took the young women into another area of the

gardens. It was secluded and peaceful, surrounded by hedges, and had a few benches and some pretty flower beds. A small pond was in the middle of the area, and Lily thought she saw some small fish in it.

"Are you going to chaperone?" Ava asked Claire with a smile.

"No, I think I can leave you to it."

"Even with my being a foreigner?" Ava said 'foreigner' with mock distaste.

"Oh, if you turn out to have nefarious motives, I'm confident we can take you," Claire said it with a smile to Ava, but her tone had just enough iron to make the threat clear. Ava just continued to smile at Claire and watched her walk away in amused fascination. She continued to stare after Claire disappeared from sight.

"Huh. She really left! I was sure she was going to do that chameleon thing and come back to keep an eye on you."

"Do I need to have an eye kept on me?"

"No," said Ava, sitting on a patch of grass in the sun. "But surely they should monitor my intentions."

Lily sat next to Ava, and the two remained in comfortable silence, lying down on their backs and drinking in the warmth.

"Do you feel it?" asked Ava after a while, her eyes closed.

"Feel what?"

"Your power."

When Ava had used her implant to scan Lily earlier, Lily had found she could connect to her power more easily. She checked now, and it was the same. When Ava used her implant, it was like her power was already on, rather than her having to reach for it and engage it.

"Yep, it's there."

"I've done my job, then. You're welcome."

Lily smiled. She was enjoying relaxing with Ava, particularly with the pressure she now constantly felt to develop her abilities. When she was with Ava, somehow that all fell away.

"So, how are you doing? Really," Ava asked.

"I'm okay. Mainly just frustrated. Everyone keeps telling me I have all this power and should have all these amazing magical talents, but I can't do anything. And when they try to help, they act like it should be as simple as breathing, but I just don't know how to do it. And then I just worry that I'm going to let everybody down."

Ava rolled over onto her stomach and looked at Lily. "You need to stop putting so much pressure on yourself. I know nothing about how to use magical abilities, but I know that if you're under too much pressure, it's difficult to do anything well."

"Thanks, Ava," said Lily.

"Yeah, I know, it's easy enough for me to say." She sat up and fiddled with a leaf. "I look at it kind of like walking. It's easy for all of your advisors, 'cause they learned magic when they were kids. When you look at kids learning to walk, it's fun. An adventure. And if they fall down, that's okay, they just get up and try again. But when you think about adults who are injured and have to learn to walk again, it's harder. They get frustrated. They know what they should be able to do, and the ramifications if they can't."

Lily remembered Ava had been in the military, and wondered if she was thinking about friends who had been hurt.

"Why don't you relax into feeling your power, really connect with it, and then reach out with it and see if something manifests?"

"I thought you knew nothing about magical abilities?"

"I don't. But it sounded good, right?"

Lily threw some leaves at Ava, who batted them away good-naturedly.

"Do you have a better idea?"

"Well, no..."

"Okay then, let's give it a go. I'm terrified that Claire will come back and think we've just been goofing off."

Lily laughed at Ava's mock fear and then stood up, shook herself off, and prepared to concentrate. Ava told her to close her eyes, and she did so, feeling a little silly and self-conscious as she did. Ava moved behind her, murmuring for her to focus on her centre. Lily felt Ava's hands touch her gently on her back and high on her stomach, just below her breasts.

"Wait, I feel something. It's like hands are touching me..."

"Shut up and focus."

Lily focussed on the feeling. It was different to how she normally felt when she connected to her power. She felt light, anxious, but not in a bad way. Like butterflies were in her chest.

"Keep focussing," murmured Ava, "I'm going to use my implant to scan you."

Lily suddenly felt her power explode within her. She focussed on it and tried to maintain her control over it. Comfortable with that, she then gently tried to increase and decrease the intensity. Excited when that worked, Lily reached out with it to see how far she could push it, and what would happen.

"I knew it! You *are* here," exclaimed Ava.

Lily opened her eyes and saw Claire had materialised, sitting on a bench off to her right, where she had apparently been for a while.

"I was just curious to see how you were progressing," said Claire innocently. "And whether you could see me with your implant."

Ava and Claire bantered back and forth, but Lily wasn't concentrating on them. She had stayed connected to her power despite the interruption, and she reached out with it now and found she still had the same control over it she'd had when focussing intently. She flexed it eagerly. Maybe she was getting the hang of this after all.

24

Lily ducked as a duster flew past her head.

"Your Majesty, the point is not for you to physically avoid the objects, but to deflect them magically."

"I know that Addison," said Lily, ducking again as a small ornament whizzed by her, urged on by Giles. "But in the absence of being able to do so, I'd really rather avoid being hit in the face."

"Maybe you should use more objects?" Addison suggested to Giles, who nodded and used his mind to gather all the small objects he could find in the Lodge. Before she could protest, he hurdled them all at Lily, who tried to duck and bat the objects away with her hands. Though she avoided most of them, a pen managed to break through her defences and smacked her on the nose.

"What is going on in here?"

All three turned, the expressions of guilty schoolchildren on their faces.

"Lady Octavia! You've returned!" said Addison excitedly, moving towards the older woman.

"Your powers of observation are astounding," said Lady

Octavia drily, keeping her eyes on Lily. "And what is it that I have interrupted you all doing in here?"

"We are training Her Majesty for the Trials," said Giles.

"Ah. I have not observed the Trials in some time, but I do not remember the part where small objects are tossed at the individual in question for them to avoid."

Giles and Addison flushed.

"Yes, well, Her Majesty is yet to manifest any powers, and in your absence..." Giles began pointedly.

"Thankfully, as you have observed, I have returned. Your Majesty," Lady Octavia called to Lily sharply, "with me, please."

She turned and walked out of the room without waiting for Lily. Lily watched her leave and realised with a start that she was meant to follow. Throwing an apologetic look to Giles and Addison, Lily hurried after Lady Octavia.

After a few minutes, they reached their destination; the outdoor courtyard. Lily was embarrassed to discover she was slightly out of breath, whereas the older woman seemed perfectly fine.

"Now, we must get down to it. With the Trials approaching, we have little time."

"Where have you been?" Lily asked boldly.

"I have had business to attend to—"

"With the oracle?"

"Yes. Now—"

"What's the oracle? Or who?"

Lady Octavia looked at Lily with an exasperated expression. "Your Majesty," she began in a patient voice that sounded as if it was hard to maintain, "we really don't have a lot of time between now and the Trials, and we need to maximise our time together to best prepare you."

Lily noticed that Lady Octavia seemed awfully

focussed on the lack of time available and wondered why she seemed so agitated. Allowing that they really hadn't spent that much time together, Lady Octavia had not struck Lily as the type of person to become unduly stressed.

"Your Majesty," Lady Octavia got Lily's attention again, and Lily realised she had become lost in her thoughts. Lady Octavia sighed. "You will be told everything you need to know when you need to know it, but for now, we must train."

Lily was hesitant to delay what she had been longing for since she arrived in Highacre, but she couldn't help but clarify, "So just to be clear, you're saying that I will be told who or what the oracle is at some point?"

"Focus!" Lady Octavia snapped. With a sigh, Lily meekly walked to the centre of the courtyard, where Lady Octavia was pointing.

"Now," said Lady Octavia in a more subdued voice, wearing an expression that was somewhat apologetic for the outburst, but that also indicated she would broker no further deviations from the task at hand. "How far have you progressed?"

Lily explained to Lady Octavia that she could now access and control her inner power, but so far had failed completely in her attempts to manifest any abilities. At Lady Octavia's order, Lily demonstrated her control over her power.

"But see?" Lily gesticulated wildly and grandly. "No abilities. Nothing. It's *so frustrating*. Nothing anyone has done has made a difference. I just can't do magic. Something about being born and raised in another dimension must have stuffed me up. We just need to face it. I don't have any magical abilities. I'll never pass the Trials and if the Trials don't kill me, the assassin will. Or best case, I can just go home whenever they can get some more of that felixium stuff."

"Oh, pull yourself together."

"Excuse me?" Lily turned to look at Lady Octavia, stunned.

"People are depending on you, child. Millions of people. All of whom will suffer under the current regime and that idiot Prime Minister's warmongering. And none of whom have a handy porthole that they can just pop on through to safety and a warm meal. You have a duty to the people of Highacre, whether you like it or not. And to all the people who have been helping you. What about your advisors? Do you think the Prime Minister will leave them be after you toddle off home and abandon them to their fate?"

Lily gaped at Lady Octavia. She had certainly not been expecting that onslaught. But was the old woman right? Was she letting everyone down? She didn't want to leave Highacre, but if she had no magic... What more was she supposed to do?

"If everything is so dire, then surely someone as important and powerful as yourself should have been here, doing everything in your power to help me. But you've been... where? What have you been doing that is more important than this?" Lily asked.

Lady Octavia looked ready to respond, but her eyes suddenly softened, and she considered Lily with an almost maternal gaze. "A life in service is a very difficult thing, Your Majesty. Something I know well, and something you will most certainly discover."

Lily felt slightly wrong-footed about the direction the conversation had taken. She waited for Lady Octavia to continue, but the older woman seemed lost in her thoughts.

"What do you mean?" Lily asked eventually, trying to sound interested rather than demanding an answer.

"Oh, child," said Lady Octavia, calling two armchairs into existence and lowering herself into one. "In youth, you look for a cause. A purpose, the thing that will be your contribution to the world. But the more you dedicate yourself to that cause, the more you focus on being the one to see the outcome realised."

Lady Octavia removed her glasses and began cleaning them.

"The truth is that any cause worth serving will have longevity that far surpasses our tiny lives. The cause will always outlive its servants, but the servants rarely realise this until the end. The result is that we never achieve the version of success we chase." Lady Octavia rose from her chair and began to pace.

"The secret is that true success is being a good steward. Furthering your cause while it is yours to steer, and then ensuring that it survives beyond your time. You have much ahead of you, child. Much will be asked, and much will be taken. And you're very right. The least I can do is to help you as much as I can in the time we have."

Lily watched the older woman with concern. She suddenly seemed very old and tired, as if she had lived a thousand lives. The change was startling. Lady Octavia usually carried herself with the energy of a much younger woman and with a confidence that left no one with any doubt about who was in charge.

Lily envied her that. Her own presence didn't have the same effect. Not yet. *But I will.* Smarting though she was from Lady Octavia's earlier words, Lily knew they were true. She couldn't abandon her advisors, her people. There was no other option. She would do everything necessary to develop her powers.

Lily looked back at Lady Octavia, concerned. If she was going to get her magic to work, she would need Lady Octavia's head in the game.

Lady Octavia was lost in her thoughts. The girl who would be queen was right. She should have helped her more. But she had been so focussed on finding all the prophecies, thinking that would be vital to their success. And maybe it would be. Who knew? Not her, and as she now knew, she would not be around to discover if her time had been well spent, or whether she had wasted days, weeks, and months on a pointless pursuit and doomed the princess to die.

Her thoughts drifted to her discussion with the young girl. It felt like eons ago, but she supposed that any discussion of your own death must, by necessity, take on an ethereal quality.

I saw you die.

Lady Octavia had faltered uncharacteristically at the girl's pronouncement before falling back on the stiff upper lip that had seen her through the dark times in her life.

"Well, go on then," she had replied. "Don't leave me in suspense."

"It will be... sooner than anticipated."

Lady Octavia herself had witnessed the pronouncements of many people's demise in the oracle's dreams. And indeed, in many cases, she had subsequently witnessed the prophecies come true. *It is somewhat different when the death is your own.*

Lady Octavia knew she was not young and was under no false illusions about her longevity. Still, hearing of one's impending demise was sobering. Pulling herself back to the present with an effort, she realised Lily had asked her something.

"Hmmm?"

"I asked if you were alright. You seem... pensive."

Lady Octavia nodded. "A good term, and fitting in the circumstances. However, at present, reflection will not help us achieve our task. We have limited time, and so we had better get cracking."

25

AUSTIN

THE BARBELL CLANGED NOISILY in the empty gym as Austin racked his weights and reached for his water bottle. Normally, working out made him feel better, cleared his mind, and helped him relax. But lately, his head kept spinning busily and nothing he did seemed to quiet the buzzing.

He was a little worried when he'd been told that Her Majesty's training would be suspended in the lead up to the confirmation hearing. But he'd rationalised that this was reasonable. She had to study intensely to ensure that she could answer any question from the council, and it was entirely possible that some of the politicians would look to deliberately trip her up.

But now the hearing was over, and he was being told that she had to concentrate on the Trials and so her sessions would be reduced—and that others would join her for the few sessions she did have so she could both train with Austin and continue training for the Trials. It hadn't been lost on him that they had not offered him any one-on-one training with Her Majesty to help develop her abilities, as the other advisors had.

Austin lay back down on the bench and prepared to lift

the barbell again. He was being sidelined; he was sure of it. But why? Had they discovered his past? He had been haunted by those pesky rumours since the war, but they had dwindled to almost nothing over the past few years. Perhaps it had been premature to think they were gone.

Finishing his set, Austin got up from the bench, grabbed his towel, and wiped the sweat from his face. He needed to calm down. Surely, if Jason had heard the rumours, he would have sent Austin packing. There would have been some line about reducing the number of people with access to Her Majesty and he would have been stood down as non-essential. In a way, that would have been better, because then he would know what Jason knew and where he stood. In the back of his mind, he worried he was being sidelined because someone had discovered his current role. But it couldn't be that. If they knew what he was doing, what he had done, he would have likely been arrested, or worse.

Of course, even if they just dismissed him, he would lose the access to Her Majesty that he currently enjoyed. And the Patriot would not be happy about that. He kicked lightly at a kettlebell, pushing it with his foot until it almost toppled and then fell back into its upright position. Where was the Patriot, anyway? His sudden silence was another source of Austin's current stress. He hadn't received a note or letter from him in weeks. Was he upset? Had he somehow learned that Austin's privileged position in the palace and his access to Her Majesty had lessened? Did he think that this was because of some failure on Austin's part? Perhaps he was disappointed and thought Austin wasn't up to being his right-hand man after all. The thought made him sad. He felt the familiar feelings of failure surface and threw himself back down on the bench for another set, even though he hadn't completed his rest period.

Heaving the bar back onto the rack with a grunt,

Austin lay under it for a beat before getting up and packing away the weights. He had left a few notes for the Patriot over the last couple of weeks, just like he had been doing since before Her Majesty's return. Sure, lately it wasn't as valuable as his usual information, but it didn't appear that his notes had even been disturbed. To be fair, normally Austin wouldn't have bothered the Patriot with that level of stuff, but he was looking for some sign that he hadn't been abandoned now that his utility had evaporated.

He tried to reassure himself that there must be more links in the chain between him and the Patriot, and it was one of those links that was broken. Indeed, if the Patriot himself was wandering around the palace retrieving Austin's notes, then he wouldn't need Austin's insights in the first place.

Austin left the gym and headed to his room, located just down the hall. He entered his ensuite and disrobed for the shower, first trying steaming hot water, and then an ice-cold blast to clear his worries. Drying off, he tried not to be frustrated that his concerns remained. The irony that his usual routine, training Her Majesty, would have helped enormously to distract him was not lost on him.

Austin dressed in khakis and a red plaid shirt. Why he was dressing relatively formally, he did not know, other than the fact that a lifetime habit of dressing in a manner suitable for a military mess facility was difficult to break. He checked himself in the mirror and decided to go and see if his latest note had been taken, or at least looked at. No harm in checking, and really, what else was he going to do?

Turning to leave his room, Austin was stunned to see that an envelope had been pushed under his door. That definitely hadn't been there when he came in. He hurried and picked it up, opening his door and looking outside. He stood still, listening for the sound of footsteps that would tell him the deliverer was close by.

Nothing.

He stood a while longer than was necessary, then stepped back into his room and shut the door. He then pressed his ear to the door in case the mysterious postman had waited for him to return to his room before moving on.

Disappointed to have missed the drop, and perhaps his chance to come face-to-face with the Patriot himself, Austin turned his attention to the envelope. It was bare, and he opened it, careful not to damage whatever was inside.

He unfolded a note with familiar handwriting. It was from the Patriot; he had not been cast off after all!

Austin held the note with reverence, as if it were some lost, ancient text that could fall apart at any minute. His hands even shook slightly, his emotions a jumble of relief and excited anticipation. He took a second to calm his mind. He wanted to savour reading the note, and make sure he didn't miss any detail.

Exhaling shakily, Austin realised he had been holding his breath. He skimmed the note, checking to see if he was still in favour. Then he read through it again, more carefully. The Patriot apologised for his long silence and assured Austin that it was because of the requirement to go to ground for a bit, and nothing to do with Austin's work, which was, as always, an exemplar that the Patriot held up for the cause.

Austin didn't like to think himself the kind of person who needed praise. He had scorned those peacocks in the army who were always seeking commendations or medals. Austin had always thought a soldier's focus should be on his job. Nonetheless, much as he hated to admit it, his chest swelled with pride at the idea of the Patriot talking to the hierarchy and foot soldiers of the nationalist movement and extolling the virtues of Austin's work. He couldn't help but picture himself there with the Patriot, shrugging off the praise they would all be jealous of. *Just doing my job, no big deal.*

The Patriot foreshadowed to Austin that big things were coming and Austin should be ready. It was imperative that he ensured he remained at the palace, and with enough trust from the other advisors so as to be able to move around freely.

Austin thought of Jason and experienced a sudden spike of anger. Jason was a nice enough bloke, but he was just too much like those dumb-as-rocks senior non-commissioned officers that had treated Austin like dirt when he was a junior officer. Like they knew everything, and he was an idiot just because they had been in the army longer than him. That didn't count for anything. He had been smarter than them when he joined. Clearly, they'd been fixated on getting their jabs in while he was junior because he was basically on their level already, and with every day he'd surpassed them.

He could easily outsmart Jason. He was a tactician whereas Austin was a strategist. He could run rings around Jason easily. He suddenly thought of Naomi, the new girl Jason had working for him. She seemed smart enough, and he wasn't sexist, but Austin hadn't met a woman he couldn't charm and manipulate.

Austin smiled, buoyed by the note. His earlier self-doubt evaporated and was replaced with a self-confidence that oozed from every pore. He could do this, and it was going to be easy.

26

THE WIND RUSTLED THE LEAVES, stirring the small branches and keeping the temperature warm but pleasant. The canopy kept some of the morning's moisture in, and the stream bubbled happily along, jumping over rocks and heading to wherever it was that the stream went.

Lily wondered where it did go. Maybe she could convince Austin and Jason to let her follow it under the guise of a hike for morning exercise one day. She smiled as she lay back on the large rock by the stream and absorbed its warmth. If they wouldn't let her, then she'd just ask Addison to take her.

Her smiled faded as she realised it was unlikely that Addison could take her anytime soon. Not before the Trials, anyway. She didn't have her lessons with Addison anymore, as most of her time was being taken up by Lady Octavia, who was trying to help her develop her abilities. Lily was slightly surprised to find she missed her lessons with Addison. It was as if her calming powers infused her whole being, creating an aura of safety around her. Or maybe it was just that something about her reminded her of her mum back home.

"What's on your mind?" asked Ava, turning lazily onto her stomach.

"Nothing." Lily sighed happily. "Enjoying the sunshine. And the break."

In between her lessons with Lady Octavia, Lily's advisors had decided it was best if the so far almost completely unsuccessful training with her advisors and friends continue. When Addison asked Lady Octavia whether they should do this, Lady Octavia had looked at Addison as one might regard someone who was wondering whether they should eat cardboard. Lady Octavia's response of, "If you must, dear," had affirmed in Lily's mind that Lady Octavia thought the training was a complete waste of time.

Addison, however, appeared to have missed this nuance and taken Lady Octavia to have supported, or even encouraged, the idea. And so it was that Lily found much of her time monopolised by pointless hours of trying to achieve what she had yet to accomplish.

At any rate, today, noticing that Lily seemed to have less patience with both the pointless training and Edmund's sporadic attempts to impress her, Ava had managed to convince Addison to let them go off alone and train together. Having led Lily into the woods, she then announced that today was a rest day.

"Everyone knows that rest days are essential to any kind of training."

Perhaps seeing the slightly nervous look on Lily's face, Ava allowed that if Lily's advisors, in their clear expertise regarding the development of magical abilities, felt that a rest day would not be of assistance, then Lily should tell them they had been experimenting to see if states of extreme relaxation had a positive effect on the generation of magic.

Lily had laughed and pushed her guilt to the side, relaxing with Ava and eventually believing that she did deserve a break. The pressure on Lily seemed to be constantly growing, and it seemed like even the usually unflappable Lady Octavia was starting to feel that Lily should have manifested something by now, and they were both feeling the stress. Lily had noticed that, if nothing else, the training had helped her connect better with her power. She now no longer felt as if it was something separate to her that she had to look for, connect with, and use. It was an inherent part of her that she could call on, like any other part of her body or mind.

Of course, no one thought that this would get her through the Trials, and so what, months ago, would have been cause for celebration, was instead shrugged off in favour of encouragement to keep working on her abilities.

Lily heard an excited yap and some splashing in the stream. She rolled over to watch Kevin excitedly jump in and out of the stream and then zoom around in circles. The small, fluffy creature had come snuffling out of the bushes as Lily and Ava headed into the woods.

Lily was not entirely sure how he had managed to get out of the palace, but then, she wasn't entirely sure how he had managed to get into the palace in the first place either. He had stayed with them as they walked through the woods, and after Lily and Ava lay down by the stream, spent his time oscillating between snuffling in the bushes, lying down and resting, and jumping in and out of the water before tearing around like a crazy thing.

Every now and then, he popped over to Lily and gave her leg or arm a little lick before heading off again. That made Lily happy, as if he were checking in on her before getting back to his sniffing.

Lily enjoyed being with Ava. It was just easy. She was comfortable in the silence that they had lapsed into, but also enjoyed their easy conversations. After Ava had announced that it was a rest day, they had chatted about everything from their pasts to everyone in the palace to what Ava might do when she returned to Meridia. They had carefully avoided anything related to the Trials or Lily's inability to do anything that vaguely resembled magic, but Lily felt she could probably even discuss that with Ava without feeling the stress and pressure that threatened to overwhelm her whenever her advisors raised the topics.

Ava noticed Lily watching Kevin, who was now stalking leaves and pouncing on them when they least expected.

"He's pretty cute," Ava said.

"Yeah, he is," said Lily, smiling.

"I am a little surprised that your advisors let you keep him. At least in the palace."

"I'm the sovereign. They don't *let* me do anything," Lily said, yawning and only half-serious.

"Oh, do excuse me, Your Majesty," said Ava. She bowed her head as much as she could while sitting on the ground.

"That's more like it," Lily joked. "But why would they have a problem with Kevin?"

"He's a pelotromo. They can be quite dangerous."

Lily laughed and then caught sight of Ava's expression. She was smiling back at Lily, but clearly serious. Lily looked at Kevin and then back at Ava.

"I know everyone keeps saying that, but I mean, look at him. He's cute, not terrifying."

Kevin was currently on his back, rolling from side to side and trying to catch a butterfly with his tiny paws.

"Well, of course he's all cute and fluffy now. But when they're threatened or scared, they grow to a massive size."

Lily considered Kevin, who could easily fit in one of her hands. "So, like a really big dog?"

"More like a woolly mammoth."

Lily looked back over at Kevin in surprise. He had given up on the butterfly and fallen asleep, tiny snores emitting from his tiny nose.

Ava must be joking.

He was so little and cute, she couldn't imagine him being dangerous. Though, Addison *had* been wary when they first saw him, and her advisors had reacted in alarm when he turned up in the palace. But if he really was that dangerous, surely they wouldn't have let her keep him. It seemed ridiculous to put so much effort into protecting her from faceless assassins when she could be crushed to death in her bed if Kevin had a bad dream. She looked suspiciously at Ava, who laughed despite herself.

"I swear I'm not pulling your leg."

"Well, what do they look like when they're massive? Do they get fangs or scales or claws or something?" Lily was finding it difficult to comprehend being scared of Kevin.

"No, they look exactly like he does now. Just massive. And they can still move like he can now, but as you can imagine, it's slightly more alarming when they might prance and frolic you to death."

Lily laughed despite herself. She tried to imagine a huge Kevin towering over her. His cute little licks might not be so cute if he were ten feet tall. Ava considered Kevin, too.

"I must say, I've not heard of one going quite this long without blowing up before. I would have expected him to have done that when you first came across him in the woods. Lots of hikers see them in the wild because they walk too close and spook them and then find themselves suddenly face-to-face with a massive fluffy puppy. Lots of hikers are also crushed to death after suddenly finding themselves face to face with a massive fluffy puppy."

"So, are there no domesticated pelotromos?"

"Well, there are some. But usually on farms or in zoos, you know? They have special enclosures that look ridiculous when the pelotromos are at their normal size because they have to be big enough to allow for when they blow up. I thought I heard something about Valmead enchanting an enclosure to prevent them from becoming huge. I might ask Alexei about it."

The two women drifted into silence again, watching Kevin as he woke up, rolled over, let out a little yip, and bounded off into the bushes after something that neither of them could see.

"Maybe he's defective and can't blow up?" Lily wondered out loud. *Maybe that's why he likes me. We're both defective.* "Or maybe," said Lily, suddenly defensive of Kevin, even though she was the one suggesting he was faulty, "he's a super-intelligent pelotromo and so can better assess threats. He knows I'm not going to hurt him, and so he just stays little."

Ava said nothing. She smiled at Lily's protectiveness of her little friend and rolled over on her back and closed her eyes.

"I'd kind of like to see giant Kevin," said Lily. "I think he'd be pretty cute. Maybe I could ride him like a horse!"

Ava laughed. "Are you going to ride him into battle? What happens when you're mid-charge and he shrinks again?"

Lily had to admit that would be inconvenient. "Okay, so no riding, but he'd still be cute."

"Yes, cute," said Ava, a note of sarcasm in her voice. "You see what he's doing now?"

Kevin burst out of the bushes and jumped into the

stream, bouncing through the water before cutting two tight circles and re-entering the bushes.

"Imagine a woolly mammoth coming at you like that."

Lily laughed at the image.

"Yeah, okay, it's funny to imagine. Look, I'm just saying. He may not be angry and looking like he wants to kill you, but he also may happily pounce your body into a pulp."

27

"Again."

"This is stupid," Lily muttered.

"Excuse me?"

"Nothing."

Lily sighed and tried again to focus on somehow making magic happen. She imagined it would be like attaching wings to someone's back and telling them to fly. There would be a lot that they would have to figure out beyond just flapping them, not to mention learning to use the muscles required.

Although at least they would know what part of their body to use and what they were supposed to be doing. 'Just do magic' did not seem to be working for Lily. Nonetheless, she continued to try to focus on drawing from her power to 'do anything, literally anything'.

Though not overly helpful to achieving their current aim, Lady Octavia's directions did tell Lily that the older woman was as frustrated as she was with her lack of progress. She had asked Lady Octavia whether she had helped other people with their magic. Lady Octavia replied she had, and with excellent results. Lady Octavia did not add that never before had it been so difficult to get results, but had reminded Lily that none of the people she had helped in the past had been unable to access their power or abilities until they were adults.

"This is stupid," Lily said again, but this time aloud. She sighed and paced around the courtyard.

"Stop your complaining and focus," said Lady Octavia.

"Focus on what?" Lily asked, frustration overwhelming her.

Lady Octavia went to respond but caught herself. Lily watched her regain control and avoid whatever outburst she had been on the precipice of. Lily was slightly disappointed. Not that she wanted Lady Octavia to yell at her, but she would have been interested to see the ever-calm Lady Octavia lose her composure.

"Alright, let's get specific."

"Finally."

Lady Octavia shot Lily a dirty look. "As I've said previously, it is not advised to lead someone in the discovery of their abilities, as it can stunt development."

"Yeah, but my development can't really get more stunted, can it?"

With a real effort, Lady Octavia did not respond but instead told Lily to focus on the vine on the courtyard wall.

"Picture it as the source of all your issues. That vine is the reason you cannot perform magic. Focus on destroying it."

"How?"

"Don't care. Burn it, freeze it, blow it up. Just *do* something."

Lily did just that. She stared at the innocent vine with all the contempt and frustration she could muster. She focussed on the frustration of not being able to do magic. On the frustration she felt when everyone else indicated that it was easy. On the frustration that Lady Octavia should be able to help her, but seemed unable to do so, and was now herself frustrated at Lily for not being able to do magic.

She decided that fire would be the most satisfying response. She envisioned burning the vine, the source of all those frustrations, to the ground. Lily breathed in deeply and thrust her hand out at the wall, yelling as she did. She imagined a fire ball emerging from her hand and flying at the vine, hitting it and exploding, enveloping the vine in a coating of fiery doom.

The only thing that surprised Lily more than the fact it worked was that instead of a ball, she only managed a weak stream of fire that emerged from her hand and, by the time it reached the vine, merely singed the leaves. She stared at the vine for a second and then turned to Lady Octavia, beaming.

Lady Octavia was still staring at the vine, her expression betraying the fact that she had not really expected that to work, before she mirrored Lily's expression of joy and crossed to her with a triumphant smile and took her hands. "Okay, what else?"

They spent the next two hours working together to see what else Lily could do. Lily couldn't remember ever having worked so hard but enjoying it so much in her life. Together, they found Lily could summon lightning, turn invisible (or at least slightly opaque), and read Lady Octavia's mind.

Lily's abilities were all very weak. Like the fire, every-thing she manifested was far from the images in her mind of her performing magnificent feats. While she could read Lady Octavia's mind, she could only read what Lady Octavia wanted her to read, and even then only one word at a time, and Lady Octavia had to be really focussed on that word. Lady Octavia had assured her she really could summon lightning, though when she tried all she heard was a distant rumble that she wasn't entirely convinced hadn't been Lady Octavia's stomach.

Lily was trying very hard not to be discouraged. She felt like she was being difficult. Displeased that she couldn't do magic and now displeased at the strength of her powers. Lady Octavia could tell, and reassured Lily that she had made enormous progress, especially when consideration was given to how much work it had taken to get there. She encouraged Lily to be proud of her achievement and distracted her by trying to teach Lily as much as she could about the abilities she was discovering.

"Thoughts can appear to the reader as words or pictures, or can be heard in the reader's mind as if the person were talking to them. Interestingly, in experiments, readers report that the voice they hear speaking the thoughts is the same as the thinker's voice, and this is true even if the reader has not heard the thinker's voice before.

"However, thoughts need to be interpreted with caution. Some thoughts are memories, but are tainted by a person's point of view, as well as hindsight. Sometimes people will think about what they wish they had done, or what they would have preferred happened. And of course, some thoughts are not memories but future intentions, or even fantasies that have no reflection on reality. This," Lady Octavia said, leaning in, "is precisely why mind reading is not admissible in court proceedings. Of course, popular culture does like to portray mind readers helping the police and solving crimes. And it's not unheard of that the police might use a mind reader to help them, but their information is rarely relied upon."

Lily liked this version of Lady Octavia. She was happy and enjoying imparting her wisdom. Lily was enjoying learning about the different ways that abilities manifested. She learned that types of magic were grouped together, such as elemental magic, and then, within those groups, different people could do different things. Lady Octavia used Lily's stream of fire as an example. Some people could shoot balls of fire, some could do streams, others still could manipulate fire, but only if it was already there.

Lady Octavia suspected that Lily would have more than just one ability in each elemental grouping, and after Lily had shot a few more streams of fire around the courtyard to reassure herself that she could replicate her ability, they took some time and found that Lily could, in fact, also shoot fireballs, and could manipulate the fire once she had shot it, directing the fireballs around the courtyard and dancing them in the air.

"Right. Your Majesty, well done." Lady Octavia beamed at Lily and Lily felt her chest swell with pride. "You have really done an amazing job and even just in this session, your abilities have grown magnificently. If you keep at it, you will be extremely powerful by the time you reach the Trials, and you will have no worries in passing them."

"Yeah, it'll be a breeze after we have a few more lessons!"

"Ah yes, well," Lady Octavia began, and Lily felt her heart sink. "As it happens, I must go away again for a bit..."

"What? But you only just got back. And I've only just been able to do magic. You need to stay and help me. Please."

Lady Octavia looked at Lily. Lily could see reluctance in her eyes, and a profound sadness. Lily could tell she didn't want to go.

"I can't yet explain to you why I must go, or where I am going. But you will be told eventually—"

"When the time is right," Lily interrupted, finishing

Lady Octavia's sentence, letting her know that despite her disappointment, Lily understood.

"Keep up your training. Run through the drills I have taught you, and make sure that each session you solidify your abilities and try to discover a new one. By all means, practice with your friends and advisors, but be sure not to reveal to them the true extent or range of your abilities."

"What? Why? And how am I supposed to do that?"

"It's for your safety. If there is someone with ill intentions within these walls, so far they have not harmed you. It is possible that while you have not shown any great magical power you have not been seen as a threat. But you do have great power, Your Majesty. You may be the most magically powerful person Highacre has ever seen. If that is realised by those who mean you harm, they may decide that it is in their best interests to dispose of you while you are not yet at the height of your power. To kill you now before they lack the ability to do so."

Lily nodded mutely. She hadn't thought about it like that, but of course Lady Octavia was right. She was perhaps in the most dangerous position she had been in since arriving in Highacre. Not yet powerful enough to protect herself, but enough to show that she would be a threat to those seeking control of the country.

But it seemed counterintuitive. Now that she had magical abilities, she would need to practice to develop them to a point where she could take care of herself. But in doing so, she may also paint a massive target on her back. Perhaps it was safer to not use her abilities?

"You *must* practice," said Lady Octavia, seeming to read Lily's mind. "It is imperative that you achieve the full extent of your potential. Practice with your advisors, but use it as an opportunity to develop control over your abilities rather than grow their power. Just because you can create a gigantic fireball doesn't mean that you should, and occasionally you will want to use your abilities subtly.

"Also," Lady Octavia hurried on, "as you develop new abilities, there is no need to let your advisors know. Practice the new ones on your own. I will tell Addison that I have left you with very specific drills that you are to run through on your own and that they require significant concentration and so you are not to be disturbed while you practice. That should ensure that you have a couple of hours a day to yourself at least."

"Can't you just tell me what abilities I have?" Lily asked, not for the first time. "Isn't that your whole job, anyway? Then I can focus on bringing them out."

She knew the answer, but the idea of Lady Octavia leaving had given Lily an air of desperation. She was worried she would not be able to develop her abilities without Lady Octavia's help.

"You know this, Your Majesty. If I tell you what abilities you have the potential to develop, you may subconsciously limit yourself. Imagining an ability can stymie its growth. It is better that they come to you through your work. It is so very important, Your Majesty, that you do not limit your power."

Lily began to ask Lady Octavia questions, but the older lady ignored her, gathered her bag, and moved to the archway.

"I must go, Your Majesty, but I will return in time for one final lesson before the Trials. By that time, you will have developed your abilities and we will delve into some more advanced topics. This lesson will be of utmost importance and will not only help you with the Trials, but will see you well through your reign."

"Not to oversell it or anything," Lily said, smiling, a

little uncomfortable. Lady Octavia did not return Lily's smile. If anything, she looked slightly sad.

"I wish I were. You are a strong woman, Your Majesty. You do not need my help, but any I might give, I am honoured to do so."

And with that, leaving a slightly stunned Lily in her wake, Lady Octavia swept out of the courtyard and was gone.

28

To HER DELIGHT, Lily found that after having broken the seal, so to speak, on her abilities, she could use them relatively easily, and her practice sessions went extremely well. She realised that her work on her power, as Lady Octavia had assured her, had not been wasted. Because she had developed the core of her magic, her abilities were much easier to develop, grow, and discover.

Sitting in her room at night, Lily worked on some of her less destructive powers. She had found that she could move some objects with her mind. She had, with some work, been able to summon her hairbrush from the bathroom while lying on her bed and had even been able to move more than one object at once.

Often, she would lay in bed at night practicing with multiple small objects. It was something similar to juggling and required significant concentration, but Lily had managed to fly several objects around the room at once, sending each to a different place. Despite her attempts, she didn't seem able to lift anything much heavier than a hardback novel, nor move anything farther than about fifty metres from her, though her dexterity was improving with practice.

Lily had also been working on her mental abilities, trying to read the mind of the guards outside her door. She found that not only could she now read their minds from her own room without even seeing them, but she had some level of mental manipulation. She had sneezed while reading the mind of an unfortunate guard and he had needed to leave due to a sudden migraine.

She wished Lady Octavia was around so she could ask her about it. Or at least available to talk to. But she reassured herself that at least she'd be able to ask all her questions at their next lesson before the Trials.

Lily was also working on her more obvious abilities, which were the ones she had decided to share with her advisors. They had all been suitably impressed and excited when she had demonstrated her fireballs. She could also now summon a small flash of lightning, regardless of the weather, but while it was pretty, it wasn't altogether useful.

She had also turned slightly translucent for Addison and Claire, and they had agreed that she must have some latent invisibility but that clearly it was not one of her strengths. In actual fact, Lily had found at night that she could now turn completely invisible. She had left her door open and then exited her bedroom and walked right up to Jason without him seeming to realise it, even waving her hand under his face while he was reading some documents.

She walked over to the guard outside her door, vaguely remembering that he was supposed to be able to see invisible people, or at least sense that they were there. Nothing. She returned to her room, excited by her progress and her new skill, with only the tiniest of voices in the back of her mind suggesting that the revealer being unable to sense her was a bad thing.

Returning to the Lodge from a particularly fun training session with Ava, Alexei, and Edmund, Lily stopped in her tracks when she heard Addison and Giles talking as if they were next to her. She looked around the corridor, but she was alone, other than Naomi following along at a respectful distance. She checked the walls to see if there was a vent or something that might carry the sound. Nothing. Still, their hushed voices sounded to her as if they were right there.

"Is everything alright, ma'am?" asked Naomi.

"Oh, yes," said Lily, wanting to focus on what Addison was saying, "I just thought I heard something, that's all."

They continued on, Lily listening as Addison voiced her concerns that they would be discovered. Giles was less worried about that, and more worried that they weren't making progress. Who might discover them and what they needed to make progress on was not mentioned.

Lily strode towards the Lodge door, flinging it open and startling Addison and Giles, who made a little squeak of surprise.

"What's going on?" Lily demanded, sick and tired of all the cloak and dagger nonsense.

"Oh! Your Majesty, Giles and I were just discussing a particularly vexing household matter..."

"No, you weren't," interrupted Lily. She focussed as hard as she could on Addison, trying to read her mind. Addison's thoughts appeared to Lily as pictures. Some were still images, while others appeared like the immersion imagery from the machine that allowed Lily to learn about her family. She saw Addison's desire not to have what she was doing discovered by Lily, but the images also showed Lily that her overriding concern was disappointing the queen—her.

"Your Majesty," Giles began, drawing Lily's attention to him. His thoughts came to Lily as his voice in her head.

They were trying to uncover the traitorous advisor and having no luck. Giles was worried about what mischief they could do undetected, as well as the fact that nothing they seemed to do had yet unmasked the person.

"Are you the traitors in our midst?" asked Lily, mostly to try and disguise her now well-developed mind-reading ability. "Or are you trying to identify the traitor?"

Addison, who had blanched at Lily's first question, visibly relaxed at her second and nodded eagerly. "We've been trying to monitor everyone. Talk to them. See who's acting out of the ordinary."

"But they're all acting as if nothing has changed," added Giles with an air of desperation. "We had thought, with you being back, that the guilty party would have to change *something*, do something that gave the game away. But they haven't, and so all we've done is to bring you here, put you in danger, and we're none the wiser."

Lily was touched. She had felt so bitter when she first got here at the idea of these people toying with her life, not caring about the risks to her and just solely focussed on achieving their aims. To be fair, it did seem that Giles and Addison were still focussed on achieving what they felt they needed to, but she hadn't before realised how much they cared about her and her safety, or how guilty they felt about the situation they had put her in.

"The thing is, Your Majesty," Addison continued hesitantly, "the main person who is acting quite oddly is Lady Octavia. She's continuously off to who knows where, when her focus should be on preparing you, especially now with the Trials coming up. What if she's being bribed to stay away and not help you? Or worse, she's in on whatever plot is underway?"

"I don't think she's the one," Lily said gently, trying her best to reassure Addison.

"If she is, I mean, what can we do? She's the detector. That's basically like being untouchable, isn't it? Who would we even go to about it?"

"Addison. It's not her."

"But, how do you know?"

"Just trust me, I'm sure about this." Before her last lesson with Octavia, Addison might have swayed Lily and caught her up in her paranoia. But she felt as if she had come a long way in understanding Lady Octavia, and somehow she just knew, beyond doubt, that Lady Octavia was on her side.

Addison looked mollified. Not entirely, but she clearly felt much better knowing that Lily, who had spent the most time with the older woman, was so sure that she was legitimate.

"Have either of you spoken with Jason? Or Naomi?" Lily gestured at the guard, who was standing by the door pretending to not be listening to their conversation. Her expression was almost an eye roll that neither Giles nor Addison had approached those in charge of Lily's security, not to mention the investigation, with their concerns. Giles and Addison both looked abashed.

"Er, no. No, I'm afraid we didn't think of that..." Giles looked very uncomfortable.

"Do you have concerns about them?" Lily whispered.

"No! No, not at all. No, I'm afraid we just didn't think..." Giles' sentence died in his mouth and he shrugged, looking at Addison for help.

"Tell you what," Lily said, saving Addison from having to think of something to claw back some level of dignity, "why don't we all go and find Jason now, and you can tell him everything you've both seen and thought of in relation to your suspicions about the other advisors. He can add your observations to his investigation and take it from there."

Addison and Giles hurriedly agreed that this was the best approach, and they all set off, Naomi leading them to the operations room where Jason's office was located. They found him talking to Claire, and Lily felt Addison and Giles tense up; they clearly had not expected the etiquette advisor to be there. Eager to keep the momentum, Lily asked Claire to speak with her and moved away from the rest of the group, allowing Addison and Giles to speak freely with Jason and Naomi.

"Yes, Your Majesty?" Claire looked at Lily expectantly. Lily, in asking Claire whether she could have a word, had failed to come up with a useful topic to ask her about.

"Um, I was wondering if you had, er... I wanted to talk about, um, flowers."

"Flowers?"

"Yes. Um, for my coronation."

Lily had no idea why she said flowers, but having said it, decided that there was nothing for it but to commit fully and so met Claire's politely confused look with expectant enthusiasm, as if she wanted nothing more right now than to talk about flower arrangements.

Claire, still looking slightly bemused at Lily's sudden interest in a topic that had never before captured even the slightest part of her attention, began to give Lily a rundown of the types of flowers under consideration, where those flowers might be used, such as in arrangements or decorating the bannisters, and what kinds of arrangements were available. Lily recalled a lesson with Claire where she had explained that there were different types of arrangements and what they were most often used for. Lily also recalled being bored stupid in that lesson.

Unable to focus on Claire's explanation of the different

types of tulips and what they might signify on different occasions, Lily decided, slightly recklessly, to practice her mind reading skills on Claire. Surely Claire must find flowers every bit as boring as she did. Trying to keep her expression neutral but interested, Lily reached out with her mind, tentatively feeling around for Claire's thoughts, careful to avoid alerting Claire to her presence.

Reading minds for Lily was like reaching out with your hand and touching vibrating circular bands of metal or rubber that surrounded a person's head. When she reached out with her mind, she could see the bands around different people, like a separate layer or lens over her normal sight. All the bands were different and vibrating at different speeds and energy levels. They were different shapes and sizes, and though she didn't know why, when she saw them in her head, they were also different colours and had different scents.

Lily had found, during her training with Lady Octavia, that when trying to read minds, you had to reach out with your mind and touch the band. If you grabbed it roughly, you would disrupt the natural vibrations, and the person would know that something had happened. But if you could make contact with the band softly, you could read everything that was there and the person would never know.

Lily had practised with the guards outside her room, but she had a strange feeling that intercepting a bored, tired mind's thoughts might be easier than reaching into someone who was alert, and possibly aware of what it felt like when someone tried to read their mind.

Despite this, Lily was pleased with how subtly she made contact with Claire's band, and so was shocked to hear Claire's somewhat amused voice in her head, *Your Majesty, it would appear that your abilities are developing quite well!*

Lily, thrown off by being busted by Claire, not to mention Claire talking to her in her head, was completely unnerved by the fact that Claire also continued on talking about flowers as if nothing strange had happened.

"I'm sorry Your Majesty, is something wrong?"

"Ah, no, sorry. Please continue."

That's right, Your Majesty. Claire's voice sounded in Lily's head again. *There is an art to mind reading while carrying on a conversation. Best to practice when there's nothing at stake. No, don't nod, Your Majesty.*

Lily didn't like this at all. It took an extreme level of concentration to respond to the appropriate conversation in the right way. Remembering her expression should reflect the floral conversation, she steeled herself and tried again.

Better. Now, you will need much more practice at entering minds and reading their contents. Powerful mind readers can often erect mental barriers to prevent access to others. You might think about learning how to do that too. And sooner rather than later.

Lily focussed on asking Claire, with her thoughts, if she would teach her, but Claire just kept on with her inner monologue of improvements Lily needed to make. She was getting annoyed, and apparently it showed.

Careful, Your Majesty. You need to keep your face neutral. Dandelions rarely provoke such frustration. As I have said, I can detect lies. That is classed as a mental ability. Those of us with mental abilities are usually much more adept at detecting mental incursions.

I am not, however, a mind reader, and therefore I cannot read your thoughts. I can merely leave mine open for you to read, and by focussing on what I want you to know, I can ensure you read the thoughts I want you to read. This is a tactic that people with mental abilities like me, who cannot erect mental blocks, can employ to prevent mind readers from accessing thoughts we do not wish them to access. That, and clearing one's mind.

Suddenly, Claire's thoughts cut out completely, and Lily was left with Claire's verbal description of the pros and cons of elliptical arrangements versus cascading ones. Lily felt as if she was in the mental equivalent of an empty room.

I learned how to manage that through much tedious meditation, thought Claire, suddenly re-emerging in Lily's head. Lily saw over Claire's shoulder that the discussion between Addison, Giles, Jason, and Naomi was wrapping up. Claire noticed too.

Please feel free to engage me for practicing these skills if you think it might help, Your Majesty. I am not the traitorous advisor and will be happy to assist you in any way.

Seeing Lily's expression, she added, *If I were the traitor, with how strong your abilities are already, you would no doubt discover me soon anyway. Therefore, it is in both of our interests for you to develop your mental abilities as quickly as possible so you can smoke out the rats without risk to yourself.*

Lily nodded gratefully at Claire. She was touched, if not slightly taken aback, by Claire's generous and selfless offer to allow Lily access to her mind, with the ultimate aim of Lily being able to access things that Claire wouldn't necessarily want her to access, and without Claire knowing that she had accessed them.

As Claire turned and led the way back to the larger group, an uncomfortable thought popped into Lily's mind. What if Claire *did* have mind reading skills? She might be such a powerful mind reader that she could easily block Lily's access to whatever she didn't want Lily to see while playing at not being able to. If that was the case, then Lily would only learn what Claire wanted her to learn about mind reading. She could be the insider, and Lily would never know.

29

LADY OCTAVIA

Lady Octavia sat in the palace courtyard in an easy chair she had conjured out of nothing. She was uncharacteristically nervous, picking at the lint on her sleeves. She pulled out her pocket watch, an old but well-maintained engraved silver timepiece, and checked it for the fifth time that minute. *I may as well just keep it out at this rate.* The thought came grudgingly as she put it back in her pocket. They were late.

Having picked all the available lint off her sleeve, Lady Octavia thought to pull out her knitting. It would be pointless, trying to finish the sweater, but it would give her hands something to do. As she went to reach into her bag to retrieve her needles, the person for whom she was waiting loomed in the archway.

"You're late," she said, annoyed.

"I wasn't aware we had an appointment." The amusement in their voice grated on Lady Octavia's already frayed nerves. She stood, smoothed out her dress, and adjusted her jacket.

"I do not have the time nor the inclination to entertain witty banter, long-winded explanations, or nugatory attempts at deception. You are here to kill me, and it is the height of ill manners to have kept me waiting."

The figure left the archway and entered the courtyard, moving closer to Lady Octavia, though maintaining a reasonable distance between them.

"Are you so ready to die, Octavia?"

"Of course I'm not ready to die," Lady Octavia snapped, "as if that matters to you. But punctuality is a good measure of a person." She sniffed. "It seems apt that a murderer would be tardy."

The figure circled Lady Octavia, maintaining the distance between them, regarding her with a level of intrigue. How could she know they had come here to kill her? And why would she not fight?

"Have you given up, Octavia?"

Their use of her name bothered her. Like they were friends. Like they were *still* friends.

She laughed mirthlessly. "Oh no, I have not given up. I am just under no illusions about what the outcome of your visit will be."

Lady Octavia turned towards the figure and took a step in their direction.

"But if you think I'm going to make it easy for you, you are sorely mistaken."

With a crack, a burst of pure energy shot from Lady Octavia's hand and knocked her would-be murderer to the ground. They recovered more quickly than they should have and came at her, swinging a small wooden club. Lady Octavia took a blow to the head and stumbled back, dazed.

This is how I am killed? A wooden bat?

Lady Octavia reached out to ward off another blow, glaring at the object as if it had personally offended her. She tried to knock the attacker to the ground again, but this time they were ready for her, and they dodged right. Lady

Octavia frowned. Her energy bolt should still have had an effect. Perhaps this person had some kind of shield?

The two continued, trading physical and magical blows. At first, Lady Octavia felt in control of the fight. She was keeping her attacker on their toes, and occasionally landing blows with her energy bolts. But she felt her grasp on her ability slip with each blow to the head. Her attacker dodged her latest bolt and smacked her hard with the club. Stars exploded behind her eyes. She couldn't hold out much longer.

Her attacker threw something hard at her legs, connecting with her right knee and causing Lady Octavia to drop, landing heavily on her left knee. Her attacker simply watched as she struggled, but ultimately failed to rise again.

"Don't grow old," she said.

"Still providing advice, even now."

"It wasn't advice. It was my wish for your future."

The attacker barked out a laugh at the unexpected insult.

"Go on then," said Lady Octavia, lifting her head, her shoulders back. "Let's get on with it."

Her attacker approached, and when she sensed they relaxed, assuming victory, she fired the strongest bolt of energy she could summon at their stomach. Crying out in pain, her attacker doubled over. Lady Octavia took the opportunity to scramble to her feet, leaning heavily on the wall for support. It wasn't dignified, but she was standing.

Her attacker approached again, wary this time, lips curled in a snarl. The niceties had been dispensed with. This was it. The end. Lady Octavia stood as straight as she could manage and took a deep, steadying breath. She closed her eyes and, smiling, thought of home.

Lily walked down to the courtyard, excited about seeing Lady Octavia and going over all the questions she had for her to make sure she didn't forget any. She was trying not to be too curious about what she might learn today, Lady Octavia's foreshadowing of the importance of this lesson echoing in her mind. She was also quite pleased with herself and the progress she had made with her abilities and had been picturing the reaction from Lady Octavia when she saw how far Lily had come.

Entering the courtyard, Lily saw it was empty, which was fine. She was a little early because of her excitement. She paced about slowly, trying not to let her excitement show too much, but burning off some of her nervous energy. Having wandered over to the far corner of the courtyard, she noticed a scuff mark on the ground. It looked fresh. *Odd.* Lily had thought that only she and Lady Octavia used the courtyard for her training, and Lily rarely came down to this end of the open area.

Curious, she looked at her surroundings a little closer. There was a singe mark on the wall that she hadn't noticed before. Though, that didn't necessarily mean it hadn't been there. She felt the wall. It was warm to her touch, but it was a sunny day. The specific spot felt slightly warmer than the rest of the brick, but not to the extent that Lily felt sure she wasn't reading into it. She glanced at her watch. Time had passed without her paying attention. Lady Octavia was late. Lady Octavia was never late.

Lily's eyes now darted around the courtyard, looking for more signs of something amiss. She could see some more scuff marks, a place where a vine looked to have been scraped, and some suspicious drops that looked like blood. *I wish I could see what happened here.*

Lily reached out, as she had been doing the past weeks in developing and discovering her powers. She tried to focus the way she did when trying to read minds. Perhaps she could read the memory of a place? Unlikely, but worth a try.

The first thing she noticed was a wave of emotions. It was overwhelming, so many emotions on top of her own. She let them go and steadied herself. This time, ready for the onslaught, she reached out and tried to pay attention to what she felt. The emotions hit her again, but she was prepared and able to handle it. They were conflicting. She felt anxiety, excitement, betrayal, confidence, grief, glee, and determination, all at once.

Two people then?

She tried to reach out further, beyond the emotions. She felt for the courtyard, and particularly the areas where she thought she had noticed something out of place. Suddenly, two ghost-like flashes appeared, but vanished before she could see what they were. She took a deep breath, steadied herself, and tried again. The ghosts reappeared, strobing slightly, but she could see that there were two people, and they were fighting. Lily used every ounce of patience she had, knowing through her recent practice that she needed to take her time to make this new ability work.

She took several breaks, but eventually witnessed the two figures fight; the aggressor got some early hits, then the other gained the upper hand, almost looking to be in control of the fight and on the verge of winning. Then, ultimately, the aggressor overpowered the other.

It frustrated Lily that the images weren't of a great quality. She couldn't see what the figures were really doing, if they were using magic or other means to fight, or even whether they were male or female. Lily thought that the figure that had wound up on the ground was Lady Octavia. It sort of looked like her, but she couldn't discount that it was her bias since she knew she was supposed to meet Lady Octavia here. She tried again, focussing on the other figure, and cursing when it was still as distorted as the last time she had watched. She could hardly identify a blob.

Giving up on being able to identify the figure, Lily pushed forwards to watch the rest of the scene. She expected to see the Lady Octavia figure get up, or otherwise be restrained by the blob. But it didn't move. The pictures strobed forwards and Lily watched as a stilted slideshow of images showed the blob lift Lady Octavia, carry her to the courtyard entrance, and unceremoniously dump her in some cart or box or maybe a wheelbarrow, and then they were gone. Finally, it dawned on Lily that the blob was disposing of the body.

The body.

Lily panicked slightly. *Maybe she was just unconscious.* She wanted to find help, but without being able to see the blob more clearly, she wasn't sure where to go. Jason, maybe. She had already put her eggs in that basket. If he was against her, then she had already made that mistake. Would it matter, anyway? The blob knew that Lady Octavia was kidnapped or dead. Would it alter their plans if everyone else knew it too? Would that be a bad thing? Perhaps the blob had made a mistake, and they could rescue Lady Octavia, revive her somehow.

Lily crossed to the entry and looked for the wheelbarrow. Kneeling, she touched the ground. There were no wheel marks, but it looked like something had been placed there recently. *Something heavy.* At that moment, Claire and Addison arrived, startling Lily, who had been so focussed on the ground that she hadn't noticed them.

"Sorry, Your Majesty, we didn't mean to scare you," said Addison as both women curtsied. "We've come to get you ready for the Trials."

"Now?" asked Lily, distracted. "They don't start until tomorrow morning."

"The Prime Minister has just announced that they've been brought forward. They'll start tonight instead."

"What?" They now had Lily's full attention. "He can do that?"

"Yes, they have sometimes done it in the past to ensure that the participant is using their true skills and is not being assisted or relying too much on preparation. And for the shock factor," Addison admitted. "It goes over well with the crowds."

"But, if they 'sometimes do that', then why on earth have we not been preparing with that in mind? I should have had Lady Octavia's lesson yesterday!"

"Oh yes, how did that go?" asked Addison enthusiastically, seemingly oblivious to Lily's mood.

"It didn't."

"What do you mean, Your Majesty?" asked Claire, more attuned to Lily's stress.

"She never arrived. I think something terrible has happened to her. She's been hurt, or worse. Maybe kidnapped."

Lily looked back around the courtyard, avoiding eye contact with Claire and not wanting to say out loud that the woman might be dead. She suddenly felt on the verge of tears and didn't know if they were for Lady Octavia or the idea of having to start the Trials now. Maybe both.

"Oh dear," said Addison, wringing her hands and looking around as if the courtyard might tell her what had happened too. "We'll have to..." she faded off, not completing her sentence and looking at Claire for help.

"Lady Octavia is a very powerful and resourceful woman," Claire started in a reassuring voice. Addison nodded enthusiastically at Lily. "If she is still alive, she will survive a little longer while we get you to the Trials. If she is dead" —Addison let out a small squeak of alarm and stopped nodding— "then we can't help her anyway."

Claire took Lily's arm and led her from the courtyard, Addison following in their wake.

"You must focus, Your Majesty. Nothing is more important right now than you completing the Trials. I know Lady Octavia would agree with me. Addison and I will take you to your rooms and I will speak with Jason while you prepare and let him know what has happened. We can do no more than that right now."

Lily nodded. Claire spoke with such surety that it made Lily feel she was doing the right thing. And she was right; Lily herself couldn't help Lady Octavia. Other well-trained people like Jason were best placed to do that. And no one *but* Lily could do the Trials. Jason would make sure that someone investigated what happened, and once Lily completed the Trials, she would help in any way she could.

Trying not to feel guilty, Lily let her advisors guide her to her room and tried to focus on not having a panic attack.

She needed to pass the Trials.

She *would* pass the Trials.

She would be queen.

30

Despite her nerves and anxiety at the reason for the trip, Lily glued herself to the window, taking in all she could of this strange country that had become home. She was told they would drive through the centre of town and then out into a slightly rural sector on the fringe of the city. She had driven through the town centre before, on her way to the Tower for her confirmation hearing, but they were taking a slightly different route today and she remained fascinated by the buildings and shops and signs.

It was late afternoon, and the sun was low in the sky. All sorts of people were out on the streets. Some were hurrying along, maybe heading home, or perhaps off to complete some last task before their day ended. But today, most people seemed to walk in groups, talking and laughing and going to enjoy fun, social things that Lily didn't know about. These were her people. The thought felt strange, but also right.

The surrounds changed first to suburbs, where everyone seemed to be out in their yards, playing with kids or talking to their neighbours. It was so nice and normal. Lily had a sudden pang of homesickness. After a while, the buildings became more sparse, and Lily felt the homesickness increase, thinking of her family's farm and wondering what her parents and siblings were doing.

As they neared their destination, the sun was towards the end of setting. It was harder to see out of the window, which increasingly reflected her pale, worried face back at her. Lily eventually turned her attention to the front of the car and saw they were heading towards a vast structure that was a bizarre mix of modern stadium and colosseum. Circular in shape, it had huge walls with spotlights spread at regular intervals that were shooting beams of light up into the sky. She was sure that it was pretty and exciting for everyone else, but to Lily, it gave her the impression of bars on a cage or prison cell.

Lily's nerves were in overdrive, and too soon the car was descending into an underground car park. The car stopped and Lily was whisked out and taken to a large changing room with bench seating around its perimeter.

Her advisors entered and they surrounded her, offering last-minute advice in low undertones that failed to mask their own nerves. They shot her concerned looks and wrung their hands. It wasn't helpful to Lily, who was trying her best to remain as calm as possible, but she reminded herself that her advisors had been through a lot themselves to get her here, and if she failed, then they were all screwed. At least she was in charge of her own destiny and not reliant on someone else not stuffing up.

As she watched her advisors, she wondered if the traitor was here among them. Was it one of the politicians? They surely stood to gain more power from any transition to a less hereditary form of government. Although she supposed that any of the advisors could probably have been persuaded to help the other side. Everyone had their price.

Austin shot her a reassuring smile and wandered over to

talk to Jason and Naomi. She appreciated his unflappable demeanour and that he had recognised that the group worry session wasn't helping. Maybe she should ask Addison for a blast of her calming magic? Tempting as that was, Lily grudgingly admitted to herself that some stress was probably a good thing.

With an effort, she brought her mind back to the task at hand. It did not matter right now who the conspirator was. All that mattered in this moment was passing the Trials. She realised Giles had been speaking to her, explaining what was going to happen.

"I'm sorry Giles, what was that last bit?"

"When they come and get you, you will go through that door there, into the centre of the area floor. It is there that each of the Trials will take place. The judging panel will determine whether you may return here in between each Trial for water and a bathroom break, but that's completely at their discretion, and they are guided by what serves the Trials best."

Lily nodded. She would not expect to return to the changing room.

"Okay, great, but what was that bit you were saying about TV?"

"Ah, yes." Giles looked as if he had meant to gloss over that bit. "The Trials are supposed to be open to the public. The stadium is quite full. And, ah, I understand the Prime Minister declared a public holiday to enable people to travel to be here."

Lily thought of all the people she had seen on her way to the arena. They were probably all happy to be coming to watch the spectacle.

"And it will be televised."

"All over Highacre?"

"Yes, and uh, internationally..."

Lily closed her eyes. She had never wanted to be a reality TV star. The crowd would be intimidating enough. She tried not to think about the entire world watching and had a sudden urge to be at home with Ava, Alexei, and Edmund, watching some poor other person going through the Trials.

Too soon, she was escorted through the door that Giles had indicated and into some kind of small antechamber. Before her were two massive wooden doors, and she could hear the excited cheers of the crowd on the other side.

She shuffled uncomfortably. The floor was coated in sand. Why had no one told her there would be sand? Her sneakers weren't the best footwear for sand. She wondered about taking them off and then decided it was probably best to get an idea of what the Trials consisted of first.

Jason was with her, and though he kept shooting her sympathetic looks, he didn't say anything, and for that she was grateful. She didn't feel like talking right now. Nor receiving any more advice, or well-meant words of encouragement.

She could hear the garbled voice of the announcer and the crowd reacting as he worked them up, building excitement for the main event. Suddenly, his voice rose, and the crowd roared.

The door in front of her opened and she stumbled out, blinded by the arena lights and deafened by the crowd. She jumped as several explosions rang out and watched numbly as confetti and streamers fell like snow. As her eyes slowly adjusted to the light, Lily saw the stadium was indeed full. Row upon row of spectators were on their feet laughing and cheering. Higher up, Lily could see a ring of private boxes, all with glass separating those within from those without. Several large screens hung high above the crowd, currently displaying various advertisements.

Despite her legs having turned to jelly, Lily somehow walked out into the middle of the arena. The announcer, having introduced Lily before she entered the arena, now turned to introducing the judging panel. Her advisors had told her that the panel was steeped in tradition.

The original panel members had been selected because of their strong magical abilities, as well as being revered for their wisdom. Membership of the panel had become like a peerage and was passed down through familial lines, justified on the basis that power tends to follow bloodlines. Her advisors had been silent as to whether wisdom did the same. It struck Lily that Highacre seemed perhaps overly wedded to nepotism, though it was not lost on her that she was obviously benefitting from that herself.

As the announcer introduced each member of the panel, they stood and gave a small wave of acknowledgement to the crowd.

"Lord Witherington!" A short, fat, jolly-looking older man stood, though it was hard to tell as he seemed to remain the same height that he had been sitting down. Addison had told Lily that he was a necromancer. Lily had difficulty imagining the smiley, red-cheeked man raising the dead.

"Madam Huber!" A duplicator, someone who could create multiple clones of themselves, Madam Huber was the exact opposite of Lord Witherington. Rake thin and wearing a serious expression, Lily thought her face might crack and shatter into a million pieces if she ever tried to smile. She gave the barest of acknowledgement to the crowd and resumed her seat.

Lily stared at Countess de Boulevard when she stood next. Looking like a child of twelve, complete with pigtails, Addison had informed Lily that her ability was that she aged incredibly slowly. She was in fact closer to one hundred and twenty, but she waved excitedly at the crowd and eagerly stared at Lily once she was again seated.

Baron and Baroness Traunt completed the panel. Addison had confided that it caused quite a stir when the families of two of the panel had married and expected to keep both their seats. Three other families had objected, and something akin to a mafia war broke out for a few years, but ultimately the Traunts had emerged victorious.

The baron looked a bit nerdy to Lily, but apparently he had thermal imaging vision and had proved quite useful during the war, earning himself both awards and the respect of his peers. He now was fairly high up in the medical sector. His wife was a frumpy middle-aged lady wearing an apron who had, having acknowledged the crowd with a cheerful wave, resumed her seat and began crocheting. Addison had told Lily that the baroness could cause a person to explode just by looking at them.

The announcer then welcomed the adjudicator, who was something of a referee, and Lily watched as a short, bald man walked quickly towards her, acknowledging the crowd with an impatient wave and swatting at something buzzing around his face. As he got closer, Lily could see it was a tiny flying camera. Though he managed to hit it, knocking it out of his way, she saw it right itself and follow him from a safer distance.

"Your Majesty," he said with a sharp nod of his head. "I am Harold, and I am the adjudicator for the Trials today. I will make sure that you understand the rules for each event and what you must achieve to successfully complete each one."

Lily found it slightly off-putting that something that her advisors had been clear was a very dangerous tradition was being treated as a sporting event. Harold was even dressed in a black-and-white striped top and had a whistle around his neck.

"I am also the designated safety warden for the Trials. I can monitor your vitals," he said, tapping his eyes, and Lily assumed his magical ability would somehow let him do that, "and if I form the opinion at any time that any trial or part thereof may cause you lasting damage or may cause you to perish, I will stop the trial and you will be deemed to have failed."

Lily clocked the term "lasting damage", and her nerves increased slightly. Harold sighed to himself and looked like he was mentally preparing for something frustrating. He turned and nodded towards the booth where the announcer was, then stood beside Lily.

The announcer's voice exploded throughout the arena again, informing everyone that Lily would first face the Trial of Courage. Harold got Lily's attention and leant in to be heard over the cheers of the crowd.

"In this trial, Your Majesty, you will be pitted against a 'threat'. This 'threat' might be anything at all, and you can address this 'threat' in any way you so choose."

Harold was using air quotes every time he said 'threat'. It was slighting annoying.

"You will be deemed to have failed the trial if you leave the arena, either via the doors, teleportation, or flying. Though you may fly or levitate to the height of the lights above the arena."

Lily briefly wondered whether she could fly, levitate, or teleport.

"Now, the killing of civilians is not permitted in this trial—"

In this *trial?*

"—and that includes death by way of accident, sacrifice, or distraction. There are protective barriers in place between the audience and the arena itself, and also on the structure to prevent its collapse, so don't think to deal with the 'threat' by bringing the building down on it..."

Lily had not considered that as a course of action and wondered if someone had actually tried to bring the entire arena down in the past.

"...but it's best you don't aim anything at the audience or building in case your abilities are stronger than the protective barriers. Like I said, accidental death will still result in you failing the Trials."

And the deaths of a bunch of innocent people...

"Do you have any questions, Your Majesty?"

Lily shook her head and watched as the camera zoomed in close to Harold's face again. He swatted at it angrily.

"These things, however, are fair game. If it were up to me, you'd get extra points for each one you destroyed. Okay." He looked up at the booth and gave a thumbs up. "Ready."

"Ladies and gentlemen," boomed the announcer, "let the Trials begin!"

31

Harold walked swiftly off to the side of the arena and Lily wondered whether she was supposed to follow him for a split second before she realised he was getting out of her way. The Trial of Courage was about to begin.

The lights in the arena dimmed slightly, and the lighting took on an ominous red tinge, eliciting "ooohs" and gasps of excitement from the crowd. A small murmur of nervous chatter broke out as Lily stood in the centre of the arena, waiting for the first Trial to unfold.

Lily's eyes darted around the arena on high alert for any movement. Her mind raced through everything she had learned about her newfound abilities as she tried to catalogue which ones might be useful in a situation where she was 'faced with a threat'. She could shoot fire, and her control over that ability had grown significantly, unbeknownst to anyone else. Lily could now easily control the fire once she shot it from her hands, directing it where she wanted it to go. She could also stop it and have it hover in mid-air, separate it into multiple balls or jets of fire, then send them in multiple different directions. Her practice with 'juggling' multiple objects with her telekinetic skills had really helped with that.

Lily also mentally checked off her ability to summon lightning. She would be fine if the Trial of Courage required her to put on a lighting display, but otherwise she doubted the ability would be much help. Lily was having difficulty thinking of any protective abilities that she had manifested. She could turn invisible, and she was actually pretty good at that now. Lily supposed it might come in handy, but she would still be vulnerable if anything hit her.

Having mentally run through her current abilities, she then turned her mind to trying to imagine any abilities she hadn't yet manifested that would be helpful right now. Lily had found that in developing new abilities, if she focussed on a general theme, any abilities she possessed that were relevant to that theme would emerge. The closer the ability was to what she envisaged, the stronger it would appear at first. Lily thought about having rock solid, impenetrable skin. If she could combine that with her invisibility, she might be in an excellent position to pass the trial.

An almighty roar rang out, breaking Lily's concentration and turning her insides to liquid. She looked around and saw an enormous, terrifying scaled beast. It was as big as a dinosaur, with a gigantic mouth filled with more teeth than any animal should need. Its eyes, glaring at Lily, were red and glowing ominously like the lighting in the arena itself. It reared up on its hind legs, slashing at the air with the huge, talon-like claws on its front feet. Slamming those feet back down, the beast lunged to its right with another roar, whipping its previously hidden tail around and displaying the huge ball of spikes at its end.

Turning towards Lily, the beast took a couple of steps and then jumped, easily clearing ten feet and landing just a few metres in front of her. The ground reverberated with the impact.

Lily swallowed thickly and with an effort, pulled herself together and focussed on the task at hand. She let fly with three large, white-hot fireballs in quick succession while running backwards to buy herself some space, all the while keeping her eyes on her target. To her surprise and immense dismay, the beast opened its mouth and lazily gulped down her fireballs.

What the...?

"Thaaaaat's right, folks! Our fire-eater is hungry! Her Majesty will have to think quickly to get herself out of this one!"

Thanks for the tip.

Lily ground her teeth, aggravated by the announcer, who sounded like he was enjoying the show. A roar blasted her from behind, and Lily turned in horror, realising that there were two fire-eaters in the arena with her. She heard the crowd shout with excitement and felt sudden fury at each and every one of them. Conveniently ignoring her earlier desire to watch some other poor sod undergo the Trials instead of her, she decided that everyone watching was sick and needed a hobby that didn't involve watching her get ripped to shreds by two massive killing machines.

A lunge from both fire-eaters at once brought Lily's attention slamming back to the task at hand. Swearing profusely in her mind, she darted away from the beasts' claws and mentally checked through what other elements of nature she could use here, now that fire was out. Water, earth... maybe she could call on an earthquake to split the ground and swallow them up? A small voice in the back of her head—which sounded an awful lot like Lady Octavia— nagged her not to limit herself, to think more broadly.

Ignoring the voice, Lily dove to her right as one of the

fire-eaters lunged at her. She dove again, falling into several rolls as it followed up with a swipe at her with its tail. She felt the air whoosh passed as it barely missed her. Lily closed her eyes and searching for a distraction, raised her arms, calling to the sky in desperation. With a deafening crack, two bolts of lightning punched down and hit each fire-eater.

Lily stared in complete shock, never having achieved forked lightening before. *I guess stress does help develop abilities.* Shaking herself back into motion, she jogged to her left to increase the distance between her and the fire-eaters. Lily kept her eyes on the fire-eaters to see how they reacted. Neither fire-eater seemed overly bothered by the lightning. They did not appear to be in pain, but the electricity seemed to have rendered them both temporarily paralysed.

Lily took the opportunity and ran to the side of the arena to ensure she was facing both fire-eaters, and neither was behind her. She focussed intensely on making her skin impenetrable. As she ran, one fire-eater recovered enough to take another swipe at her with its tail. Lily heard the swish as if time had slowed down and braced herself for impact, her mind screaming for rock-solid skin. She felt a tingle but had no idea if a convenient ability had emerged, and then all was pain as the thick tail slammed into her, sweeping her off her feet. Lily crashed into the arena wall, the crowd gasping and cringing. The wall shuddered as Lily was embedded into it, fissures breaking out all around her body. She stayed nested in the wall for a beat before she fell out and thudded to the sand.

Her body, where the fire-eater's tail had struck, was a mix of burning and numb, and her head ached from the sudden impact with the wall. She wondered what was broken or ruptured inside her and tried not to panic. She didn't know why the impact with the wall hadn't killed her.

A slight fear grew that Harold had saved her, but she had failed the Trials. One fire-eater bellowed, and she pushed herself shakily to her hands and knees, looking at the imprint she had left in the wall. It wasn't a perfect outline of her body, more like a chalk drawing from a television murder show, as if something had protected her.

The crowd screamed as the fire-eaters noticed she was still moving and started quickly advancing on her from both sides, trying to capture her in a pincer manoeuvre. Lily hopped up and ran between them, ignoring her aches and pains, ducking and weaving, trying to dodge their claws and spikes and teeth. She jumped as high as she could, hoping for flight and found, inconveniently and with bitter disappointment, that she barely even cleared the fire-eater's tail.

Ensuring she kept moving, Lily tried to figure out how the hell she was going to defeat the monsters. She wistfully thought of all her sword training with Austin and how useful one of those swords would be right about now. One of the fire-eaters lunged at her, snapping its jaws, and Lily dove off to her left, avoiding its teeth. On the other hand, maybe she didn't want to be close enough to use a sword on these things. Taking a chance, Lily closed her eyes and summoned all the lightning she could and aimed it at just one of the fire-eaters.

Four massive electrical bolts crashed into the fire-eater in quick succession, rendering the beast unconscious. Lily tried to block the roar of the other fire-eater from her mind as she raced to figure out what to do with the now-incapacitated one.

I need something sharp.

Lily again thought of Austin's swords, now regretting not trying to summon one earlier. But even if she could connect with one from this distance, which she thought highly unlikely, she very much doubted that she could get it here before the fire-eater regained consciousness. Or she was eaten by the remaining one.

Lily glanced around, keeping an eye on the fire-eater prowling to her left and looking for something, anything that she could use. A glint of light high up caught her eye. She saw some men in suits laughing and toasting in one of the fancy boxes. A sudden urge to throw something at them distracted Lily from her task, but she dismissed it. Aside from not helping her stay alive, she wasn't meant to aim her abilities at the arena.

A thought struck Lily. She wasn't meant to *collapse* the building, but that didn't mean she couldn't... With all her focus, Lily tried to summon the glass window of the box. It was too big for her to move, but her telekinetic pull shattered the glass, and she was able to gain control of a number of the shards. Ignoring the shocked screams of the crowd, Lily instinctively aimed the flying glass at the unconscious fire-eater.

Several large pieces embedded in its neck with dull thunks. The pain seemed to be rousing the beast, and Lily realised that with the fire-eater's thick skin, the embedded glass would not be enough. She ran to the right, avoiding an attack from the other fire-eater and, feeling slightly nauseated, Lily reached out with her mind for the glass again and pushed the shards across and out the other side of its neck. With a sickening guzzling sound, purple blood gushed from the fire-eater's neck, and it slumped to the ground, the tension leaving its body.

Lily heard the crowd reacting to the gore and also heard a cry of outrage from the other fire-eater. She thought she heard anguish in the cry too and looked over at the monstrous creature. It was glaring at her, clearly preparing to attack.

Taking inspiration from the unlikely source of Edmund,

Lily reached out to the remaining fire-eater with her mind. Maybe she could control it as he did his tiny birds. It was more difficult to penetrate the creature's mind than a human's. Finally, after some hasty poking and prodding, she broke in and found that it was not like a human's at all.

Lily watched the creature cautiously, seeing it notice the incursion and react by looking around for the source of the sensation. She gently felt around and, unable to find a way to control it, she looked for the creature's thoughts, or some way to communicate with it.

After a little while, Lily gave up trying to understand the complex framework and instead, on a whim, tried opening herself to the creature, as Claire had done with her. For a second Lily thought it hadn't worked, but then emotion came flooding along the mental bridge she had forged with the fire-eater. The overwhelming emotion was fear, and Lily tried to project calm and safety, steadfastly ignoring the fact that she had almost decapitated its buddy.

Images flowed into Lily's mind, and she both saw and felt the fire-eater's life story. Mere flickers of life in the wild were all it could remember before it was captured and caged in a zoo enclosure. It was a reasonably large enclosure full of trees and water, but when viewed as the only space for a large animal to live in, it was tiny.

She, the fire-eater, was female, had eventually been joined by the other fire-eater. The other fire-eater had been aggressive, and not the mate she would have chosen in the wild, but it was good to have company, and they had eventually reached a comfortable routine where they were able to coexist well. Though she hadn't thought she would be, she was very upset at the death of the other fire-eater. She was also understandably very concerned about what was about to happen to her.

Lily focussed on their connection, willing it to carry an

understanding of Lily's intentions to the fire-eater. Suddenly, to Lily's surprise, she felt rather than heard a question.

What are you going to do to me?

I don't want to hurt you, Lily thought at the beast.

But?

Well, I need to defeat you. Otherwise a lot of people are going to die. I need to complete these tasks to stop that from happening.

I don't want to die either, the creature whispered in her mind.

Lily felt as if she had been punched in the stomach. A small voice in her head suggested that reaching out to the creature had been a mistake. She should have just killed it as she had the other one. Lily pushed the voice away angrily, ashamed of the thought. She was vaguely aware of some confused murmurings in the crowd. The action had suddenly halted just when it was getting exciting.

Lily stumbled on the solution with a start, wondering how she could have been so dense, and whether if, had she been smarter and tried this earlier, she could have saved the other fire-eater. Trying not to dwell on that, she reached out to the surviving fire-eater again.

Listen, the rules say I have to defeat the threat. Now, if you're no longer a threat, then they'll have to agree that the "threat" has been defeated, right? she asked.

The fire-eater considered Lily's logic. Lily waited impatiently while the beast mulled it over. She felt bad for wanting to hurry this along. After all, if Lily was wrong, the consequences for the fire-eater were going to be much worse than they would be for Lily. Lily felt the fire-eater acquiesce to her plan and felt through their bond a resignation within the animal that though this might go horribly wrong, if she didn't take the chance, Lily would just try to kill her anyway.

The fire-eater, with one last howl, lay down in the sand to the surprise of the crowd. Lily, hoping that the fire-eater hadn't changed its mind and decided that this was actually a really easy way to win, walked over to the animal and stroked it gently on the nose.

The crowd went wild, and the lights in the arena suddenly returned to their normal white and increased in intensity. Lily could see the judging panel nodding to each other, and the announcer boomed the confirmation of Lily's success in the Trial of Courage over the cheers and applause.

Lily exhaled a sigh of relief and hoped to have time to rest before the next trial. She watched a team of people jog over to the corpse of the unlucky fire-eater. Surely cleaning up that mess would take long enough for at least a bathroom break. Unfortunately, the team executed a complex yet synchronised set of movements with their hands and the dead fire-eater, complete with blood, disappeared from the stadium floor. It was as if there had never even been a battle there at all.

Lily saw a separate group of people head towards the fire-eater with long poles that looked like electric prods and start to herd her towards the door. Lily could feel the fear of the fire-eater, as well as pain and anger as one of the group poked her with a prod.

"Hey!" Lily called to them. "No one is to harm this fire-eater. Am I understood?"

The group looked anxiously amongst themselves, being sure to keep a careful eye on the dangerous beast snarling at them.

Lily turned to the fire-eater and thought, *Will you go*

Lily projected as much confidence as she could muster. She tried not to focus on the slivers of doubt in her mind. Could she order the fire-eater released into the wild? Would that truly be the best thing for her, if she'd lived most of her life in captivity? She pushed the inconvenient thoughts away. She was going to be queen. That was the whole point of the Trials, anyway. If she couldn't order the release of the fire-eater, then there were probably bigger issues. At the very least, she could order someone to brief her on what the options were.

The fire-eater looked at Lily for a while. Long enough that Lily first worried the fire-eater could sense her doubts, and then that the fire-eater hadn't heard her thoughts at all. Finally, the fire-eater nodded at Lily and slowly moved towards the exit. The group of herders jumped when she moved and went to take their places and begin prodding her, but Lily yelled at them, ordering them to simply go with her, and they reluctantly complied.

Lily watched as the door shut and hoped that she would be able to keep her promise of freedom.

32

"LET's hear it again for Her Majesty, folks!"

The crowd roared. The noise was overwhelming, and she wondered now why she hadn't heard them much while battling the fire-eaters. It seemed impossible that she would be able to block out that kind of volume.

"One down and what's up next? That's right, it's the Trial of Illusions!" The announcer drew out the word "illusions", making it sound spooky. The crowd "oohed" and "ahhed" appropriately, excitement buzzing in the air.

Lily saw Harold approaching. She wondered where he had been throughout the Trial of Courage. She didn't remember seeing him. Had he been there, and she had merely blocked him out as she had the crowd? Or had he been watching from some safer, more sheltered position?

"Excellent work, Your Majesty," said Harold in a tone that showed no enthusiasm for her efforts at all and, if anything, sounded slightly apologetic. "We'll now move straight into the Trial of Illusions. The same rules apply as for the last trial. You must stay within the bounds of the area, and in this trial, as it is all about illusions, attacking anyone will result in an automatic failure. We've had a few of those in the past," he said, suddenly jovial at the memory. "Once someone flinched and blasted a trial administrator to oblivion." He smiled as if that was an amusing mistake that one might make from time to time.

Harold asked Lily if she had any questions, but she was too surprised by his attitude towards exploding administrators and worried about what could possibly be worse than the trial she had just endured to think of any.

As Harold walked away, Lily heard the announcer's voice booming.

"A reminder folks, for your viewing pleasure, our conjurers will be extending their illusions to ensure you can see exactly what Her Majesty sees! But remember, any interference will see you immediately removed from the arena."

As the announcer finished talking, the lights again dimmed, and this time tinged a royal blue.

Suddenly, Lily was surrounded by five creepy, hooded figures. They had appeared from nowhere, forming a circle around her, each perhaps five metres away from where Lily stood, and equal distance from each other. Lily braced herself, waiting for the attack.

She gave a small squeal. Looking around, Lily saw she had been enclosed in what seemed to be an empty transparent box. She reached out and touched the pane in front of her. It was glass, and cool to the touch. She looked around, confirming that there was no way out. She felt a slight pang of claustrophobia, but she wasn't ready to panic. Yet. She couldn't see any holes or gaps in the structure that might show a way for oxygen to get in. But all in all, if the only thing the Trial of Illusions required of her was for her to find her way out of a glass box, then this might be her favourite trial.

Lily felt something hairy brush her leg. Her stomach

dropped, and Lily looked down. Her mind screamed. Her body froze. The biggest, hairiest spider she had even seen was beside her foot, one leg on hers, another raised as if it was trying to decide how to climb Lily. Lily stepped as quickly as she dared, one pace away from the spider. One pace was all the box allowed. She heard a hiss and felt rather than saw something move out of the way of her foot. She looked over to see a large black snake slither away from her, then rear up, annoyed at almost being stepped on. A beetle scurried over Lily's foot.

Suddenly, everywhere she looked disgusting and terrifying creepy crawlies were appearing at an alarming rate. Spiders, snakes, cockroaches, centipedes, either hairy or slithery and all creepy and multiplying before her eyes. Suddenly the box felt tiny, and she was hyperaware that there was nowhere to go.

Lily felt something large slowly crawling up her back. She was instantly paralysed, unsure what to do about it. She couldn't move around to shake it off, and she didn't want to grab it. The idea of slamming her back into the glass to kill whatever it was didn't appeal to her either. What if it didn't die, and she just made it mad? But standing still wasn't working for her either. She could now feel bugs and spiders crawling up her legs. A small snake wrapped itself around her ankle.

A high-pitched ringing dominated Lily's mind, blocking out all useful thoughts and her ability to reason, to rationally find a way out of this mess. She wished that this wasn't happening, that she was anywhere but here. That this wasn't real. That this was all in her head. *Of course it is you idiot, this is the Trial of Illusions.*

The thought snapped Lily out of her panic and back to reality. A brief feeling of shame and embarrassment flitted through her mind that she was so taken with fear that she had all but forgotten why she was here and what she was supposed to do. Though as a massive, hairy, black-and-orange spider crawled onto her shoulder, she forgave herself somewhat for panicking. She could feel its weight on her shoulder and the hairy legs as they brushed her skin. She could even hear the disconcerting clicking noise it was making, probably with its pincers. For an illusion, this felt incredibly real.

On a whim, as more of a distraction than an actual plan, Lily reached out to the spider with her mind, as she had with the fire-eater. Instead of finding a full being as she had before, Lily found an empty shell. She could see a very thin external layer that was what she could visually identify as a spider, but beyond that, nothing. No vibrations, no energy. Looking closer, Lily saw the finest of threads extending from the spider to one of the hooded figures outside of the box, who had his arms outstretched towards Lily.

Trying her very best to ignore the masses of creepy crawlies now crawling all over her body, including her head, Lily fixed her eyes on a large centipede crawling up the glass in front of her. It was the same as the spider. Empty on the inside, with a delicate thread leading back to the hooded figure. The spider tapped her on the cheek with a leg, and she turned her attention back to it. Trying to maintain her focus, she looked for its thread and tried to touch it with her mind. She took hold of it, feeling its delicacy, but also its strength. With a pull, she severed the thread from the spider, and the spider disappeared from her shoulder.

Lily had all but forgotten about the crowd, but she heard them echo her shock at the sudden disappearance of the large orange beast. Lily started working at the larger insects, reptiles, and arachnids in the box, but quickly realised that for all the ones she was dispelling, more were taking their places. She looked at the hooded figure in anger and frustration. The figure ignored her, busy filling the box with horrors. *The box!*

Lily focussed on the box, fumbling with it mentally for a while until she found its threads. With a mental slice, she severed them. The glass disappeared and the creepy crawlies spilled out onto the arena floor and began running in every direction.

The crowd screamed, and the four other hooded figures looked distinctly uncomfortable. Two even took a step back. Lily focussed on a group of the crawlies still at her feet and used the same slicing technique to sever the threads of all of them at once, and they all disappeared. She removed another group before the hooded figure realised he had been defeated and lowered his arms. The rest of the bugs and critters disappeared, much to the relief of the crowd. The figure gave a small, slow nod and took a deliberate step back.

Lily looked up at the crowd, smiling. She gave a small wave, though was bitterly thinking about how it had all been amusing for them when she was locked in a box with all those things, but not so much when they were out and about. Suddenly, the ground fell away, and she plunged into ice-cold water. Lily immediately panicked, thrashing around and kicking to get back up out of the water. She saw the ice closing over her and doubled her efforts, though she seemed to go nowhere. A tiny part of Lily's mind wondered when she had been transported to an arctic region. The rest of Lily's mind ignored that voice and focussed entirely on getting out of the freezing water.

Lily's chest was pounding, her lungs screaming in protest. She wouldn't be able to hold her breath for much longer, and her limbs were slowing, numbing in the extreme cold. She kicked desperately, pulling with her arms. Against her will, her lungs won out, and she opened her mouth, gasping for air.

And air she got. It was difficult to get the air in, as her lungs, like the rest of her, were frozen, but she could breathe. Lily wondered if she could breathe underwater and checked her throat for gills. There were no gills, which meant one of three things had happened. The first was that she had been teleported to some frozen region and thrust into icy water, developing the magical ability to breathe underwater as a result. This seemed unlikely, since Lily herself was not permitted to leave the arena. It would be a tad unfair if the administrators of the trial could send her away.

Option two was that a pool of frozen water had been hidden under the arena floor and they had plunged her into it. This was more likely than option one, but Lily felt that the most likely scenario had to be option three. A pool of frozen water seemed to defeat the whole "illusions" part of the Trial of Illusions, and therefore she decided that the second hooded figure must have fooled her mind into thinking that she had been dunked through ice and trapped in the water below.

Lily calmed herself. She could breathe and so she took deep breaths, telling herself that there was no need to panic. She severed the ice's thread and kicked her legs, propelling herself towards the surface. Just as she was about to break through, Lily's predicament changed. She wasn't sure whether she had broken the illusion by realising it, or whether the hooded figure had altered it, but as she looked around, she wished she was back in the water.

Lily was tied to a large log that reached high above her to the sky, and all around her feet were logs, branches, twigs, and all sorts of flammable substances. *This is an illusion.* But, pulling at her arms, she found they were firmly fixed behind her back, tied to the pole. As she struggled, she could feel the metal ties around her wrists bite into her skin. The panic rose within her. *This is an illusion. This has to be an illusion.*

The flames burst into life all around her, and she squealed despite herself. It was so real. Lily could feel the heat and smell the smoke. She doubled her efforts in trying to escape. The metal cut her wrists, and she could feel the blood dripping onto her hands. *Stop.* Lily made a forcible effort to stop herself. She *knew* that this was not real, could not be real. It had to be an illusion, which meant that she could stop it, but fighting it physically would not work.

Lily tried to ignore the flames and concentrate on what she knew she could do that might help her. With a bang, the flames doubled in size, burning her now, licking hungrily at her legs and hands. It was significantly harder to write this off as an illusion as her skin bubbled and blistered. Lily focussed and reached for her ability to control fire, directing the fire to die. The fire shrunk, and Lily felt instant relief. Her relief was short-lived though, as almost immediately the fire redoubled in size and burned stronger, as if annoyed at her attempt to kill it.

Lily couldn't help it; she screamed. The smoke entered her lungs and burned her throat. She threw her head back, hitting it on the pole. She looked at the sky, trying to find fresh air. The pain in her legs and arms was now extreme. She panicked and flailed, but one part of her mind remained focussed on the problem, and the current problem was that she needed to think.

Lily looked inward, searching for her pain receptors. Locating them, she tried to switch them off. *Yes, I know being burned alive hurts, thanks.* Try as she might, she could still feel her skin burn, though focussing her mind on her task had reduced her panic. With some room to think, Lily looked down at the flames and realised that they weren't burning her at all. There were no burns on her legs, no blisters or cooked skin. However, she could still smell burning flesh, and the smoke. Again, she reached out with her mind. There was no living thing per se to reach out to, but she focussed on the whole scenario. Under closer examination, suddenly it all looked flimsy, like a child's drawing of a house compared to the architect's designs that her senses were seeing. As she examined it with her mental ability, the illusion shattered and fell away.

The crowd gasped and applauded enthusiastically. Lily stood stunned for a second, not having expected to defeat the illusion so easily, and then tried to shift her posture to a confident one, as if she had expected that to happen all along. As she waved at the crowd, the hooded figure nodded and took a step back. Lily saw this out of the corner of her eye and braced herself for whatever the next one would throw at her. She had managed terrifying creatures, extreme panic, and pain. She was sure she could deal with whatever the next guy dreamt up for her.

"Oh Lily, what have you gotten yourself into now?"

Lily whirled around to her right so quickly she almost fell. "Mum?"

"You don't really think you can be queen of an entire nation, do you?"

She whipped back to her left. "Dad?"

Her mother and father took a few steps closer to each other, both standing in front of her with that look of sympathetic pity on their faces that she knew so well. How were they here? They must have been brought in for the Trials.

"How did you...?"

"Now love, look," her dad began patiently, "it's marvellous that you've stepped up to get this done, it really is..."

"But we all know that you're not going to be able to do

this long-term," her mum finished, a kind, yet patronising look on her face.

Her dad glanced with a smile at her mum, nodding in agreement. "You've never been a leader."

"You've never really been much of one to stick with anything, have you?" Her parents laughed softly. It wasn't unkind; it was the kind of gentle approach her parents often used for difficult discussions. Like when Lily thought she might become a pilot. Her parents had let her run with that idea for a bit until they explained the amount of math and physics involved. They had gently, like they were now, pointed out that she wasn't terrible at math or physics, but that they certainly weren't her best subjects, and perhaps she'd like to do something that played to her strengths. And before she knew it, Lily had been refocussed on something else.

"Not that that's a criticism," added her mum, the way she did when criticising something. "It's just that, well. There's a lot of people who'd be relying on you here, wouldn't there, love? A lot of people who might be let down, even hurt, if you didn't succeed."

"Is it really worth risking them on this whim of yours?"

Lily looked at her dad. *Whim?*

"I mean, we get it." Lily's mother nodded in enthusiastic support of her father. "You've had a lot of this thrust upon you. And really, you've done a pretty good job holding it together so far. But we all know that this isn't for you."

"It's really not, love."

"So why not hand it over to someone else..."

"Someone qualified."

"Someone qualified," Lily's father agreed with her mother. "Which, really, you're not."

"You don't have any qualifications, do you sweetie?"

Lily's mother said with a laugh. Like it was a joke. Lily didn't join in. Her mother's comment had hurt.

"Oh, darling," said her mother, seeing her face fall, "it's true, but that's okay. You're good at plenty of things. Just not this."

"No, why don't we just leave this to the professionals and you can come on home. Maybe help your mother in her store..."

"She could be Elaine's assistant!"

Lily's parents nodded eagerly at each other like this was the best idea. *Elaine's assistant?* Did they really think all she was capable of was being a helper for her older sister? Doubt crept around the edges of Lily's mind. Maybe that was all she was cut out for. She had failed at everything else.

"You'd be good at that, love," said her father, meaning it, "and let's face it, you've not really been much chop at anything else."

Hearing her father echo her doubts stabbed at her chest, and she blinked back the tears that were threatening to form. A small part of her mind had risen up, offended that he had said that, but it was beaten back by her own self-doubts, validated now by her father.

"I have to stay," Lily said in a small voice. "They need me."

Both her parents burst out laughing at that. "Need you? Who *needs* you?" laughed her father.

"Oh Lily, dear," Lily's mother said, wiping the tears of laughter from her eyes, "no one needs you."

Lily stepped back as if she'd been slapped in the face.

"Oh, I'm sorry, love, but really. You can't finish university, you can't hold down a job..."

"You're not good at the farm like your brother, or the shop like your sister..."

"You've got no actual skills or hobbies, and you need other people to sort things out for you."

"Like this." Her father gestured around the arena. "How many people did it take to get you to figure out how to use your own abilities?"

Lily's heart sunk again. That one she couldn't just shake off. It had taken an army of people to get her up to scratch to even consider attempting the Trials. Like everything else, she had been terrible at it on her own. Hadn't been able to figure it out or get it done. Only when Lady Octavia helped her was she able to develop her abilities. She was a failure. She knew it, and who knew her better than her own parents? If they thought she was a failure, then it must be true. She would fail these Trials, just like everything else, and then what? The Prime Minister would arrest her advisors and the country would fall into whatever fascist chaos the Prime Minister had in mind.

And what if she succeeded? Her parents were right; she wasn't qualified to run a country. Whatever had possessed her to think that she should be in charge? People relied on their leaders for things like education and healthcare and food. And it would only be a matter of time until Meridia and Valmead realised she was a fraud. Cold sweat beaded on Lily's brow. Between disease and famine and war, she could be responsible for the deaths of thousands. Millions, even. Maybe it was better if she just withdrew.

"You should bow out gracefully, love," said her father, reading her mind. "Just walk away, and then everything will be fine."

"It will?" She sounded like a little girl, even to her own ears.

"Yes, love," her mother reassured her, "everything will be fine if you just walk away."

Lily was hurriedly blinking back tears now. They were

right, of course. She couldn't do this. And it wasn't fair to all those who had helped her. All the effort they put in. If she left now, it would be better for them in the long run. They could surely find someone else, someone better, to help them.

Still, she felt bad. Like she was letting them down. Lily looked up into the stadium, looking for her advisors. Mainly, she realised, looking for Ava. Ava had always been so positive about what Lily could do. She felt bad about showing her to be wrong and letting her down.

Lily squinted at the stadium. It was weird and blurry.

"Now love, how about we go together?" said her father, drawing her attention back to her parents. Lily looked just beyond them to the hooded figures. They were blurry too. She blinked a few times, but nothing changed.

With a click in her mind, Lily looked back at her parents, angry now.

"Lily, love, what's wrong?" Her mother looked genuinely concerned about her. Lily looked at her mother with her mental focus, as she had with the previous illusions. She wasn't a shell like the creepy crawlies, but there was something off about what Lily found. It was... like an echo. Lily looked for a thread to sever like the others, but there was nothing there. Her faux parents started moving towards her now, more intense and trying to draw her back under their spell, their manner becoming more aggressive the less attention she paid them. She examined them again. It was like they were there, but not. Like... a memory?

Was the hooded figure in her mind? What had Claire said about mental barriers? Lily drew her focus back into her own mind, then imagined pushing a mental wall from the centre out to her skull and taking everything that wasn't supposed to be there with it. She felt some resistance and pushed harder. Her parents were in her face now, screaming at her, though she couldn't make out the words; her focus was purely on expelling the hooded figure from her mind.

With a final mammoth effort, she felt him move, and completed the push, focussing now on maintaining the barrier to ensure he remained out of her head. With a final, disappointed look at Lily, her parents vanished, and suddenly the crowd returned to a sharp focus, their cheers blasting though Lily's head. She blinked and looked around, slightly disoriented, as if she had been in a dream.

Lily did not even have time to acknowledge the crowd before she felt deep slashes in her back. She checked to ensure her mental block was still in place, but only felt more slashes and something dripping down her back. Lily turned and saw the next hooded figure slashing his arms in her direction and screamed as gashes appeared on her arms and chest. She touched the blood. It was real. He slashed again and Lily felt the panic rise, but forced herself to calm. She had already overcome so much. She could do this.

More pain than Lily had ever known existed slammed down on her body. Gasping at the shock of it, she collapsed to her knees. Waves and waves of crushing pain enveloped her, like terrible cramps ripping through her entire body. She felt like her body was folding in on itself, and then as if she was being drawn and quartered. Sharp pain, like a hundred knives stabbing into her, exploded everywhere, especially in her head. For what felt like forever, Lily was unable to focus on anything but the pain. She was aware of someone screaming. It might have been her, but she didn't know.

Through her bleary, tear-filled eyes, Lily saw a figure beyond the hoods. Harold! *Thank God he's coming to stop this.* Lily felt sudden relief, but a niggling voice reminded her that if Harold stopped the Trials, then she had failed and all was lost.

Ignoring Harold, Lily focussed on holding onto her awareness. She was writhing on the ground, and something inside her hung onto that one solid fact that existed beyond the excruciating pain: that she wanted so badly for the pain to stop. She focussed on it and repeated it until that was all that was running through her mind. *Make the pain stop.* After an age, Lily felt the pain subside slightly. She took advantage of the break and doubled her focus on making it stop, but that only wasted precious time and energy she didn't have. Magic wasn't making a wish. That hooded figure in front of her with his arms outstretched—he had to be the source of her pain. *Bastard.*

Lily reached out for his mind and crashed inside, not worrying in the slightest about whether or not he knew she was there. She fumbled around, noticing the figure trying to keep his focus on her despite being in some discomfort himself. Lily was perversely pleased to think her intrusion might be unpleasant for him.

She examined his mind, the now-familiar structure easy to navigate. Lily first located his power, then followed that to find his ability. Something distracted her. This was a real mind, but something about it recalled the echo that was her parents. Her hesitation cost her. The hooded figure redoubled his efforts to cause her pain and also began erecting a block and trying to force Lily from his mind. *No, I am stronger than you.*

She pushed back, knocking through the mental block, locating his ability, and with a mental motion akin to flicking a switch, she turned it off. The pain ceased immediately, and the sudden exhilaration of feeling pain-free momentarily stunned Lily. The hooded figure looked confused by Lily's sudden relaxed state. He thrust his arms out futilely a few times, struggling to affect her. Using so much effort, his arms shook, and he tilted slightly to the side with the strain. Lily didn't feel a thing. The figure looked at her somewhat forlornly before letting his arms fall.

Lily noticed that the crowd, who had been watching in voyeuristic excitement as she had been tortured for their enjoyment, had begun murmuring curiously, wondering what happened. Proud of having defeated the hooded figure, Lily was taken with a little whimsical urge to play it up for the crowd. She dropped to a knee, yelling and grabbing her head. Out of the corner of her eye, she saw the hooded figure look at her hopefully and heard the crowd draw a collective intake of shocked air at the renewed pain.

"Just kidding," said Lily, standing back up and giving a little bow. The figure looked annoyed both at being beaten and at Lily's showmanship, but the crowd erupted into delighted applause and cheering, enjoying the display. The figure pulled his arms back inside his cloak and took a step backward.

Lily turned to the final figure. She took a deep breath, ready to take on whatever he threw at her. She had beaten the others and endured far more than she ever thought she could. She was ready.

The figure stared at her for a beat, then turned to the judging panel and gave a small nod. They huddled together, talking in low voices. The crowd started a curious murmuring, and Lily wondered what was happening. Was he seeking permission for some new, unheard-of horrible test to subject her to?

Finally, the panel looked again at the hooded figure. They nodded solemnly, and Lily put aside her resentment and prepared to face whatever came next.

The hooded figure nodded at her, pulled his arms out of his robe, and performed a complicated swishing manoeuvre with them. To Lily's shock and surprise, as one, the other four hooded figures bowed at her and disappeared. A sudden realisation hit her—they had all been duplicates of this final hooded man. Having dispelled his clones, the man simply nodded at Lily and walked towards the arena door. The crowd started cheering, louder than they had throughout the Trial.

Lily listened to the announcer proclaim the results. She had completed the Trial of Illusions. Just one trial remained between Lily and the crown.

33

"One to go folks! And it's a Highacren favourite—the Trial of Endurance!"

Harold hurried out to Lily, flinching at the roar of the crowd, patting his pockets as if looking for something.

"Well done, Your Majesty," he said distractedly. "Okay, now we just need to attach this." Harold darted forward, pressing something cool to Lily's temple. She reached up as he stepped back, feeling a small silicone dot stuck to her skin.

"What is that?" she asked.

"It'll allow the audience to see what you see," said Harold as if that should answer Lily's question. She was about to demand more information when Harold produced a small familiar disk.

An immersion device.

Lily opened her mouth, but Harold raised a finger and looked up, indicating she should listen to the announcer.

"For tonight's Trial of Endurance we have a very special treat! A Highacren legend. A true hero. A moment in history, etched forever in our minds and in every Highacren heart."

"Get on with it," Lily muttered earning a glare from Harold.

"Tonight, Her Majesty will follow in the footsteps of greatness... And reach new heights."

There were murmurs of excitement in the crowd now as some of the audience began to understand the announcer's cryptic clues.

"That's right ladies and gentlemen, tonight's Trial of Endurance will see Her Majesty repeat the flight of Fletcher Vantage and hike to the summit of Mount Harakka."

The announcer paused for the crowd to cheer and whoop.

"Now we all know the tale of heroism and grit that saw one man save a nation, but just in case we have any international visitors here with us, or our school system is not what I remember it to be," he paused indulgently for laughter, "allow me to recap. The year is 1567 and it's only a few years after the founding of this great nation. The union of the city states was fresh, and most still operated independently. However with political turmoil in Valmead, the world was on the brink of war once again.

"When the Valmeadian ships landed unexpectedly at Ulmer's Rock, Highacre needed to rally the combined might of our fledgling nation. The beacon had to be lit."

The crowd again burst into applause, some people screaming 'light the beacon'.

"With the threat already on our shores, most though it was too late—there was no way anyone but a flyer could make it all the way to the top of Mount Harakka in time and all the flyers were monitoring the border with Meridia. But one man thought otherwise. That man was Fletcher Vantage."

More applause and Lily saw Harold check his watch

impatiently, apparently now agreeing with Lily's desire for the man to get to the point.

"Fletcher, with the fate of his country on his shoulders didn't wait for permission. He grabbed a torch and started running. He made it to the beacon in a record three hours and twenty seven minutes. Fletcher Vantage put the needs of his country first and refused to stop in order to save Highacre. Her Majesty will need to do the same to pass her final trial tonight."

As the crowd roared in excited anticipation, Harold leaned closer so Lily could hear him.

"You've used an immersion device before, I assume? Good. As you know, any living things captured in the memory will not notice you, nor will you be able to interact with them. This device will allow you to use your powers, for obvious reasons. Once you are within the device, everything is permitted and your time will start as soon as you take a step. However, if you pull yourself out of the immersion prior to completion you will be immediately disqualified and fail the Trials. Do you have any questions?"

Lily shook her head. She wasn't looking forward to a three and a half hour hike up a mountain, but this felt like the least complicated trial. The lights in the arena dimmed again, and this time glowed with a greenish tinge. Harold handed Lily the device and Lily pressed the button.

The arena was immediately replaced and Lily blinked at the sudden change from night to day. She could hear the crowd faintly in the background, cheering. She'd never noticed noises from outside an immersion device before, though she'd never used one in proximity to anywhere near this much background noise.

Lily glanced around, seeing a lush forest. The thick canopy blocked the mountain from view, but a path lay before her, largely flat. She could see it start to rise a few hundred meters away before it turned and was hidden from view.

I've got this, she told herself confidently. Lily took a deep breath and began jogging down the path. As she exited the trees, she took in her view of the mountain and almost stopped dead in her tracks.

I absolutely do not have this.

The mountain extended before her, impossibly high. So high, in fact, that she couldn't see the peak through the clouds. Sheer cliffs were everywhere on its face and she began to panic that her assumption of an easy to follow, heavily signposted track was incorrect.

A man rushed passed her, sprinting and holding a torch aloft. *Fletcher?* Of course, the immersion device was a replay of his scaling the mountain. Lily increased her pace to try and keep up with him. Obviously she would need to at least match him to complete the Trial, but he would also show her the path.

Feeling reassured to not have to navigate alone, Lily tried to steady her breathing as the path rose sharply in front of her and Fletcher led her up the sharp incline to a small plateau. Lily saw Fletcher slow and reduced her pace, relieved to be able to catch her breath and trying not to think of what was to come.

She followed Fletcher around a corner and was met with an almost vertical rocky path lying with huge boulders either side.

"You have got to be kidding me," she said angrily, glaring as she tracked the path still further up and out of sight to the right. She closed her eyes and took a deep breath. She was not prepared for this. Lily had never scaled a mountain in her life. The closest she came was the large hill on her family's farm, and she had already doubled that height coming up what she now realised was a gentle rise below her.

Lily was grateful for Austin's training, though that had been focussed on combat, and sprinting. At most, she had done a few middle distance runs, and that meant she had handled the initial ascent with relative ease. But looking ahead... Her training wasn't going to help her here.

Lily looked over at Fletcher. She was thankful he'd stopped briefly, but now she needed him to get going so she could see how he approached the climb. Fletcher was similarly looking at the path with an unimpressed expression on his face. He glanced about, as if checking to see if anyone was watching, and then clicked his fingers, disappearing.

"What the—" Lily exclaimed, looking around in alarm. She heard a quiet pop, and saw Fletcher materialise at the top of the rocky incline. With a relieved look at not having to make the climb, Fletcher turned and started jogging further up the mountain.

Allowing herself the comfort of reciting every swear word she knew, Lily took a deep breath and began scrambling up the path, panicking at losing sight of Fletcher. Her feet scrambled on the small rocks, her hands looking to grab on, but the rocks were all loose, and simply came away. She dug her feet in, trying to get traction, and did the same with her hands, plunging them into the rocks and pushing herself up the path. The rocks tumbled down the mountain below her as she slipped and slid, making slow progress. About halfway up the incline, Lily paused, catching her breath. She looked back, depressed to see how little progress she'd made for the time and effort, though the start point was now far below, only the tops of the trees in sight.

Lily turned and continued scrabbling up the path, gaining inch after painstaking inch. Her left foot slipped and her knee banged painfully into the rocks on the path before she began to slide down. She grabbed out, looking for anything to stop her descent, but the rocks didn't help and she couldn't find the ground under them. Crying out in pain and frustration, Lily managed to halt the slide mere meters from where the rocky path began.

This is stupid. Lily closed her eye and breathed. What did it matter if she could scale a mountain? Lily's eyes flew open. It didn't matter. The Trials were all about magic. Perhaps she had to emulate Fletcher in more than just time.

Lily tried imagining herself teleporting. She didn't move. Lily clicked her fingers like Fletcher had. Nothing happened. She looked at the point where the normal path resumed and imagined herself standing there. But she didn't even feel a tingle that might indicate magic was trying to work. Swearing, Lily forced herself to start climbing again— there wasn't time to wait there hoping for a convenient ability.

As she dug her hands and feet into the rocks, Lily expanded her focus on potential abilities. They had mentioned flyers in the story—could she fly? Apparently not. Maybe levitate? Nope. Lily's foot slipped again, but she thrust herself forward with her other leg, feeling with relief the compacted dirt of the normal path with her hands. Moving carefully, Lily hefted herself out of the rocks and back onto stable ground. She brushed herself off as she pushed herself into a jog, eyes scanning above for any sign of Fletcher.

Her knee ached, but didn't seem to be damaged, and so she tried to increase speed despite the sharp incline. *At least it's not almost vertical.* Lily rounded another corner and cursed herself. The path wound around on itself, zigzagging up the mountain sharply. She could see Fletcher jogging a couple of levels from the top and while she was grateful he hadn't, she wondered why he hadn't simply teleported to the top of the path. Or the mountain for that matter.

Lily pushed herself on, trying not to think about how much further she might have to go and darting glances up the path to try and keep Fletcher in view. Gasping for breath, she saw him reach the top of this section and continue running along the path out of view to the left. Ignoring the stitch in her side and the burning in her calves, Lily tried to increase her speed, but found she could not. Following the path to the right and the left and the right again, she kept her eyes on the ground in front of her, willing herself forward and trying to keep her ragged breathing in check.

Where did he go? Lily was on the top path now, following it as it wound around the mountain. It was still at an incline, but not a steep one, comparatively, and Lily was grateful for the opportunity to get her breath back. She felt blisters forming on her heels and the sweat was beginning to chafe. Again, she pushed herself to find a power that would help with this task and again she found nothing.

A distant pop caused Lily to whip her head around, finally spotting Fletcher now high above her on a different section of the path.

"No!" she cried in frustration, seeing Fletcher jog out of view. She sped up to try and make up time, but as she rounded a corner, the path veered into a forty degree incline. Lily slowed to a walk. She put her head down and pushed herself to continue at speed.

Lily reached for her power, finding it there, but still, none of the abilities she reached for manifested to help her. Lily paused to wipe the sweat and tears of frustration from her face, taking a moment to look out at the view that she had largely ignored so far. It was stunning. Was there a view of this country that wasn't?

Lily felt pride well up in her chest. This was her country. Her people. She frowned at the smoke in the distance. The Disputed Region. What had the announcer said? The flyers were in the Disputed Region monitoring the border. Looked like more than monitoring was going on. *The ships!* Lily turned her gaze south, looking for the strange landmark that was Ulmer's Rock. Scanning the horizon back and forth, her eyes found the vertical plinth jutting out of the otherwise flat landscape and followed it to the coast, seeing small black smudges against the sand of the beach.

Lily frowned. She felt the urgency to get to the beacon, but this had happened in the past. A mere memory. Turning back to the path, she forced herself to continue up the mountain, glancing up hopefully for a glimpse of Fletcher, but the man seemed long gone.

The beacon is in the past, but Highacre is in peril again now. She needed to get up the mountain. She needed to match Fletcher. Her people needed her. Spurred on, Lily felt her aches and pains fade, her focus solely on her goal. *Do it for your people.*

She heard a distant roar and felt like the crowd were there with her, cheering her on. She wondered what it looked like back there. They would see what she saw on the screens, but was her body just standing there, or was she moving—scrambling up an invisible incline. She mustn't be moving. She thought back to her other ventures into immersion devices. When she'd exited the memories, she'd been right where she had been when she entered. Hopefully her blisters would remain in the device when she left.

What felt like several hours passed and every time Lily rounded a corner thinking she must be almost there she was crushed to see another expanse of mountain jutting up in front of her, ridiculously high and appallingly steep.

Finding herself in front of another precarious rocky incline, Lily dropped her head back, staring at the sky, energy gone.

I can't do this.

All the motivation of helping her people had long since evaporated. She wanted to help them, sure, but this task was impossible. She was going to fail. She hadn't see Fletcher in what felt like hours—the man had probably lit the beacon and gone home for tea by now. When were the judges going to call it and pull her out to tell her she'd failed?

Her stomach felt acidic. She'd let them all down. Her advisors, her people, her family. She was supposed to be the last hope, secreted away to save the country if the unthinkable happened. But it had happened, and she was not up to the task. Lily stared at her hands accusingly. Why had her magic failed her? Why didn't she have some ability that would help with this task? She was supposed to be the most magically powerful person of their age, but she couldn't leap up a stupid mountain in a single bound. What good was she?

The metal disk felt heavy in her pocket, and not for the first time, Lily's hand brushed over its outline. She'd clearly failed, so why not press the button and get this over with? She pulled the disk out, looking at it. Would it really be so bad? Surely there was a way to challenge the results of the Trials. Or at least the Prime Minister's invocation of them. Her advisors could find a loophole to see her still become queen.

As she turned the disk in her fingers, she heard the crown again. They deserved someone better. Someone who wouldn't give up. *Someone who can climb a mountain, apparently.* And maybe that was the answer. She could stay and help Minister Bellingham challenge the Prime Minister for his position. She'd be a better leader anyway. She was strong. And Lily could even help them figure out who was behind the assassinations before she left.

Lily's heart sank at the idea of leaving. She looked around at the view again. The view of Highacre. Of home. This was her home now. And they were *her* people. Lily glared at the path. A stupid mountain wasn't going to stop her from doing everything she could to help them.

Grunting, Lily pushed herself to take the incline at a run, ignoring her sliding feet and focussing on propelling her body forward. She heard the crowd roar and it gave her energy. She dug her feet in one side at a time, doing the same with her hands, repeating the motion. Foot, foot, hand, hand. Just keep moving. Suddenly she was at the top, flopping onto the dirt and rolling onto her back.

The crowd roared again, louder now. But it was different. Lily strained to listen over her breathing. Screams. Panic. Something was wrong. Lily glanced up at the never-ending mountain. She would fail if she left, but the screams were louder now. Was this a part of the test?

Lily felt a deep rumble vibrate through her body. Glancing around in alarm, she saw nothing wrong. The mountain looked normal, only a light breeze ruffling the leaves of the sparse bushes. *Not here—my body.*

Mind made up, Lily pulled the immersion device out of her pocket and pressed the button.

34

Chaos.

People in the stands were running in every direction, screaming and crying. Dust and smoke filled the air, and Lily could smell fire. She turned to the right and saw an entire section of the arena had collapsed. Most people were running away from it, but some were trying to move the enormous concrete slabs in a vain effort to free those trapped underneath. Pops and explosions sounded out, and a loud bang was accompanied by screams as the rubble shifted, more concrete falling on people.

Lily wondered what had happened to the building and her mind connected the vibration she had felt. *Maybe an earthquake?*

She watched, still stunned as two people in black walked up to a man trapped at the top of the collapsed section. They stood out not only from their clothes, but they were moving slowly where everyone else was panicking. Having just decided they must be emergency services, Lily squealed as one raised a pistol and shot the man in the head, his body slumping but still caught in the debris.

Not an earthquake. An attack.

"Ma'am!"

Lily turned to see Jason and Naomi running towards her, pistols drawn.

"We have her," he spoke into his lapel microphone. "Bring the vehicle around now."

The relief Lily felt at seeing her bodyguards and knowing she was safe felt at odds with watching the people in the arena screaming and crying and running in terror. She looked back at the collapsed section as Jason and Naomi positioned themselves to escort her out.

"No."

The bodyguards didn't register Lily's voice, so focussed on getting her to safety.

"No," she said louder, pulling her arm from Naomi's grip.

"Ma'am—" Jason started.

"I'm going to help them. I *need* to help them."

"Negative, we have to get you out of here."

"No, Jason. But you can come with me. Keep me safe. Or better, help me help them."

Before they could argue, Lily started running toward the rubble, her bodyguards automatically keeping pace behind her. She could feel Jason considering throwing her over his shoulder and running for the exit.

"On the left," Naomi called.

"Green light," Jason replied, and Naomi put a bullet each into the heads of three armed black-clad people who were about to climb the stairs to another section of the arena.

Lily heard Jason talking into his lapel microphone, updating someone about the situation, confirming hostile targets. She scanned the rubble and saw a woman desperately trying to free herself and two children, all pinned by the collapse. A small girl sat by her side, clutching a dirty teddy bear and crying.

"Ma'am," Jason grabbed her arm, bringing her to a halt. His eyes scanned the area before he pulled her over to an area near the collapsed building where two large slabs of concrete had fallen to create a barrier. "Wait here. Do not move."

Without waiting for Lily to ascent, Jason and Naomi moved to the corner and began returning fire. Lily pressed her back against the concrete. She hadn't even noticed whoever was firing at them. Maybe this hadn't been such a good idea. She peered around the side, again seeing the family desperately trying to free themselves. Lily cast her eyes further, examining the devastation. Three more black-clad figures were walking on the sand toward the family.

"Jason!" she called, but he and Naomi were desperately returning fire. She returned her gaze, seeing the terrorists walking casually, spotting the family and grinning at each other.

Lily darted out of cover and sprinted to the family.

"Help us, please," begged the mother, spotting Lily.

Lily looked at the three who were trapped. The little boy's leg was under a slab of concrete, but the mother and her daughter appeared to have been caught between two slabs that had fallen together. They were in the gap between the concrete, but it was too small for them to squeeze out.

Lily rushed forward and grabbed the woman's arm, pulling with everything she had, but the woman barely moved.

"Try her," she grunted. Lily grabbed the girl's arm and pulled as the mother pressed herself against the concrete, trying to make as much room as she could, but it was no use.

"Well, what have we here," a man leered. Lily looked

up and saw the terrorists watching them with interest. "Sitting ducks."

"Fish in a barrel," suggested another man.

"Dead meat," leered the woman.

"Take my girl and run," said the mother in a low voice to Lily. "Please."

Lily looked at her. She saw the terror in her eyes. The fear for her children trapped with her. The resolve that at least one could be safe. Lily looked back at the terrorists, casually pointing their pistols and discussing who would be first. She turned back to the mother.

"No," said the woman firmly, seeing the resolve in Lily's eyes. "Please. Save her."

"I can't leave you," Lily apologised.

"Time's up," called the female terrorist, aiming her pistol. Lily threw herself over the trapped woman and her children, her skin scraping on the chunks of concrete, her body tensing for the bullet she expected in her back.

"What is she doing?" one of the men asked, baffled by her actions.

"Does she think that'll stop us?" the other queried, also perplexed by Lily's actions.

"What did you think that was going to do?" called the woman in a mocking tone. "What? Are you bulletproof?"

Lily's insides froze. Diving on the family in the heat of the moment seemed like a good idea, but with the adrenaline seeping out and the mocking of the terrorists, she felt stupid. Like she had made a deadly mistake.

"Well let's find out," the woman said, her voice serious now. A crack and Lily felt a sting in her arm and warm liquid coating her skin.

"Shit shot," one of the men commented. The woman bit back, claiming to have intended to wing Lily, angry to have her marksmanship questioned.

As the terrorists argued, Lily pushed herself up. The trapped woman grabbed her, shaking Lily and urging her to grab her free child and leave. But Lily was staring at the terrorists. They were right—what had she hoped to achieve by protecting them with her body? She was still mentally on the mountain, where none of her magic was useful. But here, faced with this threat, Lily had magic. And it was useful.

With a slash of her arm, Lily blasted the three with a wave of fire, knocking them off their feet and setting their clothes and hair alight. Their laughter turned to screams and they began rolling frantically, trying to extinguish the flames.

Jason and Naomi sprinted to Lily's side, staring at the three burning people.

"Quick, help me," Lily gestured to the trapped family and the three of them braced against the concrete, straining to lift as the mother and daughter tried to wriggle free. Closing her eyes, Lily focussed her energy on the slab she was pushing, imagining it lifting as she did with all the small objects she could move telekinetically.

Hearing a cry of relief, Lily looked to see the mother and daughter squeezing out and embracing on the sand.

"Mummy!" the little girl who hadn't been caught in the collapse ran to her mother's arms. Lily smiled at sight, but then her eyes narrowed as she saw one of the terrorists climb to their feet and stagger towards them. Two shots rang out and the figure fell. Naomi ran over, her pistol trained on the bodies, and checked each to ensure they were no longer a threat.

"What do you think?" Lily asked Jason who was examining the boy whose leg was caught under the slab. Jason shook his head at her.

"I can't tell if his leg is crushed, or if the sand has cushioned it somewhat and it's just pinned. But if we move the concrete, or him, he might die."

"If we leave him here, he might die too," Lily said looking around. Naomi was back with the mother and her daughters, trying to convince them to get to safety. The mother was refusing, unable to leave her son.

Lily ran to the bodies, trying to ignore the smell and the horrific burns, refusing to comprehend that she had done that to them. That she had just killed three people. She grabbed their pistols and returned to the mother.

"If you're staying, take this. Naomi will show you how to use it."

Lily ran back to Jason as Naomi gave the mother a quick run down on the pistol.

"We've done what we can for them. We need to get rid of the terrorists so that people can come in to help everyone who's hurt and trapped."

"We need to get you out of here," Jason pleaded again, seeing her arm and pulling out a small bandage from a pouch on his belt. He handed Lily some gauze and indicated to her head, which she realised she had cut when shielding the family. She wiped the blood—just a scratch.

She shook her head. "I'm staying. Help me clear the area."

He nodded, tying off the bandage, uncomfortable with Lily in danger, but recognising that an argument helped no one. Naomi rejoined them and Jason spoke into his microphone, relaying their plan.

"Okay," he turned to Lily and Naomi. "Guards and police are working their way through the arena. We'll clear the destroyed area. Ma'am, you will be in the middle and you *will* follow my directions." Jason stared at Lily until she nodded and then they turned, leaving the family and climbing onto the rubble.

They worked their way through it, every now and then shots firing from Lily's left or right as Jason or Naomi spotted a terrorist and took them down. Lily realised why Jason wanted her in the middle, as anyone she saw was dispatched by her bodyguards before she could so much as summon a fireball.

They passed the injured and trapped, offering them the only comfort they could—assurance that help was coming. Occasionally they stopped, one applying first aid while the other two faced out, scanning for threats.

Eventually they came to the outer edge of the broken arena and saw two large armoured vehicles parked near the site of the explosion that had caused the devastation.

"Right, Naomi, you take the right. I'll take the left, and Ma'am, you stay here and provide overwatch."

"You mean, just stay out of it?"

"No, top cover. We need to clear those vehicles and if someone tries to jump us, you take care of them."

Lily frowned at Jason. "I feel like this is safer," she said, turning and sending two massive fireballs at the vehicles, engulfing them in flames. "See? Now we're all safe."

The rear doors burst open, figures falling out of each and rolling on the ground. Some of them extinguished their flames quickly, and turned toward the group, readying their weapons.

"Well, now we're still going to have to take care of them," said Jason, a slightly patronising tone in his voice. "And now they know where we are. That's why I wanted the element of surprise."

"Sorry," Lily said, rolling her eyes. "I still think that was safer than the two of you creeping around down there trying to take on armoured vehicles."

They all ducked down as shots began to ping around them.

"I'm just saying, Your Majesty, that you don't kick the hornet's nest. You need to make sure you take care of the threat."

There was a whooshing sound before an ear splitting bang as both vehicles exploded. Their metal frames twisted, shrapnel flying off and shredding the remaining terrorists. The wrecks lifted from their tyres before landing heavily back on the ground, rolling onto the now incinerated and ragged bodies.

"I think the threat has been taken care of," Lily said.

35

Lily, Jason and Naomi sat on a bench in the changing room that Lily had used before the Trials. Each was drinking water, staring into space, their cuts and injuries seen to by medical staff and either healed or dressed. The arena had been secured and the rescue effort was well underway with most of the easily reached people having been extracted from the debris and transported to hospital.

The three jumped as the door opened, Lily's advisors rushing in and fussing to see if she was alright.

"I'm fine," she battered them away, only mildly annoyed to see them stop only when Jason nodded to confirm she was. "What happened?" she asked.

"Terrorists," said Minister Bellingham. "Looks like a Meridian group. We've dealt with them before, but not in years."

"And not this big," said Addison, her eyes wide.

Lily jumped as the door opened again. Baroness Traunt and Lord Witherington entered hesitantly.

"Apologies, Your Majesty, we don't mean to interrupt," said Baroness Traunt.

"Not at all, come in," Lily said, gesturing for them to join the group.

Minister Bellingham nodded respectfully at the Baroness. "Heard you got a few of them, Gertie. Good show."

The Baroness nodded, embarrassed. "Of course. We all did what we could."

An awkward silence fell before Lord Witherington cleared his throat. "Terrible catastrophe. Just terrible," he shook his head, his body wobbling slightly. "And you were doing so well, Your Majesty."

Lily nodded blankly at him. She had almost forgotten about the Trials—the whole reason they were there in the first place.

"I know it might not seem so important in light of the attack, but we thought we should inform you of the outcome.

"The outcome?" Lily asked, her mind still on the tragedy she had witnessed.

"Of the Trials. Despite everything, you—"

"Clearly failed."

Everyone turned in surprise to see Reginald Toth striding through the door.

"The requirements were clear—to pass the Trial of Endurance, she had to remain in the immersion experience until given clearance to leave. She voluntarily withdrew. She failed."

Lily glared at the joyous grin on the Prime Minister's face. Dozens of his citizens had just been killed and injured in an attack on his soil, and here he was, elated because Lily had failed a test.

She stood, but Claire put a warning hand on her shoulder.

"Ah, yes. Well, that is one way to look at it," Lord Witherington said hesitantly.

"It's the only way," asserted the Prime Minister happily.

"Well, it's just..."

"That's not how the panel sees it, Prime Minister," said Baroness Traunt firmly.

"Excuse me?" snarled the Prime Minister, glaring at the plump woman.

"How we see it is that Her Majesty was set a task. That task was to 'put the needs of Highacre first, and refuse to stop in order to save Highacre'," she recited.

"I thought it was to get up the mountain in the same time as Fletcher Vantage," said Lily, confused.

"Yes, well, you were supposed to think that," said Lord Witherington, pleased with himself that their ruse had worked. "But the test was for you to not give up, and keep going up the mountain."

"To the top?" Lily asked.

"Oh no, the immersion device was modified so that the mountain never ends."

"What?" asked Lily, annoyed despite her mind telling her there were bigger problems.

"You didn't give up. You kept going for the good of Highacre, and so the panel agrees that you passed the Trial of Endurance and therefore have completed the Trials," he smiled sadly at Lily.

"She can't have passed the Trial of Endurance," snarled the Prime Minister, squaring up to the timid Lord Witherington. "Because she voluntarily withdrew. You can't deem her to have retrospectively completed the Trial before she withdrew."

"The panel feels," the Baroness took a step toward the Prime Minister, who took a step back. "That Her Majesty's efforts within the device not only achieved the requirements of the Trial, but that her withdrawal upon hearing her people in distress coupled with her actions in running toward danger and saving the lives of many Highacrens more than satisfy the intent of the Trial."

"Yes, and where were you, Reginald," asked Minister Bellingham dangerously, taking a step toward the Prime Minister. "Where were you while our queen was running toward the fight to help her people?"

"She's not the queen," he hissed automatically. "And I was doing what a leader should do."

"Hiding out the back?" suggested Baroness Traunt.

"Remaining safe so as to direct the rescue efforts. Remaining safe," Toth's voice rose, now sure of his response, "so that resources didn't have to be diverted from the rescue efforts to ensure my safety."

"Needn't have worried about that happening," muttered Minister Bellingham.

"But the point is, the rules of the Trial were clear. Voluntary withdrawal for any reason was automatic failure. She withdrew. She failed."

"The panel disagrees," said the Baroness. "And I think you'll find our decision is final."

"I do not accept your decision," Toth sneered, confident now and taking a step toward the Baroness. "And perhaps we need to reexamine the configuration of the judging panel."

"Fill your boots," the Baroness laughed, while Lord Witherington paled slightly at her side. "Doubt we'll have the Trials again in my lifetime. Countess de Boulevard might be upset though."

"And where is the Countess?" the Prime Minister asked.

"I believe she's with the rest of the panel, informing the

media of our decision and conveying our deepest sympathies to the victims and their families."

Minister Bellingham snorted in delight as Reginald Toth's face turned an angry shade of purple.

"This is not over," he spat at the two judges. "Not by a long shot," he glared around the room, settling his eyes on Lily.

It was almost an automatic reaction now. Lily's eyes connected with the Prime Minister and her mind reached into his. A flash of images flew down the connection as Lily was vaguely aware of the Prime Minister ranting at the group.

He was clearly going a mile a minute, and his thoughts were fractured and angry. But in and amongst the images, she was able to pull out some less fractured parts. There was a reel of her during the Trials that was overlaid strongly with anger. Lily found it odd watching herself as if on television. She moved on, determined not to be distracted.

Suddenly, she found herself watching a scene that must be downtown Burlaron. There was something off about the image, grainy, like watching something that someone had filmed off a television. Lily started as she realised she was watching the king of Highacre, her father. Turning to look at her eldest brother, she was struck again by how much he looked like their father. He had the king's features. The king was giving a speech to a large crowd, and the atmosphere seemed light. Suddenly, two shots rang out and the king and his son fell.

Lily knew she flinched, but thankfully the Prime Minister was still raging, so it was feasible that she was responding to something he'd said. Luckily, no one seemed to notice, and Lily found her way back into his thoughts. She noted she seemed to be able to read his thoughts as quickly as her own, and what might have taken minutes if she had watched the images in real time had fluttered through her head in mere fractions of seconds.

The image was still grainy, but now was clearly the queen and her daughter, Princess Emily. *Why is the Prime Minister thinking about the assassination of my family?* Lily watched as the queen, her mother, laughed and chatted with some dignitaries before addressing a smaller crowd than had been gathered for the king. They were at the harbour, and the queen was in front of a ship. Perhaps launching it? The shots were sudden, just like the assassination of the king and prince, but this time, Lily had been expecting them and covered her reaction. She tried not to think about the fact that she had just, in a matter of seconds, watched her parents and two siblings shot in the head.

The images changed again and she saw, as she now expected, Prince Liam and Princess Sarah at the football game. Lily remembered a bomb hidden in a sports bag had blown them up, and clocked that there were five to ten such bags scattered around the pair. Just as suddenly as the other times, the image blacked out and then all Lily saw was smoke. As it cleared, she saw multiple bodies scattered around, all horribly injured and covered in blood.

The Prime Minister's memory now widened, and she could see that he had been watching footage from security screens. There were a bunch of serious, well-dressed people around the table at which he was sitting. Lily deduced he was remembering the briefing he'd received following the attacks. Lily was less shocked by the footage she had just witnessed and more by the Prime Minister's emotions. He was happy. Lily could feel a sense of achievement, of a plan going right. Had he been involved in the assassination plot? Lily felt nauseous.

She was about to pull out of his thoughts and focus again on the present when she saw another image, this one less realistic, perhaps a fantasy. It was Lily waving at the crowd after completing the Trials. A shadowy figure appeared behind Lily and slit her throat. Lily involuntarily touched her own throat. While watching an image of her blood spraying from her throat was unpleasant, it did not overly shock Lily. If the Prime Minister had been involved in the plot against her family, it made sense that he would want her to suffer the same fate.

The image flickered again, this time to the Prime Minister talking to someone in the palace halls. It looked like the lower corridors, as the lighting was terrible, and the person Toth was talking to was hidden in the shadows. She heard the Prime Minister's voice in the memory. *You promised that we'd be rid of them all.* She summoned all her remaining energy and tried to shift her perspective in the memory, to follow its thread to discover the person's identity. Every effort frustrated, Lily wondered what lengths he had gone through to block the person's identity in his mind.

Lily exited the Prime Minister's mind, rage threatening to explode from her. She glared at the angry little man. Claire had told her they could not use mind reading as evidence against a person, but she now knew he was in some way responsible for the deaths of her family, and that he was out to get her. She resolved to bring him down. With a small start, she remembered that was the main point of her becoming queen anyway. But now it was personal.

Reginald Toth finished his ranting, somehow quelled to silence by the angry look on Lily's face.

"Prime Minister. Your objection is noted. Until you or anyone else can show me evidence to indicate that the judging panel's decision is anything but final, I believe we will assume it is. Now excuse me, I need to address my people."

Lily turned, trying to ignore the look of shock and anger

on the Prime Minister's face as well as the stunned looks of her advisors, and walked to the exit. Jason and Naomi followed her, and she sensed rather than saw their smiles.

She crossed the carpark, walking through the exit and up the driveway. As she crested the top, Claire caught up to her and touched her gently on the shoulder. Lily blinked at the sudden blinding flashes of cameras but listened intently to Claire's advice on what to say and how to say it. Her other advisors joined them and were about to add to her advice when the Prime Minister bustled past and walked right up to the makeshift podium that had been erected for Lily. He held his hands up for silence and waited for it before he began.

"Citizens of Highacre, I firstly want to acknowledge the terrible tragedy that has occurred here tonight, and extend my deepest sympathies to the victims and their families. Our thoughts and prayers are with you."

He continued on, taking pains to acknowledge the first responders and medical personnel, before eventually getting around to what he really wanted to talk about.

"As you saw tonight, just before the despicable attack, Her Majesty withdrew from the final Trial, thus failing to complete the task and subsequently her confirmation. Her Majesty's failure to complete the Trials only highlights the overwhelming need for greater stability for Highacre, particularly in the current security environment. Thankfully, I have been planning for all contingencies and just this afternoon by an almost unanimous vote, the Parliament passed a new Emergency Powers Act."

Lily looked at the politicians. Jeremy Toot looked benignly happy, though Lily could not be completely sure that he had heard the Prime Minister, but Minister Bellingham looked shocked. "I didn't know," she spluttered, "they did not call me to vote..."

"This important piece of legislation provides the prime minister of Highacre a wide array of powers in the event of an emergency, and an expanded suite of powers to ensure the day-to-day security, stability, and prosperity of Highacre.

"Never again will we suffer the devastating uncertainty that the power vacuum left by the tragic deaths of the royal family brought upon our glorious nation. We will not be so easily manipulated by our adversaries in the future. The assassination of our head of state will not bring our country to its knees."

Lily considered it her preference to not have the head of state assassinated at all, however, she recognised her bias in the matter. Nonetheless, she felt secure in her distaste for the assassination of the royal family being referred to as an "easy manipulation". She glanced at her advisors and could tell they were all similarly upset by the speech. The Prime Minister was clearly exaggerating the effect of the assassinations, though she did not doubt the uncertainty felt when they thought the entire family had been wiped out.

"Shouldn't I stop him?" Lily hissed at Minister Bellingham.

She shook her head. "The vote has already happened. Interrupting now may play into his narrative: he is steady, you are emotional. My advice is to hold and we'll address it later. The main issue is his claim that you failed, but the judges have already stated our case on that."

Lily nodded. Angry as she was at the Prime Minister, she took Minister Bellingham's advice about how he could manipulate the situation, and fixed an expression of benign interest on her face as she listened to him.

"Never again will we be dragged to the brink of war because of uncertainty of leadership and the nobbling of our country's steward. And with these new powers, and in light of Her Majesty's failure here tonight, I will remain in the role of Highacre's steward."

Curious mutterings broke out in the crowd, and Lily saw several reporters looking surprised and raising eyebrows as they listened intently to the Prime Minister.

"We have all witnessed Her Majesty's display here tonight, and though I know we all applaud her heroic attempts to help, she did, nonetheless fail the Trial of Endurance and is thus not confirmed as the rightful queen of Highacre. I will meet with my cabinet in coming days to discuss what this means. But I do believe it is the right outcome for our country.

"Her claim to the throne was legitimate. It was proven that she is the daughter of our late king and queen. And no one wishes more than I that they were still with us..."

Bullshit.

"But tragically they are not, and it was not only ridiculous but dangerous that we had to entertain crowning a queen who does not know our country." The Prime Minister let this hang in the air as he theatrically looked around the gathered crowd. "She does not know Highacre. She does not know her people, or their suffering. She did not suffer through the war with us, did not hurt as we hurt, endure as we endured."

Lily noted a few heads nodding in the crowd.

"He's discrediting you. Setting the stage to challenge the panel's decision. Even if that goes against him, he's already pointed out why you shouldn't be queen," Minister Bellingham whispered to Lily.

"She is very new to our land," Reginald Toth continued. "And this is not her fault, but it is the truth. Of course, she has a trusted team of experienced advisors who would have helped her"—he gestured at them over his shoulder, seemingly acknowledging their expertise while painting Lily as incompetent—"but her best friends in Highacre are foreigners! I do not mean to question the royal advisors' methods, but in a crucial transitional time when Her Majesty should have been learning anything and everything about her new home, about her people, the people she intends to rule, surely it was not in the people of Highacre's best interests for their queen to be so heavily influenced by outsiders?"

Muttering broke out anew, and Lily saw some shaking heads and even some dubious glances thrown her way.

"But our new legislation will ensure that no matter what, sufficient power in Highacre will remain with a true Highacren. It will ensure that a steady hand remains on the wheel of the ship and continues to guide us through the water, be it clear skies or storms. And no matter the influences and intentions of any monarch, the people of Highacre will be protected and their interests promoted."

Applause broke out somewhat spontaneously. Some merely polite, out of respect for the Prime Minister's position, but a not inconsequential amount was clearly enthusiastically in favour of his speech. Lily quietly fumed. The Prime Minister had just told everyone that she was akin to a foreigner, possibly explaining why she was consorting with them, and that even if she did become queen, he would be behind everything she did. That if at best, she was incompetent, he would fix everything and run the show, and if at worst, she was a foreign plant, he would protect them from her. He had set himself up perfectly to claim any credit for anything Lily did well and to lay blame, earned or otherwise, at her feet.

Lily had not noticed Jason and Naomi at her side, but they were there, subtly positioned to protect her or get her out as required. She felt a pang of gratitude towards them.

"For the meantime," the Prime Minister continued, not, as Lily had hoped, finished with his speech, "I will retain all of my emergency powers. This will ensure a stability, particularly in light of tonight's tragedy. I will of course only remain in power until such time as we have a confirmed sovereign and have conducted a thorough handover with them." The Prime Minister smiled broadly at the crowd, acting every part the paternal figure, protecting them all and selflessly looking after their best interests. Lily thought she might throw up.

Several large armoured vehicles suddenly pulled up, causing the crowd to jump and move out of the way. Lily felt Jason and Naomi tense and heard Jason muttering into his lapel microphone.

"The Act also provides for the establishment of the Highacre Special Police. I have designed this unit based on my own assessment of our weaknesses during the turbulent period leading up to and in the wake of the assassination of the royal family. The HSP is an elite unit that will answer only to the prime minister of Highacre. This separation from the monarch will provide a currently missing layer of protection for the head of state, as it will ensure that we have a unit that cannot be compromised, even if the sovereign is. In fact, I deployed them here tonight to neutralise the threat and return security to Highacre."

Bullshit.

Lily watched as dozens of militaristic black-clad figures jumped out of the armoured vehicles carrying semiautomatic weapons. They were all wearing balaclavas and were quite intimidating. She had not seen a single person dressed like that tonight. Except, of course, for the terrorists themselves.

The HSP moved into positions around the podium, some flanking the Prime Minister, clearly for appearances, but the rest buffered the crowd back a couple of metres, demonstrating their efficiency. Lily had to admit, given the events of the evening, the Prime Minister standing on the podium surrounded by his own personal security force with the smouldering arena in the background was quite impressive.

"This is a new era for Highacre. An era where the people of Highacre are safe, secure, and protected. An era where Highacre comes first."

36

THE NEXT FEW weeks passed in a blur of preparations for Lily's coronation. There was a furious media battle about whether Lily had, in fact, passed the Trials or whether she had failed and lost her claim to the crown. Minister Bellingham assured her that polling showed the public on their side, but when challenged by Lily allowed that the other side probably had their own polls indicating the public agreed with Toth.

Lily had ordered her advisors to find an unbiased panel of experts to scrutinise the legislation to determine whether or not the judge's ruling was legitimate. This made them nervous—if they found evidence that Toth was right... But Lily insisted. She didn't want to steal the throne. Thankfully, the experts agreed that it was open for the judge's to determine that Lily had completed the Trials, and in doing so, she had been successfully confirmed as the sovereign. All that was left was the coronation to make it official.

Lily had flashbacks to the preparation for her confirmation hearing as her advisors bustled around getting everything ready and they sent her all over the palace for fittings or decoration selections or rehearsals.

The attack on the arena remained the focus of the news. A small terrorist organisation in Meridia had claimed responsibility for the attack, causing anxiety throughout Highacre. The Meridian Liberation Front had not been active since the last war where they had run an allegedly unauthorised campaign against the citizens of Highacre, behind the front lines of the conflict.

However, from her daily security briefing, which she had insisted on despite Giles's reluctance, she knew that the MLF had reached out to the government of Highacre, claiming they were not responsible for the attack, nor for claiming responsibility. Without the Highacren Intelligence Agency available to look into the matter, it remained unclear whether the MLF was actually behind the attack, but trying to sow confusion, or if the attack had been conducted by someone else who was now trying to frame the group.

Lily couldn't help comparing her memory of the terrorists with her memory of the Prime Minister's new private security unit. She knew that the Highacre Special Police had been ensuring their presence was felt. They had been operating largely within Burlaron, but reports of their activities throughout Highacre showed they were a large organisation with significant reach. It was Jason's assessment that their current activities were designed to ensure she knew just that.

All descriptions pointed to a highly trained, well-equipped, and powerful force. Which was good if they were acting for the good of Highacre. However, Lily felt sure that at best the HSP would be used solely to protect the Prime Minister's best interests. At worst, to violently provide fodder for his propaganda. And that made their efficiency and effectiveness alarming. Lily privately met with Jason and Naomi and asked them to work up options to brief her on what, if anything, could be done if it became necessary to take down the HSP, and how costly such action would be. Lily doubted very much that the HSP would simply lay down their weapons, and that meant that many people could die.

While the attack on the arena and the threat of the HSP loomed large, Lily was more immediately concerned about the lack of information about what had happened to Lady Octavia. She had insisted that Jason devote resources to locating her mentor, despite his opinion that Lily's own security was a higher priority. The more days that passed with no news of her fate, the more worried Lily became. Though still clinging to a shred of hope that Lady Octavia might be alive, that they had not even managed to find her body set alarm bells ringing in the back of Lily's mind. If she was dead, why hadn't they found her body? What was gained in hiding it? And if she was still alive, why couldn't they find her? Lily tried not to think too much about what they might be doing to her.

Between her concerns about the Prime Minister and his HSP, terrorists, Lady Octavia's fate and the preparations for her coronation, Lily lost track of time and was surprised to discover halfway through getting ready one morning that she wasn't simply having another fitting, but the day of her coronation had finally arrived.

Once the preparations were complete, Addison, Claire, and Giles rushed her through the palace corridors on the way to the throne room for the ceremony. Lily was moving as fast as the horrendous dress they had squeezed her into would allow, having unsuccessfully argued that the tradi-tional dresses would better serve Highacre in a museum, so all the people of Highacre could all get to see them.

"Very benevolent, Your Majesty, however any such changes you wish to make to this tradition will have to come after you have been officially crowned." Giles had worn a little smirk that faded immediately upon seeing her face.

"Well, it's also a security threat. What if someone is planning another attack? If I need to get away quickly, I should wear something a little more movement-friendly, right Jason?"

Unfortunately, Jason had not been really listening to their discussion and responded by assuring everyone that he and his team could move Lily to safety even if she was encased in concrete. By the time he saw Lily's expression and realised that this was the wrong answer, he could not backtrack, and Giles had left Addison and Claire to entomb Lily in the monstrosity.

Lily had thought that there couldn't possibly be a worse dress than her dress for the royal ball, but the dressmakers of Highacre proved her wrong. This one was both more gaudy than the other, and more restrictive in movement. And also more itchy, which really just put the icing on the cake. Lily had eventually insisted on wearing a pair of her workout tights underneath. This had helped with the itching, and she felt better being able to put some of her belongings in the side pockets of the tights. She grabbed the contents of her jacket pockets and transferred them to her tights without thought. Only after she had the dress on did she realise that there was no way for her to access the pockets, and therefore her lip balm, tissue, immersion device, and the disc that Jenkins had given her, which she had taken to carrying everywhere mostly out of habit, were really only with her for moral support.

On what should have been one of the happiest days of Lily's life, she found she was truly miserable. And the fact that they were late and therefore trying to rush was doing little for her mood.

As Lily, Addison, Claire, Jason, and Naomi headed

off towards the coronation, taking a confusing maze of back corridors and smaller hallways. Lily, trying to focus on anything but the huge crowd she was about to encounter, became lost in her thoughts and almost bowled straight into Jason and Naomi when they stopped suddenly.

Jason took a couple of steps forward as Naomi moved protectively in front of Lily, who shuffled slightly to see what the interruption was.

"Frank? You're not supposed to be in today..."

Frank ignored Jason, his eyes boring into Lily, whose stomach dropped. Next second, Lily was staring down the barrel of a pistol. Jason and Naomi exploded into action as the corridor filled with chaos. Lily was pushed to the side, Naomi shielding her with her own body as Jason shoved Frank's arm to the side, the pistol discharging. The explosion was deafening in the confines of the corridor.

"They're coming from the other end!"

As Addison and Claire ran past to intercept the new threat, Naomi grabbed Lily and pushed her away from danger and into the entrance of a separate corridor.

"Hide here, Your Majesty. I am going to help Addison. Trust no one—Frank is a palace guard." Naomi looked over her shoulder, worry etched on her face. "You are not under any circumstances to get involved in the fight, but if anyone approaches you, call for me, and feel free to blast them with fire in the meantime."

Before Lily could protest, Naomi was gone. She heard yelling and crashing and saw flashes of different coloured light. Afraid, Lily crept back from the opening, further into the corridor.

She noticed that a panel in the wall about halfway down the hallway was poking open. *A hidden door.* Without thinking, Lily turned away from the chaos and headed for it.

As she approached, she saw that there was an odd blueish glow leaking from the room behind the panel.

Lily poked her head inside and saw a medium-sized room awash in the blue light emanating from the machine in its middle. As she made her way inside, she realised it was the interdimensional travel machine that she had seen before, when she met Jenkins. But it was on! Had someone gone through? Or was someone coming back? And either way, how did they get the felixium to power it?

"It is impressive, isn't it?"

Lily started, not having realised that anyone else was in the room, and was surprised to see Ezra emerge from the shadows.

"Oh, um, yes. Yes, it is. What are you doing here, Ezra?"

"Oh, I heard Jenkins was testing the machine and thought I'd swing by to see it in action before I head off to your coronation." He tipped his head to Lily.

"Where did you hear that?" Lily asked. She felt off-balance and confused. The transition from the unexpected attack to Ezra calmly observing the interdimensional travel machine was jarring. A small part of her mind began ringing an alarm.

"Oh, here and there." Ezra waved her question away before adding conspiratorially, "Addison is a font of information."

This was all very strange. Lily turned towards the door, but she could only hear faint voices. She hoped that meant her advisors had subdued the attackers. She turned back to face the ambassador. Ezra shouldn't even know about the machine, but here he was in the room with it like it was no big deal. And where was Jenkins? Lily could not imagine anything that could draw him from the room, let alone leave the machine unattended while powered on. Perhaps he had gone through the machine and into another dimension? But that seemed wrong, too. Surely he wouldn't go through without someone here to make sure everything was fine from this end. And that person certainly wasn't Ezra.

As if prompted by her thoughts, Jenkins entered the room, a frown on his face as he studied a handheld device.

"Shouldn't be on. Jenkins didn't turn it on. No one else should know how. No felixium anyway." He stopped suddenly. "No felixium. But machine is on—"

"Jenkins!" Ezra greeted the scientist jovially, startling him from his thoughts.

Jenkins stared at Ezra and Lily in shock, unaware that they had been standing there watching him. His eyes settled on Ezra and he tilted his head to the side, considering him. "This is not good."

"I'm surprised you're here, Jenkins. I heard Giles sent some men to go and look at that cave in the forest."

Jenkins dropped his device. "The cave?" His eyes grew large in alarm.

"Yes, they headed that way just a few moments ago. Something about sorting out an issue . . ."

Jenkins turned abruptly and headed for the door, muttering, "No, no, no."

Ezra watched him leave, looking supremely happy with himself.

"Ezra," Lily said in a low, quiet voice. "You shouldn't be here."

Before he could answer her, voices grew louder outside the door through which Lily had entered, and suddenly Ava and Alexei appeared, looking around in wonder.

"What is this place?" asked Alexei, a note of awe in his voice. The two of them spotted Ezra and Lily and moved towards them. Lily noticed Ezra appeared annoyed at the intrusion, but the expression left his face almost as soon as it registered.

"What are you two doing here?" Ezra asked. Though he sounded pleasantly surprised, he couldn't entirely keep the sharp note out of his voice. Ava caught it too, shooting Ezra a fleeting questioning look that faded as he responded with a barely perceptible shake of his head.

"We're lost," Ava explained, smiling. "We were heading to the coronation and tried to take a shortcut. We were wandering through these little hallways for a while." She shrugged at Lily. "They all look the same. Anyway, we saw the blue light and decided to take a look. Thank goodness you're here, Your Majesty. Clearly, we're not late." She smiled cheekily. "Nice dress."

Lily shot her a dirty look and then wondered what to do about the three foreigners who were now examining the interdimensional travel machine that was meant to be a state secret, with one of them clearly in possession of more information about it than he should have.

Lily was rescued from her consideration of this awkward situation by the entry into the room of a mysterious cloaked figure. Everyone in the room started at its appearance. *Of course, what else can go wrong?* Lily looked around for another way out of the room, immediately alarmed after the encounter with the rogue guards. Everyone else hesitated, wrong-footed by the lack of action or comment from the figure, who was just standing there staring at them. Lily assumed it was staring, but its hood was pulled low and its face in shadow.

"What do you want?" she demanded of it, determined to take action since no one else seemed inclined to do so. Lily's voice was slightly higher than she had intended, giving away her fear.

The figure raised an arm, a pale hand emerging from its sleeve, and pointed directly at Lily. The others turned to look at her, recoiling from her slightly.

Before Lily could think to do anything, the figure lunged at her. Lily tried to dodge to her right, but her dress would not cooperate. The figure grabbed her arm. Whoever was under that cloak was very strong. They pulled Lily towards them, as if trying to grab her around her body. Lily struggled and called out for help, in her panic immediately forgetting all of her training in hand-to-hand combat and magical prowess.

Suddenly, the figure stumbled against her, but lost its grip slightly. Lily turned and could see Alexei fighting the figure, trying to pull it off her. She looked to her right and saw Ava recovering herself and preparing to jump into the fray to help Lily. Ezra was off to the side of the room, looking on with a horrified expression.

Lily was jerked and flung around as both Alexei and Ava now tried to free her from her assailant's grip, the cloaked figure unwilling to let her go. It roared in frustration and flung Lily roughly, moving this way and that to shed its attackers. They were a mess of bodies, grabbing and pushing and pulling. Lily couldn't even tell who was who anymore.

Suddenly, the figure let go, and Lily felt herself careening across the room. She had no idea what direction she was moving in. She felt herself collide with something heavy and heard Alexei and Ava grunt. They should have stopped her, but they were off balance too, and grabbed onto Lily and each other in a futile effort to steady themselves. Lily had the momentum, and so clinging together, all three of them stumbled backward, towards the machine. The next thing Lily knew, she was surrounded by a brilliant blue light. She felt a familiar pulling sensation, and then . . . black.

EPILOGUE

THE CLOAKED figure dashed out of the machine room and down the corridor, veering off into a storeroom that was normally locked. Only then did Austin remove the cloak, stashing it behind a broken statue where there was a crack in the wall.

He ran his hands through his hair. That had not gone like he'd planned it. He pulled out the note from the Patriot to see exactly how badly he had messed up.

The Patriot had been sending him notes regularly since he had foreshadowed the big things to come. And he hadn't been overselling it. The Patriot's plan was in motion. Everything in Highacre was about to change. Austin thought back to when he had received his first note. It was after his old army friend took him to a nationalist rally "for old times' sake". It was supporting the movement about Highacre for Highacrens and calling for the end of preferential treatment of refugees and an overemphasis by the Parliament on foreign affairs.

The next day he had received his first note signed by "A Patriot", which he had dismissed as a joke until he mentioned it to his buddy, who was impressed and clearly a little jealous that Austin had received the note and not him. His buddy had said that the Patriot was very high up in the ranks of the group that was trying to lead a nationalist revolution, if not the leader.

He opened this latest note.

My Loyal Ally,

Your service to the cause has always been exemplary, and now we need you more than ever. I cannot go into details here, but our enemies have convinced the queen that we are traitors. She cannot be allowed to proceed to her coronation before we can right this wrong and ensure she understands our aims. Once she knows our goal, she cannot help but join us in its pursuit.

You must go to the room that is hidden off the third hallway near the bust of St. Vitious. The door will be open for you. Push her through the machine emitting blue light. She will be met on the other side by some fellow patriots who will take care of the rest, and she will be returned once she is on our side.

Good luck!
A Patriot

He had been more convinced than ever that the Patriot was high up in the government—he would have to be to know about the interdimensional travel machine.

That made it even worse that everything had gone wrong. The queen had been there as promised, but he had not expected the ambassadors to court. He was pretty sure the Patriot would not have wanted him to push them through the machine with the queen.

Well, there was nothing he could do about it now.

Whoever was at the other end waiting for the queen would just have to deal with the extras. And really, he had probably done them a favour. His buddies in the Nationalist Party said the Prime Minister was posturing for war, and the ambassadors going missing would surely only help with that.

He thought about trying to get a message to the Patriot, but he seemed to find out everything that happened, whether or not Austin tried to report back. Perhaps it would be better if he left it. Maybe the Patriot wouldn't hear about his mistake. Or at least, if he was mad, Austin would have had time to make sure his report showed that he had no other choice. Perhaps he could even come up with a reason why he did it, like it was planned. If he showed he was proactive, used initiative, maybe the Patriot would bring him in further and make him one of the movement's generals.

Ultimately, Austin decided that there was nothing more he could do, and so he smoothed down his clothes, checked that the corridor outside was clear, and hurried off to mingle in with the crowds waiting for a coronation that would not happen.

Ezra maintained his horrified expression until Austin left the room, and only then did he approach the machine. Damned bumpkin. Only Lily was supposed to go through the portal. Perhaps he should have been more specific in his note, though he hadn't expected the ambassadors to court to show up. Alexei he did not really care about, but losing Ava was . . . problematic.

He examined the machine, looking for some way to reverse Ava's travel, but could not see anything even vaguely useful on the face of the machine, and he had to get going.

He moved to the door, listening for signs of activity outside. Surely they had noticed that Lily was missing by now. Finally, he heard the frantic voices and footsteps heading this way.

"Help!" Ezra called, bursting out into the hallway. "Help me, please!"

"It's Ezra!"

"Ezra, what's wrong?"

Giles, Addison, Claire, Jason, and the new female body-guard rushed towards him. They looked panicked and tousled.

"Oh, thank goodness." He made a show of trying to calm down and catch his breath, pointing towards the room he had just exited. "In there. I followed a cloaked figure . . ." At that, the two bodyguards broke off and entered the room, sweeping it for threats, before looking back at Ezra, who had followed them in with the rest of the group.

Claire glared at the glowing machine. "That shouldn't be on."

"Mr Ambassador, are you okay? We need to be going. The queen—"

"That's what I'm trying to tell you," Ezra interrupted Jason with his best pleading and panicked voice. "I saw a cloaked figure. He looked suspicious, and so I followed him. He came in here. The queen was here with the ambassadors to court. She seemed to be showing them that thing." He pointed at the machine, smiling internally beneath his frantic expression. Let them believe she was telling her friends state secrets.

"The cloaked figure, he rushed at them and they fought, and then the queen and ambassadors all went through the middle of that machine and disappeared! Where have they gone?"

The advisors burst into action. Jason told the new bodyguard to go and find Jenkins, while Giles went to the machine to examine it. Addison stayed by Ezra's side, as did Claire, which was annoying. She was far too switched on.

"Addison, where did Ava go?" He almost whispered his question, eyes wide, willing tears to well.

"Ezra, it's okay. It'll be okay." Addison reassured him. "She's with the queen. She's probably safer there than we are. Some of the guards have joined the other side."

Ezra frowned, considering the new complication. It would have to wait, and with the queen out of the way, he had bought a little time. But if he was going to succeed with his plan, he would have to move fast. Ezra bowed his head, as if overcome with emotion, and smiled. He had work to do.

BOOKS BY K.T. HOLDER

<u>The Highacren Prophecy</u>

Regent (free prequel novella)

Royal

Return

Reign

Rogue (free bonus chapter)

<u>The City Chronicles</u>

Rise of the Divvinium (free prequel novella)

City of Stone

City of Shadows

Echoes of the Divvinium (free bonus novella)

City of Sorrow

ACKNOWLEDGMENTS

It's been such a journey to get here! Royal is my first step in a new direction of my life. It's something I started before I knew I could write a book, and before I believed I could dare to make my dream a reality.

Royal specifically, and the entire series, mark a massive life change for me in giving up the work I thought I'd be doing forever and refocusing on something I'm passionate about, but has less stability. But life's too short to not try and follow your dreams!

The first person I need to thank is my amazing wife. She re-read this story through soo many iterations it may as well have been several books and she never hesitated to read it again. Without her belief in me and unwavering support I wouldn't be where I am today. Thank you so much for everything and I'm so lucky to explore life with you.

I also need to thank my pups. They're the best writing companions a girl could have and without the rhythmic snoring I wouldn't be able to concentrate half as well.

A huge thank you to Courtney at Elevation Editorial. Getting your first book edited is scary, but Courtney made the process so much fun! This is a better book (and series) because of her help, support and suggestions.

Thank you to the team at GetCovers for the amazing covers for all the books in this series. They are so awesome and the team is so easy to work with.

And the biggest thank you is for you! Thank you so much for reading my book! I can't tell you how much it means to me that you took a chance, and I really hope you enjoyed it.

If you did enjoy the story, please consider leaving a review on Amazon or Goodreads, or really anywhere you like! They really can make a difference, especially in helping other people find my books, and it'll go a long way to letting me keep writing stories for you.

Feel free to to head over to my website (www.kthold er.com) where you can sign up to hear about book releases and other fun things! If you sign up, you get Regent, an exclusive prequel novella, for free!

You can also get updates by following me on Facebook and Instagram, and I'm also on Goodreads and BookBub!

Thanks again!